MW01491351

LADY OF FIRE

LADY OF FIRE

A Medieval Romance

A "clean read" rewrite of *Pagan Bride*, published by Bantam Books, 1995

TAMARA LEIGH
USA Today Best-Selling Author

Text copyright © 2015 Tamara Leigh
All rights reserved.
No part of this book may be reproduced, or stored in a retrieval system, or transmitted in any form or by any means, electronic, mechanical, photocopying, recording, or otherwise, without express written permission of the publisher.

ISBN: 1942326130
ISBN 13: 9781942326137

TAMARA LEIGH NOVELS

CLEAN READ HISTORICAL ROMANCE
The Feud: A Medieval Romance Series
Baron Of Godsmere: **Book One** 02/15
Baron Of Emberly: **Book Two** 12/15
Baron of Blackwood: **Book Three** 2016

Medieval Romance Series
Lady At Arms: **Book One** 01/14 (1994 Bantam Books
bestseller *Warrior Bride* clean read rewrite)
Lady Of Eve: **Book Two** 06/14 (1994 Bantam Books
bestseller *Virgin Bride* clean read rewrite)

Stand-Alone Medieval Romance Novels
Lady Of Fire 11/14 (1995 Bantam Books best-
seller *Pagan Bride* clean read rewrite)
Lady Of Conquest 06/15 (1996 Bantam Books best-
seller *Saxon Bride* clean read rewrite)
Lady Undaunted Late Winter 2016 (1996 HarperCollins
bestseller *Misbegotten* clean read rewrite)
Dreamspell: **A Medieval Time Travel Romance** 03/12

INSPIRATIONAL HISTORICAL ROMANCE
Age of Faith: A Medieval Romance Series
The Unveiling: **Book One** 08/12
The Yielding: **Book Two** 12/12
The Redeeming: **Book Three** 05/13
The Kindling: **Book Four** 11/13
The Longing: **Book Five** 05/14

www.tamaraleigh.com

1

Algiers, 1454

Not even chains could make him look the slave.

Wearing loose-fitting chausses and a sleeveless, tattered tunic that was more ribbon than garment, the towering, broad-shouldered man was dragged to the platform to stand before the astonished crowd. Those who struggled to hold him scowled and grunted as he roared curses understood only by those who knew his language.

An Englishman, Sabine silently rejoiced. *An enraged one.*

She had not expected to encounter such a fine specimen. Though he could not be noble, for he would surely have been ransomed, he had the bearing of one of high birth.

She gripped the arm of the chief eunuch who had accompanied her to the auction. "That one, Khalid."

His eyes widened. "Mistress, he is not a eunuch."

True. The auctioneer had not prefaced the summons to bid with that information, but it did not matter. This was the one she had been waiting for these two months, and she would not allow him to slip through her fingers.

"He is the one," she said sharply.

Khalid leaned down from his great height. "Only a eunuch is allowed within the walls of a harem."

"None need know," she said as the bidding commenced.

Khalid shook his head. "This man is fit only for the quarries. There will be others better suited to your purpose." Of which only he, her confidant these past ten years, knew.

"The time that remains to me is swift-footed," she said, a creak in her voice. "Do not deny me this. It may be my only chance."

The corners of his mouth tightened. "Upon his arms and through the tears in his tunic, can you not see the stripes laid to him?

Of course she saw them, the recently acquired ones livid and swollen.

"He has been beaten and often," he continued. "That is a bad sign."

"And yet he is alive," she countered. "It means he is strong and determined. *That* is a good sign."

Khalid's shoulders rose with the breath of patience. "Mistress, a man as valuable as that is not beaten so viciously without cause. He is dangerous."

Regardless, she would have him, for she had seen none worthier to carry out her plan. "Only a fool or one too apathetic to rise up again would be devoid of such anger," Sabine retorted, "and neither of those I seek. Now buy him."

Noting the bidding had turned fierce among those who sought to acquire the Englishman for their mines and quarries, she watched the struggle that alternately lined and smoothed Khalid's face. He longed to aid her, but had good cause to weigh his loyalty against fear for his life. If the English slave could not be reasoned with...if he seduced the women of the harem...if it was revealed he was not a eunuch...

But if I lose him to another, I could lose that which is most precious to me, she excused herself for what she demanded of her old friend. "Do you not bid, Khalid, I shall."

His nostrils flared. "He will cost much, mistress."

She pulled the gold bracelet from her wrist and thrust it into his hand, then began to work a ring from her finger. "I care not what he costs."

Khalid stayed her desperate gesture with a hand to her shoulder, and grudgingly stepped forward.

Watching through the gossamer veil that hid her face, Sabine anxiously smoothed her fingers down her black cloak. Draped from the crown of her head, the garment fell straight to the ground, concealing the colorful finery beneath. It was the same for all respectable women who went out in public in this place far removed from the world she had been born into.

As the bidding escalated, Khalid adding his voice to the shouts, the slave continued to struggle against his captors.

From what well does he draw strength? Sabine wondered. What sustains his spirit?

In the next instant, he broke an arm free and slung the chain stretched between his manacled wrists into the face of one of his captors. The man shouted, stumbled back, and fell to the platform where he groped at his bloodied mouth. His companion also sprayed blood upon the air, but when he fell, he took the Englishman down with him.

As the crowd rumbled with alarm, those nearest the platform— save Khalid—hastened back as slave and captor wrestled to subdue one another.

Hands to her chest, beneath which her heart beat frantically, Sabine acknowledged that Khalid had been wise to discourage her from purchasing such a man. After all, she was no longer the young woman of twenty years ago. Had she three more years left in her, she would see the age of forty.

When it became evident the Englishman would not be easily put down, Khalid leapt onto the platform, wrenched the slave off his opponent, and brought his knee up between the Englishman's thighs.

The man threw his head back, but no sound issued from his lips. Then he dropped.

A cheer rose from the crowd as the formidable, dark-skinned eunuch relinquished the Englishman to the others who had been reluctant to come to the aid of their comrades. Then Khalid turned and searched out his mistress. Eyes lighting upon her, he frowned.

Though Sabine knew he was more strongly opposed to purchasing the slave, she nodded.

Khalid looked to the auctioneer. "I will pay no more," he said, letting his last offer stand. "Is there another who would challenge me?"

The beady-eyed auctioneer looked out across the throng. When none came forward, he accepted the eunuch's bid.

Hiding her unease behind her veil, Sabine watched as the slave was dragged from the platform.

"It is done," Khalid growled when he rejoined her. "I hope you do not come to regret it as much as I."

She set a hand upon his arm. "I thank you, my friend. Your loyalty will be rewarded."

He inclined his head. "I pray I live long enough to enjoy the harvest."

2

Feigning boredom amid excitement and fear that tangled her insides, Sabine levered up from the pillows. Though eyes bored into her as she rearranged her slender form amid a profusion of color, she did not acknowledge the slave until she was comfortably settled.

She sighed, focused on his manacled ankles, and began an upward perusal. When she reached his face, his indignation was evident in bunched muscles and eyes shot with rage.

Mentally, she prepared herself for flight lest he defy his chains and the guards holding him, but then she saw him sway.

She swept her gaze to Khalid. Though his expression was impassive, his sparkling eyes confirmed he had drugged the man in such a way that, though the mind remained alert, the body was severely limited in acting upon its urgings.

Relieved, she motioned for the guards to withdraw.

They bowed and slipped into the shadowed corners of the tent to keep watch. And watch was all they could do, for they knew nothing of the English language. Unlike Khalid.

Sabine lowered her feet to the carpet that covered the earthen floor, straightened, and sauntered forward.

"I am Sabine," she said in accented English that evidenced the nineteen years she had lived among the Arab people. "By what name are you called, Englishman?"

He narrowed his lids.

Confident he could do her no harm, she placed herself before him, rose to her toes, and peered into a hard countenance divided into two distinct halves. Whereas the right was unblemished, the left was scarred by a blade that had perfectly traced the high cheekbone there.

She shifted her attention to eyes of a shade approaching amethyst. And frowned. On whom had she seen that rare color? Finding no match in her memory, she considered his hair. It was dirty, hanging almost to his shoulders, and appeared to be bronze in color. As for his face, one would not call it handsome, but neither was it unattractive.

Pity, she thought, *he might give his life to achieve the goal I set him.*

Firmly telling herself he would succeed, if for no other reason than to preserve his own life, she set herself back on her heels, causing the miniature bells about her ankle to tinkle like the laughter of children. A moment later, the sprightly sound was answered by the harsh rattle of chains.

"Harlot!" the slave rasped, shoving his great body against her.

Instantly, Khalid and the guards were upon him. The latter held him by the arms while the eunuch landed the back of a hand across the man's face.

The slave did not flinch.

I am in no danger, Sabine told herself as she struggled to calm her pounding heart, but not until the guards began dragging the slave toward the tent opening did she find her voice.

"Leave him!" she commanded in Arabic. When Khalid protested, she quieted him with a shake of her head. "You have made it so he can do me no harm."

With obvious grudging, the eunuch ordered the guards forward. "Seat him there"—he motioned to a stool—"and take yourselves from the tent."

They forced him to sit and withdrew.

"They will talk of the slave's defiance," Khalid warned. "If you intend to continue on this perilous course, mistress, it is best done in privacy."

He was right. Emasculated men, deprived of desires of the flesh, lost much of their high spirit and unruliness. Indeed, some became quite gentle. But this Englishman displayed none of those qualities. Given the right incentive, could he feign them?

Once more, Sabine approached him. "You have nothing to fear from me—"

"Fear?" he growled. "'Tis I who should be feared. As lovely as your heathen neck is, I am quite taken with the thought of it between my hands."

Sabine was further unnerved, though more by his voice than his threat. Despite its strain, his speech seemed too eloquent for a commoner. But she shrugged off the peculiarity and pulled out the pins securing her hair veil.

"You have much to learn, Englishman," she said, and revealed tresses of a red so true no amount of henna could reproduce it.

Confusion lined his face, but he cleared it with a scowl.

"I am as English as you," she said, lowering to her knees beside him. "Just as you are a slave, so was I when I arrived in this country."

He swept his gaze over her Arabic dress. "What is it you call yourself now?"

Refusing to be ashamed of the lifestyle that had been forced upon her nearly twenty years past, she set her chin high. "I am the wife of a wealthy Arab merchant." She said it with the pride warranted for having attained such a station. She could have easily met the fate suffered by most—that of a prostitute.

"An apostate," the Englishman tossed back. "A harlot who has thrown off her religion and taken that of another so she might know greater comfort."

Sabine lifted a chain from the neck of her caftan and held forth the crucifix suspended from it. "Is it still your wish to feel my neck between your hands?"

He stared at it, returned his gaze to hers. "What is it you want from me?"

"I have a proposal I believe you will find acceptable." At his lack of response, she continued, "You seek your freedom, and if you do my bidding, you shall have it."

His anger eased perceptibly, but when he spoke, defiance was in every letter formed by tongue and lips. "Whether or not I do your *bidding,* I shall have my freedom."

Recalling what Khalid had apprised her of a short while ago, she smiled. "If that is so, why have you not escaped since you were taken? It has been over a year."

His eyes darkened further. "Be assured, every chance given me, I have defied my captors, but flesh and bone do not easily break steel. And when a man is chained to the oar of a galley nearly all day and night, he is ever in the power of manacle and chain."

Remembering her bonds that had been light compared to that which now fettered him, recalling her defiance that had been tolerated insomuch that her beauty was not devalued, Sabine stood and walked to the Englishman's back. He jerked when she pushed aside the torn material of his tunic. And again when she lightly touched a scar that ran shoulder to hip.

"Certes, you rebelled," she murmured, then came back around. "A pity there was none to ransom you. Had you a title, you would not have been made to suffer so."

"I do have a title!"

She should not have been surprised in light of his speech, mannerisms, and carriage, but she was. She looked to Khalid who nodded.

Silently, she bemoaned that she had not listened better at the auction. At the least, she should have given Khalid time to tell her all of what was known of the man. Still, it changed nothing—certainly not for the worse, for a nobleman might better serve her purpose than a commoner.

"Why were you not ransomed?" she asked.

Silence.

She turned to Khalid who handed her the documents. Angling them toward the light, she found what she sought. And saw nothing save the name at the top—De Gautier.

Feeling light of head, she gripped the documents so tightly the edges crumpled. In all of England, there could be no poorer choice of one to whom she entrusted her most precious possession. A De Gautier—unthinkable.

The coughing came on with little warning, as it did more of late. Pressing a hand to her chest, she turned to Khalid who lifted her into his arms.

He carried her to the bed of pillows, lowered her, and pressed a square of linen into her hand. With his concerned face hovering above hers, she put the cloth to her mouth and coughed up blood.

"I shall send him away," Khalid said when the spell passed.

She lifted a staying hand. "I am not finished with him." Ignoring her friend's glower, she looked to De Gautier.

Now she knew why a memory had stirred over his eyes. He had been but a child, perhaps eight years of age, when she had come face-to-face with Lucien de Gautier. Then she had been Lady Catherine, the young bride of Lord James Breville. The boy had been her husband's captive.

Though a good man, James had not been averse to using the De Gautier heir to obtain what he and his ancestors had long desired. For generations, the Brevilles and De Gautiers had quarreled over a strip of land—Dewmoor Pass—that lay between their properties. Although kings had attempted to settle the dispute, peace had always been short-lived, for neither family was willing to permanently relinquish any portion of it. As a result, enmity was amassed and, from time to time, blood was shed.

Had the De Gautier boy not proven so clever, James might have finally secured the land for the Brevilles. As the negotiations dragged on, Lucien had bided his time. Though the boy made no attempt to mask his anger, he had been allowed to wander about the castle with few eyes upon him. Thus, he had slipped out through the portcullis one night. By the time he was spotted heading for the wood, he had enough of a lead to lose his pursuers.

But that was almost twenty years ago. A lifetime, Sabine told herself as she focused on the boy who had long since become a man. Were the families still at one another's throats? Likely, for not even England's war with France that finally looked to be at an end, had lasted as long as the Breville and De Gautier dispute.

As Sabine considered abandoning her plan to smuggle her daughter out of Algiers, an idea rose amidst her fatigue. Since Lucien de Gautier did not recognize her as the wife of his enemy, she could still make use of him—providing he believed her daughter was fathered by Sabine's Arab husband.

She pushed herself into a sitting position and met his stare. "Shall we bargain?"

"First, I would know what upset you." He nodded at the documents that lay upon the carpet.

Casually, she draped a silk robe around her shoulders. "Naught upset me. Simply, I am not well."

"And, simply, you are a liar."

"I am not well," she repeated. "And for that, my coin has bought you."

His expression revealed he did not believe her, but he said, "Speak."

"I offer you freedom."

Warily, he said, "What will it cost me?"

Beneath the cover of her robe, she clenched her hands. "I have family in England. Take my daughter with you when you return."

"That is all you ask of me?"

She gave a sharp laugh. "'Twill be no easy thing. Not only will my husband not allow Alessandra to leave, but she will not go willingly."

"For what would you send her away if she wishes to remain?"

Pained by what she must reveal, Sabine took some moments to compose her words. "Soon, my daughter is to wed one of the Islamic faith, and when I am gone—and it will not be long now—there will be none to protect her."

"Then her safety concerns you."

"Aye, but neither do I wish her to have the life I have lived. Were she suited to it, it would not bother me so, but she is not."

"The life of a—"

"Life in a harem," she interrupted before he could call her that filthy name again.

A corner of Lucien's mouth lifted. "How do you propose I return her to England if she will not come willingly?"

"You will enter the harem," she said as if it were the simplest thing in the world. It was not. "There you will gain her trust, and if I still cannot convince her to leave, you will force her. All will be arranged to see you safely from this land."

Lucien's gaze moved past Sabine to Khalid. "Even I know," he said dryly, "unless a man is no longer a man, he is not allowed in that place of women."

She glanced at her old friend, acutely aware of the battle waged in the silence between the two men. Obviously, Lucien de Gautier would not soon forget his humiliation at Khalid's hands. Nor would Khalid overlook the insult just paid him.

"'Tis so," she said. "Only members of the household and eunuchs are allowed inside the harem. Thus, you must become a eunuch to enter."

Lucien bared his teeth. "If you are suggesting I become like him"— he indicated Khalid with a thrust of his chin—"I decline your *generous* offer. When I return home, it will be as a man."

"In pretense only must you become a eunuch. None but Khalid and I will know."

After a long moment, he said, "I am to trust him?"

"He is loyal to me. No word of our secret will pass his lips."

"And if I refuse?"

"Then you are of no use to me. And a true eunuch you will become."

He surprised her with laughter. "You think I do not know castration is forbidden here?"

What he said was true. The emasculating procedure was only allowed outside the Muslim nations in spite of the demand for eunuchs within it. "Laws can be broken," Sabine said. "As I do not accept my husband's faith, it would not weigh heavily upon my conscience to break that particular law."

Khalid stepped forward. "I will do it myself," he said in English. When Lucien turned his wrathful stare upon the eunuch, Khalid raised his palms heavenward. "Surely Allah will forgive so minor a transgression against a heathen."

A muscle in Lucien's jaw spasmed, but he did not unfurl his anger.

"Do not allow your pride to cloud your judgment," Sabine said. "I have given you hope where you had none."

"Then it seems I must accept your proposal."

So relieved was she that she sank back into the pillows. "You shall remain in the city with Khalid for a sennight. He will instruct you in the ways of a eunuch, and you will answer to him in all things. Afterward, he will bring you to the home of my husband, Abd al-Jabbar, and you will enter the harem."

She turned to Khalid. "No doubt he has been long without a woman," she spoke in her adopted language. "Make certain that when you bring him into the women's quarters, his desires are sufficiently quenched that he will not be tempted to touch what he must not."

"It will be done, mistress."

She returned her attention to Lucien. "I have instructed Khalid—"

"I heard."

Then he had learned their language. Though it would make it less difficult for him in her husband's home, it unsettled her. "Know this," she said, "once you enter the harem, you will not be intimate with a woman until you have fulfilled your end of the bargain by delivering my daughter to my family."

He smiled, a mocking thing that showed his teeth had survived the ravages of life at sea.

Sabine swallowed hard. "Do not fail me, Lucien de Gautier. You are very much a man, and I would not wish to change that."

His smile widened. "Be assured, I will be cautious."

3

THE MUSIC GREW louder, its vigorous beat winding around the slender woman who swayed at the center of the large room. It pulled her head back and closed her eyes, drew her arms up and spread them to embrace the rhythm. It shook her shoulders, rotated her hips, made her fingers snap.

Slowly, the female dancers hired to entertain the women of Abd al-Jabbar's harem drifted away, going to stand along the walls to watch the one who had claimed the dance for herself.

She was different from the others—her hair a flame amid the ashes, skin that should have been pale tanned and faintly touched with freckles, and the eyes she opened upon her captive audience were green and flashed with daring.

The tempo quickened, and the solitary dancer whose fine-boned body curved where it ought to, swept across the floor. Laughter spilling from her, she snatched the gossamer veil from her waist-length hair, scattering the pins that had held it in place, and drew it between her hands. Once more raising her arms above her head, she pivoted on the balls of her bare feet and whirled amid the diaphanous material clothing her limbs. And when the music reached its zenith, she gave a shriek of delight.

"Alessandra!" a sharp voice split the air.

The music ceased, and a din of female voices rose in its place.

Wrenched from what seemed a trancelike state, the dancer whipped around. She blinked at the woman who stood at the far end of the room. Then, obviously afflicted with lightheadedness, she staggered and stumbled, dropped to her knees, and sank back on her heels.

Standing between Sabine and Khalid, Lucien silently cursed the attraction in whose grip he had been since laying eyes upon Alessandra, whom he had assumed was a dancer—though with her mother's hair falling down her back, he should have known otherwise.

Here was forbidden fruit. Indeed, of all who might tempt him to sins of the flesh, this lady of fire and daring and laughter could move him nearest his downfall. His task had just turned more dangerous. Indeed, it could prove deadly.

Dear Lord, Alessandra silently appealed to the one above, *I did not mean to. But, yes, I have done it again.*

Dizziness subsiding sufficiently to allow her to focus on her mother who stood just inside the doors, she whispered, "Worse, I am caught. Again."

She drew a deep breath, blew it up her face, and stood. As she stepped forward, the musicians and dancers resumed their entertainment. Not that their audience would be captive, for the encounter between mother and daughter was surely of greater interest.

Alessandra was halfway to Sabine's side when she glanced to the right. Alongside Khalid stood a man of equal girth and height—as much a giant as the chief eunuch. Though fair of skin, he was clothed the same as Khalid, head covered with a turban, a caftan falling from his shoulders, and over that a dark robe.

Most notable were his eyes, their beauty undiminished by the brown-blue smudge ringing the right. Who had blackened it? Who had dared?

The answer was found in the strange bend of Khalid's nose, which conjured a vision of the two men locked in mortal combat. Who had come out on top? Perhaps neither.

She returned her attention to the new man whose gaze was taking a leisurely jaunt over her. At every place he lit, from her heated face to her toes, she felt singed.

Why does he stare? she wondered. *Does he mock me?*

Regardless, he was surely the eunuch her mother had purchased a sennight past. No others would be so forward.

"I would have an explanation for your behavior," Sabine said when her daughter halted before her.

Hating that she had agitated her, Alessandra leaned forward and pressed a kiss to her cool cheek. "Forgive me. I could not help myself."

Sabine's compressed lips twitched, face softened. "You must learn to control these impulses." She brushed Alessandra's hair off her face. "When Jabbar hears of this, he will likely forbid you entertainment."

And he would hear of it. Leila, the first of his three wives, was likely sending word this moment.

"It will have been worth it," Alessandra said with an apologetic smile, "for I so enjoyed the dance."

"Well, do not complain when you are once more left to your boredom."

"Would I do such a thing?"

"You would."

Alessandra laughed. "And still you will come to my defense."

Sabine rolled her eyes, took her daughter's hand, and turned her toward the new eunuch.

Up close, Alessandra was more disconcerted. There was none of a eunuch's serenity in that scarred face. Indeed, his expression was hard, as if anger had engraved it. Still, there was light in his eyes. Amusement?

"Why do you stare?" she asked.

"He is from England," Sabine said. "Thus, he has much to learn before he takes his place in our household."

Alessandra gasped, stepped nearer him. "England? Why did you not tell me, Mother?"

"I wished to surprise you."

Alessandra looked across her shoulder. "That you have done."

Her mother smiled. "I thought he could help you with your English. In return, you can teach him our language."

Alessandra winced. She was not keen on being tutored in English. Though she could converse in her mother's native language, it felt awkward upon her tongue. Not only did it lack the richness and superb delicacy of the language she had spoken all her life, there was none of Arabic's singsong intonation to soften it.

"I can teach him our language," she agreed, though she had no intention of wasting time learning more of the English her mother wished her to know intimately. She returned her attention to the man and was further unsettled when his gaze once more lowered over her.

Never had she felt uncomfortable in the clothes she wore within the women's quarters. But then, never had a man—not even her betrothed—looked at her as this one did.

Wondering what thoughts should so tug at the eunuch's mind that they should also tug at his lips, she looked down her front. Heat rose to her face as she considered what the thinly-woven material of her garments half-heartedly concealed—the swell of her breasts and flare of her hips.

Her first thought was to cover herself. Her next was that never had she felt ashamed of her body, and she would not begin now.

She tossed her head and asked in English, "What is your name?"

"He has taken the name of Seif," Sabine once more spoke for him.

"Seif." Alessandra nodded. "And his Christian name?"

"Of no consequence," Sabine said sharply. "In this household, he is Seif."

Surprised by her mother's vehemence, Alessandra turned to her. "Something is wrong?"

Sabine shook her head. "I am but tired."

Understandable considering her mother had spent the past three nights with Jabbar. Though he had two other wives and a dozen concubines, there was none he loved more than her mother. For this, Leila's dislike of Sabine was unequaled.

Alessandra put a hand beneath her mother's elbow and urged her toward the others. "Come sit."

Sabine drew back. "I am going to rest now. Perhaps you could introduce Seif to the others?"

Alessandra looked to the women of the harem. As predicted, they showed little interest in the musicians and dancers. However, the distraction provided by Sabine and her daughter had waned. It was the new eunuch who held their attention.

Knowing what they contemplated, Alessandra scowled. They were like vultures, hungry for more than Jabbar's passing attention. Even Leila, who usually hid her emotions well, appeared fascinated with Seif.

Sabine swept her gaze over the same faces her daughter looked upon. *The ice is thin here,* she warned herself. *Do not venture too far out upon it. Stay as near the edge as possible.*

Meaning she ought to remain here with Alessandra. And she would if not that the ice of her illness was thinner yet, threatening to make itself known to those who would use it to their benefit. But of greater concern was Jabbar. Not only would she spare him the pain of her approaching death, but she dare not provide him with an excuse to sooner see his son wed to Alessandra. Thus, Sabine paid the physician well to keep her secret and supply her with medicine of which she was very much in need at this moment.

"Go, Alessandra," she said.

"Very well." Her daughter turned to Lucien. "Come, Seif."

As he stepped forward, Sabine caught his arm. "Do not forget," she whispered. "No one is to know of my illness, especially my daughter."

He dipped his head. "None will hear of it from me."

Wishing she had greater confidence in his words, she dropped her hand. "Forget not our bargain."

"How could I?"

She watched him follow Alessandra. Though one would have to be blind not to notice her daughter's unusual beauty, never before had she seemed so provocative and sensual.

Lucien had also noticed. Though he had striven to keep his face impassive while watching Alessandra dance, Sabine had caught the light in his eyes and seen the flaring of nostrils and spasming of jaw muscles.

Was it possible he had not quenched his desires these past nights? Khalid had not spoken of that aspect of Lucien's training, and she had not felt compelled to ask since the eunuch had assured her the Englishman was ready to come among the women. But was he?

Even if her plan succeeded, would her daughter reach England untouched? Or would this giant of a man spoil her? And what if he discovered Alessandra's true identity?

Oh, foolish plan of mine, she silently lamented. But though tempted to abandon it, the alternative was worse. Concern over whether Alessandra reached England with her virtue intact was preferable to knowing the sort of life Rashid would give her. And once she was on English soil, she could escape Lucien de Gautier, if need be. It was a chance Sabine must take.

Khalid came alongside her. "The Englishman will be watched," he said.

She grimaced at the sight of that splendid nose knocked askew. Though Khalid had told her Lucien and he had come to an understanding and there would be no more trouble between them, she was not convinced—especially if De Gautier had not quenched his desires.

"Khalid, you ensured he was well sated, did you not?"

His lips thinned.

She drew a sharp breath. "You said he was ready."

"Apologies, mistress, but there are some things a man cannot be made to do, especially one as strong-willed as that. No matter the variety, and it was a wondrous selection, he turned away each prostitute delivered him—said never had he paid for a woman's embrace and he would not start in our wretched country."

Sabine momentarily closed her eyes. "We may be doomed, then."

"As told, he will be watched."

She jerked her chin. "Do not fail me, Khalid." With one last glance at her daughter and the man who stood alongside her, she withdrew from the room.

Attempting to block her awareness of the new eunuch, Alessandra focused on the dancers. She admired their colorful garments and the trinkets about their wrists, waists, and ankles that flashed color and sound with every movement.

How I envy their freedom! she silently bemoaned. *If only I could be as unfettered!*

Struggling to still the restlessness that tempted her back to the dance floor, she crossed her arms over her chest. But her body began to sway.

Only when a hand pulled her back did she realize she had stepped forward.

She snapped her gaze to the long, tanned fingers encircling her wrist, jerked her chin up. "Release me," she demanded in English.

Seif raised his eyebrows.

She tugged at her hand. It was futile, though not because his hold was tight. Indeed, his touch seemed almost a caress.

Jolted by a sensation that slid down her spine, she hissed, "Do you not let go, I will call the other eunuchs and have you removed."

"The dance is forbidden you, mistress. I but assure you do not further displease your mother."

Though Alessandra was grateful he had prevented her from compounding her crime, there was no reason for him to continue to hold her. "That you have done," she said. "Now release me!"

He drew his thumb across the inside of her wrist. "I but wait for this to calm."

Her pulse leaped higher. "You are too bold for a eunuch," she fiercely whispered. "Mayhap a whip across your back will put you in your place."

His derision cleared and he released her wrist. "Forgive me, mistress. As your mother told, I have much to learn."

Were it a genuine apology, she might have made allowances for him, but she knew he merely appeased her. Too, she did not like the flutterings roused by the touch of his eyes and hand—things never before experienced and which almost frightened her. They were too much like the music she could not resist.

Amid the applause that sounded at the end of the dancers' performance, Alessandra turned away.

Seif stepped into her path. "Were you not to introduce me to the others?"

"Introduce yourself," she said and stepped around him. Grateful he did not follow, she met Khalid's questioning gaze before hastening from the hall.

4

"INSUFFERABLE!" ALESSANDRA TOSSED up her hands.

Rising onto an elbow, Sabine watched her daughter pace, her hair a splash of color against the softly painted walls. "He is that," she agreed.

"Then for what did you purchase him?"

"You are spoiled, Alessandra. It takes time for a man recently made a eunuch to accept his fate. The Englishman will come around."

"But he is not like the others."

After a hesitation, her mother said, "Given time, he will be."

Alessandra rubbed her arms. "I do not like it when he touches me."

Sabine sat up. Had it started, then? If so, how long before her daughter succumbed to Lucien's seduction? Though steps could be taken to ensure her virtue remained intact while she remained in Algiers, once she was in Lucien's hands, Sabine had only his word that he would not touch Alessandra. And his word was not enough, especially considering her daughter's heightened awareness of those things far removed from a girl's world.

Silently, Sabine cursed the illness eating through her. If not for that which often incapacitated her, she could have continued to control Alessandra's exposure to the harem women and their boastful, vulgar tongues. Now, her daughter knew by word what she had been shielded from, and it would not be long before curiosity tempted her to gain knowledge through experience.

"He touched you?" Sabine could not keep the tremor from her voice.

Alessandra shrugged. "He but grabbed my wrist."

"For what?"

Her daughter ceased pacing, muttered, "He did not like what I was doing."

"Which was?"

"I did not mean to, but...I nearly gained the dance floor again."

Sabine dropped back on the divan. "And you think yourself suited to harem life." She shook her head. "You would be better off in England."

After a long silence, her daughter crossed the room and perched on the divan's edge. "Let us speak of the marketplace. You have not told me what else you purchased besides that dreadful eunuch."

"'Tis England we will speak of," Sabine said. "There is still much I have not told you."

Alessandra's shoulders slumped. "I know enough. I am the firstborn child of Lady Catherine—you—and Lord James Breville of Corburry. My father is wealthy and noble, a good man. Though you did not know it, you were with child when you were stolen from your home and sold into slavery—"

"Enough," Sabine said. "'Tis Agnes I would speak of."

"Agnes?"

"The cousin with whom I came to live when my parents died. I was ten years of age."

Alessandra had not heard of Agnes. She leaned nearer. "Were you great friends?"

A snort escaped Sabine. "We were rivals."

"In what way?"

"Every way. Agnes was a year older and quite lovely. Her parents doted on her and gave her everything."

"And you?"

Sabine shrugged. "I was not neglected. Though my clothes were those Agnes cast off, my playthings those she tossed aside, I was mostly content."

Alessandra felt a pang of sorrow for the lost girl her mother must have been. "Did you and Agnes quarrel much?"

"Often, and like boys—rolling on the ground, kicking, pulling each other's hair."

It was difficult to believe her gentle mother had engaged in such sport. Amused, Alessandra said, "Who won?"

"Agnes. Every time. She was larger than me."

"You never bettered her?"

"Aye, though not in wrestling."

"Tell!"

Sabine smiled. "Agnes wanted James Breville. She courted him, flirted outrageously, even asked him to marry her."

"And?"

Her mother laughed. "Though I had not encouraged him, James chose me."

It seemed a fitting revenge. "He loved you?"

"He did. It mattered not that my dowry was paltry. He wanted only me."

"And you loved him as well."

Smile lowering, Sabine lifted a hand and caressed her daughter's cheek. "I cannot lie. Never did I love your father, though I did have great affection for him."

Alessandra shook her head. "But you love Jabbar. I have heard you say so."

"Aye, though it was not so in the beginning. I hated the one who bought me and sought to make me his concubine. But he was patient with my Christian ways, and so handsome my tongue cleaved to my palate each time I looked at him. Not until you were born did he touch me." She sighed. "Though I did not wish it, I fell in love with him. And he with me."

"Thus, you became his wife."

"One of three."

"And you have been happy with him, have you not?"

Happy. Sabine turned the lovely word over in her mind, wished she could wholeheartedly claim it. "At times. Unfortunately, it is a difficult thing to share the man you love. For that, I do not wish this match between you and Rashid. It is not Christian. Nor is it English."

"I am not English—"

"'Tis the only blood in your veins, Daughter," Sabine said more sharply than intended, having pointed this out many times before. "Though you have been raised amongst those of a different culture and faith, you are English and true only to the god of the Christians. Thus, this is not the life I wish for you, nor the life you could live."

"You do not know that!"

"Do I not? Who cannot stand to be long indoors, who waxes impatient when there is naught to do but sit around the fountain and eat sweets, who longs to dance and go unveiled before all, who plays pranks and grows indignant when Rashid takes a concubine to bed?" Who, Sabine did not say aloud, was becoming too curious about what other women of the harem knew of men.

Alessandra surged to her feet, the bells around her ankles sounding harsh in the tense room. "I will hear no more."

Urgency lending Sabine speed, she caught her daughter's arm. "You are too spirited and strong-willed to become one of several wives. Though you wish to wed Rashid, such a life will not satisfy you."

Hurt flashed across Alessandra's face. "You would send me away? To England and people I do not know? People like that new eunuch? Why, he has not a smile with which to smite the devil from his eye!"

Fearful Alessandra might stumble upon the true purpose of Lucien de Gautier, Sabine let tears she often contained moisten her eyes. "You know 'tis my greatest desire that you return to your father."

Alessandra dragged her bottom lip between her teeth. "But what of you? If you would send me to him, why would you not also come?"

"My place is here, with Jabbar. This is my life—"

"As it is mine!"

"Nay, Alessandra, it will never be yours. You are your father's daughter—different from those simpering, conniving creatures Rashid will wed and take to his bed, rivals who will make you consider every morsel you place in your mouth for fear it could be your last."

Sabine recalled Leila's ill-fated attempt to poison her shortly after she had come to live in Jabbar's harem. Though the woman had already bore him his first son—Rashid—earning herself the esteemed position of mother of the heir, she had become intensely jealous as Jabbar showed his preference for Sabine. Thus, Leila had tried to murder her rival.

Sabine had shielded Alessandra from such things, but the danger was ever present. And now, it was time she learned of it. "Leila is as opposed to you wedding Rashid as I am. So much that she would think nothing of poisoning your food to be rid of you."

Alessandra stared at her mother. Though she was hardly ignorant of Leila's animosity, she did not believe Rashid's mother capable of murder. "I think you exaggerate. And even were that true, Rashid would not allow her to harm me."

Sabine made a sound low in her throat. "A fortnight before you were born, Leila poisoned my food. Fortunately, as I was so nauseated with pregnancy, I ate very little. Though it was not enough to kill me, I was sick unto death. Nay, Alessandra, there is nothing Rashid could do to prevent his mother from doing the same to you. I was fortunate. You may not be."

Alessandra was so shaken that it was some time before she could form coherent words. "For this, Khalid oversees the preparation of everything we eat—the reason I am forbidden to take food from Leila."

Sabine stroked her arm. "Thus, I do not want this life for you."

"But…" Alessandra shook her head. "Why did Jabbar not punish Leila?"

"He did. He took Rashid from her and sent her back to her family. Had her son not needed her, he would not have allowed her to return, but Rashid became so distraught that he refused to eat. Day and night he cried, his small body growing weak." She sighed. "As Jabbar could not bring himself to send his son away, he brought Leila back."

Alessandra gripped her hands so hard they hurt. "Yet you would send me away."

"England is your home. There you will be safe."

Though Alessandra feared as never before, she could not accept that she must be forever parted from all she knew. "I understand your concern, but I will not leave you, nor those with whom I have been raised."

"You will leave."

"I will not." Alessandra pushed upright. "And there is naught you can do to change my mind."

"Then I will not change your mind."

Sabine's threat was not of the sort that promised to take away sweets or minor privileges. Still, Alessandra pressed, "Jabbar will not send me away, and neither will he allow you to do so."

Face flushing, her mother said, "I ask no man for permission to do with my daughter what must be done to keep her safe. I bore you, and *I* will decide your fate."

Alessandra took a step back. This was a different woman from the one who had raised her. This one was unyielding—almost cruelly.

But then Sabine blinked, and the hard lines of her face eased as if she slid back into herself. "Because I love you so much," she said softly, "you cannot stay."

Alessandra moved nearer, gripped her mother's hand. "Because I love you so much, I will resist any attempt to steal me from your side. Though I am not Arab, neither am I English. This is where I belong, and here I will stay."

"Then you will fight me."

"Pray, do not make me, Mother."

With a sad smile, Sabine said, "You know how I dislike losing."

Hoping the matter was settled, Alessandra kissed her cheek. "You are not losing. We both gain."

Sabine considered her. "There is something else we must speak of," she said. "You are not to tell Seif of your English background."

Alessandra frowned. "He is a eunuch. There is not much chance we shall engage in such a conversation."

"Nevertheless, do not name your father, nor speak of his lands."

"You have never forbidden me such. Why now?"

"It does not matter. Just do not speak of it."

"What are you hiding?" She and her mother had always been close such that, until the revelation of Leila's murder attempt, Alessandra would have said there were no secrets between. But it seemed there were more secrets, and one of them had to do with the Englishman.

Sabine laced her fingers, stared at them. "Is it not enough that I ask this of you?"

"It is not easy to accept the secrets you put between us. And you know how deep my curiosity."

"Very well," Sabine acceded, "I will tell you, but ask me no more. Though I did not know it when I purchased him, the eunuch's English name is Lucien de Gautier."

Alessandra tried to remember where she had heard it.

"He is of the same family whose lands adjoin those of the Brevilles. The family who has been at odds with your father's family for years."

Now she remembered, though the details were vague. "Continue, Mother."

"For many years, theirs was a blood feud. Before I was taken from England, it had mostly lessened to petty skirmishes and disagreements, but still their dislike for one another went deep."

"Did the De Gautiers sell you into slavery?"

"I do not know, though I have considered it."

"And as Seif is a relation, you fear he might do us harm should he discover our identity."

"It is possible, especially now that he has recently become a eunuch. I think, in time, he will settle down, but one should never knowingly cross swords with the devil."

Alessandra smiled at the comparison. "I shall say nothing of my lineage."

"Do not forget," Sabine cautioned. "You cannot know how important it is."

5

RISING BEFORE THE other women of the harem, Alessandra dressed and ascended to the roof terrace she often frequented. From there, she could observe the boats on the Mediterranean and watch the sun rise above the city of Algiers.

Her mother's husband, an intensely private man, had chosen to build his sprawling home inland, away from the city. Its location was inconvenient, as it could take a half day to reach Algiers's bustling marketplace if one traveled by donkey. However, the journey could be made in two hours upon a swift horse. Or so Alessandra was told.

Plagued as always by restlessness—Sabine claimed it was her father in her—she had been disappointed when she had not been allowed to accompany her mother into the city the last few times. In her search for a new eunuch, Sabine had been adamant that Alessandra remain behind. And they had argued over it.

Soon, though, Alessandra would be allowed to venture into the city, for she needed cloth for her wedding attire. Although she and Rashid were not to wed for several months, it would take considerable time to complete the embroidery that would adorn her costume.

She wrinkled her nose in anticipation of the endless hours of needle and thread. Though proficient at sewing, it was a chore she disliked. But, as with most things her mother insisted she master, it was a skill of gentle Englishwomen.

With the coming of dawn, Alessandra lowered to her knees and clasped her hands before her. She had only begun her prayers when a voice said, "To which god do you pray? Muhammad's, or that of the Christians?"

She jumped to her feet, spun around. "For what are you here?"

The new eunuch straightened from the wall. "I followed you."

He had been watching her all this time? "Why?" she demanded, resenting that with each step he took, the farther back she had to tilt her head.

He halted within reach and looked out across the land to where the city lay. "I thought we might begin our lessons. If I am to converse well with the women, I must know more of your language."

"It is not among your duties to *converse* with the women," Alessandra said, and her irritation deepened as she imagined how the wives and concubines must have vied for his attention after she had deserted him two days earlier. Since then, she had seen little of him, Khalid having commanded his time.

"I would not think it my duty," he conceded, "but they seem of a different mind."

That did not surprise her, though it vexed her. Drawing her cloak tightly about her, she said, "Until you have learned your place, eunuch, I have no intention of teaching you anything. You are too ill-mannered and rude."

"Because I prevented you from making more of a spectacle of yourself?"

Her dancing. "Once again, you overstep your bounds, Seif." Turning away, she lowered her lids against the brilliance of the ascending sun. "Leave me."

She listened for his departure, but the heat of his body continued to warm her back as the sun warmed her front. Thinking he would grow bored and wander off, she feigned ignorance of his continued presence. However, her body paid no heed to her pretense, as acutely aware of his proximity as if his hands caressed her rather than his heat.

Why, she wondered, *does this eunuch have such an effect upon me? And what, exactly, is the effect?* It felt like nothing she had experienced. Was it what the women of the harem named desire?

Impossible. He was not even handsome—certainly, not like Rashid.

"You have not answered my question." His breath swept her ear, making her startle.

"Wh-what question?" she asked, keeping her back to him.

"Whether or not you are a pagan. Are you, Sabine's daughter?"

The sun was not up a full ten minutes, yet she felt as if she could shed her cloak. "I do not have to answer that."

He laid a hand on her shoulder and turned her. Stunned by his boldness, she remained unmoving as he slid his fingers down her throat, hooked them around the chain encircling her neck, and pulled the crucifix from her caftan. Cradling it in his palm, he said, "Christian. Though you are still a bit of a pagan, are you not?"

She jumped back, causing the crucifix to whip out of his hand and fall against her chest. "You dare!" she stormed and reflexively pressed a hand to her throat and collarbone where she yet felt the warmth of his touch.

His eyes laughed at her. "Would you like me to return your crucifix to its hiding place?"

He knew exactly the effect he had upon her, she realized, and chastised herself for behaving the same as Jabbar's women who were too long absent attention. And never had she known such attentions that she should miss them!

Hitching up her cloak, she darted past him toward the stairs. A moment later, she came up against a firm chest and found herself wrapped in arms that had held her so near only when she was a child.

"Rashid!" She peered up into his startled face.

"You are in a hurry." He set her back from him. "I had hoped to have a few minutes with you before father and I depart for the city. We will be gone a sennight."

Insides tight with worry, Alessandra looked over her shoulder at where Seif watched with arms crossed over his chest.

Yielding to the recklessness her mother tried so hard to wrest from her, she threw her arms around Rashid's neck and pressed her mouth to his. It was her first kiss, but what should have been saved for her wedding night was nothing like what she had hoped. She strained to feel a greater thrill than that roused by the mere touch of the eunuch's hand, but there was only a whisper of something sweet.

"Alessandra!" Rashid set her back a second time. "This is highly improper. What is wrong with you?"

Shame washed over her. "I am sorry. I do not know…"

What *was* wrong with her? Why had she felt so little? Why had Rashid not responded? Had it been the same for him? Or was it propriety that held him back? She loved him, did she not? Felt the same for him that her mother felt for Jabbar?

Perhaps not. They had grown up together and, despite Leila's attempts to keep them apart, had been as close as brother and sister. Was that all there was between them? Had it not become something more?

"Is this the new eunuch?" Rashid asked, stepping past her.

Reluctantly, she followed. "He is the one Mother recently purchased."

Rashid frowned over his shoulder. "For what is he here with you?"

Alessandra grasped at the only excuse to which she could lay her thoughts. "Mother asked that I teach him our language. Since his duties are many once the household awakens, early morn seemed a good time."

He halted before Seif, clasped his hands behind his back, and considered the man whom his father's coin had bought.

From where Alessandra came to stand beside him, she silently implored the eunuch to lower his eyes in deference to the master's son. But his gaze was as sharp and unwavering as when he looked upon her.

Fortunately, Rashid was even-tempered, his ire not easily roused. In contrast, Jabbar would likely have had the eunuch put to the bastinado.

"He has more to learn than just our language," Rashid pronounced. "I think his time would be better spent with Khalid, do you not?"

"I...yes."

Rashid stepped nearer Seif. "I am Rashid, firstborn of Abd al-Jabbar," he said in Arabic. "You are?"

"Seif."

Smiling faintly, Rashid looked to Alessandra. "He learns fast."

She raised her gaze to the eunuch's. "So he does." She cared less that he had corroborated her story than that he understood more than she had been led to believe.

Abruptly, Rashid turned and strode opposite.

Alessandra hurried after him. "You wished to speak with me?"

"I had thought there might be a bauble you would like from the city," he said as he began his descent of the stairs.

She paused to look back at the lone figure silhouetted against the new sky. Though he had turned toward the city, she was certain he laughed at her.

Long after Alessandra and Rashid had departed, Lucien remained atop the roof and surveyed the home of Abd al-Jabbar. It was immense, spread out over nearly as much land as the whole of the De Gautier castle in England. Like the castle, it was fortified with walls patrolled by guards, but there the resemblance ended.

The main living quarters, a large flat-topped structure built of ponderous blocks of stone, was only two stories high. Therein was housed the hall, the kitchens, and meeting rooms for the men. Three single-storied buildings jutted out from it, one being the harem and apartments of the women, the second the bathhouse, the third the men's apartments.

Between the harem and the bathhouse lay a spacious garden with a marble-tiled fishpond at its center. Farther out were the eunuchs' quarters, the servants' quarters, the stables and storehouses. Though not as imposing as most castles in England, the mansion was more opulent with its tiled floors, arcades formed by marble pillars, and numerous fountains. Luxury, not security, had been the primary consideration in its construction.

Had he not given his word to Sabine, Lucien reflected, he could have escaped this place his first day. But he must wait on the impetuous Alessandra.

Grinding his teeth, he considered the dangerous game he played with her. He had not intended to engage in such sport. But then, previous to their introduction, he had thought her to be but a blushing girl, and he had certainly not expected her to be so lovely. Except for her warm skin tone that evidenced she was fond of the sun, it was impossible to tell that any blood other than English coursed her veins. Too, she had all the looks of her mother.

It was a long time since he had been so attracted to a woman. And that he should feel it for this one astounded him—she who moved easily among those who had made of him a slave. More, he resented being raked by jealousy when she had kissed the arrogant Rashid.

He had learned of their impending marriage from Khalid, but only from the young man's boasting this morn had he discovered that Rashid was also an offspring of Jabbar. The two were half siblings, then.

Did the Islamic faith permit such close marriages? Though Lucien had learned much of the Arab people and their culture this past year, this was an area of which he had little knowledge. Surely this was Sabine's real reason for wanting her daughter taken to England. Having remained a Christian, she could not approve of such a union.

And there would not be one. As agreed, he would deliver Alessandra into the hands of her mother's relatives in England.

Strange, but he was no longer as concerned about their escape as he had been. Though dangerous, it did not seem as perilous as the temptation he would face once the fiery young woman was in his care.

"Almighty!" he grumbled. Perhaps he should not have turned away the women Khalid had pressed upon him. Perhaps—

Nay, the course he had set himself was the right one, though it meant he must be vigilant in all things Alessandra. Were he not, he could find himself a true eunuch.

6

"Alessandra, join us!"

Idly pushing back and forth on the swing, Alessandra looked over her shoulder at the spectacle emerging from the trees.

A donkey between them, the daughters of the wives and concubines entered the garden. Though all were younger than she by four years or more, the older ones having been married away, Alessandra grinned and slipped off the swing. She had taken but a step forward when the feel of Seif's gaze halted her. With a muffled groan, she reseated herself.

"You can be the gentleman first," called Nada, an exotic, sable-headed girl.

Alessandra shook her head, telling herself it would be enough to watch the others enjoy themselves.

Quickly, Nada was readied for her ride. Dressed as a man—eyebrows thickened with kohl, mustache painted above her upper lip—a carved melon perched upon her head, she was helped onto the donkey. Facing backward, she took hold of the animal's tail that was handed to her. Then, with a single kick, away she went.

Laughing, she held tight and tried to keep her balance as the donkey trotted through the garden. As was most often the case, the melon was the first to go, cracking and spilling its seeds onto the stone path and causing the animal to leap forward. With a shriek, Nada fell into a flower bed.

How Alessandra wished Seif would go indoors! There was none better at the game than she, who almost always made the full circuit of the garden, melon and all. Lest she give in to impulsiveness, she gripped the swing ropes tighter.

A moment later, Leila's husky laughter caused Alessandra to peer over her shoulder. A hand on Seif's forearm, the woman smiled up at him.

Though the eunuch did not appear to be encouraging her, something stirred inside Alessandra. Whatever it was, it made her strongly dislike what she saw.

How soon before the still-beautiful Leila made him hers? she wondered. With the exception of Khalid, all the eunuchs had succumbed to her wiles at one time—and in one form—or another.

Leila stepped nearer Seif.

Seemingly oblivious, the eunuch shifted his regard to Alessandra. Though his face reflected little emotion, his eyes sparkled.

Berating herself for staring, Alessandra returned her attention to the game. And enjoyed it less as she struggled against the need to once more look upon Seif.

With each successive rider, the donkey became less accommodating, its irritation manifested in increased speed, quivering hindquarters, and incessant braying. Thus, it was not surprising when it kicked its hind legs and threw its rider, who landed among spiny bushes.

Alessandra launched herself from the swing and was the first to reach the wailing girl. "I am here, sweet one," she soothed as she disentangled her from the greedy thorns, wincing as she, herself, fell victim to the drawing of blood. "Hush, Pearl. You are almost free."

The wails turned to whimpers when Alessandra lifted her from the bushes and set her on her feet. As the others gathered around, Alessandra smiled encouragingly. "There now. All is better."

Lower lip trembling, Pearl sniffed hard.

LADY OF FIRE

"Ah, sweet one"—Alessandra pushed tear-dampened hair off her
brow—"it was foolish of you to play the game."

The girl's weepy eyes widened. "I have seen you play it!"

"But I am much older and more experienced."

A *harrumph* brought Alessandra's head around, and she saw that the
woman who would soon be her mother-in-law stood behind her.

A small dog clasped beneath an arm, a smile curving her mouth,
Leila said, "I think you were brave, dear Pearl."

Alessandra gasped. It was ill of the woman to encourage one who
was too young and slight to participate in the game.

"Indeed," Leila continued, "not even Alessandra has ridden a beast as
roused to temper as that one is."

"That is not true," Alessandra exclaimed.

Leila sent her eyebrows high. "Then let us see if you can ride him."

Alessandra knew she was being taunted, that she should not
accept the challenge, but she looked to where Seif stood near the
fishpond.

She would not be dancing, she reasoned, and she had not been
forbidden to take part in the garden games. Indeed, it was not unheard
of for the older women to participate. What harm in it, and why should
she care what the new eunuch thought of her?

She returned her gaze to Pearl. "Give me the man's clothes."

Excited chatter rose from the dark-browed, mustached girls as
Alessandra submitted to the preparations. Throughout, she kept her gaze
averted from Seif.

I will not fail, she assured herself. *I will keep the melon atop my head
and traverse the entire garden without mishap. I will make that insufferable man
swallow his mirth.*

Transformed into a *gentleman,* she was soon seated on the animal, its
tail in one hand. Knowing it would be a difficult ride with the donkey
in such an agitated state, she tightened her legs about him and steeled
herself for the jolt.

"Away!" Nada landed a hand to the animal's rump.

— 39 —

Immediately, the melon began to slip, forcing Alessandra to angle her head to keep it aloft.

The donkey followed the path at a brisk pace, jostling its rider. As it approached the first curve, it increased its speed and, when that did not unseat Alessandra, leaned hard into it.

Clamping her thighs tighter, Alessandra concentrated on keeping the melon atop her head, blurring her eyes so she would not be distracted.

She could not see the fishpond from her backward-facing position, but she knew when she neared it and the end of her ride. As she silently rejoiced, she nearly lost the melon. Righting it, she smiled in anticipation of her first glimpse of water.

There! She threw her hands up and let the melon fall.

Amid the applause, a yipping dog darted between the donkey's legs, and Alessandra had only enough time to register the danger before the animal bucked with such force it rid itself of its rider.

Air, of which Alessandra's desperate hands could not catch hold. Water, that parted to ease her fall but proved too shallow. Pain, for which she had no time. Not yet. First, breath.

She thrust up onto her knees and dropped to all fours when a sharp ache pierced her head. Braced on outstretched arms, she coughed to clear her lungs and, with her first, strangled breath, noted the water's pink cast.

No sooner did she acknowledge it was blood that tainted the water, than she was plucked from it.

Oblivion beckoned, merging the babble of voices such that there was only one she clearly discerned—Leila's.

"I do not know how it happened," the woman cried. "I do not know how he got away from me."

Alessandra squeezed her eyes against the pounding behind her eyes. "Ah, Khalid," she breathed, "am I going to die?"

"Nay, little one." The words were English. "You will not."

There was no more voiceless laughter, and arms that should not be comforting made her want to stay in them forever. Pressing her face to Seif's chest, she settled into his warmth and went adrift.

Cold.

Turning onto her side, Alessandra drew her knees to her chest and wrapped her arms around them, whimpering when the movement sharpened the ache at the back of her head.

She threw out a hand and groped for something to drag over her, but found only pillows. Once more hugging her shivering limbs, she startled when light forced its way through her lids.

"Mother?" she croaked.

As warm hands lifted her legs and tugged at something wrapped around them, she eased her eyes open and squinted against the light that shone in a room otherwise darkened by night.

The large figure bending over the foot of her divan was Seif, though it should not be. Once the stars came out, even eunuchs were forbidden the harem—except Khalid. She was about to ask the reason he was here with her when she remembered this was not the first time she had awakened, and each time he had been beside her mother.

He pulled the blanket free from its entanglement with her feet.

"Where is my mother?" she asked.

He stepped near, draped the blanket over her, and tucked it around her.

"Where?" she pressed, as much to know the answer as to distract herself from his touch.

He straightened to his overwhelming height. "I would think she is sleeping."

"Then why are you here?"

"Your mother and Khalid ordered me to sleep outside your apartment until Jabbar's return. They are concerned for your wellbeing."

The accident.

Alessandra remembered the sensation of flying through the air. Next, breathing in the water, coughing it out, seeing it stained with blood. Then the arms that had lifted her and held her close.

She drew a hand from beneath the blanket and touched the bandage wound around her head. "How did it happen?"

"Leila's dog frightened the donkey."

The warmth that had begun to move through her receded as her mother's disclosure of days earlier, and Leila's taunting that had enticed Alessandra into mounting the donkey, melded. Had it been an accident, or had Leila set out to harm her as Sabine had warned?

"Was it an accident, Seif?" she said between teeth that had begun to click.

He removed his robe and also fit it around her. "Your mother does not believe so."

Alessandra gripped his arm. "What do you think?"

"It may have been an accident. It may have been deliberate."

"You do not know which?"

He lifted her hand from his arm, slid it back beneath the covers. "As your betrothed told, there is much I have yet to learn of your language."

Fearful he meant to leave, she said, "Is it late?"

"It is quite early. In two hours, it will be day again. Sleep now, and I will summon your mother at first light." He turned away.

"Do not go!"

He lifted the lamp he had brought within and looked back. "My place is outside your door, mistress."

"Can you not stay until dawn? I am cold and…" Unable to believe the shameless thing she was about to say, she lowered her eyes. "…I need your warmth."

He was silent so long she thought he must have slipped away, but when she looked up, he watched her.

"It would be improper," he said, "and I would not wish to feel Khalid's whip across my back."

Nor would she wish him to feel it. "I should not have asked." She turned her face opposite. "I am sorry."

More silence, then she heard his advance. When he halted alongside the divan, she looked around. "What is it?"

He extinguished the lamp and, amid the dark, urged her across the divan.

Alessandra clutched the cover to her chest. "But I thought——"

"It will be our secret." He seated himself beside her, put his back to the wall, and pulled her up against his side.

It was a mistake to have invited his trespass, and yet she could not bring herself to send him away.

She breathed in his scent that was unlike any she had known. His skin and clothing wafted no hint of spice or perfume, nothing to mask his odor that was so strangely pleasant she could only liken it to Rashid's prize stallion.

She loved the smell of the high-strung, temperamental beast, and had buried her face in his neck the one time she had been allowed so near him. How she had longed to bend low over the stallion's neck and feel and hear his labored breathing as he turned still air into wind, but no matter how she begged, Rashid said it was dangerous and would not even take her up before him. Still, she was certain he would eventually yield and the powerful stallion that so reminded her of this man—who was no longer a man—would carry her away.

"If you relax," Seif said, "sleep will come more easily."

With a nervous laugh, she eased the stiffness from her spine and settled more deeply against him. "Do you know what I am thinking?" she asked.

"I do not."

"How like a horse you are—a great stallion who runs with the wind."

"Is that so?"

"Rashid has such a stallion named Altair. It means flying eagle."

"Does he fly like an eagle?"

"I am certain he must, though I have not been allowed to ride him."

"And you would like to."

She sighed. "Very much. But Rashid says Altair will not tolerate a woman rider."

"That is true of some stallions."

"I do not see why. I can sit a horse the same as Rashid." Seif need not know her experience was limited to donkeys, nor that she had only been astride a gentle horse with Rashid at her back and controlling the reins.

"You think so?" the eunuch asked.

Alessandra yawned, closed her eyes. "I am certain of it." Relaxing the hand with which she held to the front of his caftan, she lowered it to his lap, and as she began to drift, felt Seif shift as if uncomfortable.

His hand turned around hers, fingers brushed the skin of her palm and wrist that had never before seemed so sensitive. Then his mouth was in her hair, warm breath caressing her scalp. "And I am certain you would find neither a stallion, nor a man like me, as easy to control as you think."

"Still, I would like to try."

Something rumbled from the chest beneath her ear, and he said, "Sleep, Alessandra."

"I thank you for staying. It is kind of you." She yawned again.

As Alessandra settled into sleep, Lucien breathed in her perfumed hair and acknowledged that what had made him stay was more the desire to know the feel of her than kindness. And, again, he wondered what he was getting into. This was not part of the bargain struck with Sabine. Indeed, he risked emasculation were he discovered abed with her daughter, no matter how innocent it might be. And considering the path his mind kept wandering down, it was nowhere near innocent.

He sighed. A wise man would not place himself in such a situation. But still he could not bring himself to slip away now that she slept. Too much, he liked the feel and scent of her. More, he admired her spirit—refreshing in light of the women with whom he had previously associated.

There had been quite a few, though he could not link names with the blurred faces he called forth. Even the two to whom he had been betrothed were as indistinct as the others.

Absently stroking Alessandra's hair, he wondered at his failing memory.

7

SABINE REFUSED TO believe her daughter's fall was anything other than a deliberate attempt to harm her. Thus, Alessandra found herself in Seif's company thereafter.

He followed her everywhere, excepting those places he was not allowed. It would not have been bad had she not shamed herself by pleading with him to stay with her three nights past—and had she not continued to feel the sense of loss with which she had been afflicted upon awakening alone the morning after. Blessedly, he had yet to speak of the incident.

Now, feeling healed after the rest her mother had insisted upon, Alessandra decided it was time for a bath. At the hour of the day when most of the women congregated in the bathhouse, she left her room.

As she walked past Seif, he stepped from the wall, and his shadow fell over her. Only when the sulfurous vapor greeted her near the bathhouse did it occur to her he might follow her inside. Though she had never felt uncomfortable disrobing in the presence of those eunuchs who watched over the women, the thought of doing so in front of this one disturbed her.

At the door, she turned. "You may wait here. I will not be long."

"The baths are not forbidden me. I tended them my first day here."

Then he knew the state of the women inside. "You will wait here," she repeated and gave her back to him.

Seif's hand fell to the door, preventing her from opening it. "If you go inside, so shall I."

Alessandra turned back around. "No harm can be done me in the baths."

"Unless it is forbidden me, I am to go where you go. That includes the baths. Am I any different from other eunuchs?"

She wanted to tell him he was very different, but she had yet to understand what set him apart from the others. After all, it was only a feeling, one that appalled and confused her.

"Very well," she said, "you may accompany me."

She was pleased by the surprise that flashed across his face. Clearly, he had expected her to forgo her bath.

He pulled open the door and stood back to allow her to precede him.

In the antechamber, a servant girl greeted her. "You are better, mistress?"

"I am. I but require a bath to wash away these past days."

From a table laden with various items, the girl removed a thick bathrobe, a towel, and high wooden clogs.

"You may go ahead," Alessandra instructed Seif.

"I will wait for you."

She would have protested, but he considerately turned and strode to the door that led into the baths. Uncertain as to how much time she had before he looked around, she tossed off her clothes, thrust her arms into the robe the girl held for her, and slipped her feet into clogs that would spare her the heat of the marble floor. Then, taking the proffered towel, she hurried forward.

"You are prompt," Seif said.

Now closer to his height, though she still had to angle her head to meet his gaze, Alessandra said, "You expected otherwise?"

With a bit of a smile, he reached for the door.

The bathhouse was spacious, a large pool at its center, marble sinks spaced along the walls for bathing.

As expected, most of the harem women were present, their curious gazes falling upon Seif and Alessandra as they entered. While some were being bathed at the sinks, others languished beside the pool, eating sweetmeats and engaging in idle talk, bodies shamelessly exposed. Only two—one of them Nada—had ventured into the pool whose warm water caused a haze to cloak the bathhouse.

Alessandra was thankful for Leila's absence. As first wife, she had a private bathing chamber, but it was not unusual to find her gossiping here.

"You should have worn pattens as well," Alessandra whispered to Seif.

"Pattens?"

"Clogs." She nodded at hers.

He grimaced. "I have not the grace, nor the tolerance, to balance upon such silly footwear."

"The other eunuchs wear them."

Peering through the haze, he considered the two who kept watch over the women. "So they do."

"Alessandra!" Nada called.

Alessandra looked to the girl whose bare shoulders were visible above the water.

"You are well?" Nada asked.

Alessandra inclined her head. "I am healed."

"Allah is merciful!" Nada turned and swam opposite.

God is merciful, Alessandra silently amended, knowing better than to speak it aloud.

When the servant girl who stood ready to bathe her beckoned, Alessandra said, "Wait here. This I do alone," and stepped away from Seif.

Though his feet did not follow, his eyes did. She knew it as surely as she knew she would soon be as unclothed as the others. Hoping the haze would dull his vision, she kept her back to him as the servant began to remove the robe the heat caused to cling to her skin.

"Do not!" Alessandra snatched the lapels closed.

"Mistress?" The girl clasped her hands at her waist. "Have I offended?"

Alessandra did not understand the bout of modesty that ought to be reserved for Rashid when she came to their nuptial bed, but she was so overwhelmed by the thought of Seif seeing her bare body that the warm air grew thick, and she felt almost ill.

"Mistress?" The girl's eyes sparkled as if she might spill tears.

"You have not offended. I am chilled, that is all." Alessandra touched her head that was yet tender. "I suppose I am not entirely healed, but still you can assist with my ablutions." She lowered to the stool before the sink.

Immediately, the girl began gathering up Alessandra's hair and securing it atop her head. When she moved to the sink to retrieve soap and towel, Alessandra looked over her shoulder.

Seif was where she had left him, but he had turned to the side. Arms crossed over his chest, he appeared fascinated by the gleaming fixtures that carried water into the bath house. But as he had surely seen them when last he was here, she wondered if his interest was a means of affording her privacy—unaware she had not shed her robe as was the normal course of bathing.

As if feeling watched, he looked around. His gaze held hers a moment, then he moved it down her robed figure. On the return to her face, he paused upon her nape that was no longer curtained by her hair, and which she had heard was an exquisite place to feel a man's kiss.

When his eyes once more settled to hers, she could barely breathe, but though she longed to break the contact that stretched between them like a taut, unraveling rope, she could not.

If his eyes could so affect her, what might his hands do if ever she allowed them to touch her as boldly? Those things the wives and concubines spoke of when their conversations turned to lovemaking?

For shame, Alessandra! she silently rebuked. *You ought not to have such thoughts—not of Rashid, and certainly not of this eunuch!*

As the rational reminder banished sensations she should not feel, an outlandish thought crept in. *Or is he a eunuch?*

Was it mere coincidence her mother had purchased an Englishman to replace the eunuch who had fallen into disfavor? Eunuchs were not so scarce that Sabine would have had to settle for one so inexperienced. And then for her to force his company upon Alessandra…

The appearance of a concubine at Seif's side broke their eye contact, and Alessandra turned forward again.

"Is your chill gone, mistress?" the servant girl asked where she knelt at Alessandra's feet.

It was long gone, but to admit it would be to consent to the removal of her robe. "I fear not."

With a sympathetic smile, the girl slipped the clogs from Alessandra's feet. "Then I shall bathe you one limb at a time, and when you are clean, I will henna your hands and feet. Then you will feel yourself again."

If only she *could* feel herself again. She did not like the turmoil she had been suffering since Seif's arrival, nor that she had such sinful feelings for the eunuch when she had none for Rashid.

A half hour later, scrubbed clean, hair washed and hanging damp down her back, Alessandra rose from the stool and tightened the belt of her robe.

"You are leaving?" the girl asked. "What of the henna I promised?"

"Another day. I am still chilled." It was even more of a lie now considering the perspiration dotting her brow, but she could not stand to sit still any longer.

Avoiding looking toward Seif, she approached the women clustered at the pool's edge and lowered herself beside Hayfa, second wife to Jabbar. Raising the hem of her robe, she sank her feet in the water.

Hayfa, whose once slender body had grown heavy with overindulgence, scooted near and flicked the robe's sleeve. "You will faint if you insist on wearing that."

"I have taken a chill," Alessandra said, hoping to quell the whisperings about her remaining clothed. "When I am warm again, I will remove it."

Hayfa leaned close. "Tell me of this new eunuch. What type is he?"

She knew what the woman referred to, but could not keep her cheeks from coloring with embarrassment. "I can tell you nothing."

TAMARA LEIGH

"Hmmph," grunted a concubine who had been listening. "Is it not you with whom he has spent these past days?"

The woman made it sound as if she and Seif were lovers! Though Alessandra knew she should not allow herself to be drawn into this conversation, she felt a need to defend her innocence. "He has been given the task of following me wherever I go and sleeping outside my apartment. That is all."

From the women's expressions, it was clear neither believed her, making Alessandra's palms itch to smack their smirks away.

"If it is true our innocent Alessandra knows nothing of his type," Hayfa said, "perhaps she should ask him."

"Ask him yourself," Alessandra said.

"I think she is frightened of him," Hayfa submitted. "See how she keeps herself covered in his presence. Perhaps he has warmed her cold English blood, and she knows not what to do."

It was too near the truth. Though Alessandra wanted to ignore the challenge, she hastened to her feet. "I am not frightened of him," she said and started toward Seif.

Legs braced apart, hands clasped behind his back, he watched her approach through narrowed lids.

She halted before him and looked up with what she hoped was indifference. "Hayfa"—she nodded at the woman—"wishes to know what type of eunuch you are."

Puzzlement lined his brow. "Of what do you speak?"

She groaned inwardly. He surely knew to what she referred and but played with her. Knowing she could not return without the information, she said, "She would know if you are the type who can make love to a woman and yet not spoil her with a child the master would deny as his"—how she hated the tremble in her voice!—"or the type who has been...altered such that he can do neither."

His eyebrows lowered over his amethyst-colored eyes. "How do you know of such things?"

— 50 —

So great was her discomfort that she nearly fled, but as she had come this far, she gestured to the eunuch who stood on the other side of the pool. "As Hayfa often boasts, Yusuf is able to give pleasure without getting her with child. Thus, he is of the first type of eunuch."

"Has he given you pleasure as well?"

Her knees nearly buckled. That he would suggest—

She tamped down her outrage with the reminder it was the same as Hayfa and the concubine alluded to. That a young woman could reach the age of eight and ten and remain untouched was almost unheard of in a land where girls were often wed by their thirteenth birthday. Alessandra would have been wed as well had her mother not interceded time and again. Thus, she was chaste among women who had long known a man's touch and pitied her for her lack of experience.

Though the denial had been upon her lips, instead she lied. "I am no maiden."

His eyes bored into hers as if he might see the truth of her words, but finally, he said, "And I am no Yusuf. You may tell Hayfa and her friends I am the same as Khalid."

Alessandra caught her breath. This day, she had entertained the possibility he might not even be a eunuch, and now to be told he was one in every sense of the word...

"I do not believe you."

He shrugged. "Though you claim to have no maidenly senses left to offend, I do not think your mother would like it if I offered proof."

Flushing toe to scalp, presenting the very real possibility she might be overcome by heat as Hayfa warned, Alessandra whirled and made as swift a retreat from the bathhouse as she could manage.

Long after she had enclosed herself in her apartment, she still felt Seif's laughter and heard that of Hayfa and the concubine.

As Lucien exited the bathhouse, Sabine returned to the shadows where she had slipped upon witnessing Alessandra's flight. Hand to her chest, she searched the Englishman's profile as he strode past, certain he had the answers to the questions spinning through her mind.

What had been the cause of Alessandra's haste? Why the flush upon her skin that could not be solely attributed to heat? Why her trembling lips and the tears in her eyes?

All manner of imaginings plagued Sabine, each tied to Lucien de Gautier and none without foundation. He had been in the bathhouse as Alessandra bathed and had undoubtedly seen what was denied Englishmen until they wed the lady.

What had happened between them? Certainly nothing untoward with the others present, but something.

The coughing came again, but she suppressed it until Lucien was out of sight. When she released it, wheezing and gasping breaths threatened to prostrate her. Desperate to muffle the terrible sounds, she lifted the skirt of her caftan, pressed it to her mouth, and lurched toward her apartment.

Providing she could reach it without calling attention to herself, she could lie down and clear her mind enough to determine what to do.

A moment later, Khalid's concerned face swam before her and he lifted her high in his great arms. "Hush, mistress," he soothed. "I am here. Give over to me."

Clenching fistfuls of his robe, coughing into his chest, she was mollified by the knowledge that, as always, he would take care of everything.

8

"E<small>NTER</small>!" A<small>LESSANDRA CALLED</small>. Without turning from the latticed window, she motioned her visitor forward. "Come see."

A moment later, she wished she had not, struck as she was by an awareness of the man she had left in the bathhouse an hour past. Had she known it was Seif, she would not have answered his knock.

"What is it?" he asked, his arm brushing hers as he came alongside.

She drew her arms nearer her body, nodded at the two romping in the garden. "There."

"Ah, gazelles."

"A mother and her baby. It is the first I have seen of the little one since its birth."

Seif made a sound of acknowledgment, then said, "I have come to apologize."

She kept her gaze fastened upon the gazelles. "For?"

"I should not have been so forward with you."

"That is true."

"Then you accept my apology?"

She sighed. "Mother says allowances must be made for you, so that I shall do."

"What sort of allowances?"

As seemed to be becoming a habit regarding him, she wished she had said less. She shrugged. "You are English. Thus, you cannot know our ways."

"How are your ways different from mine?"

She reflected a moment. "I do not know exactly, only that they are."

He chuckled, a sound made new by the fact it came from him. "The differences are great, mistress. For instance…" He gently pried her fingers from the lattice she gripped.

Surprised that he would touch her again, and so soon after apologizing for being forward, she tried to pull free.

"…it would not be mortally untoward for a man to kiss a woman's hand in England." He drew hers to his mouth and pressed his lips to the inside of her wrist.

A shiver raced up her arm. "Do not," she breathed.

He smiled. "Here, one could lose his head over so small a thing."

Providing he survived the loss of other parts of his anatomy, Alessandra reflected. "Which is what will happen if it is known what you do," she said.

His hold on her hand lightened, and though she could have pulled free, something inside her bade her remain still.

He put his head to the side. "Will you reveal me?"

She moistened her lips. "I would not wish to see you harmed for…" His eyes having lowered to her mouth, her next words were mostly breath. "…so small a thing."

His eyes returned to hers, the pupils of which had dilated, leaving only a narrow ring of violet. "And if it is no small thing?"

She was sure she did not understand what he meant, and yet she longed to be nearer, for her first real kiss to be given by his mouth. She swallowed. "Let me go."

He opened his fingers.

She did not retreat, and the hand he had kissed remained lifted toward him.

"You are still here, Alessandra."

Perhaps it was her name on his lips, deeply spoken as if she were not the only one incapable of movement, but when she was able to move, she stepped nearer, slid her arms around his neck, and lifted her face to his.

"Tell no one," she said and pulled his head down.

Seif's mouth upon hers was nothing like the kiss with which she had surprised Rashid. It was more like that of which the women spoke—a thrill that went to her every edge, a longing for no end to it, an ache for more.

"Seif," she breathed.

"I am Lucien," he rasped and pulled her so near there was no space between them. Sliding his arms around her, he pressed a hand to the small of her back, the other to her nape, and threaded his fingers up through her hair.

So very dangerous, and yet it was her voice that beseeched, "More, Lucien."

And Lucien's voice that said, "That is enough." He released her and stepped back.

Alessandra put a hand to her lips and stared at the man she had kissed, a slave into whose arms she had gone without thought of consequences. Without thought of Rashid.

Hurriedly, she crossed to her dressing table. "You should not have done that," she said, though she knew it was more her doing.

Seif—rather, Lucien as her mother had also revealed—moved behind her but did not touch her again. "If you would salve your conscience," he said, "consider it but a demonstration of the differences between our cultures."

She picked up her comb and began tugging it through her hair. "Is that what you consider it? Merely a lesson?"

"And desire for what is forbidden me. I *can* still feel such want."

Slowly, she looked around. "You desire me?" She did not mean her words to be whispered. They were. She did not mean to sound hopeful. She did. And it shamed her, for it made her seem like a child promised a toy long denied her, one she was afraid to believe was truly within her grasp.

"I would not have touched you otherwise," he said.

More hopeful. More shameful. More dangerous. How she longed to return to his arms!

End this now, Alessandra, she silently demanded. *No good can come of wanting something you cannot—and should not!—have.*

She set the comb down, turned to face him. "I am promised to Rashid. There can be no more of…what we did."

His mouth bent upward. "It is you who controls what happens between us, mistress. I am but a slave."

Why was there no comfort in that? She slipped past him and crossed to the center of her apartment. "Then I have nothing over which to be concerned."

He raised his eyebrows. "Naught," he said and leaned back against the edge of her dressing table.

"Is there something else you wish to discuss, Seif?"

"Your mouth."

She blinked. "What?"

"I am curious about it—that it is untried though you are no longer a maiden."

She had hoped the lie that she was not virtuous would remain where it had fallen in the bathhouse, but here it was. Inwardly cringing, she wondered why he believed her mouth was untried. After all, he had seen her kiss Rashid atop the roof. And though she had attempted to place the blame for this day's intimacy at Seif's feet, it was *she* who had initiated their kiss—one she had enjoyed. Did this mean that, though he claimed he desired her, the kiss had not been to his liking? Had the press of her lips been uncertain? Awkward? It *was* he who had ended the kiss.

Hating how off balance he made her feel, she said, "We shall not speak of things that will not happen again, Seif."

He inclined his head. "As you would, mistress."

"Then we are done here."

He straightened from her dressing table. "I had thought we might begin my lessons."

She almost laughed. "It is obvious you have already acquired a sufficient grasp of our language."

He retrieved her comb. "I know not what this is called."

She hastened forward and took it from him. "A *misht*." She returned it to the tabletop.

"And this color?" He flicked the skirt of her yellow caftan.

"*Asfar*. I—"

"What is the name of that which lines your eyes?"

Self-consciously, she ran a fingertip beneath her lower lid. "*Mirwad*." He looked around as if for something else to inquire about.

Alessandra sighed and crossed to her divan. "If you are determined to remain," she said as she arranged the strewn pillows, "tell me how you became a slave."

Silence descended and did not lift once her pillows were in place. Seating herself on the edge of the divan, she raised her eyebrows.

His face had darkened, creating a sharp contrast against the white of his turban, and the light in his eyes and smile upon his mouth were gone.

"Have I asked something I should not?" A futile question, for it was obvious her inquiry was unwelcome.

He turned, strode to the door, and was gone so completely it was as if he had not been here.

But he had been. Alessandra ran fingertips across her mouth. Most definitely, Lucien de Gautier had been here.

Lucien contained himself until he gained the privacy of the garden. Then he slammed his fists into the bark of a tree until, knuckles scraped raw, pain cast a shadow across his rage—one of sufficient length and breadth to allow him to begin to straighten out his thoughts.

He put his back to the tree and stared at the scalable wall that stood between him and freedom.

Since arriving at Jabbar's home, he had not allowed himself to dwell on the horrors suffered during his captivity. However, Alessandra's innocent question had freed memories best locked away.

"Curse her! Curse all women!" he growled. They were a faithless lot, and Alessandra numbered among them. Though promised to another, she had touched and kissed him—

After you set out to seduce her, spoke the voice of discernment he had often ignored this past year. *Thus, are men not also a faithless lot?*

He ground his teeth. He had come to Alessandra's apartment only to apologize, but seeing her sunlit hair tumbled about her shoulders, witnessing her delight over the gazelles, standing so near her...

He had wanted to feel her tresses between his fingers and her curves beneath the shapeless caftan. He had wanted to understand the impetuous workings of her mind and to burn his fingers, if need be, to feel her fire. He had wanted her to wipe away this past year that had embittered and hardened him more than all the years spent battling the Brevilles. And so he had tempted her.

He closed his eyes, murmured, "We are a faithless lot, indeed."

Though he would never trust a woman with his heart, this present anger had nothing to do with the fairer sex—all to do with the nightmare of slavery. *That* was where it belonged.

9

At the end of a sennight, Jabbar and Rashid returned bearing gifts of silk, jewelry, and gilded slippers.

Amid the buzz of women flaunting their new finery, there was music and dancing in the hall. Trays laden with pastries and sweetmeats were borne by servant girls, though they were largely ignored by the women who were too elated to indulge.

All were dressed for the occasion of the master's visit, each hoping to catch his eye so she might be the one with whom he spent the night. As usual, there was little modesty about them. Their light, colorful trousers and vests allowed glimpses of breasts and buttocks, thighs and ankles. Their hands, feet, and hair were hennaed and faces heavily made up.

Seated at the far end of the hall was Jabbar, who surveyed all with a faint smile. On his left sat Rashid, on his right, Sabine. Unlike the others, Alessandra's mother wore a caftan. The garment was elaborate, its silver and gold threads catching light, but it revealed little of her figure, evidencing she remained Jabbar's favorite. He did not need tantalizing glimpses of her body to desire her and, most likely, it was she with whom he would pass the night.

Though Alessandra enjoyed such occasions, her pleasure this afternoon was overshadowed by the present Rashid had brought her.

Removed from the others, she fingered the cloth that would be fashioned into a wedding gown. It was beautiful and would complement her hair and complexion, but she was disappointed that she had not been allowed to choose it herself.

'Tis a small thing, she told herself.

But was it? It represented the day she would truly become a woman—the beginning of the rest of her life with Rashid as first wife.

"First," she whispered and determinedly turned her thoughts to the trip into the city that had been denied her. It would have been a break from the monotony of the harem, long hours spent in the marketplace haggling with vendors and seeing sights she had not laid eyes upon in two years. And then there was the freedom, of which she had so little and constantly dreamed.

Perhaps her mother was right. Perhaps she was not fit for such a life. But would England be different?

"You do not like the cloth?"

She looked up at the man who was now Lucien to her, though only in her thoughts. Since he had walked out on her several days past, the air between them had been strained, and only this day had it begun to ease.

"What, Seif?" she asked.

Hands behind his back, he nodded at the fabric.

"I do like it," she said with as much enthusiasm as she could muster. "It is lovely."

"For your wedding?"

"How did you know?"

"A guess only."

Looking away, she pretended interest in the group of women to her right.

"If it is not the cloth that makes you unhappy," Lucien said, "what is it?"

She eyed him. "You think me unhappy?"

"Not even the music and dance interests you."

True. At the very least, her feet ought to be tapping. "Sometimes I feel as if…" She searched for English words to express herself. "As if I cannot get a full breath. As if a great weight is upon my chest."

He frowned. "You are ill?"

"I do not speak of an ailment," she said, and immediately thought of her mother and the reason Sabine had yet to shake off her cough. "This comes from my head, making me restless and impatient for..." She gave a short laugh. "...freedom, I suppose. Doubtless, you have experienced such yourself."

He smiled tightly. "You feel enslaved?"

She pondered the word, shook her head. "It would be unfair to name it so harsh a thing."

"What would you call it?"

"I do not know."

Lucien's gaze shifted and, following it, Alessandra saw her mother approached.

As the eunuch returned to his place against the wall, Sabine lowered to the divan alongside her daughter. "Are you not going to show me what Rashid brought you, Alessandra?"

This was the first time she had seen her mother in two days, for she had allowed none but Khalid within her apartment. Alessandra had not been overly worried, for she had grown accustomed to her mother locking herself away. She had been doing so for nearly two years now, offering only the excuse of needing time alone with God. Though it sometimes made Alessandra feel abandoned, she had learned to wait it out, as had Jabbar.

Now, peering into Sabine's pale, drawn face with its darkly shadowed eyes, she was not sure she should have stayed away. She pressed a hand over her mother's. "You do not seem well."

Sabine grimaced, drew fingers through her hair. "Better?"

"You know that is not what I mean. You look ill."

"It is always difficult when Jabbar goes away—worse, when Leila takes advantage of the situation and tries to harm you."

That might be some of it, but not all. "What of the cough? You still—"

"I have yet to speak to Jabbar about what that woman did, but when I have him alone this eve, I shall."

"You yet suffer from a cough," Alessandra pressed. "Has the physician nothing to rid you of it?"

Sabine looked across the hall. "He says I need not worry, that it will pass."

"But he is old. Perhaps we should summon another physician."

Sabine sighed. "You weary me with your needless concern. Let us speak of other things."

From the set of her mother's face, Alessandra knew she would get no further. Blowing out her breath, she settled into the abundance of pillows. "Of what would you rather speak?"

"Khalid tells me you and the new eunuch are getting along better." Her mother's smile did not reach her eyes, further convincing Alessandra something was amiss. And Khalid likely knew what it was. Would he tell her if asked?

No, he would never betray her mother's confidence, not even to her daughter.

"Did you not hear me, Alessandra?"

She met Sabine's gaze. "It is true. Seif and I are becoming accustomed to one another."

"I am pleased. He has guarded you well these past days."

"There is something curious about him," Alessandra mused.

Sabine stiffened, said tautly, "What is that?"

Even more curious was her mother's reaction. Alessandra stole a glance at Lucien and saw he watched Jabbar and Rashid. "I do not know, but I intend to discover what it is."

"He is an Englishman, Alessandra. It is his culture that makes him a curiosity. Accept it and leave it be."

Had Sabine not been so desperate to impress that upon her, Alessandra might have allowed herself to be led down that path. But there was something here she was not meant to see, and it made her wonder if her suspicions about whether or not Lucien was, indeed, a eunuch were founded. "Mother—"

"The cloth is for your wedding gown?"

In the midst of Alessandra's struggle over whether or not to continue to seek an answer, Leila boasted loudly, "It is me Jabbar desires."

Alessandra followed her mother's gaze across the room.

"I had but to press myself to him to know," Leila continued. "I vow, this night he will come to me."

The women with whom she surrounded herself tittered and glanced at Sabine.

Such taunting was not unusual, though Leila's words often proved empty, but her posturing always angered Alessandra who knew it saddened her mother to share Jabbar.

Will I be as gracious once Rashid begins taking other wives and filling his harem with concubines? she wondered. *Will I be able to subdue my restlessness? Quell the longing to know greater freedom? Overlook my faith that dictates marriage between one man and one woman?*

Sinking her teeth into her lower lip, she looked around and met Lucien's amethyst gaze. And feared that four times she would fail.

10

❧

What does my mother not mean me to see?

Over the next two days, the question so often nibbled at Alessandra that she struggled not to snap at annoyances and small offenses. And that it might relate to the question of whether or not Lucien was truly a eunuch further curdled her disposition. Thus, she determined she would have an answer.

It was bold—and dangerous—but she gathered the courage to do the task she had set herself. Clothed in the colors of night, she climbed out her window and lowered herself amid the garden's fragrant bushes.

The moon was high and full, illuminating the path she must parallel to gain the eunuchs' quarters and making it imperative she exercise caution lest a guard caught sight of her. Though it could not have taken more than a handful of minutes to cautiously traverse the garden, it felt tenfold that.

Upon reaching the gate, she eased it open and winced when its hinges creaked. Lest she needed to make a hasty retreat, she left it ajar.

Staying low, she hastened toward the low-lying building that housed the eunuchs. As she neared, excitement rippled through her. It was a long time since she had undertaken such an adventure, and the opportunity would have been denied her had Jabbar not dismissed Sabine's accusations against Leila. After speaking with those present in the garden that day, he had pardoned his first wife of wrongdoing. Thus, Lucien had been excused from the duty of guarding Alessandra's apartment and now slept in the eunuchs' quarters where he would not be required to clothe himself head to toe.

Thankful she was slender, Alessandra squeezed behind the bushes that lined the back of the building and picked her way along the wall. At each window, she peered inside to determine which of the eunuchs slept there. Aided by the slant of moonlight, she eliminated one after another of those who most often passed the night unclothed, shoulders and backs bare above light coverings.

Beginning to wonder if Lucien had been given quarters elsewhere, she felt a rush of relief when she peered into the last room. Though he faced away from her on a pallet against the far wall, she knew it was him from the width of a bare back crossed with shadows. Only Khalid was as large.

She considered the first obstacle—the covering down around Lucien's waist. As children, Rashid and she had stolen into the eunuchs' quarters one night and found the first—and last—of the men they had happened upon completely bared. Alessandra had hoped to find Lucien in a similar state, but she would have to venture within to have her answer. More disconcerting, his covering must be drawn back. Could she do it without awakening him?

She eyed his tapered hips, the wide expanse of back and shoulders that swelled with muscle, told herself she did not feel any of the sensations that warmed her, reminded herself to whom she was betrothed.

I do this only to gain the answer denied me, she reminded herself. *Naught else.*

Naught else? a voice derided, questioning her restlessness that had grown since Lucien's arrival. Before, she had been able to stifle it sufficiently to bring it under control. Now, his glance that seemed to see into her soul, his touch that made her lose her breath, his kiss—

Naught else! she rebuked and raised her gaze to Lucien's uncovered head that was mostly in shadow. What color was his hair? It looked somewhere between yellow and brown. Having only been exposed to dark and red hair, she longed to see it better. And she would if she could finish what she had begun.

Returning her gaze to his back, it struck her that the shadows upon it were not uniform as they should be were they thrown by what she had assumed were the lattice coverings. A glance left and right confirming this window, unlike her own, was not fit with lattices, she wondered how his back came to be criss-crossed with dark lines.

The answer struck, though surely not as fiercely as the whip that had scarred him.

As if her own back burned with the cruel punishment, she imagined the pain of such torture and better understood the anger she had glimpsed when she had asked how he had become a slave.

It nearly made her abandon her quest to know if he was a eunuch, but she had not come this far to leave the question unanswered.

She placed her hands on the windowsill and carefully hoisted herself onto the ledge. Crouching there, she watched Lucien to ensure she had not disturbed his sleep. When the breath moving his shoulders remained constant, she lowered to the floor and crept forward.

Squatting at his feet, she peered up his body into his shadowed face. He continued to sleep.

She eyed the narrow space between pallet and wall and wondered how she was to move him onto his back without awakening him. If she lightly stroked the soles of his feet—

She gasped, for neither could she blame nonexistent lattice coverings for what moonlight revealed. Sliding her gaze down the vertical groove that ran the length of his right foot, then across the horizontal groove, she identified that which had been burned into the bottom of his foot—a crucifix.

For what purpose? Was it an English custom? Her mother had not spoken of it and certainly did not bear the mark herself, but that one would daily tread upon a symbol of one's faith seemed sacrilegious. It disturbed her, and combined with the possibility of awakening him, tempted her to abandon her quest.

She wavered, then slowly straightened and turned away.

The air stirred at her back, and a muscled arm fastened around her waist. As she was swept backward, she pressed her lips to keep from crying out, instinctively knowing she had more to fear from those outside the room than the man who had seized her.

She landed on her back upon his pallet and was immediately pinned beneath him.

"You could wake a sleeping baby," Lucien growled, his eyes glittering above her.

"Get off," she wheezed.

He raised himself, though just enough to allow her to draw air deep. "For what are you here, Alessandra?"

As she could conjure no believable excuse for intruding upon his privacy, there was only the humiliating truth. "That I might learn whether or not you are the eunuch you claim to be."

The coarse breath that moved the hair at her brow ceased, and she felt his disbelief. Or was it disapproval?

When he finally spoke again, it was with reproach. "You are too brazen, a danger to both of us."

His words chafed. "As neither my mother nor you will speak to me in truth, I determined to discover it myself." The moment the words were out, she wished them back in, for they were childish.

"You truly believed you could learn the state of my body without awakening me?"

What had roused him? Her gasp when she had seen what was burned into his foot? "I had but to draw back the cover to know," she said. "Had I not changed my mind, I would have succeeded." She shifted beneath him in an attempt to move him off her.

He clamped his legs tighter on either side of her. "You would not have, for I am not so foolish to sleep bare knowing I shall need every moment should death come calling in the night."

She frowned. "You wear trousers?"

"Indeed."

At this moment, it was of great comfort.

"And I was awake long ere you entered my room."

Alessandra snorted. "That I do not believe."

Despite the dim between their faces, she saw his eyebrows rise. "It would have been better for you to climb the wall than to use the gate."

She startled. Was it possible one could sleep so lightly to have heard that slight creak of hinges? If he had caught it, had the guards?

"Did you know it was me?" she asked.

"Only when I caught your scent at the window—attar of the orange blossom. The others prefer roses or jasmine."

Why did it both excite and alarm her that he knew her smell? She pressed her hands to his chest. "Please, Lucien, get off."

"Lucien?" Was that a smile in his voice? Likely, for when they had kissed, he had demanded she speak it rather than his eunuch's name. He lowered his head and his lips brushed her ear. "Has no one ever warned you of the dangers of playing with fire, Alessandra?"

His words and warm breath kindling that which she had only ever felt with him, tempting her to turn her mouth to his, she said, "I wish to return to my apartment."

"Without discovering that which you came for?"

She would have affirmed it, but he pressed his mouth to a place just beneath her ear. "Oh," she breathed.

He kissed her jaw, drawing her nearer the flame she would be a fool to pass her fingers through. But fool that she was, she turned her face and touched her lips to his.

Lucien hesitated. He had told himself he would only teach her a much-needed lesson, but the taste of her made him want more.

Just a bit further, he promised himself. And angled his head to better fit his mouth to hers.

She gasped into him, and that small, feminine sound moved him nearer a place he did not mean to go.

Only a bit further, he told himself. And deepened the kiss.

She parted her lips.

Not much further, he silently intoned. And felt the pained hunger of one long denied sustenance.

More gasping, pressing nearer.

Far enough, Lucien.

Sinking nails into his chest, sliding hands into his hair.

Too far! Cease now, else you will not only provide the answer she seeks but ruin her.

He stilled. Would he ruin her? Though her mouth was inexperienced, she claimed she was no longer a maiden.

You but seek an excuse to go where you should not, Lucien de Gautier!

He lifted his head, and when she opened eyes that drank in moonlight, asked, "With how many men have you been?"

"I…" A whimper escaped her. "Pray, do not stop."

She was too desperate—as of one who tastes the sweet and, having no experience with the consequences of overindulgence, gives herself over to it. "The truth, Alessandra."

He felt the scrape of her fingernails across his scalp as she curled her fingers into his hair. "Only you, Lucien."

Then otherwise virtuous. He pitted the wants of the flesh against his honor—as well as Sabine's threat to see him emasculated if he violated her daughter—and drew back. "We are done."

Her arms tightened around his neck. "Why?"

Hearing the hurt in her voice, he said gently, "Such a gift should not be given lightly. 'Tis for the man you wed." Though he was to ensure that man was not Abd al-Jabbar's son, to allay her suspicions about his purpose here, he added, "If we do not stop now, Rashid will know he is not the first to lie with you. And should—" He clenched his teeth, chastised himself for nearly pointing out that if she too soon grew large with child, it would go worse for both of them. Had he spoken it, she would have proof he was not a eunuch.

Hearing her swallow, knowing she choked down tears, he touched her face. "I will not make more a mockery of our faith than already I have done."

"But—"

"Shh!" He closed a hand over her mouth, turned his head, listened. But whatever had piqued his senses was either gone or had never been. Cursing himself for allowing the feel of her to make him forget the danger pressing in on all sides, he removed his hand from her mouth. "You must return to your apartment."

Alessandra searched his shadowed face. Though her heart beat wild with the fear of being caught with him, she was more inclined to weep. She had thought she knew herself, but where this man was concerned, she felt foreign. There was no reason to wish to be with him or risk her relationship with Rashid whom she adored. And yet, with each passing day since Lucien's arrival, Rashid became more the brother he had once seemed, rather than the man that the young woman she had grown into had dreamed of wedding. So what did she feel for Lucien?

Desire, she told herself. And for this, Jabbar quickly married off his daughters and was displeased with Sabine's delays in wedding her own daughter to Rashid. *Naught but desire.*

Alessandra pulled her arms from around Lucien's neck. "Forgive me. It is my shame that I am no better than the others who would use you for the same purpose."

"You are not like the others," he said low. "Were you, I would not touch you."

Then he thought it more than desire that drew her to him? She longed to set him right, but the air of urgency with which he moved off her reminded her that this was not the place or time to speak of such things, nor to satisfy her curiosity over his scars and the cross burned into his foot.

When he gripped her arm and raised her to standing, she saw he did, indeed, wear trousers—yet another reminder. "I *will* know the truth of you, Lucien," she said as she set to ordering garments gone askew.

"Of what use would I be in a harem were I not a eunuch?" he said.

She lifted her gaze up his muscular chest. "Do you know my mother wishes me to go to England? That she opposes my marriage to Rashid?"

"I am but a slave. Why would she discuss these things with me?"

Alessandra searched his face upon which moonlight shone, traced the scar with her eyes, then with the hand she lifted between them. He jerked, and though he did not put distance between them, she heard the sharp breath he drew.

"Why do you answer my question with another?" she asked. "To avoid speaking the truth?"

She was to receive no answer, for the door was thrown wide and a light thrust inside the room.

Alessandra swung around to face the two who stepped inside.

"What do you here, Alessandra?" her mother demanded, face bright with anger.

"I..." Alessandra glanced at Lucien. Finding him expressionless, she looked to Khalid for help, but his usually placid face evidenced he was no less furious than her mother.

Sabine strode forward, pushed her daughter aside, and stepped so near Lucien she had to drop her head nearly all the way back to peer into his face. "I warned you. Now you will suffer the consequences."

Alessandra placed a hand on her mother's arm. "He has done nothing wrong. I came to speak with him, that is all."

Sabine's head snapped around. "In the middle of the night?"

"I could not sleep."

"And so you stole out the window of your apartment? Tell me, Daughter, what could not be said in the light of day? What requires that you stand so near him? That you touch him?"

What was there to say that would not be a lie yet acceptable enough to cool her anger? Unfortunately, all Alessandra could lay claim to was the blame. "Whatever you think happened, Mother, the fault is mine. Is it not I who came to him?"

Sabine looked from her to Lucien, back again. "Are you still virtuous, Daughter?"

It was so blunt a question Alessandra caught her breath. Had Lucien not had the good sense—the honor—to stop, it was a question her mother would not have to ask.

She raised her chin. "You think I would shame you by giving this eunuch what is to be my husband's?"

Her mother stared. "Answer me."

"You can be assured Rashid will find me untouched on our wedding night."

"I would know now," a smug voice spoke from behind Khalid.

They all turned toward Leila who had draped herself against the door frame, her expression triumphant. Worse, beyond her stood Rashid, his face a mask of torment as he stared at Alessandra.

Regret burned through her. She had betrayed and hurt her friend, the man she was to wed.

Leila straightened, sauntered past Khalid, and placed herself before Alessandra. "On the morrow we will send for the physician. And you had best be chaste, for not even your mother can prevent the punishment due a whore."

Sabine shoved Leila aside. "There is no need for a physician. My daughter speaks true."

Smiling broadly, Leila brushed the sleeve of her robe where Sabine had touched her. "Soon, we will know for certain." She turned her attention to Lucien, and her eyes glowed appreciatively as she swept them up his bare torso to the bronze hair touching his shoulders. "What punishment for this eunuch, Khalid?"

Reminded of his duty, the chief eunuch stepped forward and gripped Lucien's arm. "He will be placed in confinement until it is known whether he has done wrong."

"Hmm." Leila drew a fingernail down Lucien's chest. "Has he not done wrong in being alone with Alessandra?"

"Fifty strokes of the bastinado," Rashid said, striding forward.

"Nay!" Alessandra cried, distantly noting the other eunuchs gathering outside the door. "He has done nothing."

Leila stepped in front of Alessandra. "My son, heir of Jabbar, has spoken."

Alessandra's next thought was to plead with Rashid, but his face warned it would be futile—a face she hardly recognized. Brightly colored, lips twisted, it was no longer handsome and familiar. It was frightening.

"Mother," she implored through a blur of tears.

Sabine shook her head. "It is done."

"Come." Khalid urged Lucien from the room.

Alessandra swung back to Lucien. Their eyes met, and in the depths of his she saw something feral pulsed there, warning of the clash to come a moment before he thrust Khalid away.

In spite of his strength, the odds were against him. One word from Khalid and the other eunuchs surged into the room. Lucien fought them, inflicting brutal blows, but he was soon overpowered and dragged to his feet.

"Now, Englishman," Rashid shouted, "you will learn respect!" The sound of flesh striking flesh resounded around the room. Again and again.

Alessandra turned into her mother's arms and pressed her face to her shoulder. She had done this to Lucien. Could he ever forgive her?

Finally, silence, then Rashid ordered, "One hundred strokes of the bastinado."

"Two hundred would be better," Leila suggested.

Alessandra pulled out of her mother's arms and ran to Rashid. Averting her eyes from Lucien who was held upright by the eunuchs, she cried, "Pray, Rashid, do not do this. It is wrong!"

His eyes searched hers for something she prayed he would not find. Then he repeated, "One hundred strokes."

"Why do you cry for him?" Sabine asked when the sun shed its first light over the land.

Eyes swollen and tender, her daughter looked up. "It is my fault."

Sabine lifted a tress of Alessandra's hair and watched it curl around her fingers. "That is not the only reason you cry."

Where she lay with her head in her mother's lap, Alessandra wiped the back of a hand across her eyes. "I do not understand why it hurts so much."

"Could it be you feel something for Lucien de Gautier that you do not feel for Rashid?"

"I do have feelings for him, but I do not understand what they are."

Sabine closed her eyes. "Does your heart beat fast—painfully so—when he is near?"

"Sometimes it is difficult to breathe."

"Does he come upon your thoughts often, disrupt what you are doing?"

"Even when he is not within sight."

"What is it like when he lays a hand upon your arm?"

Alessandra shuddered. "I want more."

"Could it be love?"

"I do not know. Do you think it possible?"

Sabine sighed. "Only you can be certain, Alessandra, but remember this. Regardless of what happens, Lucien is your father's enemy. He is not to be trusted. And he is a eunuch."

Alessandra searched her face as if seeking a lie there, then closed her eyes. "His pain must be unbearable, and his scars…"

Sabine seamed her lips. Only if Rashid had stayed to ensure punishment was given as ordered would Khalid have carried it out to its full extent. Otherwise, her friend would lessen the severity to be certain the Englishman was able to complete the bargain struck with her.

"…terrible," Alessandra whispered.

Sabine drew a deep breath. "Try not to think on it, Daughter."

11

H AD ALESSANDRA NOT been so preoccupied with Lucien's fate, the humiliation would have pierced her soul. Instead, the impersonal hands examining her went mostly unnoticed.

"She is intact," the physician pronounced.

Sabine's sigh of relief startled Alessandra back to the present. Yanking a cover over her exposed limbs, she looked to her mother. "You did not believe me."

Quickly, Sabine crossed to her side and put an arm around her. "Forgive me."

Alessandra chastised herself for adding guilt to her mother's burdened shoulders. Sabine was right to doubt her. Had Lucien taken what was shamelessly offered him, Alessandra would have denied it in hopes of saving him from punishment.

She forced a smile. "There is nothing to forgive."

"Mistress," the physician addressed Sabine, "I will inform your husband the wedding may go forward."

She inclined her head and the man strode from the room.

Alone with her daughter, Sabine said, "Come, let us dress you."

Alessandra allowed her to attend to her needs, her every thought centered on the man who had been made to suffer for her reckless abandon of the night past.

How did he fare? she wondered and conjured a ten-year-old memory of the cruel punishment she had witnessed. Though her mother had forbidden her to go near the stables while the manservant was put to the bastinado, curiosity had made her rebel—and was responsible for the nightmares that had visited her for months thereafter.

The man's feet had been locked between two pieces of wood and raised high so that only his neck and shoulders rested on the ground. Using a short stick, a guard had delivered blows to the soles of the servant's feet. The man had thrashed on the ground, his screams so loud that no matter how hard Alessandra pressed hands to her ears, she could not entirely block the sound. Blessedly, the man had lost consciousness halfway through the thirty strokes of his sentence.

Lucien was larger, younger, and far stronger than the manservant had been, but could he bear more than three times the punishment? Would he be forever disabled?

Had she any tears left, Alessandra would have wept again.

Outfitted in a long caftan, trousers, and slippers, she yielded to the pressure of her mother's hands and sank down upon the stool before her dressing table. Staring at her reflection in the mirror, she wondered how she might learn of Lucien's well-being. She did not dare seek him herself.

"What are you thinking?" Sabine asked as she brushed the snarls from her daughter's hair.

Alessandra met her gaze in the mirror. "Lucien."

"You should not call him that. Here he is Seif." Sectioning her daughter's hair, she began to braid it.

"Where is he?"

"Likely returned to the eunuchs' quarters."

"I wish to see him."

Sabine's jaw clenched. "And have him suffer further punishment?"

"I must know," Alessandra whispered.

Her mother met her eyes in the mirror. "Khalid will bring news soon."

Shortly, a light tap sounded on the door, and when Sabine called, "Enter!" it was the chief eunuch who stepped inside. However, it was not word of Lucien he carried.

"Mistress, the master requests your presence in the hall."

Alessandra felt her mother tense, knew the summons boded no good. But as the matter of her chastity was settled, what else was there to discuss?

"What of Alessandra?" Sabine asked.

"She is to accompany you."

Sabine quickly secured the braid with a ribbon, then helped Alessandra to her feet. "Come, Daughter. Jabbar awaits."

Silence hung over them as they made their way to the hall, so intense Alessandra though she might scream. Hands clenched, lips pressed, she followed her mother into the great room.

Jabbar beckoned them forward.

Other than servants, Rashid and his mother were the only occupants of the hall where they stood on opposite sides of Jabbar.

Alessandra looked first to her betrothed and was surprised when he gave her a reassuring smile. Here again was the boy she had grown up with, the one with whom she had shared laughter and adventure. But though it seemed the vengeful man of the night past was gone, she would never forget what he had become.

She shifted her gaze to Leila. She should not have been startled by the lovely face hatred had turned hideous, but she was. And when their eyes met, Alessandra knew she would never again question her mother's fear of Jabbar's first wife. Indeed, she was fairly certain it had been no accident that the woman's little dog had frightened the donkey.

Alessandra and her mother halted before Jabbar.

"Alessandra, come forward," he said.

She obeyed and lowered to her knees before him.

He laid a hand to her head. "Though you are born of another man, you have been like a daughter to me."

She longed to smile, her affection for this man shadowed only by her worry over Lucien.

"Thus, I have long overlooked your behavior and gave Rashid permission to wed you against my better judgment. I do not doubt you will be a difficult wife, but as he has chosen you, I will not stay him from doing so. However, it is time you accept the customs of our people and shed those of your mother's."

Alessandra raised her head. "I do not understand. I wear the costume of the Arab people. I—"

"I speak of your conduct. No more will you venture out-of-doors without an escort, nor uncover yourself to darken your skin. You will observe the mealtimes and remain seated when there is music and dancing. Never again will you leave your apartment after dark. You will show respect for men and keep your tongue firmly in your mouth unless a question is asked of you. You will join the others for prayers—"

"She is a Christian!" Sabine protested.

Jabbar considered her. "So she is." He turned to Rashid. "Would you have her convert?"

Rashid shook his head. "Though our children will be raised in the faith of Islam, this I will not ask of her."

Jabbar returned his gaze to Alessandra. "Do you understand what is required of you henceforth?"

She felt caged. Enslaved. For a moment, she imagined mounting a swift horse that would carry her far from here, but as difficult as it would be to assume the role Jabbar demanded of her, this was all she had ever known and she would not abandon it—regardless that her mother wished otherwise.

She lowered her chin and stared at the colorful tiles beneath her knees. "I understand."

"I am pleased." Jabbar dropped his hand to her shoulder and gently squeezed it.

Believing the interview was at an end, Alessandra started to rise, but he urged her back down. "There is more."

She looked up. "More?"

"I give you five days in which to prepare yourself. Then you and Rashid will wed."

"Five days!" Sabine cried. "Jabbar, it is too soon."

Exhibiting his usual tolerance for the Englishwoman he had taken to wife, he shook his head. "That is what you have been telling me these past four years. Did not the events of last eve convince you Alessandra has been too long without benefit of the marriage bed?"

"But nothing happened that she need be ashamed of. The physician—"

"Yes, she is untouched, but for how long? She grows restless to know what you have denied her. Thus, she shall marry my son."

For some moments, the only sound to be heard was Sabine's strident breaths, then she gasped, "The wedding dress. It will take many weeks to complete."

Jabbar heaved a sigh. "Alessandra is nearly your size. With minor alterations, she can wear the dress you wore when we wed."

"But she should have her own. And what of the celebration? There is no time—"

Jabbar thrust to his feet. "Five days," he barked and left the hall.

12

After endless hours in the bathhouse, where she was bathed and groomed, though not to distraction as she wished, the last thing Alessandra wanted was to attend the women's celebration known as "henna night." On this, the eve of her wedding, she longed only for her mother's company, but that would be frowned upon. Hence, she submitted to the women who came for her in the late afternoon.

Sabine at her side, she was led into the hall. Even those who typically shunned her greeted her warmly. Leila was the only one who distanced herself.

Within the vast room were music, dancing, and trays laden with every food imaginable. There were bowls filled with flowers, the heavy scent of frankincense and myrrh, and a table heaped with bride gifts. As nearly all the women wore brightly colored garments that showed their bodies to best advantage, the room was a rainbow of shifting colors. Most noticeable, though, was the hum of excitement.

Alessandra was far from casting off the anxiety of these past four days, but she smiled as she was guided forward and seated in her place of honor at the center of the hall. Immediately, the younger women surrounded her, wielding pots of henna, cosmetics, hair oils, and aromatics for the body. Giggling and chattering, they began the ceremonial decoration of her person.

With a wooden stick, henna was applied to her palms, the insteps of her feet, and her face, the latter being the most painstaking of the procedure. While the intricate, lacy patterns were traced on her brow and cheeks, Alessandra sat as still as possible. But it was so ticklish, the women reprimanded her several times for twitching her nose and mouth.

While the henna dried, body oils were touched to her skin and her hair tended to. Grimacing and grunting as her tresses were tightly fashioned into nine braids, Alessandra looked about the hall and saw her mother conversing with Khalid.

If not that the eunuch's normally expressionless face was creased with distress, it would not have been unusual, but something was amiss.

Had further ill befallen Lucien? Following their meeting with Jabbar four days past, Khalid had reassured Sabine and her that Lucien fared well and would not be long in healing. Blessedly, as Rashid had not stayed to witness the entire sentence, Lucien had suffered only twenty strokes of the bastinado. However, Khalid had also told of Rashid's plan to sell the Englishman the next time he journeyed into the city.

Alessandra longed to go to Lucien and beg his forgiveness, but time and again she stayed the foolish urge and tried to be content with the infrequent news Khalid brought.

"There!" Nada thrust a hand mirror in front of Alessandra. "What do you think?"

Two thick braids hung on either side of her hennaed face, six from her crown, and one from the nape of her neck. "Lovely," she murmured and returned her thoughts to Lucien.

Disappointed by the lack of enthusiasm, Nada made a mewl of disgust and began to peel the dried henna from Alessandra's face. Once the residue of paste was wiped away, all that remained of the ceremonial preparations was the application of cosmetics.

To a restless Alessandra, it was a waste of time, for they would have to be reapplied on the morrow, but it was useless to protest. This was the women's night, and they would be satisfied with nothing less than everything.

Finally, she rose from the stool. The women exclaimed over her, touched her hair, admired the orange henna stains, and breathed deeply of the fragrant scents wafting from her hair and skin.

Telling herself there would be time aplenty to discover the cause of Khalid's distress, Alessandra yielded to the women, certain they would soon drift away and immerse themselves in the revelry.

It took longer than hoped, but at last she was free to seek out her mother.

"You look lovely, Daughter." Sabine patted the cushion beside her.

Alessandra sank down on the divan. "Has something happened to Lucien?"

Sabine glanced around to be certain none were privy to their conversation. "Why do you ask?"

"I saw you speaking with Khalid. He seemed troubled."

"It was nothing. All has been taken care of."

"And Lucien?"

Eyes fixed elsewhere, Sabine said, "Be assured, it had naught to do with him."

Alessandra followed her gaze to Leila.

"A dangerous woman," Sabine murmured. "An even more dangerous mother-in-law."

"I will be cautious," Alessandra assured her.

Her mother looked back at her. "There is no need."

"But have you not told me—"

"So I have." Sabine flicked an impatient hand. "She is a viper and will stop at nothing to harm either of us."

"Then why should I not be cautious?"

Her mother leaned near. "After tonight, you will be gone from here."

Alessandra jerked back. "I will not! I have told you—"

"Do not speak so loud!" Sabine rasped. "And try to smile."

A look around the hall revealing her outburst had not gone unnoticed, Alessandra pretended an interest in the dancers. "I am not going," she whispered. "I will not leave you."

Sabine squeezed her hand. "You cannot stay amid such danger."

Alessandra peered sidelong at her. "If you can survive it, I can."

"I have been fortunate, but one day, my luck will end."

"Nay." Alessandra shook her head. "You are too wise. Indeed, methinks you may live forever."

Sabine stared at her daughter's profile, wondered if she should have revealed her illness to Alessandra. Would knowledge of it make a difference? Move her to do what must be done?

In the end, she came to the same conclusion she always did. It would make her daughter more determined to remain at her side. And when the sickness finally took her, it would be too late to send Alessandra to England. She would be wed to Rashid, quite possibly with his child growing in her belly.

If not that Khalid caught her eye and gave the agreed upon signal, Sabine would have pursued the argument. Instead, she nudged Alessandra. "Go. I wish to see you dance one last time before you wed."

Her daughter's eyes widened. "You are granting me permission?"

Sabine shooed her away. "Enjoy yourself. When you are wed, Rashid will not allow it."

Slowly, Alessandra rose. "You are sure?"

Sabine also gained her feet. "Go quickly before I change my mind."

Still Alessandra hesitated, then she hurried away to join the dancers.

"It is done," Khalid told Sabine as they watched her daughter take up the dance.

"You saw her?"

"I did. It was hidden in her vest."

He spoke of Leila and the lethal drug he had earlier discovered missing from his closet of medicines.

"What did she put it on?" Sabine asked.

"Dates. Those on the platter the girl brings you." Khalid jutted his chin at the servant girl who threaded her way toward them. "I will take them to Jabbar and show him Leila's murderous deceit."

"No. That will not stop the wedding. And even if Leila is removed, eventually, another will take her place."

Khalid narrowed his eyes. "What do you propose, mistress?"

"Let the girl bring me the food. This night, Leila will have one small triumph."

"Mistress, you do not intend—?"

"I am dying, Khalid. Whether it be this day or a month from now, the end is the same."

"What of Alessandra?"

It deeply grieved her that her daughter might see her in the throes of death, but there seemed no other way. "It will serve to convince her the dangers are real, and once I am gone, she will see there is nothing for her here."

Khalid growled low. "Nothing except the only life she has known."

"She will go with Lucien," Sabine said firmly. In spite of her misgivings over trusting him with Alessandra, she had come to realize their mutual attraction could be the bond that held them together until they reached England. She only prayed Alessandra would not reveal she was a Breville.

Unaware she bore death upon her arms, the girl set the platter of beautifully prepared food on the nearby table. "For your daughter and you, mistress." She bowed, turned away.

My daughter, Sabine inwardly raged as she considered the half-dozen gleaming dates. She drew a deep breath, chose a sweetmeat instead, and carried it toward her mouth. "Does Leila watch?" she asked.

A muscle in Khalid's jaw clenched. "Yes, mistress."

Sabine slowly chewed the sweetmeat, slowly swallowed, more slowly considered the dates. And chose the plumpest. "I have prepared a bag for Alessandra's journey," she said. "You will find it beneath my dressing table."

"I beg you, mistress"—Khalid's voice was tight with what she knew were tears—"do not do this."

"You have been a good friend. As promised, all except that which I give my daughter and the Englishman is yours."

"Seif is more than capable of forcing her to go with him," Khalid reminded her of their original plan.

Sabine rolled the sticky fruit between thumb and forefinger. "She holds her breath, does she not?"

Nostrils flaring, hands tight at his sides, Khalid glanced at where Leila reclined. "She does."

"I wonder how long she can go without air before she faints," Sabine mused and lifted the poisoned fruit to her lips. Holding it there, she waited for Khalid to turn his coal-black gaze upon her. When he did, she said, "Do not mourn me, old friend. At last, I shall be free of pain."

Something warm and loving, as of deepest friendship, passed between them, then she turned her regard upon her lovely, vivacious daughter. She waited, and when she felt something akin to peace—the nearest she could come—she took her first bite of the poisoned fruit.

And so I win, Leila, she silently gloried in her triumph.

Unhurriedly, she ate the remainder of the date, and four others. "A pity she did not put poison on something else," she said as she licked the juice from her fingers. "I have never been fond of dates."

She lowered herself to the divan that would be her deathbed, made herself comfortable among the pillows, and folded her hands over her abdomen. "Of course, they were intended for Alessandra, were they not?" It was well known her daughter had a passion for the little fruits.

Khalid poured a goblet of honeyed lemon juice and passed it to her.

Wondering when she would feel the beginnings of death, Sabine sipped the cool liquid and reached to the platter again. "This"—she nudged the last date—"you must take to Jabbar."

A gleam in his eyes, Khalid said, "He will feed it to Leila."

He probably would, and that was good. Even if Lucien de Gautier failed her, an almost unthinkable event, Leila would not be given another chance to harm Alessandra.

"Will it be long, Khalid?" she asked when several minutes had passed.

"Though it is deadly, it is slow to act."

She should have known Leila would not choose something that would deprive her of the pleasure of a slow death. "Is it painful?"

"It is, but if you do not fight it, the pain will be less."

There was not much comfort in that, but it was good to know what to expect. Looking past the dancers, she picked out Leila's flushed countenance.

Poor woman, she mused, *she knows not whether to celebrate or lament. She has what she has ever wanted, and yet not all to which she aspired this eve.*

Sabine's wry smile slipped when she caught sight of Alessandra making her way toward her.

"It was wonderful!" her daughter exclaimed as she neared. "I do not think I shall ever forget this night."

For a different reason, Sabine hoped she would not.

Alessandra dropped down beside her, poured herself a drink, and quickly drained the goblet.

"Why do you waste your time with me when you could be dancing?" Sabine asked, gliding a hand over her daughter's arm. As she did so, it occurred to her this was the last time they would touch. Vision blurring, she looked away.

Alessandra, who had not felt like laughing earlier, did so now. "Even I must rest sometime, Mother." She leaned sideways, planted a kiss on Sabine's cheek, and reached for the last date. Only to have it snatched from beneath her fingers.

"Khalid!" she exclaimed. Never had she seen the chief eunuch take food in front of the harem women.

He smiled, a tight thing that did not reach his eyes or soften the grooves alongside his mouth.

"You are behaving most strange," Alessandra said.

He shrugged. "I am hungry."

She eyed the fruit. "Then why do you not eat it?"

"I would enjoy it in private."

It did not seem as if he sported with her, and yet what other explanation was there? She stood, held out a hand. "If you are not going to eat it now, surely I ought to enjoy it?"

He crossed his arms over his chest.

It had to be a game he played. Smiling, she looked down at her mother, in the next instant crouched beside her.

"What is wrong?" she gasped, searching Sabine's contorted face.

"I—" Her mother's voice broke, and she lurched against the pillows, threw her head back, and wheezed.

Khalid yanked Alessandra to her feet and thrust her aside.

"What is wrong with her?" Alessandra cried.

He knelt alongside the divan and drew Sabine into his arms.

She convulsed again, rasped, "Pain!"

"Mother!" Alessandra dropped down beside Khalid. "What is happening?"

Drawing short, jerky breaths, Sabine opened her eyes. "Poison." Her hand trembled violently as she raised it to Alessandra's face. "I warned…"

Alessandra caught her mother's hand and pressed it to her heart. "What do you mean?"

Sabine's gaze flickered over the faces of those gathering around, and when they settled upon her rival, she cried, "Leila." Then she convulsed again, snapping her head back and causing the muscles of her throat to bulge and veins to rise.

All of her trembling, Alessandra stared at Rashid's mother whose face radiated satisfaction, then she thrust to her feet.

As if the others knew her intent, they cleared a path for her all the way to Leila. Alessandra halted before the woman. "You did this."

Leila raised her eyebrows. "I know not what you speak of."

Alessandra lunged, and the two fell to the floor, Leila taking the brunt of the fall upon the hard tiles.

"Murderer!" Alessandra raked her nails down the older woman's face and neck.

Leila retaliated with a slap that snapped her attacker's head to the side, then caught Alessandra's braids and wrenched them.

Physical pain nothing compared to what shredded her heart, Alessandra bunched her hands and drove them into Leila's sides. Distantly, she heard the woman's cries, distantly she felt herself being tugged and pulled. Then she was dragged off Leila and back against a firm chest.

"What are you doing, Alessandra?" It was Rashid.

"Release me!" she screamed, straining and thrusting her body toward Leila who struggled to her feet.

Rashid wrapped his arms tight around her. "Cease!"

She jerked her chin around and met his gaze over her shoulder. "You are not my master! Loose me!"

Shock swept the anger from his eyes. "Alessandra, what——?"

A shout of denial resounding around the room, Rashid turned her with him to see Jabbar fall to his knees beside the divan.

"No!" he shouted and dragged Sabine's limp form out of Khalid's arms into his own.

The bones also went out of Alessandra. If not for Rashid's support, she would have crumpled to the floor. "Mother," she croaked as the man whom none had ever seen shed a tear buried his face in Sabine's hair and began to sob.

"I do not understand," Rashid said as if to himself.

"Release me," Alessandra demanded. "Now!"

His arms fell away.

Legs feeling as if they might collapse, she stumbled forward and sank down beside Jabbar.

As he continued to weep and deny that the woman he loved was lost to him, Alessandra pressed a palm to Sabine's back and prayed her heart yet beat. It had to. If Jabbar would only quiet, she would feel it.

Swallowing so hard it hurt, she lifted her mother's wrist, stopped breathing, and strained to feel life jump beneath her fingers. Nothing.

"Mother," she choked, then dropped her chin to her chest and arms to her sides, and sank back on her heels.

Though grief demanded a greater outlet than the tears streaming her face, she sealed her lips against the sobs and howls that filled her throat so full she felt it would burst. Shaking her head, she began to rock herself back and forth.

Minutes passed. Perhaps hours.

Alessandra did not know. She knew only that her mother had been carried away and all sent from the hall, and it was into this pounding silence that someone came to her.

He lowered beside her and, with gentle murmurings, stroked her hair. She did not know him. Did not want him here. Wanted to awaken and have all be as it was, no matter how the bars of her gilded cage chafed.

Not until the one at her side tried to draw her to her feet did she lift her head. She stared at the dark-headed man and, for a moment, was comforted by the familiar face. But that comfort was quickly replaced with fear.

Here was the son of the woman who had murdered her mother. He had Leila's heavy-lidded eyes, her mouth, and the same high forehead. He was of that one's blood which ran so hot with jealousy only murder could cool it.

"Come." Rashid's eyes were deceptively kind. "I will see you to your apartment."

She wrenched her arm from his grasp, cried, "Do not touch me!" and began to crawl away.

He gripped her shoulder. "Alessandra, it is Rashid."

She fell onto her side. Freed from his hold, she wrapped her arms around her head and curled in on herself.

His body brushed hers where he came down beside her, and again he beseeched, "It is Rashid."

She knew that. How she knew that! "Leave me be!"

When he tried to pull her into his arms, she lashed out, slapping and scratching while some pitiful, keening sound scored her throat and stung her ears.

She did not realize he had moved away until Khalid's voice warmed her ear. "Mistress, put your arms around my neck. I will carry you to your bed."

Chest convulsing with shallow breath, she peered up into his dark face. The grooves there were deeper and more numerous, and his eyes...

So much sorrow, so little light.

"My mother," she whispered.

"She is at rest, little one. No more harm can be done her."

"Truly?" she said on a sob.

"Is that not what your god promises?"

So He did. Still, it was little solace for one left so far behind. Desperate to be comforted by this man who deeply felt her loss, she slid her arms around his neck.

When he lifted her, she pressed her face into his shoulder so she would not have to look upon that other one—he who was born of a murderess.

13

Surfacing from a sleep she did wish to awaken from, Alessandra heard her name called and felt warm fingers slide over her arm. She groaned, rolled onto her stomach, and buried her face in a pillow.

"Alessandra!" The voice was more insistent, then she was turned and pulled up onto her knees.

Raising her head, she tried to focus on the shadowed figure who supported her. Though it was too dark to make out his features, she knew who had come to her in the night.

"Lucien! What——?"

"Quiet!"

Gripped by memories of what had happened the last time they had been caught together, she lowered her voice. "I have been terribly afeared for you. Are you in much pain?"

"No more than I am accustomed to." His voice was gruff, impatient.

She winced. "Can you ever forgive me?"

At his hesitation, her distress trebled. But then he lowered his head and pressed a kiss to her lips. "Now——"

"Ah, Lucien." She leaned against him and slid her arms around his neck. "I so like the feel of you." Her mother had guessed right. She did have feelings for him—things she did not feel for Rashid. Smiling, she touched her mouth to the exposed skin above the neck of his caftan.

"Alessandra——"

"I had the most frightening dream," she said as images filtered into her consciousness—a woman gasping for breath, the evil eyes of another.

Having no desire to dwell on perverse imaginings of the mind, for that was all they were, she shook her head to clear it. And awakened a bit more.

She frowned. "Why are you here? If you are caught—"

"We must hurry." He pulled her hands from around his neck.

She tried again to make out his features but caught only the glitter of his eyes. "I do not understand."

He lifted her from the divan and set her feet to the floor. "We are leaving this night." He turned toward the open window through which he must have entered her apartment. "We have no time to waste."

Suspicions sprang upon Alessandra. Her mother's determination to see her taken to England. The long search for a new eunuch. The purchase of an Englishman unsuited to harem life. The possibility he might not be a eunuch at all.

She closed her eyes. Was this her mother's doing? It had to be, meaning Lucien was not a eunuch in any sense. He was a man paid to play the part and whose true purpose was to steal her from the only life she had known. His touch and kisses had meant nothing to him other than a means of gaining her trust.

"Ah, nay," she lamented.

He grasped her arm and began pulling her toward the window.

She wrenched free. "I have been tricked!"

"God's teeth!" Lucien reached for her again.

She evaded him and retreated to the far side of the room beside her dressing table. "It is my mother's bidding you do," she said.

He strode toward her. "I will explain it all later."

"There will be no later." She fumbled for something with which to strike him and her hand closed over her brush. "Do you come nearer, I will scream!"

Continuing toward her, he said, "And be responsible for my death?"

She waged a battle between preservation and conscience. She could not allow him to take her from here, but neither could she sentence him to death. "Go, Lucien," she pleaded. "Take your freedom and leave me."

"I am not going without you. You are leaving this night, even if it is over my shoulder."

She swept her pitiful excuse of a weapon before her. "Then that is how you must take me."

He lunged and caught her arm.

Alessandra twisted around, raised her free arm above her head, and brought the handle of the brush down upon his skull.

He grunted and snatched the brush from her.

"I will not go with you!" she cried. "I will not leave my mother!"

His arms crushed her to his chest. "Alessandra." Though his voice was harsh, she thought she heard a ring of regret. "It was no dream. Your mother is gone. She is dead."

If not that he held her so near, she would have sworn he had punched her in the chest, for his words stole her breath.

"There is no longer any reason for you to remain here," he continued.

Memories rushed at her, too vivid to be dreams, but she shook her head. "You lie, Lucien de Gautier. It *was* a dream!"

"Leila poisoned your mother. Do you not remember attacking her?"

Well she remembered it, and though she tried to back her mind away from it, the memory clung like disease. Too real to be a dream.

"How would I know your dream if that is all it was, Alessandra?"

He could not. Still, she asked in a small voice, "My mother is dead?"

"She is. I am sorry."

Feeling grief tighten her chest, she turned from wrenching sorrow in favor of the less painful emotion of hatred. "I will see Leila dead."

"Her punishment will be just, Alessandra. Now we must leave."

"Not until my own eyes have witnessed she suffers the same fate as my mother."

He growled, swung her into his arms, and strode toward the window.

Alessandra renewed her struggles, punching, kicking, and bucking, holding back only her voice lest he once more bend—quite possibly die—to the bastinado.

Lucien hated what she forced him to do, something he had never done to a woman. He dropped her to her feet, and holding her with one hand, raised the other. "One day you will thank me for this," he said and landed a fist to her jaw.

She sucked air, fell sideways, and fought him no more.

Unable to sleep for fear of the terrible punishment awaiting her on the morrow, Leila gripped the lattice of the window and stared into the night.

These were her final hours. Although she was the mother of Jabbar's heir, which had saved her from banishment once, nothing could save her now. There had been a chance Jabbar would have sent her away had it been the daughter, not the mother, but his lust for Sabine was too great. Even without the poisoned date Khalid had produced, the end would likely have been the same.

Leila drew a hand down her face and winced at the scrapes Alessandra's nails had raked into her skin. Worse were the blows the brat had driven into her sides, making it painful to draw deep breaths.

Hatred that Leila had not believed could grow stronger swelled through her. If only it had been Alessandra's young body that had shuddered and gasped. Then, even had Leila's sentence been death, it would have been worth it. But Rashid would still wed Alessandra.

Though Leila had tried to convince her son otherwise, he was determined to have the flame-headed whore for a wife. He shared his father's same perverse desires.

Head throbbing, she pressed fingers to her temples and reflected on the victory that had nearly been hers four nights past. Hoping to discover what pleasure the English eunuch could give her, despite his rejection of her attempts to seduce him, she had sought him out.

She had gone by way of the garden, as she always did when she desired a tryst. But as she had slipped past the open gate, she had seen Alessandra climbing through the window of the eunuch's room. At first, Leila had been outraged, jealous that another enjoyed what she was denied, but sanity prevailed.

Realizing here was the way to ensure Rashid did not marry Sabine's daughter, she had given the two sufficient time to compromise themselves, then gone for her son. Unfortunately, Sabine and Khalid had arrived ahead of them.

Still, Leila had been certain the physician would give testimony to Alessandra's loss of chastity, and she had nearly gone mad when the old man had refuted it. Then Jabbar had ordered that the wedding go forward.

It would have been so easy had Alessandra lost her virtue. Rashid could not have forgiven that, for he was the same as most Arab men. The purity of his bride was all-important. So much that, had it been any but Sabine's daughter, merely being alone with another man at night, even a eunuch, would have been sufficient cause to reject Alessandra. But Rashid had been adamant, leaving Leila no choice but to use poison to achieve her end.

A sound in the night, so slight she thought she might have imagined it, had her searching the garden. There—movement. She peered closer. Though there was little moonlight, she picked out the shadowy figure of a large man.

It was not a guard, for none were that size. It had to be Khalid. Or the Englishman. As he slipped through the trees, a sliver of moonlight fell upon something in his arms before he was once more enveloped in shadow.

Red hair.

Leila had thought she would not smile again. But here was the Englishman. And Alessandra. Where would they consummate their desire? His quarters? The stables? There in the garden?

She began to tremble at the realization she was being given another chance to expose the lovers and free her son from wedding the whore.

She sank to her knees and thanked Allah for smiling upon her in her last hours. Perhaps he might even deliver her from Jabbar's sentence of death.

Though she burned to raise the alarm, she quelled the impulse, telling herself she must be patient. This time she wanted no question as to what transpired between the two. Whether or not Alessandra remained virtuous, her behavior would not be overlooked a second time.

"I have won," she whispered into the dark, tears rolling down her face. "Won."

14

As ARRANGED, HORSES had been waiting beyond the walls. Though Lucien and Alessandra had only to travel as far as Algiers, where a ship waited to take them up the coast, through the Strait of Gibraltar, and on to England, Khalid had left nothing to chance. Both animals were well provisioned should the plan go awry.

It had been a thin hope Alessandra would remain unconscious throughout the ride, and they were not even halfway into it when she began to rouse.

Pushing his mount harder, the second horse following close behind on a length of rope, Lucien held tight to Alessandra in anticipation of the fight she would give him. Though it would be easier to knock her senseless a second time, there was no immediate danger. Thus, he would not do again that which he found so repugnant.

Before Alessandra opened her eyes, she knew who held her, and his purpose. Worse, she knew wrenching pain as the events that had led to this moment rushed at her.

Lucien had not lied. No dream had stolen away her mother. That honor belonged to the vicious woman who was to have been her mother-in-law.

The desire for vengeance lending her strength to fight the grief threatening to break open her emotions, she promised herself that later she would indulge in the tears burning her eyes, the sobs straining her throat. Now she must focus on escaping her deceitful, unwanted savior.

Swallowing hard, she winced as ache shot through her jaw where Lucien had struck her, then pushed aside the fold of robe that had been drawn over her and peered up at the figure silhouetted against the night sky.

How far had he taken her from her home? Was Algiers his destination?

Not caring that she might tumble from the horse, she thrust her hands against Lucien's chest, but he merely tightened his arm around her waist until it became so difficult to breathe that she ceased struggling.

He made her wait several moments before easing his hold, and when he did, she cursed him in Arabic, raising her voice to be heard over the air rushing past them and the pounding of hooves. Whether or not he reacted to her obscenities, it was too dark to know, but she hurled insults until her throat was so raw she could issue no more.

It was then she noticed the discomfort of the ride. Cradled against Lucien, her rear end wedged between his thighs, legs dangling over one side, she had no defense against the horse's jarring movements—unlike Lucien who was able to move with the animal.

Her resentment grew, and she silently vowed he would rue the day he had made a pact with her mother.

On the final approach to the city, when Lucien slowed the horses and proceeded with caution, she spat, "How dare you take me from my home! You are nothing but a—"

"Quiet!" His arm tightened again.

She strained against it. "I will not be quiet. If it will gain me my freedom, I will awaken the entire city."

He reined the horse in, grasped her shoulders, and pulled her around to face him. "Would you prefer I strike you again?"

She opened her mouth to challenge him, closed it, shifted her sore jaw. He would do it. "You are the lowliest cur," she muttered.

He snorted. "You do not know the half of it. Now behave."

He guided the horses behind the covering of trees not far from a row of buildings that marked the farthest reaches of the city.

"We will leave our mounts here," he said, then dismounted and lifted Alessandra down.

It was still too dark to see well, but she felt his regard and knew he questioned whether she could be trusted to stay put.

"I have given you warning," he said, then turned his attention to the packs strapped to the horse and began searching their contents. He unfastened two of the four packs and dropped them to the ground, then crossed to the second horse.

Alessandra did not care what his reason was for choosing only those packs, but thinking it might cause him to lower his guard if she pretended interest, she asked, "What of these other ones?"

He glanced over his shoulder. "They were provisioned in the event of a land journey. If all goes as planned, we need only those required for a sea journey."

The moment he returned his attention to the other packs, Alessandra unfastened her robe that would prove a hindrance and let it fall to her feet. Then she ran toward the buildings. The soft ground slowed her, but neither would it benefit the man who would soon be after her. Fortunately, she stood a good chance of escape, for the soles of his feet could not have fully healed from the bastinado.

She thought she heard him behind her, but told herself it was only imagined. His best chance of overtaking her was astride a horse, and that would be too great a risk for the amount of noise it would make.

Thus, she was unprepared when his body slammed her to the ground. Dirt tearing into her palms and grazing her face, breath emptying in a rush, she cried out.

"Little fool!" Lucien raised himself from her, flipped her over, and dragged her up onto her knees.

Breathing hard, she stared into his shadowed face. "Fool? Because I refuse to allow you to take me to a place I do not wish to go?"

"I made a bargain with your mother, and I intend to keep it. Fight me all the way, but you are going to England."

"I am not!"

His own anger pulsed between them, but then he drew a deep breath and slowly released it. "Why are you so frightened of change for the better, Alessandra?"

"It is not change I fear," she lied to herself and to him, though not entirely, for she was also driven by revenge. "I will not allow Leila to go unpunished."

"Khalid will make certain she suffers like for like. Why can you not leave it to him?"

She was grateful he could not see her eyes turn to tears. "I will myself witness that evil woman drawing her last breath."

"Then what? Will you wed Rashid and spend the remainder of your days in this godforsaken place? What of the children you will raise under the constant threat of intrigues such as that which killed your mother?"

She forced grief down. "It is none of your concern. If you want to escape, go, but leave me. I do not wish to ever set foot on English soil."

Lucien caught her chin and raised it.

"Release me!" she hissed. "I loathe your touch."

"You lie. You desire me as much as I desire you."

"Desire?" Why did it pain her that he named her feelings for him something so lascivious? "Is that all you feel for me, Lucien? Lust of the flesh?"

His thumb brushed her lower lip. "What would you have me call it? Love?"

She closed her eyes, and in her struggle to not be moved by his touch, remembered her mother's suggestion that it might be love Alessandra felt for him. Though he could not possibly feel such for her, *was* that what drew her to him? He was correct in believing she desired him, but it was more than that. Indeed, whatever it was, it made this yearn of the flesh seem more like a symptom.

"I would not believe you if you called it that," she said.

He slid his thumb across her upper lip. "Then I will not. Desire it is, the same as you feel."

"You conceited—"

"Surely you have not forgotten this?" He lowered his mouth to hers.

Alessandra commanded herself to remain unresponsive, to feel nothing, but her body moved to betray her. Battling the fluttering in her chest and stomach, she forced her thoughts back in time. And as she sifted through memories, she paused upon the first day Lucien had come to her in the harem.

She heard again her conversation with her mother regarding the new eunuch. Sabine had said allowances were to be made for him, then revealed his real name and that he was an enemy of the Brevilles.

Lucien lifted his head. "Deny it you may," he said, "but Rashid will never make you feel what you do in my arms."

She could just make out the sparkle of his eyes. "I doubt you even desire me. Every word, every look, every touch was but a means of gaining my trust to lure me into accompanying you to England."

He drew the backs of his fingers down her cheek. "I do not think there is anything I would not have done to gain my freedom, but desire is not something one can force, Alessandra. It is there, or it is not."

"You expect me to believe you?"

"I do."

She did not. Determined to remain in Algiers, she embraced the only thing that might convince him to leave her behind. Disregarding her mother's warning, she said, "Then it must pain you to feel anything but hate, even if only desire, for a Breville."

He jerked so violently, it was as if she had slapped him. "What game do you play, Alessandra?"

"No game. I but reveal what my mother feared to disclose. Before she was stolen from her home and sold into slavery, Sabine was Lady Catherine Breville of Corburry—wife of Lord James Breville. I am their daughter."

In the silence, she felt his struggle. Hoping to push him nearer the edge of leaving her, she said, "We are enemies. Thus, as it would not be unseemly for the bargain struck with my mother to go unfulfilled, I release you from it."

He loosed her, thrust to his feet. "Blind," he growled. "It was there all along—her reaction to my papers, her secretiveness, your lack of resemblance to Jabbar. Almighty! I could have been on my way to England long before now. Instead, I risked all to help a stinking Breville."

Now it was Alessandra who felt slapped. But this was what she wanted, his contempt the key to gaining her freedom.

He shoved a hand through his hair. "Though I was still a boy, well I remember when Lady Catherine disappeared. How could I forget? It was the De Gautiers who were accused of taking her. Do you know our people nearly starved the following winter?"

"How could I know anything of what transpired after my mother's abduction?"

Bitter laughter sounded from him. "Then I will tell you of that dark time."

"I do not wish to—"

"James Breville set fire to half our harvest. And he would have burned all had the other half not been gathered in. Then he led raids against our villages and took what little the people had, leaving them hungrier than before."

Alessandra shuddered, told herself her father had surely believed the De Gautiers had taken her mother, for Sabine had said James was a good man. "Was it not your family who abducted my mother?" she asked.

"Upon my word," he barked, "we had naught to do with her disappearance."

Curiously, she believed him. She stood and touched Lucien's arm. "Then it is just as well I will not be accompanying you. God speed your journey."

He grabbed her wrist. "*Our* journey."

He still intended to force her to England? "But I am a Breville. Why would you wish to help me?"

"I assure you, help no longer has anything to do with it." His tone was chill. "Your mother was wise to keep your identity hidden. And you are a fool to divulge it." He began pulling her toward the horses.

"What do you intend?" she asked, suddenly fearful of this man who had become a stranger in the space of minutes, and whose ominous emotions were more than a match for her anger and indignation. Gone was the one who had moved her so deeply with his caring when she had been injured, later with his mouth and hands...

Lucien halted, rifled through a pack on the ground, and thrust garments at her. "Don these."

Alessandra did not require the light of day to know he held the traditional costume Arab women wore in public—a heavy caftan, a cloak, a concealing veil.

She gripped his arm. "Lucien, please, do not—"

He thrust her hand aside. "I will gag, bind, and carry you over my shoulder if need be. Now put these on, or I will do it for you."

She accepted the garments, murmured, "You know not what you do."

"In that you are wrong." He retrieved a length of cloth from a pack and began to fashion a turban around his head.

How was she to escape him? Alessandra wondered as she pulled on the caftan. Only when its warmth settled over her did she realize how chill she had become. Grateful, she positioned the veil and draped the cloak from the crown of her head.

With the packs secured beneath his robes, Lucien took her arm and steered her in the direction of the buildings.

"Not a word," he said as they neared. "Do you understand?"

"Lucien, can you not see how foolish—?"

He halted and pulled her in front of him. "I have no more patience. All I ask for is a yes or a no. Which is it?"

Her whole world having turned upside down—anger, grief, and fear tearing up her insides—she wanted to cry. "I understand," she choked.

"Good." He guided her forward again.

The steep, narrow streets they negotiated were nearly deserted, and when they chanced to cross another's path, they were afforded no more than a cursory glance.

Alessandra had never seen Algiers at night. For a few minutes, she arose from her misery and allowed the silhouetted city to fill her senses. It was almost beautiful. Unlike during the day when it was a dirty, teeming, exciting place begging to be explored, it radiated magic beneath the stars.

Shortly, she was forced back to her present circumstances by the smell of the sea and the clamor of a lit harbor that merely rested while the city slept. Here there were people about, mostly drunken seamen in search of another drink or a woman. They were loud and coarse, staggering and spouting vulgarities.

Slipping in and out of shadows, Lucien pulled Alessandra after him. "Where is she?" he muttered as he searched the calm waters of the harbor.

She? Was it a ship he spoke of?

"There," he said. "*The Sea Scourge*."

Alessandra followed his gaze. Unlike the others ships anchored nearby, *The Sea Scourge* was not wide of beam or long of reach, but it appeared solid.

"It is the one that will take you to England?" she whispered.

"Do not exclude yourself, Alessandra. You will accompany me."

She had not meant to provoke him. It was simply that she had not accepted she would, indeed, leave Algiers. And still she would not abandon her hope of escape.

Thinking it best to change the subject, she looked up at him. "How are we to—?"

She gasped. With the harbor light upon Lucien's face, she clearly saw the damage Rashid had inflicted upon it. Though it had clearly healed these past days, bruises and lacerations were yet evident.

"Oh, Lucien." She reached up.

He pulled his head back. "Do not."

Guilt deepening, she was grateful for the veil that hid her face. "It is my fault," she mumbled.

"Which is no less than I expect from a Breville."

His words cut, but she could not blame him for bitterness that was his due.

"Come." He pulled her into the street. "There should be a boat waiting to take us to the ship."

An old seaman, a bottle of spirits dangling from his fingers, staggered to a halt and stared at them.

Lucien continued past him, and they were nearly across the street when the pound of hooves brought him up short.

"What is it?" Alessandra asked.

He spun her around and dragged her back into the alley where he pressed himself and her against the wall of a building.

"Lucien—"

"Do you speak another word, I will be forced to strike you again!"

Alessandra closed her mouth and waited to discover the identity of the horsemen who descended upon the harbor. Had Jabbar discovered her missing and sent men in search of her? Although it seemed implausible her absence would be noted before daylight, there was a chance.

Shouted orders and the increasingly loud clatter of hooves preceded the riders' appearance.

Peering around Lucien, Alessandra saw the first of them. Though the man's profile was difficult to discern in the single moment it was visible to her, the horse identified him.

"Rashid," she gasped.

As the thought to call out to him surfaced, she was propelled farther down the alley. At the opposite end, Lucien turned her to face him.

"One of two things will happen if you alert him. You will be returned to the harem, and I will be put to death, or you will simply make my task more difficult."

He spoke true. For the offense he had committed, death was the only course. As evidenced by the damage done his face and the one hundred bastinado strokes Rashid had ordered, only a slow, torturous death would satisfy her betrothed. But perhaps this was what she needed to convince him to leave her behind. "Think you I care what happens to you?"

Lucien clenched his teeth. He did not have time to engage in verbal sparring. Provided the old seaman was coherent, he would not be long in pointing out the direction the pursued had gone. Still, he needed Alessandra's cooperation.

He tipped her chin up. "Unlike your father, you do have a conscience. You will not be responsible for my death. And though we are now enemies, you cannot deny what you feel when I touch you."

She thrust his hand away. "You do not know my mind."

"I know enough of it, and I know your body." Holding firm to her, he hurried her across the street and down another alley. Fortunately, it was a large city, and there were many darkened corners in which to conceal themselves as they traversed it.

Throughout, Lucien prayed the horses had not been discovered. It was their only hope of escape. Even then, it would not be easy. A land journey was dangerous and would take considerable time compared to travel by ship. Worse, he would have to deal with Alessandra's determination to remain in Algiers.

God's rood! he silently cursed. He almost wished she had not told him of her loathsome sire. Until then, he had been more than willing to take her to England. Now it was a struggle not to leave her behind.

What prevented him from doing just that? He knew the answer, of course—was simply loath to admit it. It was more than attraction he felt for this impetuous desert flame. What had sustained him throughout the punishment Rashid had ordered was the desire to know Alessandra beyond carnal urgings. But now…

Stay the course, anger spoke through him, *take what she gives, for how sweet the revenge of returning her spoiled to her father.*

Sweet? his conscience railed. *Until she is infected by the Brevilles, she is one in name only, and what kind of man would you be to use her so? More, what kind of Christian? And if a child results from such a union?*

Lucien's wandering thoughts were nearly his undoing. Just in time, he caught sight of the horse loping down the street they were about to cross. He drew Alessandra back into the shadows and pressed her face to his chest.

He was surprised when she melted into him, her labored breathing evidencing her exhaustion. He had pushed her hard.

"Leave me, Lucien," she whispered as the rider neared. "I will only slow you, and you will never know freedom. Never will you return to your beloved England."

He lowered his mouth to her ear. "If you truly wish to remain in Algiers, here is your chance. Call to him."

Alessandra put her head back and peered into his darkened face. It was a dare he issued, and she nearly rose to it. But she would not be the cause of his death. If she was to escape, she must do so in such a way that he would come to no further harm.

She pressed her face against his chest and waited for the rider to pass.

He did not.

The man halted his horse at the mouth of the alley and leaned forward to peer down its length. "Who is there?" he demanded in Arabic.

Lucien released her and reached inside his robes. The barely perceptible glint of light on steel revealed a dagger.

The man ahead dismounted, drew his sword, and stepped forward.

There would be bloodshed, Alessandra knew. As soon as the man's eyes adjusted to the dark, he would see them.

In the next instant, Lucien pushed her against the wall, lunged forward, and fell upon the man.

Clasping her arms to her chest, Alessandra watched the two shadows become one, heard their grunts and curses, could not discern who had the advantage.

"Dear Lord," she breathed, "do not see Lucien harmed."

The men crashed to the ground where the struggle continued until one rose victorious and moved toward her.

Alessandra took a tentative step forward. "Is it you, Lucien?"

He took hold of her arm. "I hope you are not disappointed."

Suppressing the impulse to throw her arms around him, she allowed herself to be guided around the silent form that lay in the alley.

"Is he dead?" she asked.

"I may be a De Gautier," he muttered, "but I am not so cruel as to leave a man suffering."

Shortly, he lifted her onto the dead man's horse and swung up behind her.

"We might be seen," she said over her shoulder. "Would it not be better to continue on foot?"

"'Tis a necessary risk. Once Rashid's men are spread over the city, we will not be able to reach the horses."

Those left behind that were provisioned for the land journey they must now make.

The alleys being too narrow and cluttered for the large animal, Lucien negotiated the streets, proceeding with caution and traversing side streets when other riders approached.

After what felt like an eternity, they were finally free of the city and, it seemed, all hope of her escaping Lucien de Gautier.

15

ALL THROUGH THAT day and into the night, they rode, pausing only to refresh the horses and share the food Khalid had packed for them.

Few words passed between them, Alessandra keeping grief at bay with imaginings of revenge upon Leila, his thoughts likely upon keeping hold of his newfound freedom.

Not until the sun rose on the second day did they stop for rest, Lucien having determined it best if, henceforth, they traveled by night to elude their pursuers. Though they had followed the caravan routes heading west, he now turned the horses north to the sanctuary offered by the rocky Mediterranean coast. It was there, in one of many caves, they bedded down to await the coming of night.

"I am cold," Alessandra finally admitted to one of two reasons her body could not sink into the sleep it desperately needed. Though the effort required to suppress memories of her mother's death was more weighty than the chill pervading her limbs, it was not something of which she would speak.

When her words were met with silence, she asked, "Lucien, are you awake?"

Across the dim, she heard him sigh. "I am."

She rose and, taking her blanket with her, crossed to where he lay and knelt beside him. "I am cold."

Though it was midmorning, the cave had not warmed, nor was it likely to for some time considering its west-facing location on the rocky shore.

Lucien looked up at her, but there was not enough light to distinguish his features. "What do you want?"

Resenting his deliberate obtuseness, she said, "Do you wish me to beg?"

"A Breville beg? Never."

Weary of being associated with a family she did not know, she snapped, "I am not responsible for things in which I have had no hand."

He levered onto an elbow, reached up, and pressed fingers to the pulse in her throat. "Yours is the same blood."

She shoved his hand away and started to rise, but he caught her arm. "You have not yet told me what you want."

"I want naught from you! If you are going to hate me for being a Breville, I shall hate you for being a De Gautier."

"Thus has it long been between our families," he said and pulled her atop his chest. "Would you like me to warm you, Lady Alessandra?"

Her pride urged her to retreat, but the moment his heat seeped through her clothing, she was lost. Slowly, she relaxed, savoring his warmth while wishing his arms had lost their previous appeal.

After a time, he shifted her down against his side, tugged his blanket from beneath her, and drew it over her. "Sleep now," he said. "We have a long ride ahead of us this night."

Head pillowed on his shoulder, she closed her eyes. However, sleep was elusive, this time due to her awareness of him.

"Why must we be enemies, Lucien?" she asked. "There is no ill between us."

"You are wrong. You and your mother deceived me."

"I did not do so knowingly. I knew nothing of my mother's plans, and do not forget that you deceived me in pretending to be a eunuch." Which he was not at all. Of that she was now certain.

"We deceived each other," he said, "which is what our families have been doing for the past one hundred twenty-five years."

That long, she mused. "It must end sometime."

"Not likely in my time."

"Why?"

He was slow to answer, but when he did, he sounded weary. "Alessandra, there is so much you do not know, nor understand."

"Then tell me of it."

"You will learn soon enough."

"Was my family responsible for your enslavement?" As the Brevilles thought the De Gautiers were responsible for her mother's disappearance, it followed they might have retaliated in kind.

Bitter laughter answered her. "That is a burden I alone carry."

"Tell me."

After a long silence, he said, "What do you know of the war between England and France?"

Though it was a subject much removed from everyday life in the Maghrib—the coastal portion of North Africa that included Algiers—Alessandra's mother had kept apprised of the long-standing conflict and occasionally spoken of it.

The backs of her eyes pricking as a vision of Sabine rose before her, she forced her thoughts to the war.

It had come about when the English laid claim to the French throne during the last century. Though it had not been a continuous war, for the most part, England had been victorious throughout. Only recently had it met its downfall. Now, it seemed, France would remain a separate country under the rule of a French king, and England would have to content itself with its island kingdom.

She shrugged. "It is a war that looks to have finally been lost by the English."

"Aye, a foolish war that should have ended more than a hundred years ago."

"You fought in it?"

"I did."

"Why?"

"Pride, arrogance. Thus, I crossed the channel to fight for a king who does not know his own feeble mind."

"You speak of Henry the Sixth?"

"The same."

"What happened?"

"What happened was Lord John Talbot, the Earl of Shrewsbury. The old man was impetuous—reckless. At Castillon, I and another tried to convince him to forgo the frontal attack he insisted upon, at least until our infantry arrived, but he would not listen."

The strategies of war meant little to Alessandra. Though she was versed in many subjects, owing to her mother's carefully devised studies, war had not been covered in detail. "Why would the earl not listen?"

He snorted. "If the English have a failing, it is that of stubbornness. It prevents them from knowing when the game is lost."

"It was lost at Castillon?"

"It was lost long before then."

"Then of what import is Castillon?"

"Talbot died, along with nearly all those who fought for him. They were blown apart by the French artillery. Like rain, their life's blood sprayed upon the battlefield."

Alessandra's imagination painting the scene for her, she pressed nearer him. "How did you survive?"

"I fell with the others, but mine was not a mortal wound, and I rose again to take up my sword against the French."

"Did you kill anyone?"

"Aye, one of them the eldest son of a duke. For that, I was sold into slavery following my capture."

"You were not ransomed?"

"Not by the French. The duke vowed I would suffer a fate worse than death, and it nearly was. Only after I was sold into slavery and had served several months on a galley did the captain attempt to ransom me. Then…"

"Then?"

He shook his head. "You wanted to know how I became a slave. That is all there is."

"That is not all. Why did your family not pay the ransom to bring you home?"

Lucien ground his teeth. It was a question to which he also wished to know the answer. When the ransom demand had been sent, he had thought his freedom assured. The long, agonizing months of waiting had finally brought news that the payment of monies had been denied. It had made as little sense then as it did now.

Why would his father, with whom he had been close, refuse to pay a ransom he could afford? True, he had been against his eldest son defending the English claim to the French throne, but that had been the extent of their disagreement. What had transpired at Falstaff to change that?

"Lucien?" Alessandra touched his cheek.

Hardening his jaw against the sensation her fingertips roused, he said, "I do not know why the ransom was refused, but I shall discover the reason."

She slid her hand down, laid it to his chest. "Perhaps your family did not have enough money to pay it."

"My family does not want for anything." He was unable to keep anger from his voice. "The De Gautiers are as prosperous as the Brevilles."

"Unless something changed that."

Why did she defend his family? Resenting that she did not behave like those he had been reared to despise, he said, "Go to sleep, Alessandra."

She fell quiet—for a time. "Tell me of the cross burned into the bottom of your foot."

As he had suspected, she had seen it the night she had crouched at his feet in his quarters. He drew a deep breath. "We have not many hours ere we ride again."

She slid her hand up his neck, over his jaw, and traced the scar on his face.

"What of this, Lucien?"

"Cease!" He gripped her hand and lowered it.

"I would know," she beseeched.

He had no intention of speaking of it, and would not have had he not been struck by the thought that if she knew how cruel and deadly the world outside the harem was, she might think better of escape.

"The scar on my face is the symbol of the Islamic faith—the crescent." Though he strove to speak matter-of-factly, he could hear the bitterness in his voice. "It and a hundred lashes were the reward for my second attempt to escape the galley where I was enslaved."

She shuddered. "It was intentional, then."

"As intentional as Rashid's sentence."

"And the cross?"

He could not keep his muscles from bunching. "Punishment for my third attempt."

"Why a cross? Why the sole of your foot?"

"Can you not guess?"

She shook her head against his shoulder. "I am afraid to."

"I was branded that I might forever trample the symbol of my faith."

She caught her breath. "And forever display your enemy's upon your face."

Lucien saw again the cutter's dagger, the man's smile, his glittering black eyes the moment before the blade drew the crescent. He saw the red, glowing poker and felt the searing pain as it was applied to the bottom of his foot. The scarred flesh of his back crawled as he recalled all the times his defiance had earned him the whip. In those moments, he lived again the rage that had fired his being and kept him barely sane throughout the ordeal.

He had not cried out, had not begged for mercy as many of those before and after him had done. Though his stubbornness had angered his captors, earning him greater punishment, he had not yielded.

Softly, Alessandra said, "I am sorry that my people——"

"Your people? They are no more your people than they are mine, Alessandra."

"That is not true. I was raised among them. Though I do not share their faith, I have shared all else—have embraced their ways since childhood."

"And soon you will embrace the ways of the Brevilles. Regretfully, *they* are your people."

"Then you will deliver me to my father?"

She had good cause to doubt he would, for when she had revealed her identity, he had made it clear he no longer desired to help her and had said she was a fool to divulge her sire's name. That had been anger talking.

"Perhaps not straightaway, but you will eventually come to know the man who fathered you."

"Then you do intend to use me against him. To further your quarrel."

It was no less than what James Breville would do under the same circumstances. Indeed, the man had attempted to use the De Gautier heir when, as a youth, Lucien had fallen into his hands.

Recalling the one time he had been at Corbulbury, Lucien delved his memories of the lovely, redheaded woman Breville had taken to wife. Unfortunately, during his captivity he had paid the woman little attention, intent as he had been on plotting his escape. And escape he had. A month later, Breville's wife had disappeared. Breville could not possibly know she would reappear in the person of their daughter.

"If there is gain to be had in holding you," he said, "I would be a fool not to avail myself of it." She might even prove the means by which the families finally settled their dispute—in favor of the De Gautiers.

"What is your plan?" she asked, and he heard bitterness in her voice.

"I have not one, but be assured, as we have a long journey ahead, I will devise one ere we reach England."

"*If* we reach England."

"It is my destination, and so it is yours."

And that was the last spoken of it before she went quiet.

What am I to do with her? Lucien wondered when her tense body finally grew lax and her breathing deepened. By sire only was she a Breville. Could he, indeed, use her?

At an impasse, he turned his face into her hair and breathed in her scent. In spite of the long ride's accumulation of dust and perspiration, he found her no less appealing than she had been the night of her visit to his quarters when attar of the orange blossom had revealed it was she who came to him.

Disturbed by the stirring of his body, he turned his head opposite. And tried to forget the feminine body curled against his.

16

"Is it much different from riding a donkey?"

Hoping Alessandra jested, Lucien turned from the setting sun and looked to where she stood with her back to him alongside her mount. "What say you?"

"A donkey." She smoothed a hand over the stallion's thickly corded neck. "I have only ridden donkeys by myself, never a horse."

He groaned. Considering her unruly disposition, he had assumed she would know how to handle such an animal. Too, she had claimed she could sit a horse the same as Rashid.

"There are similarities in that if one can ride a horse," he said as he strode toward her, "one can ride a donkey."

"Such is not the circumstance," she put over her shoulder.

"As well I know." He halted alongside her, took the reins from her, and turned her to face him. However, the words he had been about to speak slipped away.

As she had not donned the cloak and veil, he saw for the first time the intricate designs that had been stained upon her skin for her marriage. More, he saw the sorrow in her eyes. He had known it would be there, had felt it each time they touched, but had not expected to feel such compassion.

"When are you going to cry?" he asked.

She lowered her chin.

He crooked a finger beneath it and lifted her gaze to his. "When, Alessandra?"

"I spilled tears the night my mother was murdered." Her eyes glazed with evidence there were more to be shed. "And I am done, for they are of no benefit."

"Your mother is dead, Alessandra. 'Twould not be unseemly for you to openly grieve."

She stepped back and came up against the stallion. "I am done," she said again.

"You are not. Why will you not allow yourself to weep as other women—even men—would do upon losing someone they deeply love?"

She turned sideways and threaded her fingers through the horse's mane. "Until you came, I knew little of tears. In Jabbar's household, there was mostly happiness."

"Crying is not something you need practice, Alessandra." He laid a hand on her shoulder. "You just cry."

She ducked beneath his arm and swung around. "I do not wish to!"

"Then you would rather be eaten with plans of revenge against Leila than give your mother her due."

Her face suffused with color. "You think to advise me, Lucien de Gautier, you whose life has been filled with devising means of obtaining vengeance against the Brevilles? Do not waste your breath."

He could not argue that he was in no position to give advice while he was inclined to use her against her father. However, her cooperation was necessary to ensure they reached England safely, and if she knew the truth of her mother's death, perhaps she might give up her foolish idea of returning to Algiers.

"I had hoped not to have to tell you this," he said, "but it is time you knew your mother was an accomplice to her own death."

Alessandra stared at Lucien. "What do you mean?"

"Sabine knew of the poison—that it was meant for you, not her."

She jerked. "You lie! My mother would never submit to poison. That is suicide, and she was a good Christian."

"I do not lie. Sabine knowingly ate the dates to prove to you the dangers of the harem. It was her greatest desire that you leave Algiers."

Then it was the dates that had delivered the fatal poison, Alessandra realized. "Khalid," she whispered, remembering his refusal to hand over the last date. "He knew." Which meant he and Leila had planned her mother's death together? It did not seem possible. Yet what other explanation?

"Aye, Khalid knew," Lucien said. "He saw Leila poison the dates, but when he warned Sabine, still she ate them."

Alessandra shook her head. "My mother would not have gone to such an extreme. She was still young and—"

"She was dying."

She stumbled back. Her mother had been youthful and vibrant. True, she had suffered a bad cough, but otherwise she had been healthy.

"No," she said, "again you lie. Is it the same with all your countrymen?"

Lucien strode to his horse, withdrew a sealed letter from one of the packs, and returned to her side. "This should explain it." He thrust it into her hand. "Then, perhaps, you will abandon your quest to remain in this country."

Alessandra turned over the letter and saw her name scrawled across the back in her mother's handwriting. "Where did you get this?"

"From Khalid. I was instructed to present it when we reached England, but under the circumstances, I believe it will serve you better now."

She broke the seal, unfolded the letter, and stared at words written in Arabic. Clearly, her mother had not trusted Lucien to not read it. Though Sabine had never fully mastered the written language of her adopted country, in this instance, she had chosen it over English.

Turning from Lucien, Alessandra crossed to an outcropping of rock weathered smooth by the sea's spray and lowered to it. Hands quaking, she began to read.

My beloved Alessandra, I pray one day you will forgive me for a deception I would not have worked upon you had I another choice. As I have said time and again, you do not belong in Algiers. Your place is with your father in England. There is the world you should have been born into, and into which you better fit than in a harem behind a veil. I know you, dear one. You are restless and will ever be testing the bars of your beautiful cage, suffering punishment for it, and growing resentful that the man for whom you bear children will think little of swelling the bellies of other women. Now I will reveal that which I have kept hidden for two years. I am dying, and more quickly these past months. With the passing of each day, my cough worsens and the pain is sometimes so terrible I hide myself from you and others so none will learn of my illness. The physician says my suffering will be over soon, and I eagerly await the blessed day, though I know it will pain you and Jabbar. As I conclude this letter, I beseech you not to vex the Englishman overly much, nor forget it is imperative he not learn your true identity. To ensure your safety, I have given him instructions to deliver you into the care of my aunt and uncle, Harold and Bethilde Crennan of Glasbrook. They will deliver you to your father. Farewell, Daughter, and forget not that I love you above all I have ever loved.

Alessandra read the last sentence over and over until she felt her face crumple and the pressure of a sob that was determined to make it to her lips.

A hand touched her shoulder, and though she ached for whatever comfort Lucien might offer, her mind protested. In his arms lay dependency she could ill afford in her circumstances.

"Alessandra."

The sob broke free, and despite her resolve to ignore Lucien, she turned into his arms. As he pulled her near, she buried her face against his chest, grasped fistfuls of his cloak, and clung to him.

He let her grieve until his garments were wet through, her sobs subsided into miserable hiccups, and the day sky had mostly become the night sky. Drawing back, he sought her gaze, and when she gave it to him out of painfully swollen eyes, he said, "'Tis time we were on our way." He swept a thumb across her moist, lower lashes. "We have much ground to cover this night."

Ground that would take her farther from revenge against Leila. It mattered not that her mother would have died from her illness had she not been more quickly ushered unto death. What mattered were the remaining days Alessandra might have spent with Sabine—days that had been stolen from her by that evil woman.

And now Lucien de Gautier was also acting the thief by denying her the satisfaction of ensuring Leila's punishment. There had to be a way to convince him to leave her behind. But though she was certain it was compassion she had seen in eyes that had earlier shone with anger, would it be enough to turn him from his course?

It would not, she concluded. Lucien's plans were set.

Bitterness welled. She had been sheltered from the realities of the world, and as they seemed determined to rain down upon her without cease, it was time to brace herself and prove she was no longer the child her mother had often named her. To prove she was a woman.

She pulled free of Lucien and stood. "I have cried," she said, voice chill even to her ears. "Are you satisfied?"

Lucien was too taken aback to conceal his surprise. While they had sat in the waning of day, he had held a soft, compliant woman capable of shedding honest tears. Now, with angry words, set jaw, and flashing eyes, she had slipped back into the impetuous skin of one who was more girl than woman.

Berating himself for being a fool when he knew better than to allow a Breville to play upon his emotions, he wondered what had compelled him to offer comfort. What about her so weakened him that he fell victim to unwanted feelings?

He stood, and as he strode past her, said, "Do not be long. We ride shortly."

"You ride, Lucien de Gautier, not I. Even if I must walk, I will return to Algiers."

He halted. Had not the letter convinced her there was nothing left for her there? What vengeance did she think to work upon Leila? If she would only look closer upon the matter and be honest with herself, she would see the woman had actually done Sabine a favor. Gone was the wracking pain Lucien had witnessed. Finally, she was at peace.

Keeping his back to her, as he did not trust himself to face her again, he said, "I am in no mood to be tested, Alessandra. Do you not come of your own will, you shall learn the extent of my loathing for your family."

After a silence broken only by the slapping surf, he heard the scrape of her shoes over the rocks.

"If you succeed in forcing me to England," she said when she reached his side, "I will join with my father against you."

He curled his fingers into his palms and peered into her face that, though the features were the same as those he had looked upon that first day in the harem when she had danced as she should not have, was much changed. The innocence that had shone from her was gone. But though he wanted to be relieved that the Alessandra he had come to care about was no more, he could not ignore the pain of her passing. It seemed she was fully Breville now.

"I cannot imagine it being any other way," he said. "But do not forget that ere you can stand the side of the Brevilles, you must first escape me."

She glared at him. "Escape I shall."

"I do not doubt you will try." As he stalked off, he flung over his shoulder, "Little girl."

17

AND ESCAPE ALESSANDRA attempted several times over the next ten days of their journey.

Though it was soon apparent she was gifted with natural horsemanship, fortunately for Lucien, her mount proved less worthy than his. Thus, the chases she led him on were little more than diversions that tested his patience.

Hours of silence marked their night journeys, and when they spoke one to the other, it was often in anger. Their situation was made worse by hunger as Khalid's provisions dwindled and fresh water became increasingly difficult to find.

Had Lucien been alone, he would have supplemented their food with wild game or stolen into merchant camps erected around fresh water and availed himself of their supplies, but he could not trust Alessandra to stay put. Days earlier, he had taken her with him in pursuit of game, but she had turned the hunt for food into an argument that had scattered their quarry.

As for their days, he would have preferred they sleep apart, but each time they bedded down he had to hold her to his side to ensure uninterrupted sleep, for though Algiers grew ever distant, she seemed just as determined to return there.

Coming back to the present, Lucien scowled at their pitiful provisions. Two more days, he estimated, before they reached Tangier and a ship that could carry them to England.

His stomach rumbled, kindling his frustration. Thinking of the nourishing meat he could hunt, he looked to Alessandra who sat near the cave opening. Oblivious to his regard, she dragged fingers through her tangled hair.

There is a solution to this dilemma, he reminded himself. He had considered it before, but had been loath to carry it out. Now, as they would be without food come the morrow, he had no choice.

He retrieved a rope and advanced on Alessandra. Though she had to hear his approach, she did not look around.

So much the better, he thought and lowered beside her and grasped her wrists together in one hand. Surprise on his side, he began binding her.

Her head shot back, eyes flashed at him. "What are you doing?"

He lifted an eyebrow and returned his attention to the rope.

"Cease!" she cried, her voice echoing around the cave.

Finished with her hands, Lucien pushed her onto her back. Amid her struggling and screeching, he thrust aside her cloak and caftan and drew the excess rope downward. It was no easy task, but he captured her ankles together and bound them.

As he reached to tear a piece of material from his cloak, he realized Alessandra was cursing him in her native tongue. She spoke rapidly, but he followed much of what she said, picking out expletives with which he had become familiar during his time on the galley.

"What a brazen tongue you have, my lady," he scolded when she paused to replenish her breath.

Spouting more curses, she attempted to propel her body to the side, but he straddled her and secured the gag that ought to quiet her sufficiently should any come near the cave in his absence.

"I wish you had not forced me to do this," he said and stood.

She stilled, stared up at him.

"Sleep now. When I return, we shall have a real meal."

Were her eyes daggers, they would have dropped him where he stood. Feeling their bloodletting edges, he strode from the cave.

Alessandra was in need of sleep, but she had no thought other than to use Lucien's absence for escape. Lest he think to better secure her, she forced down her fury long enough to be certain he was gone, then she resumed her struggles—thrashing, bucking, and rolling around. But all she managed to do was dislodge the gag, sustain scrapes wherever her flesh was exposed to the rock-strewn ground, and exhaust herself.

Breathing hard where she lay in a tangle, she screamed one last time out of a throat that felt bloodied, then squeezed her moist eyes closed. It appeared Lucien no longer underestimated her, she whom he had called *little girl*.

Those words had worn her raw since he had spoken them ten days past, and not because they offended—though they did. Once she had emerged from the shock of learning the details of her mother's death, she had seen the truth of Lucien's words. And been struck by the nause-ating irony that, no sooner had she determined she would prove herself a grown woman, she had spoken as a child by threatening to stand with her father against him. Though in the days since she had struggled to think well before speaking, still words she often wished back caused him to regard her as if she were, indeed, a child.

"I am a woman," she whispered. "I must behave as one." But that did not mean she should hang her head and allow Lucien to lead her where she did not wish to go.

When she finally had her breath back, she lifted her bound wrists and considered the rope. For all her efforts, the knot had not loosened. Indeed, from the painful tingling in her hands, it was tighter.

Clenching and unclenching her fingers to restore circulation, she lifted her hands to her mouth and began biting at the fibrous rope. It was animal-like, but whatever it took to gain her freedom.

So immersed did she become in the task over what could have been hours, so pained were her jaws and teeth, she failed to register she was no longer alone until a shadow swept over her.

"God's eyes, Alessandra!" Lucien yanked her up to sitting and looked near upon the rope she had chewed partway through.

Her hope of escape trampled, she thrust her face near his. "How dare you—"

He closed a hand over her mouth. "Keep your anger to yourself, else I will leave you bound."

He would.

Curse him for the power he wields over me! she silently raged. *Curse him for being the one born a man!* Though never had she desired to be other than that which she had been born, there seemed no advantage to being a female.

"Will you contain yourself?" Lucien asked.

Teeth clenched, she nodded.

He removed his hand from her mouth and began to work the rope's knot.

Once freed, she hastened to stand with her back to him before the cave opening. "Knave," she muttered. "Cur. Blackguard."

A moment later, he pushed her back against the rock wall and pinned her with his body. "Always you push," he ground out. "What do you hope to gain? You think I will throw my hands up and allow you to return to Algiers?"

She glared at him. "I do not understand why you do not!"

"Certes, I am tempted, but I gave my word I would get you to England, and I shall."

Mention of Sabine caused Alessandra's emotions to shift toward sorrow, a place she was constantly sidestepping for how vulnerable it made her. Struggling to return to anger, she put her chin higher. But that small, defiant gesture was not enough to prevent her lower lip from trembling. As she pressed it tight with the upper, the movement drew Lucien's gaze.

It did not appear to be desire with which he regarded her mouth, but concern. He drew back a space and slid a thumb beneath her lip. "You are quite the fury, Alessandra. See what you have done to your mouth."

She knew, had felt the abrasions and subsequent swelling inflicted by the rope's rough fibers as she had tried to gnaw her way free.

"I would not think it would bother you," she said.

"It should not," he said and bent near.

She jerked, thinking he intended to kiss her. He did, but not her mouth.

He pressed his lips alongside her ear. "But it does trouble me," he said softly.

She shuddered, more from his warm breath in her ear than the touch of his lips. It felt too wonderful to allow it to go any further. And yet she could not summon the words to demand her release.

He has made himself your enemy, she reminded herself. *He tied you up like an animal! Fight him!*

"It is more than my word that makes me hold to you, Alessandra," he murmured, his breath once more shooting sensation through her. "Despite who begot you, despite how you madden and anger me, I want you."

Rashid wanted her, too, would have wed her to have her. Not Lucien de Gautier. He would bed her, and that was all. No words of love would he speak and, afterward, he would force her onto a ship bound for England, tearing her from all she knew. And revenge.

Catching hold of the anger that had consumed her during her struggle with the ropes, she said, "Why do you not force yourself upon me? Is that not what a De Gautier would do?"

She felt him tense, but he did not release her as she thought her slander might cause him to do.

He lifted his head. "You do not know the De Gautiers, and you certainly do not know me. I have never been and will never be one to force myself on a woman."

Even his breath fluttering across her stinging, scraped lips made her more aware of her body than she had ever been. "Good. Then you will never have me." No sooner was it said than a thought struck her, a shameful one of the ilk she strove to think through before speaking. "Were I to give myself to you, would you release me?"

His eyes narrowed. "Do you place such little value on your virtue that you would bargain it away?"

From the heat rising up her neck, she knew her face was destined for a shade of red. However, her embarrassment was as much for what she had not said—she valued her virtue, but were it Lucien to whom she lost it...

"For revenge, then?" he pressed. "Your virtue for a chance to witness Leila's punishment?"

That was how it sounded. Desperate and crass, hardly befitting a lady.

"In England, a woman's virtue is everything, Alessandra. Do you not have it, it is unlikely you will capture a worthy husband."

She caught her breath. "What makes you think I wish a husband?"

"It is what your father will want."

But would her father acknowledge her as his? Though her mother had said he was good and kind of heart, what of those things Lucien had revealed about the man? Providing he had spoken true.

She drew a deep breath. "It was not an offer I made you. I am curious, that is all."

"I am glad to hear it, for though I desire you, neither am I a man who pays for a woman's company, be it in coin, be it in favors."

She was not surprised. Though at her angriest there was satisfaction in thinking and speaking ill of her family's enemy, he showed little evidence of being of a perfidious bent. Indeed, though he had trussed and gagged her, it was not without cause. They needed food and, given the chance, she would have tried to escape again.

"Too," he added, "the virtuous daughter of James Breville will surely be of more value to me once we reach England."

She gasped. It was such a calculated thing to say, especially considering the place from which he had jerked her thoughts. But then, his hatred of her family went deep. Of a perfidious bent, indeed!

"You are despicable," she said. "An animal."

He released her and stepped back. "I am what my captors made me."

Keeping her back to the wall, she said, "The blame is not theirs. It is the De Gautiers'. *They* made you."

He seemed to think on her words, then said, "To a point, you are right, but enough of this. There is meat to be fired and sleep to be had ere night falls."

Unsettled that he so easily yielded, she grappled for further argument, but there was none.

Indisputably, Lucien de Gautier remained in control of her fate—one that would soon deliver her to Tangier.

18

⤳⧓⤳

DESPITE THE DANGER of being a woman alone, it was a chance Alessandra could not pass up. Thus, as she and Lucien were swallowed by the masses frequenting Tangier's marketplace, she bided her time.

Why he had brought her so far west was a question that would never be answered if she succeeded in losing herself among the crowd, for each time she had asked, he had only glared. All she knew for certain was that he was looking for something. Or someone.

Holding tight to her horse's reins as she led the animal forward, she slowed her steps and dropped back into the thickening crowd.

Soon, she told herself, allowing herself a small smile at how easy it would be to lose herself among the hundreds of women who wore the same cloak and veil of Muslim tradition. But Lucien also slowed, so much that she was forced to draw level with him again.

"Stay close," he growled in the language of his enemies.

Alessandra glanced at him. Earlier that morning, on the outskirts of the city, he had arranged the excessive material of his head cloth to cover the lower half of his face. Garbed as he was, with only a strip of tanned skin visible, he melded with those around him. However, as his amethyst eyes would reveal he was not of Arab descent, he mostly kept them cast down.

A major port bordering on the Atlantic and Mediterranean, Tangier was a place of many faces where trade between countries was rampant. Thus, a disguise would have been unnecessary if not for the possibility Rashid was still in pursuit.

Was he? Or had he given up and taken another for his wife? Long gone were the mass of braids and intricate henna markings she would have worn to her marriage bed. Also firmly in her past were her wide-eyed innocence and the mother who had opposed her marriage to Rashid. She was no man's bride now.

She sighed, moved her thoughts back to escape. The opportunity presented itself when Lucien paused before a vendor's stall that was strewn with textiles and woolens of every color.

Keeping an eye on Alessandra, he spoke in a low voice to the little man who had rushed forward to present his wares. The vendor was to be disappointed, for it was obvious Lucien was interested in something other than fabric.

Pressed against her horse by those eager to make a place for themselves in the cramped street, Alessandra prayed for Lucien to look away. When he finally obliged, she ducked and scrambled beneath her horse. Heart pounding furiously, she threw herself into the crowd and was swallowed. One black-clad woman among many, she pushed her way through the suffocating press of bodies.

She heard Lucien call her name, his voice a bellow above the excited buzz. How near he was, she did not know. All that mattered was that she find her way out of his reach.

As she hastened past stalls, merchants, and patrons, she tried to ignore the regret burrowing through her. If she succeeded, she would never again know Lucien's touch, the masculine scent of him, and the sensations he roused. He would be lost to her—a man for whom she continued to harbor feelings, despite all the discord.

Had the gap between them not widened so terribly when she had told him she was a Breville, she might have cast off her longing to see Leila punished, and even set aside the fear of what awaited her in England. But it was too late. Lucien might desire her, but he disliked her, and she had every reason to feel the same way about him. If only she could...

Tears blurring her vision, she slipped into the shadowed alley between two buildings. Breathing hard, she leaned back against a wall and stared at the patch of daylight whence she had come.

She was just beginning to relax when Lucien's tall, broad figure blocked the light.

Holding her breath, she tensed for flight lest he draw nearer.

He did. "Alessandra," he called as he entered the passageway, wide shoulders brushing the walls on either side.

She thrust off the wall and ran opposite. For once, she had the advantage of size, easily negotiating the tight space that hindered Lucien—until her foot caught on something and she fell facedown.

Veil torn away, cloak askew, dirt upon her lips, she scrambled to her feet and lunged toward the light.

The street she emerged upon was not as busy as that of the marketplace. Had it been, its advantage would still have been limited, for her red hair had come uncovered. No longer was she one of hundreds.

Men stared as she ran past and women scurried away as if death had come into their presence.

Alessandra spared a glance over her shoulder and gasped at the sight of Lucien who thrust aside all in his path.

Hoping to lose him among the buildings, she turned right, left, and left again. Still he came.

Why did he not let her go? Did he not realize the danger of pursuing her?

She made another sharp turn, sprinted between two crudely constructed buildings, and turned again. Though the deepening stench, poverty and coarseness of the people, and lascivious stares evidenced she had entered a less desirable part of the city, she did not turn back.

Rounding a corner, she came upon a half-open door and, without thought, leapt inside and closed it. Back pressed to it, she listened for the sound of Lucien's passing. There it was, preceded by curses.

Would he retrace his steps? Likely, but by then she would be gone.

Feeling the sting of tears, she whispered, "Farewell, Lucien de Gautier," then forced her attention upon the room in which she found herself.

It appeared to be a storehouse. Its shelves were lined with encrusted bottles, open barrels wafted alcohol fumes, and sacks strewn about the floor spilled grain upon which rats leisurely fed.

She shuddered. Only from a great distance had she ever seen the vile creatures.

Hugging her arms to her, she looked to where light shone beneath a door opposite. Beyond it were the sounds of merrymaking.

She could not stay long, must find an authority to aid her return to Algiers. Blessedly, she was not without coin. That much she had planned for by raiding one of Lucien's pouches. But would it be enough? Providing the name of Abd al-Jabbar was known in this westernmost country as it was known throughout the central Maghrib, she need not worry.

Determining enough time had passed, Alessandra straightened her cloak and envisioned the bath she would have once she secured passage to Algiers. Unfortunately, fresh water had been too precious these past weeks, and the accumulation of dirt upon her was distasteful.

After arranging the hood over her hair, she reached for the excess material of her cloak that would have to serve in place of her lost veil.

As she drew it up, the door opposite opened and light rushed in.

Her first thought was that Lucien had discovered her. But the man at whom she stared wide-eyed was nowhere near his size.

"Thief!" he cried.

She spun around, but as she pulled open the door she had come through, it was thrust closed and she was hurled across the room.

Landing among the scattered grain and the screech of disturbed rats, fear flooded her. The man thought her a thief, and thieves were treated harshly in the Muslim world.

The hand she might well lose was grabbed at the wrist and wrenched so forcibly that she was propelled upright.

"Cease!" she cried in Arabic. "I have stolen nothing."

The man's brow furrowed as he looked from her red hair to her eyes, nose, and mouth, then he dragged her from the storeroom and into a room packed with tables and chairs. The handful of men seated there looked up from their drinks.

Kicking and scratching, Alessandra did not cease until the man holding her grabbed her hair and forced her head back.

Desperate, she looked about what was surely a tavern in hopes of discovering one sympathetic face among the leers. There were none.

"Master, a thief!" her captor cried.

A heavy man, darker than most Arabs, likely of mixed race, rose from a nearby table. "A prostitute," he said, raking his black eyes over her. "Perhaps she can pay for what she has taken."

Alessandra was slow to comprehend his meaning, but when he halted before her, pushed her cloak aside, and ran a hand over her chest, she understood. "Do not!" she cried.

He smacked her across the face.

Cheek burning, she said in rapid Arabic, "My father is Abd al-Jabbar. I was stolen from him a fortnight past. He will richly reward you for my safe return."

Silence fell as the men digested her claim, then the room burst with laughter that breathed the foul scent of alcohol upon her.

Of course they did not believe her. Not only was she of obvious European descent, but she was disheveled.

"A whore and a liar," the dark man said and reached for her again. "Come, let us see your wares."

"I have coin," she said, knowing it was only a matter of time before it was taken from her. "I will pay—"

Hands fell upon her body, and she cried out with fear for what this man meant to do, anger that there was nothing she could do to prevent it, and despair over what she had lost in fleeing Lucien. Despite his deception and that he had refused to return her to Algiers, he had been safe.

Heavenly Father, she silently beseeched, *forgive me for being so foolish to believe it possible to escape without mishap—to venture alone into a mans' world and remain unscathed. Pray, deliver Lucien unto me!*

Other hands touched and pinched her. Vile words were spoken that nauseated and terrified her.

Withdraw, she silently urged. *If you cannot remove yourself in body, remove yourself in mind.*

But her mind would not be parted from its companion, and so caught up was she in the heinous act to come that she was only vaguely aware when the pouch containing her coins was taken.

"Lucien," she gasped amid tears. "Lucien!"

As if in response, a man rose from a table in the back of the room, but it was no bronze-headed giant. As he advanced on her, surely intending to violate her, two others followed.

"Enough!" he spoke in the lingua franca recognized by the Arab-speaking people, his heavy accent evidencing he was of French descent.

Alessandra's assailants pulled back, allowing her to look nearer upon the handsome, dark-headed man. In European dress, he and his men stood out among the many draped in shapeless robes. Hope surged through her. Might he aid her?

He stopped several feet distant and considered her with an appreciative gleam in his eyes. "What price for this woman?" he asked.

She was to be sold?

The tavern owner waved the others back. "You would pay to have her first, Monsieur LeBrec?"

The Frenchman shook his head. "I will pay to have her to myself. I share with no man."

Though his words offered little comfort, compared with the others, he seemed respectable. Perhaps she could convince him of her relation to Abd al-Jabbar.

The tavern owner grinned. "You are a selfish man. And when you are finished with her?"

"You know my business, Asim."

"Indeed," Asim murmured, then named an exorbitant price.

"Too much," LeBrec said. "Look at her. She is no prize. And smell…"
He sniffed the air. "It will take much purging before she is of use to me."
He offered a quarter of Asim's asking price.

Asim thrust Alessandra in front of LeBrec. "Look, friend, she is of
fine frame and slender of limb." He swept a hand down over her. "Much
pleasure she will bring you."

"She smells worse than thought," LeBrec said dryly.

Alessandra nearly spouted indignant words, but she could not afford
to anger the Frenchman.

Asim leaned near Alessandra, breathed in her scent, and lowered
his price.

LeBrec argued it, and shortly an agreement was reached at less than
half the original figure.

Asim took the money, pushed Alessandra at LeBrec, and lumbered
off. The other men also dispersed.

LeBrec pulled Alessandra's cloak closed. "You need not fear me. You
are safe now."

Attempting to see beyond his wonderful smile, she said in a voice
flushed with relief, "*Merci, monsieur.*" He did not seem an animal, but
would he aid in her return to Algiers? If so, at what price?

"So you know my language, eh?" he asked.

"And English." Sabine had neglected no area of her daughter's education, endowing her with the fluency of three languages and the funda-
mentals of several others.

Grasping her elbow, LeBrec guided her to the tavern's entrance, his
companions following. "Yet you speak Arabic as if it were your native
language," he mused.

She halted. "It is. I am no liar, monsieur. I was born and raised in
Algiers. My father is Abd al-Jabbar."

He smiled wider, and the corners of his eyes crinkled. "What is your
name, *cherie?*"

"Alessandra."

"Well, Alessandra, when this grime is removed"—he drew a thumb down her cheek and came away with a smudge—"we shall know for certain, eh?"

She would have to tell him all of it, she realized. She only hoped the price of his assistance would not be her virtue.

"Come," he urged, "I will take you to my home where you can have a long bath. Then we will talk."

A bath. The dirt no longer concerned Alessandra, but the cleansing away of the feel of those hands that had sought to violate her. Warily optimistic, she placed herself in LeBrec's hands.

Pity, Jacques LeBrec thought as he leaned over Alessandra's sleeping figure and lifted a lock of her lustrous red hair.

He was taken with the beautiful, impetuous young woman who had emerged from the filth to grace his table hours earlier. She was refreshing, her manners impeccable and testimony to her incredible story, and of which he now had written proof.

He let the tress fall, then straightened and looked at the letter he had found among her scant belongings. It was from her mother, and its poignancy had gripped him when he had read it minutes earlier. He retrieved it, folded it, and tucked it inside his overtunic.

When he looked again at Alessandra, he stirred in remembrance of the shapely figure he had glimpsed beneath the diaphanous material she had been clothed in following her bath, and that was now hidden beneath the blanket pulled over her. But only a stir.

Having long ago accepted his impotence, he was not surprised. Still, he continued to hope he would find a woman capable of bringing him to life. Though it seemed Alessandra was not to be the one, she had moved him more than any other.

Just as well, he consoled himself as he turned away. *Otherwise, I might not be able to part with her. Which I must do. And soon.*

It was not like him to become emotionally attached to one of his investments, but this woman was an exception. Had he time to send a messenger to Algiers to discover the reward for her return, he would keep the promise she had extracted to return her to Abd al-Jabbar. Unfortunately, he had a sizable debt coming due.

At the door, he looked over his shoulder. In sleep, she was even more exquisite. The light sprinkling of freckles enhanced, rather than detracted, from her beauty. Her long lashes, pert nose, and bowed mouth were an artist's dream. And her spirit, that transcended slumber, was irresistible. It was no wonder this Lucien she pretended to hate was so determined to take her to England. No doubt he knew how to pleasure a woman. And himself.

The bitterness that Jacques had long ago come to terms with crept back in. It tore at him, hardening him against feelings that were determined to interfere with what he must do.

No matter, he tried to convince himself. If Alessandra could not satisfy the elusive passion of his body, she would satisfy the one passion in which he could easily indulge—gambling.

19

"THERE IS AN auction today," Jacques said as he assisted Alessandra from the carriage that had delivered them to the marketplace.

She assured herself her veil was in place, then peered up at the man who had generously made himself her guardian three days past. During that time, he had proven himself a gentleman—unlike Lucien, she reminded herself as she was assailed by longing.

"Auction?" she said.

Jacques set a hand to her back and guided her forward. "*Oui,* a slave auction."

She tensed. It was at such an event her mother had purchased Lucien, and she found the thought of attending one unappealing. "I have never seen one," she murmured as he led her toward a stall brimming with cosmetics.

"But today you shall, *cherie.*"

Alessandra wanted to object, but held her tongue for fear of offending this man who had been kind to her. If not for him, a terrible fate would have befallen her. Now she had only to wait for Jabbar. As Jacques had sent a messenger two days ago, she would soon be restored to all that was familiar.

Telling herself it was what she wanted—wishing she did not have to remind herself of it—she looked to the vendor who pressed pots of kohl and rouge upon her.

She shook her head, but Jacques tossed a coin to the man who scooped up the cosmetics and handed them to her.

She thanked him and placed them in the pouch beneath her cloak.

Next, Jacques led her to a small stall where trinkets blinked in the sunlight.

"This would look lovely with your hair." He dangled an intricate silver necklace before her.

"It is beautiful."

"Then you must have it."

"I have no coin," she reminded him.

He smiled. "It would please me to buy it for you."

Although she had agreed to allow him to purchase caftans—the reason for the outing—she was uncomfortable with his offer. The garments were a matter of comfort and modesty that the silken trousers, chemise, and vest he had loaned her did not permit. And though she had been given no choice with the cosmetics, the necklace was even more of a luxury.

"You have already shown me more kindness than I deserve. Thus, I cannot accept it."

He reached for his purse. "Consider it repayment for your companionship these past days."

"It is you who should be thanked. If not—"

"You will wear it for me tonight. I insist, *cherie*."

"And *I* insist otherwise."

His face darkened so suddenly she nearly stepped back. "You think I expect payment in flesh?" he snapped, causing the merchant to quiet.

Alarmed, she said, "I do not mean to sound ungrateful, Jacques. Certes, I am appreciative of all you have done for me."

Abruptly, he turned away.

She touched his arm. "Forgive me for offending you."

He kept his back to her until his shoulders no longer moved with the turbulence of whatever had roused him to anger. When he once more faced her, his expression and coloring were nearly normal, there being just enough evidence of the anger he had turned upon her to feed the foreboding in her breast.

"Humor me, will you?" He held out the necklace.

She nodded. "Very well, but I shall repay you as soon as I am able."

Displeasure flitted across his handsome face, flitted off. "This I know."

Once he had worked the merchant down to the price he was willing to pay, he pushed aside Alessandra's cloak to secure the necklace about her throat.

Reminding herself he was European and, therefore, unfamiliar with the strict decorum of the Muslims, she swallowed her discomfort at being revealed before strangers while he fastened the clasp.

"I knew it would suit you," he said with a thin smile.

Grateful for her veil, she pulled her cloak closed over the filmy garments. "*Merci,* Jacques."

He turned her around and led her between the stalls. "You are a strange one, Alessandra."

"How is that?"

"You are different from other women I have known."

"Have there been many?" The moment she said it, she wished she could take back the words. They were too bold and personal.

As if unaffected by her query, Jacques said, "I have known many. Though few were virgins like you."

Alessandra halted, forcing him to stop to keep hold of her. "How do you know that about me?" It was not something they had discussed. In fact, considering the tale she had shared with him, she would not have been surprised had he assumed otherwise.

He urged her forward again. "I know the face of innocence." He turned off the main street and down a narrower one. "Though yours is no longer in full bloom, the prize has yet to be taken."

His words and behavior embarrassed her. More, they worried her, for this Jacques deviated considerably from the one she had come to know in the comfort of his home. What had changed?

"It surprises me," he continued, "that this Lucien you speak of did not take your virtue in all the time you were together. Or that you did not surrender it to him."

Alessandra would have halted again, but his lengthy stride would not permit it. "You cannot know that," she said.

Down another street he pulled her, at the end of which lay a large, decrepit building. "But I do, for it is my business."

Something was very wrong. "Your business?" She recalled he had said something similar to the tavern owner. "I do not understand."

He kept his gaze fixed ahead. "All will be explained momentarily."

She looked to the building that was far removed from the market-place. What of the caftans he had promised her? Were they not the purpose of their outing?

She dug her heels in and pulled free of his grasp. "Where are you taking me?"

"You will see." He reached for her.

She jumped back. "You are behaving strange, Jacques. I will go no farther until you have told me the reason."

"I have a surprise for you. Would you ruin it by forcing me to reveal it before its time?"

She stood firm. "I must know."

He sighed, then grabbed her and lifted her high against his chest.

"Put me down!" she shrieked and struggled to break free.

He stumbled but did not relinquish his hold. Though Lucien would dwarf him, Jacques was no weakling, his stout, broad-shouldered frame surprisingly muscular beneath his clothes.

Alessandra fought him all the way, and not until she was dropped into a chair did her blows fall only upon air. Well past concern for her modesty, she threw off her veil and the constricting cloak. "How dare you!" she hissed as she peripherally took in the filthy room into which he had deposited her.

"I am truly sorry, *cherie*," he said, his breathing labored where he stood over her. "It is with much regret I do this."

Alessandra was wrenched by his betrayal, for she knew she was being cast before wolves. Jacques had never intended to help her. All along, he'd had other plans for her. Still, she had to hear it from him.

"What is it you do, Jacques?"

He averted his gaze. "Understand, *cherie,* it is business."

The business of knowing whether or not a woman was virtuous. "What business is that?"

He returned his gaze to hers. "Slaving, Alessandra."

She closed her eyes. How was she to escape? And if she managed to, what new dangers awaited her? Her mind dredged up the ravishment from which he had self-servingly rescued her. Was there no safety for a woman alone in the world?

Her chest and throat tightened. All was lost, not only her mother and home, but Lucien. Lucien within whom beat a heart of compassion, whose face she yearned to see, in whose arms she longed to be. He hated the Breville in her, but now that she most acutely felt his absence, his loathing no longer seemed such a terrible thing. An obstacle only. And the revenge she longed to take upon Leila…

Strangely distant, almost trivial. Sabine was gone, and though Alessandra would ever embrace her mother's memory, the mourning would eventually ease. What might not ease was the life ahead of her. Her mother had done her best to ensure it would be a more tolerable one than that of the harem and veil, but Catherine Breville's daughter had rebelled. And now this…

She suppressed a sob.

"Wipe your tears, *cherie*." Jacques thrust a crisp kerchief at her.

She slapped his hand aside and scrubbed her eyes across her forearm. "Why, Jacques?"

His smile was apologetic. "You will bring a good sum—an innocent with tresses of fire who speaks the Arab language." He reached to her hair but grasped only air.

The chair upended by her hasty retreat, Alessandra stepped over it to put distance between them. "You are despicable! A man who is not a man. A weasel!"

As if she had landed a terrible blow, his lungs emptied with a rush, hands snapped into fists, color flooded his neck and face. "I could have sold you into prostitution!"

She laughed. "I should be grateful you mean only to sell me into slavery?"

"Many will vie to bring you into their harem. Surely you prefer one lover to many?"

"I prefer none!"

Lower jaw thrusting, he dropped his gaze to the floor between them.

Alessandra glanced at the door he had carried her through. He would overtake her before she reached it. However, there was an open pathway to a door on her left—her only chance, though she had no notion of what lay beyond it.

She ran, heard Jacques shout her name and the sound of his boots on the wooden floor, but nothing would turn her from her course.

Nothing except the large woman who appeared in the doorway.

Alessandra slammed into her, cried out when rough hands clamped around her forearms.

As she strained to break free, the woman ran eyes over her, then boomed in uncultured French, "You could have lost her, dear Jacques."

"Not with you slugging about," he snapped and reached to reclaim Alessandra.

At that moment, she would have willingly gone to him, the known preferable to the one who examined her as if she were a sweet morsel.

Sidestepping Jacques's attempt to relieve her of Alessandra, the woman said, "Surely you are not having second thoughts. This one will free you of your debts. Or nearly so."

He turned away, asked over his shoulder. "How much?"

The woman released one of Alessandra's arms, gripped her captive's chin, and pressed her head back. She considered the face, then the hair. "A bit too red, do you not think?"

"Do not play games with me! What can you get for the wench?"

Tears burned Alessandra's eyes. *Chattel. That is all I am to them. Cloth on a bolt.*

"I cannot know for certain, but you will not be disappointed."

"Do it today," Jacques said and strode opposite.

As Alessandra peered sidelong at him, straining to keep him in sight, the woman called, "It would be better to wait. Word will spread, and you will obtain a higher price."

He halted, looked around, but not at Alessandra. "I said *today*!"

The woman heaved a foul-smelling sigh. "As you would."

"And Edith…?"

"*Oui?*"

"The necklace goes with her."

Alessandra had forgotten about it. As greedy eyes flitted over the silver collar, she reached to tear it from her neck, but the woman loosed her chin and caught her arm against her side.

"Do you understand, Edith?" Jacques pressed.

"It goes with her," she grumbled.

Jacques resumed his course.

Alessandra had no intention of begging him, and yet as he was about to pass through the doorway, his name burst from her. "Jacques!"

He paused and his shoulders hunched. "*Pardon, cherie,*" he said without looking around. Then he was gone.

With a mix of fear and rage, Alessandra fought the hands holding her.

"If that is to be the way of it," the woman said. She thrust Alessandra back against the wall, squeezed a calloused hand around her captive's throat, and did not let up even when her prey ceased struggling.

The loss of air sprayed colors against the backs of Alessandra's lids. Lovely colors despite the strain and pain that called them into being.

Even lovelier was the black that ran over them, promising to deliver her from this nightmare. But not the plaintive voice in her head.

What have I done, Lucien? Dear God, what have I done?

A man who is not a man.

That was what she had said of him, though she could not know how true she spoke.

Staggering in his haste to exit the building in which he had sentenced Alessandra to slavery, Jacques stepped to the side and leaned back against the wall.

It should not be such a hard thing. But it was, and more so after their time in the marketplace.

Curse her! Why could she not be like the other grasping creatures who had surrounded him all his life? He should not have had to push the necklace upon her, a fine piece of jewelry meant to serve as an apology. Rather, she should have asked for more—earrings, a bracelet, a belt of shimmering coins. But it was as if she had known what awaited her and sought to employ guilt to alter his plan. And such guilt! Deeper than that with which his mother had controlled him, the devil rest her soul.

Alessandra's face rising before him, he closed his eyes, but it was clearer, more vibrant, behind his lids.

It had cut him to see the gratitude, admiration, and trust with which she had regarded him these past days replaced by accusation, loathing, and fear. Indeed, he had been tempted to remain the champion he had pretended to be these past days. But then Edith had reminded him of his debt and who he was—Jacques LeBrec, slave trader, gambler unextraordinaire. For that, he had rejected the woman's suggestion that the sale of Alessandra be delayed. At a time like this, he could not afford to reshape his character. Thus, it had to be today or he might change his mind. And then where would he be?

20

Had she not been such precious merchandise, Alessandra bitterly reflected, she might have ended up much the same as the girl with whom she shared a cell.

Clutching the accursed necklace still fastened around her neck, she stared at the girl's bruised and swollen face that not even sleep could soften. And shuddered. It could as easily be her had Jacques not ordered that she be auctioned this day.

An hour past, she had awakened here—one of many cells, but separate from the others. From her tearful companion, a dark-skinned girl of ten and five who spoke halting Arabic, Alessandra had discovered the reason for the segregation. With the exception of the children, they alone were chaste. The other captives, a teeming mass of bodies pressed into cells filled to capacity, were men and women of varying races and languages. Though some were vocal about their captivity, most seemed resigned.

What had it been like for Lucien, a man of greater strength and will than any of those before her? Hell. The same—no, worse—than that in which she found herself.

She imagined his giant's wrath. The threats and curses that had surely battered those who dared make him their slave. His restless pacing in a cell he had likely shared with no others. His broad hands grasping the bars and straining their ability to contain him. His fists bludgeoning all who ventured near.

And now he was free, likely on a ship set sail for his precious, chilly England. Would she ever be free?

She gripped the necklace so tight its edges cut into her palm. As it was the only thing of value she possessed—the worth of the cosmetics negligible—she had quelled the childish desire to rid herself of Jacques's conscience-easing gift. Bereft of jewels, it was not overly valuable, but it might aid in her escape if an opportunity presented itself.

A commotion at the far end of the warehouse gave way to a procession of men clad in various dress. They followed one whom Alessandra's companion had earlier identified as the auctioneer, the same who had beat the girl several days past when she had refused to rise from her bed of straw to allow buyers to look nearer upon her.

Dry mouthed, Alessandra watched their advance into the bowels of this market of human flesh. The buyers—a select number granted the privilege of preview before the auction—gathered before each cell to listen to the auctioneer extol the qualities of the occupants, then moved on.

"Oh, Lucien," Alessandra breathed. Always it came back to him. Every notable twist and turn in her life was a result of the unforgettable man she had spurned in her bid for freedom. If only he had caught her in that alleyway…

No cloak to cover her, she shortly suffered the leers of the auctioneer and his buyers who stepped near the bars to better see her figure through her light garments.

Determinedly, she sat erect on the dank straw she had gathered into her corner.

Naught to fear, she told herself in an attempt to calm her fiercely beating heart. *Not yet.* The price for her virtue was too high to permit any to sample her.

Bright blue eyes and a wicked smile drew her attention to a man of good height and carriage. As his gaze lapped her curves, he smiled wider.

Alessandra struggled not to respond to his brazen regard, but it turned her anger inside out and she jumped to her feet and lunged at the bars. "Curse you!" She thrust her hands between the iron rods. "Curse you all!"

Her nails scraped air, the blood of her intended victims maddeningly out of reach.

Laughter burst from the rake's throat. "Sweet mother of mercy," he said in crisp English. Then, fluid as the warm waters of the Mediterranean, he stepped forward and caught her wrist before she could snatch it back. "Imagine this one in your beds!" he said, switching to lingua franca as he reeled her in until her side was pressed hard against the bars.

"Release me!" she demanded.

Ignoring the auctioneer's scowl, her tormentor slid his other hand up her arm, brushing aside the sleeve of her chemise.

The others drew near again, faces lit with interest as the rake advanced on her body.

"English swine!" she cursed.

Fingers coming to rest on the flesh of her upper arm, he leaned in and whispered, "You will be in my bed by nightfall."

Through her wild tumble of hair, she glared at him. "With a knife."

His eyebrows jumped. "Promise?"

Alessandra stared. This man was dangerous, possibly more so than Lucien. Were all Englishmen the same?

She had been straining so hard against the rake's hold that when he released her, she flew back and landed in her corner, startling the girl into wakefulness.

"Make ready, my lady," the Englishman taunted. "The day will be long. The night longer."

Bile burning a path from her belly to her mouth, Alessandra watched him and the others leave, their parting glances filled with lecherous imaginings. Though she wanted to cry, to scream, to pound her fists, she drew up her knees, pressed her aching forehead to them, and turned to the only one who could save her now.

Please God, send me an angel.

Alessandra would never forget the ravenous faces, nor the fear that flayed her as she looked out across the crowd. She would not forget the three hundred and seventeen steps she had counted from her cell to the platform, nor the merciless hands that had guided her there. And the remembrance of one man would be the anchor to which all was bound—Lucien de Gautier.

She did not blame him, for she was the culpable one. Had she not fled, she might be with him on a ship bound for England. Now, gone forever, was the one to whom she might have given her heart had the barriers between them not become insurmountable.

The auctioneer's bellow startled her back to a world gone mad, and she inwardly cringed as he ticked off her qualities, somehow managing to make the word *virgin* sound foul each time he spoke it.

With a strength she had not realized she possessed, she stood with her shoulders back and waited to be divested of her clothing, as the woman before her had been. Although she longed to resist such humiliation, she knew it would be futile and would only excite the wolves flanking her.

Breaking her fixed stare, she searched the crowd for the Englishman who had earlier taunted her.

As if reading her thoughts, he moved into her line of sight and smiled his wicked smile. Then, answering the auctioneer's summons to bid, he yelled out a staggering sum that must have made the others rethink their desire to have her.

Amazed to find herself still clothed, she sent thanks heavenward, then once more broached the subject of an angel.

A rotund Turk dressed in gilt-edged garments stepped forward and topped the Englishman's price. No angel he.

An Arab raised the price higher. The farthest thing from an angel, his eyes ravishing her where she stood.

The Englishman countered. Certainly no angel, more likely a henchman of the devil.

Alessandra feared she would lose the bile in her otherwise empty stomach. Then, on second thought, she prayed she would. If that did not curb the lust of these men, nothing would.

The bidding continued, creeping and jumping higher with each shout until Alessandra's nerves jangled. Squeezing her eyes closed, she forced deep breaths into her lungs.

It was then something warm enveloped her. She lifted her lids. Violet. That was the color of the eyes into which she looked.

"Lucien," she whispered.

Mouth a thin, hard line, the man who should be long gone stared back at her from the shadowed folds of his head cloth. Still wearing Arab dress, he would have melded with the others if not that his proportions set him apart. But even if he had been on a level with those around him, Alessandra would have known of his presence.

She offered him a tentative smile—of apology, regret, gratitude.

His face remained impassive, showing no evidence of the emotions beneath it. For certain, he was still angry with her for running from him.

Refusing to look away for fear he would disappear, she felt the ashes of her soul smolder with hope, then turn to glowing embers.

She would not have believed angels capable of assuming flesh, but in Lucien, one had found a way.

Heart lightened, she waited for him to offer a sizable portion of what her mother had given him. She had seen the coin, as well as pouches of Sabine's jewelry. Though Alessandra had rarely had dealings with money, it had appeared Lucien had been given a king's ransom. More than enough to assume the role of savior.

When would he? she wondered after some minutes passed, during which he did not bid. And why did he persist in maintaining a blank expression, offering no reassurance even by way of a turning of the lips?

"To Captain Giraud!" the auctioneer announced.

The warmth surrounding Alessandra turned chill. She tore her gaze from Lucien and landed it upon the other man—the rake who had vowed to make her his. Was it possible she belonged to this one whose mocking eyes held terrible promise of the night to come?

It was not. In spite of Lucien's hate for the Brevilles, he would not forsake her. Would not have attended the auction unless he meant to free her.

She looked back to where he stood. *Had* stood, that space now horribly vacant.

"Lucien," she gasped, searching the crowd for a glimpse of him. That was all she had before he went from sight.

"Lucien!" She lunged forward.

As hands dragged her back from the edge of the platform, she struck out, her knuckles contacting soft flesh, then bone that shot pain up her arm.

A slap jerked her head back, and she was flipped over a shoulder. As she was carried down the steps, she pummeled the man's back and told herself Lucien would not be so cold and unfeeling, that he would not leave her to ravishment when it was within his means to deliver her.

But he had turned his back on her. Had revenge against her father hardened him to her plight? Had he only come to see her off to the hell she had dug for herself?

Tears scalded her eyes. To have been so close, only to discover how far she truly was, shook the adult foundation she had done her best to lay over that of a child. Vowing she would not succumb to its crumbling, she fought down the evidence of her misery.

Dropped to her feet, she saw Captain Giraud striding toward her, wearing the same smile that had first fired her anger.

Soon he will discover the poor bargain he has made, she told herself. *He will regret every gold piece paid for me.*

He halted before her. Eyes gleaming, he taunted, "'Tis as I said, hmm?"

Needing no reminder of his threat to bed her, Alessandra launched herself forward, causing him to stagger beneath the thrust of her weight. Quickly regaining his footing, he grasped her arms and started to set her back from him—providing all the space she needed to land a nasty blow.

Too late, the man who had carried her from the platform interceded. Though he clearly tried to contain his expression, his lips quivered as he held her and waited on the Englishman who bent over his pained anatomy.

Slowly, Captain Giraud straightened. When his gaze met Alessandra's, she hissed, "It is also as I said."

"Once you are on my ship," he growled, "you will learn the folly of your actions, wench."

His threat leaving its imprint on her closeted fears, she tossed back, "As shall you."

Jacques stared at the boat that grew smaller as it was rowed toward an impressive merchant ship bearing the name *Jezebel*.

As he continued to watch, Alessandra rose up and hurled herself to the side. Expecting her to plunge into the waters of the Mediterranean, he held his breath, but the English captain caught her around the waist and hauled her down and onto his lap.

Though they were too distant for Jacques to make out their exchange, he was certain Alessandra spewed curses. The boat rocked, but continued on as if nothing untoward had occurred.

In spite of the ache inside him, Jacques smiled. Though Alessandra would find herself the mistress of *Jezebel*'s captain, she would be fine. Indeed, she was bound for England where her mother had said she belonged.

Assuring himself his conscience was eased, he turned and stepped into the waiting carriage.

21

Footsteps. His.

Gripping the stool she had determined was the best weapon available to her, Alessandra pressed herself against the cabin wall and spread her legs for balance. And just in time, for the ship pitched again.

Were they leaving port? She knew nothing of the captain's plans, for he had not spoken to her since they had exchanged threats following the humiliation she had dealt him in that most private of places. His silence had suited her, for her mind had been awhirl with plans and devices by which she might thwart his efforts to take what she had only ever been tempted to yield to one man—one treacherous, vengeful man.

Her unwelcome visitor paused outside the cabin door, and she heard the sound of keys being sorted. Then one rasped in the lock, and the mechanism released with a soft click.

For the dozenth time, Alessandra calculated where the blow must land to assure the man was incapacitated long enough for her to flee.

The moment that light, shadowed by the one who pushed the door inward, reached into the darkened cabin, she pushed off the wall and swung her weapon.

It struck the man hard, the force of the blow causing her to lose her grip and sending the stool crashing to the floor. The captain's body did not follow as anticipated. Rather, the arm with which she had wielded her weapon was snatched and she was yanked forward.

"I am grateful for my height," drawled a heart-stoppingly familiar voice.

Alessandra jerked her chin up, picked out familiar features and bronze hair. Even his facial scar was visible in the muted light. Was she dreaming? Or had her mind twisted on her?

Aching to know for certain he was flesh, she reached with her free hand and traced the crescent.

Believe the warmth beneath your fingers, she told herself. *Believe he did not abandon you. Believe there is a place in this angry giant that yearns for you as you yearn for him.*

She cried out and collapsed against Lucien's chest, and when he released her arm, wrapped both of them around him. Sobbing, she grabbed handfuls of the back of his tunic and held tight for fear he might vanish again. Angels had a way of doing that.

She did not know how long she shuddered and reveled in the hands that stroked her arms, back, and head as if she were a child—a child she would not mind being named providing he never let go—but finally she quieted.

"Alessandra."

She tilted her head back and met eyes she had thought never to see again. "You did not—" She gulped. "You did not forsake me."

"I could not, though God knows I was tempted."

Refusing to be offended, she beseeched, "Forgive me," then rose onto her toes and set her mouth upon his. She breathed in his wonderfully solid body, filled her nostrils with his masculinity and the scent of the sea upon his skin, sought a response.

He did not give one, and she knew it was anger that held him from her—anger for who she was and what she had done.

He pulled back, and when she opened her eyes, said, "You were expecting the good captain, eh?"

She startled, grabbed his arm. "We must hurry, else he will discover us. He is evil and—"

"Is that right?" Amusement softened his voice.

She frowned. Why was he so calm? Should he not be spiriting her away from the ship? Had he overwhelmed Giraud? If so, what of the crew?

"You do not understand," she said.

"But I do." He released her and turned away. "You have naught to fear. All is as it should be."

Frowning, she watched him cross to the lantern she had earlier put out. His large hands, which should have been graceless, easily lit it.

Lucien wore tunic and hose that showed him to be more of a man than any caftan or robe could, and his hair was pulled back from his face and secured at his nape with a leather thong.

It was the European mode of dress. Jacques LeBrec had dressed similarly, though his clothes had been finer and more embellished.

Lucien moved to the chest whose contents she had failed to discover, but only for lack of a key, which he now inserted in the lock. He lifted the lid, removed a gown of purplish red and an under gown of dark green, and returned to her.

"Change your clothes." He lifted one of her arms and turned the garments over it. "Then we will go above deck."

"I do not understand."

He turned away. "You will."

Something creeping forward from the back of her mind, Alessandra said, "Lucien, why did you bring me all the way to Tangier? Oran was less than half the distance." She spoke of the coastal city they had skirted partway into their journey. When Lucien had insisted on continuing to Tangier, she had thought he chose to go farther west to throw off Rashid's pursuit. It had suited her, giving her that much more time to devise an escape. Now she did not think she had guessed right.

A hand on the door, Lucien looked back. "I will explain later."

"It's Captain Giraud. He is the reason you insisted on coming to Tangier."

He inclined his head. "Nicholas is my cousin."

Surprise supplanted the relief Alessandra had felt upon discovering Lucien had not forsaken her, then anger. "That knave is your cousin?"

He sighed, closed the door, leaned against it. "It was necessary, Alessandra."

"Necessary?" Heat rippled over her neck and into her face. "You allowed me to be sold like a piece of horseflesh. That miscreant you call cousin taunted me. He——"

"Calm yourself!" Lucien strode to her. "For all we knew, Rashid had made Tangier ere the auction and he, or one of his men, could have been among those in the crowd. Thus, it was too great a risk for me to show my face, one that could have set death upon my heels and seen you returned to Algiers with none to carry out your mother's wishes."

Alessandra stared up at him. He was right. Had he bid for her, he would have drawn attention. It was wrong of her to fault him for exercising caution.

Yet he had allowed her to believe the worst even when she had been whisked away from the auction, and his ruthless cousin had not enlightened her. These past hours locked in his cabin had been horrid with wild imaginings.

"Your cousin," she said. "Do you know the words he spoke to me and the lascivious looks he cast upon my person?"

Lucien's scowl rose toward a grin. "I can imagine."

"You need not, for I will tell you. He said he would have me in his bed this night."

"That is his bed." Lucien nodded at the cot suspended between wooden supports. "And that is where you will sleep. Not a lie."

"But he insinuated…" Her face warmed further. "He set out to frighten me."

He shrugged. "Doubtless, he took it upon himself to teach you a lesson."

"What right——?"

"We should have sailed two days ago, Alessandra." He planted his feet apart to counter the ship's movement. "Your escapade has cost him much in time and profit. Now his cargo will not reach England before the other ships bound for its ports."

It was the least he deserved for the terrible fright he had given her, Alessandra reasoned. However, guilt followed, and she cast her eyes down. "I am sorry."

"As you should be."

She set her teeth to keep her jaw from trembling. How was it that no matter how hard she tried to cast off the child in her, the little one would not be shed? Could she do nothing right?

Lucien tilted her chin up, and she caught her breath at the compassion in his eyes. "It is done now," he said. "Soon you will be in England as your mother wished."

The mention of Sabine caused her emotions to go further aslant. "Yes," she choked. "As she wished."

Lucien touched his lips to hers, drew back. "Dress now. The sky promises a spectacular sunset."

Lips tingling from the brief contact, she looked down at the garments over her arm. They appeared to be as her mother had described, close replicas of the sketches Sabine had made of English costume.

The gown, with its V-shaped neckline and waist, gathered sleeves, and dagged hem, could have been the same as her mother had worn as James Breville's young bride. In no way did it resemble the shapeless caftans Alessandra was accustomed to wearing in public, and it was a far cry from the gossamer vest and trousers of the harem.

"Something is wrong?" Lucien asked.

"I have never worn such clothing."

His eyebrows rose. "You require assistance?"

She nodded. "Will you show me?"

If the stool had struck his head as intended, he could not have looked more surprised. But he said, "I will."

It was reckless, Alessandra knew, but she could not bear the thought of him leaving, even if only for a short time.

She handed him the garments, turned, and unfastened her vest with trembling fingers. She dropped it on the cot, then lifted the front of her chemise and hooked her thumbs in the waistband of her trousers. As she slid them down, her heart beat with jumps and jerks she was certain Lucien could hear.

She stepped out of the trousers and, smoothing the chemise down her legs, turned.

He slid his gaze over her. "You are a siren, Alessandra Breville. A flame-headed siren who would lure me to my destruction. Is that your intent?"

She searched his face. "I would lure you, though not to your destruction."

"What, then?"

In that moment, she longed to speak of love, but that was as a girl would do, flitting about and proclaiming feelings she did not truly understand. A woman, though...

A woman would think through that which moved heart and mind, sometimes in opposite directions. A woman would give due consideration to the consequences of bestowing such precious, vulnerable feelings upon a man.

Determined to rise above the girl who had shown time and again she could not be trusted, Alessandra said, "After what happened this day—worse, what nearly happened—I do not wish to be parted from you again. With you, I am safe. I know that now."

He lowered his gaze to her throat, lifted a hand and touched the necklace. "As you were not safe with LeBrec?"

Reminded of the Frenchman's guilt-easing gift, her skin suddenly burned where it lay against her. She reached up and fumbled for the clasp.

Lucien's hand stayed hers. "Did he touch you?"

Dare she hope it was jealousy darkening his eyes? That it mattered to him whether or not Jacques—

She stilled.

How did Lucien know of him? She did not think Jacques had been at the auction. Certainly, she had not seen him there. "How is it you know of him?"

"Did he touch you?" he repeated.

Then she would have to answer first. "Though he proved despicable, he behaved the gentleman. Undefiled, I was worth far more."

His lids dropped over his eyes. When he lifted them, relief shone from the violet depths.

Alessandra searched his face. "It matters to you?"

He hesitated, then said, "It matters."

It was a start, and for now it would have to suffice, for she did not think he would give more. "How do you know of Jacques?" she asked.

His mouth tightened. "Tale of the redheaded wench caught stealing the stores of a tavern spread quickly, though too late for me to intervene. By the time I learned what had happened, LeBrec had you ensconced in his home."

"Why did you not come for me there?"

"His walls are high, his guards many. And as you did not know what he intended, I was certain you would fight me. I had to content myself with what news the servant girl, Bea, brought."

The shy Circassian girl who had tended Alessandra's bath and grooming. In spite of Bea's timidity, her eyes had been watchful. Now Alessandra's understood the reason.

"As LeBrec has a reputation for leaving innocents intact," Lucien continued, "it seemed safer to take you at auction."

She lowered her head, stared at his chest. "I will not fight you anymore, Lucien."

"I know."

"I will go to England with you as my mother wished."

"It is already done."

She looked up. "Done?"

"We have set sail. There is no turning back."

So final. England drew near while Algiers receded. Gone was the life she had known. Before her was a life that might swallow her whole. And at the center of it was Lucien. What were his plans for her?

"What of me?" she asked. "Will you use me against my father?"

"Nay," he said after a brief hesitation. "I will give you over to old man Breville as soon as we reach Corburry."

"Then I am not to be the instrument of your revenge?"

His bitter laughter warmed her brow. "It seems fitting enough revenge to give you to him. We shall see how he handles what I have endured these past weeks."

Then he simply wished to be shed of her. To hide her misery, she averted her gaze.

"First, the under gown," he said. "Lift your arms."

She did as bid, and he lowered the garment over her.

As its hem settled to the floor, she considered the modest, relatively heavy garment. "This will suffice," she said.

"It will not," he countered. "As you are one woman among many men, utmost modesty is in order."

Of course. It was not a harem through which she would be moving, but a ship full of men from a world far removed from hers.

She raised her arms and he lowered the outer gown over her head. It was heavier than the first and wonderfully roomy—until he began buttoning the bodice. Its tightening diminished her breath, and the brush of his fingers across her chest stole it completely.

"It fits well," he said, looping the last button.

"It does?" Though the skirt was voluminous, the bodice was not proportionate. If she breathed deeply, the buttons might burst free. "I have no freedom in it."

Without comment, he belted the high waist.

She squirmed. "Even less now."

He arched an eyebrow. "In English society, there is no place for a woman to wear caftans and trousers."

She peered over her shoulder at the garments she had shed. "What of a veil? I cannot go before men without one."

"Ladies of gentle birth dress as you are now, Alessandra. Some wear headdresses, but veils are of Muslim women."

It was as her mother had told her, yet it was still foreign. Nervous, she knit her fingers. "And I am of gentle birth?"

Lucien smiled. "By parentage only."

Rejoicing in the lightening of his mood, she stepped close. "Lucien, do you remember the kisses we shared?"

The tightening of his mouth caused the scar along his cheekbone to pucker. "I am not likely to forget."

As he would not forget who her father was, his eyes told.

"Nor am I," she said on a sigh. Consoling herself with the thought it would be many weeks before they reached England, time in which to change his mind about her, she swept past him.

And fell short of the door by several feet. Truly fell. Having trod on the hem of the under gown, she plummeted.

She had only a moment to contemplate the cleanliness of the floor before Lucien scooped her upright and began brushing her down. "You must either raise your skirts or shorten your stride," he said. "Preferably both."

She plucked at the skirt. "'Tis too long. The hem will have to be raised."

He straightened. "The hem is where it should be for a proper English lady. You will have to adjust."

She wanted to tell him she was neither proper, nor an English lady, but decided to hold her tongue. A needle and thread would solve her problem more easily than changing her behavior. In the meantime, she would keep the skirt raised.

"I am ready," she said.

22

"I owe you an apology," Alessandra said, and Lucien nearly smiled when she pointedly lowered her gaze to Nicholas's hips.

Jezebel's captain, more handsome than his cousin, though of less stature, said, "That you do, my lady."

Yanking up the hem of her skirt, Alessandra stepped from Lucien's side, paused to catch her balance when the ship listed, and placed herself before the captain. "Given."

Frowning at her peculiar form of apology, Nicholas sent an eyebrow high and looked to his cousin.

Lucien shrugged.

Returning his gaze to the woman responsible for delaying his departure, Nicholas inclined his head. "Accepted, my lady."

"There is something else I owe you."

"Indeed?"

She struck him across the face. "You are no gentleman, Captain Giraud."

Lucien struggled against the impulse to intervene as the imprint of her palm rose on his cousin's cheek and the man's hands curled into fists. Captain Nicholas Giraud, former corsair and, more recently, Christian-turned-renegade, was not one to allow such offenses to go unpunished—especially with his crew as witnesses.

Hoping he would not have to insert himself between Nicholas and the little fool who seemed oblivious to the anger many would have heeded as a call to flee, Lucien held.

Of a sudden, a smile broke through Nicholas's lips, and he loosed laughter that carried across the ship on the wind that filled the sails.

Alessandra gasped. "You think it good fun what you did to me?"

He laughed louder, and when he had enough, met Lucien's gaze and raised his palms in surrender. "Better you than me, Cousin." With a shake of his head, he strode toward the bow of his ship.

Lucien stepped to Alessandra's side, casting his shadow over her. As he stared at the top of her head, he marveled that the anger and frustration of these past days, which had become nearly unmanageable, should be so greatly lightened.

"I do not know why I did not anticipate that," he said.

She looked up. "He deserved it."

Lucien took her elbow and guided her from the aftercastle to the steps. "I have much to teach you ere we reach England."

"Such as?"

"If you wish to continue being called a lady, you must behave as one."

On the last step down, she halted. "You think I do not?"

"Behave as an English noblewoman? I *know* you do not."

"But I am not—"

"You will be." Before long, she would be in England, known by her sire's name, and her standing would be that of a lady.

She nibbled her lower lip, asked, "Are ladies in England so very different from ladies of the Maghrib?"

Not wishing to miss his first sunset of true freedom, he urged her forward. "Come to the rail, and I will explain."

For the first few steps, there was space between them, but then she pressed as near his side as she could come without causing him to trip over her.

Doubtless, she was discomfited by the stares of the crew, for Nicholas had dragged her kicking and cursing onto the ship hours earlier and the men had enjoyed laughter and jokes at her expense. Now that she was dressed in European finery, they looked at her anew, though with little more respect than before.

Did she long for a veil behind which to hide her unease?

Lucien settled his forearms on the railing and let the wind do with his hair as it pleased. And it pleased mightily—tugging at it, freeing strands from the leather thong.

More happily, it played amongst Alessandra's hair, tossing its unbound length across her face and into his own until she gathered it and tucked it into the neck of her gown.

"How different are the ladies of England?" she asked again.

He stared ahead, narrowing his eyes on the place where the ocean swallowed the sun. "Very," he said. Though numerous examples came to mind, he said, "The donkey game you played—a proper lady would never attempt such foolishness."

"And if she did?"

He glanced at her. "Likely, her papa would bundle her off to a convent."

"For riding a donkey backward?"

"For riding a donkey at all."

Her shoulders slumped. "How tedious."

Lucien turned to her. "Not at all. There are many diversions."

She also turned toward him. "Such as?"

"Hunting, hawking, dancing—"

"Dancing?"

"Aye, to dance well is an essential accomplishment of the nobility. You must learn—"

"But I know how to dance."

He shook his head. "I speak of dances unlike those to which you are accustomed. Very different, indeed."

Her face fell. "Tedious, then."

Perhaps compared with the erotic dance he had watched her perform. However, European dance had something hers did not—the interaction of male and female, man and woman, lovers…

"Not so," he said.

"Then?"

Lucien had the urge to show rather than tell. Would she flow, her body following his? Or would she be stiff and awkward, resistant to his lead?

He swept his gaze over her figure, remembered how it had moved that first day when she had given herself to the music. Nay, never stiff, never awkward. But perhaps resistant to another's lead.

Returning his gaze to her face, he paused upon the hollow at the base of her throat where LeBrec's gift nestled. He had forgotten about it. Jealousy that Alessandra had assured him he had no reason to feel threatening his hard-won serenity, he lifted the necklace.

Ignoring her start of surprise, he rotated it and unfastened the clasp. "Do with it what you will"—he pressed it into her hand—"but never again wear it in my presence."

She closed her fingers around it. "I wanted to tear it off, but it was the only thing of value I possessed, and I thought it might aid in my escape." She lifted her face, and the setting sun made fire of her hair. "I thank you that I no longer need it," she said and flung it down into the white-crested waves. "Monsieur LeBrec is no more."

Everything in Lucien tightened as he looked upon a face that hardly resembled the one she had worn at auction when men had vied to buy her for their pleasure and her pain. Though he knew it would be best not to feed the jumble of feelings he had for this beautiful, freckled waif, he could not.

"Give me your hand, Alessandra."

Though a suspicious light entered her eyes, she slid her fingers over his. "Aye?"

"I will teach you the European style of dance."

"Here?" She swept her gaze over the crew, most of whom made no attempt to hide their interest in the only two passengers aboard *Jezebel*. "Would that not be unwise?"

"There are private dances, and there are public ones. Naturally, I will not demonstrate that which is best learned behind closed doors."

She blushed prettily. "Oh."

Lightening his grip on her left hand, he led her forward. "This is known as the estampie, the noblest of all dances."

"A rather dull dance," she said a short time later as, side by side, they once more worked through the slow, grave steps. The instruction was not going well, and Lucien suspected the reason for her stuttering stops and starts was her yearn for lively movement.

"Relax," he said. "You make it more difficult than it needs to be."

"If only it were more difficult," she bemoaned as he led her across the deck. "Can we not dance closer, with your arms around me?"

He laughed. "'Tis not the manner in which English nobles dance. Such things are not permissible, except, perhaps, among the peasants."

"As we are not yet in England, what harm in affecting we are peasants?"

"You will like the farandole better," he said. "Though it is a group dance, it has more movement." To demonstrate, he whirled her around, turned her again, and swept her across the deck.

"Lucien!" she gasped as he passed her under his arm.

He coiled her into a spiral and unwound her. "Better?"

"Much!"

Within minutes, she had mastered the half-dozen steps that always came back around to the first.

"Can we not dance the peasants' dance?" she asked when next he came near her.

Lucien looked to the crew, most of whom had turned their attention to their duties, then reeled her to him and slid an arm around her waist.

"Never in England," he said and settled a hand to the small of her back and urged her forward until they were nearly chest to chest.

He moved her across the deck, their bodies pressing, withdrawing, and pressing again. No more stuttering steps, no more muttering, no more scowls. And when he brought her to a halt, she said, "Again!"

"First, a break." He released her waist and, holding her left hand, led her into deepening shadows where none could see and eased her back against the mast.

Wide-eyed, she whispered, "Do you mean to kiss me?"

He lowered his head and covered her mouth with his.

Alessandra sighed and pushed fingers through his hair.

Feeling as if he were falling into her, knowing it might be impossible to extricate himself if he let it go further, Lucien ended the kiss and pulled her into another dance.

She laughed and, uninhibited, floated in his arms.

As night descended, Lucien silently vowed he would no longer think of her as a spawn of James Breville. From this day forward, she would simply be Alessandra—not that there was anything simple about her. Indeed, the thought came unbidden to him, she could be the key to peaceably settling the dispute between the Brevilles and the De Gautiers.

Danced out, weary, belly full of strange foodstuffs that politeness had prevented her from refusing, Alessandra stepped into the dimly lit cabin and halted. "There are two cots now. Before, there was only one."

Behind her, Lucien closed the door. "The second is mine."

She looked around. "I did not know you intended to share the cabin with me."

"Do you object?"

More than anything, she wished him near. "I do not, but is it proper? It would not be were I yet under Jabbar's protection, and from what I know of England, I cannot imagine it is acceptable there."

"You are right. However, space is limited, and there is no other whom I trust to keep you safe from the crew."

"But what will they think?"

"Most improper thoughts, but you will less likely suffer their attentions if they believe you belong to me."

The silence between them grew thick with longing. Hoping it was not hers alone, Alessandra wished she did belong to Lucien. And he to her.

"Worry not what crusty men of the sea think," he finally said. "Once we reach England, you will not see them again. It is only the English nobles you must needs impress."

Mouth gone dry, Alessandra crossed to the cot that would be hers. "I do not know that I will be able to sleep in such a contraption. It looks uncomfortable."

"It is not. Shall I show you how to mount it?"

"Would you?"

"Aye, but first you should remove your gown."

She looked over her shoulder.

He raised his eyebrows. "If you sleep in it, it will be a mass of wrinkles." Then, rather than offer to assist her as he had done when she had donned it, he turned aside.

Meaning she was not the only one to feel the longing? That now, alone with her and with night upon them, he thought better of the intimacy inherent in undressing her?

Telling herself it was good he played the gentleman the same as he had done before Nicholas during their meal, she set about freeing button after button from its bothersome loop and dragged the gown off. Clad in undergown and chemise, she folded the gown and placed it atop the trunk.

"I am ready," she said.

Lucien crossed to her cot. "One hand here." He took it and placed it on the far rail, "the other here." He closed her other hand over the side rail she stood alongside. "Then a knee up and roll your body into it. Simple."

"Or humiliating," she said as she lifted a leg over the side of the shifting cot.

Lucien placed one hand on the back of her knee, the other on her hip, and gave her a boost.

Landing facedown on the soft mattress, she held tight, certain the swinging cot would dump her on the cabin floor.

Blessedly, he steadied the cot. "Now turn over."

She released her handholds and slowly made her way onto her back.

"As I said, simple." Lucien grinned.

She grimaced. "Only because you make it so. I do not think I shall ever become accustomed to it."

"You will." He reached for the folded blanket at her feet. "The voyage will be long, and sleep is more easily had on a bed that adjusts to the ship's movement, especially when it lists heavily." He shook out the blanket and spread it over her. "I take your leave now."

She sat up, caught her breath when the cot lurched. "You said you were sharing the cabin with me."

"I am." He steadied the cot. "But now I must speak with Nicholas."

"You spoke with him this eve."

His gaze turned serious. "There are some things which are not discussed in front of ladies. Remember that."

"Cannot my being a lady wait until we reach England?"

"You cannot simply act the lady, Alessandra, you must feel the lady. And so we begin now."

She sighed, gingerly settled back on the mattress.

"I will not be long," he said. "Dream well." Then he was gone.

Though this early in the voyage, Lucien knew it was likely safe to leave Alessandra alone in the cabin at night, he locked her inside. Until he took good measure of the crew—and they took good measure of him—it was best to exercise caution. And, of course, there was Alessandra's penchant for getting herself into trouble. If she determined to explore the ship and a seaman caught her alone…

Lucien did not wish another death on his conscience.

He located Nicholas aft, where he was overseeing the setting of a sail.

"Marvelous, is she not?" Nicholas said as Lucien approached. "So calm, so placid."

Lucien knew better than to think his cousin referred to a woman of flesh. It was the ocean he spoke of.

"She is pouting, you know," Nicholas added.

Lucien halted before him, spread his legs to counter the ship's sway. "Pouting?"

His cousin grinned. "She only puffs at my sails, and all because I dared place my hull upon another's waters."

"The Mediterranean."

Nicholas nodded. "As if this ocean were true only to me." He laughed, flashing white teeth in the dim. "Imagine that, a harlot with a jealous streak."

"Perhaps you ought to find another mistress," Lucien suggested.

Nicholas scowled. "Like your Alessandra? She who will bleed your heart from you until you are less than a woman, then flit into another's arms? Vincent's, perhaps?"

Lucien's humor fell away so abruptly that only great restraint kept him from landing a blow to the other man.

It had never bothered him that his brother's handsome looks and brilliant smile drew women like bees to flowers—at least, until those looks and Vincent's shameless flirting twice ended Lucien's betrothals. To wed a woman who openly yearned for another was a humiliation to which he would not subject himself, especially when the other man was his own brother.

Lucien breathed deep. "For all your obsession with this accursed ocean, you are more wise than I."

Nicholas clapped him on the shoulder. "For a moment, I thought you meant to do me harm."

"I did."

"Then I am glad you rethought it."

Deciding it was time for a change of subject, Lucien turned his thoughts to his reason for seeking out his cousin. Since meeting up with him in Tangier, he had not had time to address the concerns that now badgered him, his worry over Alessandra having consumed him entirely.

"I would hear what you know of Falstaff," he said. "What changes have been wrought in my home since I left?"

Nicholas pushed a hand through his hair, kneaded his neck muscles. "I have been no farther than London for more than a year now, Lucien. As you know, I do not dare venture too far from my ship lest the Church clap me in irons for turning renegade."

"A fool thing to do."

Nicholas looked not the least remorseful. "At the time, it served its purpose."

"I am not going to ask what that was."

"Wise," Nicholas said, then turned serious. "When last I was at Falstaff, all was as it should be—except you were thought dead. Your father was heartbroken that you had gone to France with his angry words ringing in your ears. Indeed, it was his greatest sorrow he could not make it right between you."

Lucien nodded. For weeks, they had argued over Falstaff's heir journeying to France to fight a war his sire regarded as futile and witless. Harsh words were exchanged, and Lucien had ridden away angry and resentful. In the end, his father had proven right, and Lucien intended to bend his knee to him and admit it once they were reunited.

"I will make amends when I return," he murmured.

After a long silence, Nicholas continued, "As for the disagreement between the Brevilles and your family, it was yet being seeded and, on occasion, yielding bitter harvest. Vincent gambled away whatever he could lay hands upon, and Jervais…"

Lucien smiled at mention of his youngest brother.

"You would not recognize him, Lucien. He is a worthy knight. His shoulders are broad, his skill at arms exceptional, and when he speaks, one turns an ear to him."

"What of my mother?"

"She is well."

"Giselle?"

Nicholas grinned. "What can I say? Your little sister has a mouth on her that may rival Alessandra's. Though your mother tries to contain her, she is, at times, out of control. Very strong of mind for a girl child."

It was she whom Lucien most looked forward to seeing again. "What else?"

"That is all I know."

Lucien nodded. "Though a year can change even that."

"It can." Nicholas offered his wineskin.

Lucien accepted and, shortly, passed it back.

"Change is not always bad, Lucien. After all, it has brought you back from the dead."

What he was saying without saying it, Lucien knew, was that if things were different at Falstaff when its heir returned, he should be tolerant.

And Lucien was determined he would not disappoint. He had abided in darkness too long to sow discord among his family.

He looked out across the blue-black waters that abutted the blue-black sky. Somewhere in that unforeseeable distance lay England.

Home, he breathed into himself. *I am going home.* Feeling a settling in his soul, he bid his cousin a good eve and headed back across the deck to Alessandra.

Nicholas considered his mistress. Like the harlot she proved to be each time he came to her, she lured him, spread her arms wide, seduced him with salty kisses, was quick to betray him. And he savored every moment. Or nearly so, for at her most treacherous, she left casualties in her wake. But that was the price paid to be borne upon her.

Lucien could have his redheaded paramour. *Jezebel's* captain would make do with the occasional wench, always returning to the one who possessed his soul.

Settling his elbows to the railing, he peered across the water to the moon's reflection on the sweetest of curves. And laughed at himself. He took his feelings for the ocean too far, but for all that she was not and could never be, she was safer and more constant than a flesh and blood woman, like the one he had bought at auction at his cousin's behest.

He almost pitied Lucien—almost, for though Alessandra would surely continue to test the man who had rescued her from lifelong bondage, she was something to behold. The question was, what lay ahead for them? Of greater import, what lay ahead for Lucien?

Nicholas worked through their conversation and, coming to the end of it, grunted. There was one thing he had neglected to mention— important, though better forgotten for the time being.

Had he told Lucien of his father's illness, it would be a much longer voyage than it needed to be, for Lucien's guilt would be tenfold greater. Too, it was possible the old man had recovered—a good possibility considering what the De Gautiers were made of. But Nicholas feared not.

23

"I t is an interesting game." Alessandra wrinkled her nose as she considered the ivory cubes Lucien and she had been tossing this past half hour. "But not much fun."

He swept the cubes into his palm. "'Tis called dice, a popular game in England. My brother, Vincent, has but to hold a pair and he loses all but the clothes on his back."

Alessandra drew her knees up, rested her chin on them, and looked to the distant coast of Portugal. "I prefer chess."

"And your donkey game."

She hid her smile against her knees. "It makes me laugh. Were you not so English, you might see the fun of it."

"And were you not so Arab, you might see how ridiculous it is."

She returned her gaze to him. "These past days you have been merciless in reminding me I am English, instructing me in all manners of that culture, and now you call me Arab?"

"It must be your determination to cling to your pagan ways that confuses me," he said.

She clicked her tongue. "Have I not been a willing pupil? I lift my skirts and measure my steps. I curtsy and use polite address though I have yet to encounter one seaman deserving of such. I eat that terrible fare with a smile on my face. And I have learned your dances and suffered these gowns."

"All that, and yet you refuse to wear head cover to protect your skin." He leaned forward and tapped freckles the sun had warmed to a darker pigment.

Alessandra lowered her lashes, not to hide embarrassment, but to mask the emotion roused by his touch. Since their departure from Tangier, he had played the gentleman well. All she had of him were kisses stolen amid laughter, frustration, and uncomfortable silence. As she had from the beginning, she longed to be nearer him, but he continued to hold himself apart.

"I like the sun," she said, then stood, propped her arms on the railing, and cupped her chin in a palm.

Lucien also rose. "You will not see much of it once we reach England, especially with summer nearly past.

"Mother said it could be a cold place."

"'Tis the reason so many babes are born during high summer."

"How is that?"

Mischief brightened his eyes. "When the clouds are weeping rain and snow and the air is so chill it near bites you bloody, the best place to be at day's end is abed. And not alone."

Holding his teasing gaze, Alessandra said, "Is that what you do? Lie abed with a lover?"

He raised his eyebrows.

Jealousy, with the bite of the English cold of which he had warned, sinking its teeth into her, Alessandra said, "Of course you do," and stepped around him.

Though she felt his presence at her back all the way to the cabin, she pretended ignorance and started to close the door behind her.

His foot prevented it from settling in its frame. "I should not have been so forward," he said when she looked up. "For all that I would have you behave the lady, it seems I must learn again how to behave the gentleman. Pray, forgive me."

She gave a curt nod, tried to close the door.

When he resisted her effort, she gave a huff and pivoted.

"Still, you are angry with me," he said as he stepped inside.

Busying herself with straightening her few possessions, she said, "I am merely tired."

When the silence stretched so long it became more awkward to keep her back to him than to face him, she turned.

"What do you want from me, Alessandra?" he asked where he stood before the door.

Though the girl tempted her toward a coy response, the woman urged her to speak true, even if it left her vulnerable, her pride trampled.

"I feel for you, Lucien. I believe you know this. What I would know is if you feel for me."

His jaw shifted. "I have already said I desire you. I make no lie of it."

"That is not what I asked. Do you feel something beyond desire?"

Once more, all went still between them, but just when she thought he would not answer, he strode forward. "I know you believe your feelings are those of the heart"—he halted before her—"and you would have my feelings be the same, but it is not so simple a thing."

She frowned. "I do not see why it should be hard."

"Alessandra, as I am the only remnant of your former life—albeit recently acquired—it is natural you would attach yourself to me, especially after all you have lost and endured."

She caught her breath as memories kept carefully tucked away unfolded—her mother's agonizing death, the terrible journey to Tangier, near ravishment in the tavern, the platform upon which she had been auctioned as if she were a breeding goat.

"In England, there will be no harem to hide you from men's eyes," he continued, "nor to hide them from yours. Before you will be a wondrous selection, and among them will be eager suitors—men who are not your father's adversary."

She stepped nearer and slid her arms around his neck. "I do not want any of them. I want—"

"Alessandra"—he closed his hands around her wrists and pulled them down between them—"do not mistake inexperience and gratitude for something it is not. For both our sakes."

Heartbreak made her snatch hold of the one word that offered hope. "Both?"

He released her and turned away.

Frustration made her call after him, "I will not ask again what you feel for me, Lucien."

He looked over his shoulder. "Then you are making good progress."

Anger made her yank off a shoe and draw her arm back to hurl it.

He closed the door behind him.

The yearn to be seen as a woman made her drop the shoe to the floor and her face into her hands. But she did not cry. Would not cry.

Though tempted to forgo the nooning meal, Alessandra gathered herself together as a woman would do and left the cabin.

When she entered the galley, Lucien and Nicholas looked up from their meal of salted meat and fish.

She inclined her head and came around the table to seat herself on the long bench beside Lucien.

"Sit next to Nicholas," he said.

She halted. Had she so angered him that he did not wish her near?

"A lesson," he clarified, and she knew he had glimpsed her distress.

A lesson, she mulled as she advanced on his cousin, *not as dire as him being angry, but unwelcome, nonetheless.*

Aware of the strain between her and Nicholas, despite it having abated, she lowered herself several feet from him.

Without looking up from the meat from which he was pulling a strip, Lucien said, "Closer."

"Why?"

"Closer, Alessandra."

She edged nearer.

"More."

She looked to Nicholas. Though his attention was on his goblet, there was a smile in the corner of his lips.

Determined to upend his private humor, even at the cost of looking childish—surely even a woman could enjoy herself from time to time—she slid so near him their thighs touched. And gained what she sought.

Mouth suddenly weighted, he snapped his gaze to her.

It was Alessandra's turn to smile. "This close?" She looked to Lucien.

"No respectable English lady would sit so near a man in public," he growled, "not even her own husband."

"I must remember that," she said, though she did not move. Thus, it was Nicholas who put space between them.

Shortly, the wiry old cook came out from behind the screen in the corner. Bearing two trenchers, he set one before Lucien, the other between Alessandra and Nicholas.

She peered into the stale, hollowed-out loaf of bread that held a thick concoction in which unappetizing foodstuffs floated. "I fear I am not very hungry."

Lucien arched an eyebrow. "Still, you will eat, for there is no lesson otherwise. Now try the stew."

She lifted the spoon and reached to pull the trencher in front of her, but Nicholas's hand shot out and prevented her from doing so.

"Now what?" she exclaimed as she turned a frown upon him.

"It is also Nicholas's trencher," Lucien said. "In England, sharing food between two is common."

It was difficult enough becoming accustomed to dining among men, but to also share food?

"Did your mother not tell you of such things?" Lucien asked.

She did recall Sabine speaking of it, but it had only been talk. How primitive the reality. "She did."

"Then I need not explain further."

She sighed and scooped up a spoonful of stew. The dish proved more palatable than it looked—indeed, it was tastier than anything she had thus far been served aboard ship.

She dipped again, and her spoon collided with Nicholas's.

"You must await your turn," Lucien said.

She withdrew and watched as Nicholas took his time fishing for a worthy morsel. Finally, his spoon curved around a large piece of meat. And abandoned it.

Alessandra looked up and found him watching her.

"Mayhap you would like to choose one for me, my lady," he said.

She drew back. "Of course I would not."

"This is not a lesson in the code of love, Nicholas," Lucien said sharply.

"Most unfortunate," his cousin said. "Though it could be. You must take care not to neglect that part of Alessandra's education, Cousin."

"'Tis none of your concern, *Cousin*."

Alessandra reveled in what she read as jealousy. Was this what it would take to make Lucien reveal his feelings for her?

Deciding it was not childish to test the possibility, reasoning that even a woman must know how well she was regarded by one she well regarded, she laid a hand upon Nicholas's arm. "Tell me of this code of love."

His lips thinned as he considered her hand upon him. But when he gave her his gaze, there was light in his eyes, as if he understood her game.

"Let me think." He took another bite of stew, slowly chewed and swallowed, then said, "The code is a fine thing. A lover must submit to his lady the same as a knight would his lord. He swears loyalty and enduring service."

"And?"

"The lady offers him some favor. Of course, she must not submit too soon, for her lover must suffer, at least a little. And once she accepts him as her lover—"

"Enough!" Lucien rose so abruptly that had the bench not been secured to the floor, it would have been upended. He rounded the table, took Alessandra's arm, and drew her toward the door. "We will speak of this later, Nicholas."

As he pushed Alessandra ahead of him up the steps and into sunlight, from below came the sound of his cousin's laughter.

Skirts raised, Alessandra struggled to match Lucien's stride as he led her toward the cabin. But then he changed direction and steered her into the shadow of the mainmast.

Guessing he did not trust himself alone with her, hoping he feared he would be tempted to kiss her as she longed to be kissed, she was almost breathless when he halted.

He released her, braced his feet apart, and said in a low, strained voice, "Have you learned naught from what I have taught you?"

She also secured her footing. "I have learned plenty, and found little of it enjoyable—excepting the dances we shared and Nicholas's talk of love."

"Which he knows little enough of, he who loves none but the ocean."

"And you know more?"

His eyes narrowed. "I know what a lady does and does not discuss with a man not her husband—that the only lover a true lady takes is the one to whom she is wed."

"*We* have discussed such things," she retorted, "and if you would have me be a true lady, why do you not wed me?" She gasped as words she had not intended to speak soared from her like birds taking to flight.

Lucien's lids rose, jaw eased, furrowed brow smoothed. Then he stepped close and swept the hair out of her eyes. "Twice I have been betrothed, Alessandra, and twice I have broken my betrothal. Marriage does not bode well for me."

She could hardly breathe. He was opening himself to her—giving her a small piece of who he truly was. And she wanted more. "Why did you break your betrothals?"

"Neither woman was faithful."

"You were cuckolded?"

"Nay, but I would have been."

She frowned. "How can you know this?"

His eyes grew distant. "The way they looked at my brother. Once they laid eyes upon Vincent, it was certain they wanted him."

Though Lucien was not the most handsome of men, Alessandra thought him generous of looks and, especially, character. "You think I would do the same?"

"Likely."

So he not only regarded her as a child, but as a frivolous one. "Then you do not know me." She turned away, stiffened when he pulled her back against him, melted the moment his arms wrapped around her.

"But I do know you," he said into her hair. "I know you set out to make me jealous of Nicholas, and you did it because you believe it is me you want. But as you know, not only is there division between our families, but you have too little experience with men to know what you truly want."

Sinking more deeply against his body, she dropped her head to his shoulder and peered up at him. "I have never been more certain of anything."

His gaze stroked her face. "You are not acting the lady, Alessandra."

"Surely," she whispered, "I do not need to pretend when it is just you and me."

He tilted her face higher, breathed, "You do not," and lowered his head.

Alessandra did not feel the strain in her neck as he lingeringly kissed her, but she felt the absence of his mouth when he drew back. "Truce?" he asked as he turned her to face him.

She smiled. "Truce." And, hopefully, more.

24

"STORM A-COMIN'!" CRIED the seaman as he monkeyed down the mast.

Hands clasped behind his back, Nicholas turned and stared at the horizon that had been open and clear when last he had looked. Now, advancing storm clouds blurred the line between ocean and sky.

He had thought it would come to this—that here, in the Bay of Biscay, his dark mistress would make him pay for his betrayal with the Mediterranean. For two days, they had navigated the bay off the French coast. It was difficult and dangerous due to the prevailing winds and a strong current, but now it might prove disastrous.

Knowing he could not chance hugging near the coast and the rocks upon which his ship might be crushed, he called down to the helmsman, "Take her out!"

It would require vast, open water for *Jezebel* to weather what would surely be a severe storm. It might not prove so terrible had it come upon them in daylight, but there was only an hour remaining before night descended.

Nicholas drew a breath of the heavy air and began ordering his men. The sails were adjusted and ropes corrected, all with a deep awareness of peril—and excitement that only men of the sea could appreciate.

Once more, Nicholas considered the sky and the agitated water. "Harlot," he muttered. "What will be my reward if I win this one?"

Might he reach England before the ships that had set sail before him? Might his cargo recover the value by which it had been reduced when Alessandra's rescue had delayed his departure from Tangier? A slim possibility, but a grand challenge.

"It looks serious," Lucien called.

Tempering the smile that would betray his grave expression, Nicholas turned to where his cousin mounted the steps. "A tempest. Every hand will be needed to beat it back. Think you are up to it, Cousin?"

Lucien considered the gathering clouds and remembered other storms he had braved. On the galley he had slaved on, wind and rain and saltwater had beat upon him as he and his fellow slaves fought to save themselves and their masters from the wrath of a vicious sea. Indeed, had he not been chained to his oar for a recently committed offense, one of those storms would have gifted him the same watery grave as several of the oarsmen who had rowed in front and in back of him.

"I am up to it," he said.

"Good. Where is Alessandra?"

"In the cabin." Where he had left her to practice her writing. Though her Arabic lettering was beautiful, her English penmanship was almost appalling. As usual, she had argued with him over the necessity of the exercise, but had yielded after extracting a promise that she would have a day free of lessons on the morrow.

"She is to remain there," Nicholas said.

"I will tell her and return to assist in securing the ship."

When Lucien opened the cabin door a short while later, the sight that greeted him nearly made him laugh.

"That is quite a feat," he said.

The ink-dipped quill slipped from between Alessandra's toes and landed on the floor.

"Oh!" She sat up straight. "I did not expect you to return so soon."

"Most obvious." He bent and retrieved the quill. "Is this how you earn your day free of lessons?"

She scrambled for the parchments upon which she had been practicing. "My hand cramped. Thus, while I waited it out, I thought I would see if I could hold the quill between my toes the same as I hold it between my fingers." One by one, she raised the three examples of writing for him to see.

He grimaced. "Surely you can do better than that."

She turned one around, frowned. "What do you mean? It is much improved."

He shook his head and said, "A storm is headed our way. You are to remain here until I tell you it is safe to come out."

"Oh, but I would see it!" She swung her legs over the cot.

Lucien stayed her with a hand to the shoulder. "You need only feel it, which you most certainly shall."

"But—"

"If need be, I will lock you in."

She groaned. "I shall stay put. But you will come tell me what is happening from time to time, will you not?"

"If I am able to." Which was unlikely. "Remain in the cot. It will take much of the turbulence."

As if to demonstrate, the ship lurched to the side, back to midpoint, and to the side again.

"It has begun," Lucien said.

Alessandra turned, pillowed her head on an outstretched arm, and peered up at him. "You will take care, will you not, Lucien?"

"All will be well," he said and strode to the lantern and blew it out. "'Twill be safer unlit." He crossed to the door and stepped out into the tempest that had begun to show its teeth.

Alessandra stared at the door, on the other side of which was Lucien. "Lord, protect him," she whispered, "and the crew, and Nicholas."

She smiled at that last. Though she and the enigmatic captain would never be boon companions, she had a liking for him. And she was fairly certain he liked her—grudgingly so.

Over the next hour, she tried to doze, but there was no rest to be had as the squall built, nor an easing of her troubled stomach.

Staring into the dark, straining to make sense of Nicholas's shouted orders overhead, she gripped the ropes of the cot as it pitched hard.

"Down the mainsail!" she heard.

"Down the mainsail!" another repeated, surely for those who could not hear the captain above the wind's howl.

There came a screeching sound, then a thunderous clapping as the sailcloth dropped from on high.

Immediately, the ship righted and there was calm as if the storm had ended.

Just as Alessandra eased her hold on the ropes, the ship slammed to the left, tossing her out of the cot. She threw her arms out to break her fall, slid across the floor on her belly, and came to rest in the cradle where floor met wall. Then she began to backslide.

"Dear Lord," she gasped, frantically searching for something to catch hold of. "Save us." She hooked an arm around the leg of the bolted-down table she came up against and listened for sounds above. All she heard was the pounding of the ocean against the creaking hull.

Had all been swept overboard? Lucien with them?

She prayed more fervently, promising all manner of better behavior if God would deliver them out of death's hands. Then she heard voices again, but before she could slump with relief, there came the cry, "Man overboard!"

"Lucien!" she cried.

She peered across the dark cabin to the door, wondered if she could make it there before the next swell knocked her down.

Releasing her life hold, she used the roll of the ship to move her across the floor, then scrambled upright and wrenched the door open.

Staggering down the narrow passageway, hands to the walls on either side, she wet her feet up to the ankles in water that leaked through the hatch. Finding the steps before her, she lowered to her hands and knees and began to crawl upward.

Each time a sharp listing slammed her against the wall, she righted herself until, finally, she threw back the hatch.

Spray lashed at her face and hands, the frigid wind seized her hair and whipped it into her eyes, and before her, men who were little more than shadow ran to unknown places in their bid to survive the storm.

Holding the hatch with one hand to maintain her balance, she cupped the other alongside her mouth and shouted, "Lucien!" But his name sounded like little more than a sigh on the wind.

Fleetingly, she thought of her vow to stay below, then dragged her skirts out of the way and stepped onto the deck. She gripped the nearest handhold—one of several casks lashed together. Holding to it with both hands, she suffered the storm's rage as she looked for Lucien.

"Please God," she once more called upon Him, "let him not be the one lost to the ocean. Let him show himself to me." But one shadow looked much like another, none differentiating itself by great height or breadth.

With the arrival of another great swell, Alessandra's feet slipped from beneath her, and though she held to the cask, she fell hard to her knees. It was then she heard the shout of what sounded like her name.

As she made it to her feet, a wave backhanded her, ripping her hands from the cask. Carried upon cold, salty water that swept into her mouth and nose, certain she was bound for the railing, she flailed for something to turn her hands around, but there was nothing.

I am going to die, she silently acknowledged. *Dear Lord, do not also send Lucien to this watery grave. He needs to go home.*

Something slammed around her waist and thrust her to the deck.

The wave that had aspired to sweep her into the ocean passed over the rail, but before Alessandra could drag a breath of air, another wave hit and beat upon the one stretched over her. When it also passed by, the man surged to his feet and wrenched her upright.

"Lucien?" she gasped.

He tossed her over his shoulder and ran for the hatch, reaching it just ahead of the ocean and slamming it closed behind them.

As soon as Lucien stepped into the cabin, he dropped her to her feet. "You gave me your word," he growled amid darkness. "You were not to move from here."

Vaguely aware of how cold and wet she was, she flung herself back into his arms. "You are alive!"

He disengaged her hands, only to snatch her back to prevent her from tumbling with the ship's lurching.

"Alive," he said, "but only by the grace of God are you."

"I am sorry." She pressed her face against his cold, soaked chest. "I heard the shout that a man had gone overboard and feared it was you."

"An unfortunate soul," he said, then more gruffly, "What you did was foolish. Even had I been the one to go into the water, there was naught you could do."

"I had to know!"

He grumbled something, then drew her with him to the cot and lifted her onto it.

She reached for him. "Lucien—"

"We will talk later." He removed her hand from his arm and laid it upon her breast, then surprised her by finding her mouth in the dark. "I will come back to you," he said against her lips.

Then he left her again, and she heard the scrape of metal on metal as he locked her in.

Shivering more from the fear she would not see him again than the cold of a wet, beaten body, she dragged the blanket over her, curled up, and let prayers tumble from her lips.

He came back to her, pressing his forehead to hers, touching her mouth, nose, and eyes with soft kisses, feathering fingers down her neck. But not until the cot swung and his damp body stretched out beside her did she realize it was not a dream.

Wonderfully cramped alongside his large frame, Alessandra raised her lids and, by the light of day, gazed at the man who faced her. Though his eyes were shot with red and darkly ringed from his battle with Nicholas's mistress, he smiled.

There had been times she had thought the storm would never end, but when the raging night had given way to a rough dawn and she caught the sound of Lucien's voice, she had allowed herself to drop over the edge into sleep.

Smiling with relief and gratitude, she murmured, "You kept your promise," and touched his stubbled jaw.

He turned his face into her palm and put his lips to it. "'Tis over."

She curled her fingers around the kiss. "There were no more lost?"

The curves on either side of his mouth straightened. "Only the one, but that is one too many."

"Of course. I am sorry."

He did not speak further on it, and when he closed his eyes, she ventured, "Are you still angry with me?"

"I am not. Though I ought to be."

She edged nearer, laid a hand to his chest. "Why have you come to lie with me?"

His lids lifted partway. "To hold you. It is the prize I promised myself—what kept me going." He lifted the blanket, drew it over him, and pulled her near.

Nestled against his chest that, in spite of his damp clothes, was more welcome than anything in the world, she ventured, "Will you kiss me, Lucien? Like you did that first time?"

He stiffened, but then his eyes opened to reveal their intoxicating violet and the mouth she wished upon hers once more curved. "How did I kiss you that first time?"

"You do not remember?"

"Well I remember the night you came to my quarters, but I would hear it from you."

For as bold as she had been to ask it, such fiery heat should not have risen to her cheeks. "I…you…" She sighed. "I have not the words to describe it. I can but say it was perfect."

"My other kisses have not been perfect?"

"Not like that."

His teasing smile became one of regret. "That is because they have not been as dangerous as our first one, Alessandra, though they could have easily become so."

She swallowed. "Will this one be dangerous?"

"Were I to kiss you, but I will not, for it is perilous enough being here with you—something I would not dare were I not so battered and weary."

She could not hide her disappointment.

He sighed. "You know that I feel for you, do you not?"

She caught her breath. Might he admit he loved her as she was certain she loved him? "Something beyond desire," she said, "but what is it?"

He opened his mouth, closed it.

"Lucien?"

"'Tis enough that I feel. For that, I will only hold you, Alessandra."

It was honorable. She knew it was. Unless she fooled herself. What if this was his revenge against the Brevilles—making her want him without hope of ever having him?

"Do you toy with me, Lucien?" she asked.

"I do not." Fatigue was in every syllable. "Though you may not wish it, you are a lady. And a lady is what I intend to give over to old man Breville, not a long-lost daughter whose belly grows large with his enemy's whelp."

Fool or not, she believed him.

"Now I must sleep, Alessandra. Will you allow it, or should I move to my cot?"

Assuring herself there were days aplenty to discover what he felt for her, she said, "Stay." And silently added, *Today. And tomorrow. And always.*

25

Falstaff, England, 1454

"I SEE IT!" ALESSANDRA exclaimed.

Proud and austere, the distant keep of Falstaff rose from a still fog as if floating atop a cloud. Of the walls surrounding it, only intermittent crenellations were visible, and only if one peered closely. Even the village Lucien had spoken of was nowhere to be seen, cloaked in the same curious morning haze.

Since arriving in England, Alessandra had marveled at this new land. Granted, it was chill and damp compared to Algiers, but it had an appeal all its own.

The London of lore, where the ship had anchored, had intrigued her, beckoning her to explore its crowded streets and shops. And she would have if Lucien had not been in such a hurry. To her disappointment, after securing horses and provisions, he had announced it was time to ride north.

Nicholas had accompanied them to the outskirts of the city. Far more genial since discovering he had been granted the wind to reach London ahead of those ships that had departed Tangier before his, he had kissed Alessandra's hand and waved Lucien and her on their way.

Verdant countryside and wooded forests passed by in a blur. Inns with coarse, English-speaking people had provided a place to bed down for the night. Strange food and drink, to which she had been given an introduction during the weeks aboard ship, was palatable, though more often tested her stomach.

It was an adventure, but it would soon end when Lucien fulfilled the bargain struck with her mother.

She swallowed in an attempt to dislodge her anxiety, wished she could delay the meeting with her father, ached for Lucien to first take her with him to Falstaff.

Looking at him, she saw longing in his eyes as he stared at his home. But as if aware of her regard, he blinked the emotion away and twisted in his saddle to meet her gaze.

"Lucien, I do not think I am ready for Corburry," she said.

He smiled. "More likely, Corburry is not ready for you."

He had said it before, and often with wit, but this time the comment was far less amusing. "Perhaps."

He sidled his mount alongside hers. "We have discussed this many times."

"So we have, and still I would prefer we pause first at Falstaff. What can it hurt?"

He drew a deep breath. "What awaits me there, I cannot say, but I would not subject you to more discomfort than already you face in becoming acquainted with your own family. Thus, I shall face mine alone."

Alessandra mustered a brave face. "I understand."

Lucien crooked a finger beneath her chin. "I do not think you do, but you will see it is for the best." He brushed his mouth across hers—much too fleetingly for her to respond or know better what he felt for her. Then he released her, pressed his heels to his mount, and led the way to Corburry.

The castle of Corburry was a fortress, one erected of immense stone blocks that bore ample evidence of past conflicts. Most obvious were sizable sections of the gatehouse and curtain walls that had been repaired with stone of differing shades. Less obvious were pocks and chips that, because they had not threatened the integrity of the walls, remained as further testimony of the sieges endured by the occupants.

How many of the attacks were a result of the long-standing dispute between the Brevilles and De Gautiers? Alessandra wondered, then shook off the question. At this moment, more important was how she would be received by her father.

She raised her gaze up the cylindrical keep that rose from the center of the castle. It was there her family resided, and the destiny her mother had forced upon her.

Though dear, sweet Sabine had been certain this was where her daughter belonged, Alessandra wished she was as certain.

"Something is wrong," Lucien broke into her thoughts. Mouth grimly set, gaze riveted on the castle, he touched his dagger, then his sword.

"What do you mean?"

"I can count on one hand the number of soldiers that walk the walls."

She tallied the four figures there. "How many should there be?"

His head came around. "Many, Alessandra. James Breville is not a man to take chances."

"Unlike you," she said, remembering the chances he had taken to bring her out of Algiers.

He nodded. "Unlike me."

"Do you think it a ruse?"

"It is certainly not what it should be, for it is not merely a scarcity of men upon the walls that does not suit. We should not have been allowed to draw so close. Only by stealth did my kin and I advance this near without meeting resistance."

"Perchance the castle folk are in worship 'Tis Sunday, after all." Purposely, she melded the words *it* and *is* into one, a nuance of the English language she had worked at mastering these past weeks, and which was much easier than masking the accent that marked her as a foreigner. Not that she intended to.

"You still have much to learn," Lucien muttered.

"Then teach me."

"Methinks that is better left to your father," he said and urged his horse down the rise.

Alessandra trailing, they approached the castle in clear view, finally stirring those atop the walls.

"Cover your hair," Lucien said.

"Why?" Though, initially, she had been uneasy going about in public with face and hair uncovered, she enjoyed the freedom. What she did not enjoy was the English clothing that continued to hinder her movements.

"Do as told," Lucien said.

She raised the hood of her mantle and tucked her hair out of sight. "Better?"

Without confirming she had done as ordered, he nodded as he stared ahead.

Alessandra sighed. She much preferred the Lucien she had come to know on board ship. The gentleman forgotten, he was once more a warrior—alert, calculating, predatory.

With mounting suspicion and greater caution, Lucien proceeded toward the castle. When would the attack come? he wondered as he followed the movements of those visible to him. And from where?

Though the portcullis was in place, barring entrance to the castle, the drawbridge remained lowered, and no attempt was being made to raise this all-important bastion of defense.

Might peace have come to Corburry? Immediately, he rejected the idea. Two years could not have wrought such change.

He reined in before the drawbridge, withholding his gaze from Alessandra as she drew alongside.

"Who goes?" demanded the bearded man who appeared at the portcullis.

Lucien recognized the one he had encountered in a skirmish when he had been ten and four summers aged. "Do you not recognize that who is responsible for your hobble, Sully?" he called.

Silence.

Lucien smiled a hard smile. He had come close to killing the cur that wet, miserable morn. But he had been unprepared to take his first life. Within the year, that had changed.

"Lucien de Gautier!" exclaimed the man.

"Aye. Now summon your heathen lord."

Sully grasped the bars and pressed his long face between them. "By the fury of hell, be ye a ghost, man?"

It was as Nicholas had said, that all believed him dead. "I am of flesh, the same as that which your dagger once cleaved. Now rouse old man Breville and tell him I am here."

Sully's gaze skittered to the cloaked figure alongside Lucien. "Who be that with ye?"

"Tell your lord I have brought him long-lost kin."

Sully lowered his gaze down the bit of gown that peeked from beneath Alessandra's mantle. "Do she have a name?"

"It will be revealed to your lord. Now bring him hither."

Muttering, Sully turned and limped out of sight.

"You did not tell him," Alessandra said.

"He will know soon enough."

Sully returned minutes later. "Lady Breville requests you proceed to the keep."

"Lady Breville?" Alessandra whispered.

Lucien regretted he had not informed her of her father's remarriage. "James Breville's second wife," he said and saw hurt flicker over her face.

He returned his attention to Sully and the unthinkable invitation. Only once, as a youth, had he been inside those walls, and then it had been as a captive. Did the Brevilles think him foolish enough to enter their viper's nest a second time? And why would they risk it? Even Lady Breville would know better.

"What of Lord James?" Lucien asked.

"Ah…" Sully shuffled his feet in the damp earth. "The lord'll be along shortly."

Then he was elsewhere. Perhaps burning off his midday meal by pillaging and plundering De Gautier villages.

"We shall await him here," Lucien called a moment ahead of a squeal that heralded the ascent of the iron portcullis.

Lucien drew his sword, watched as Sully ducked beneath the gate and traversed the drawbridge.

Wide of shoulders and chest, but painfully short of stature, the man halted ten feet distant from Lucien. Stroking the dagger at his waist, he eyed the sword raised against him. "Come back from the dead, did ye?" The rounding of his cheeks was the only evidence of a bearded smile. "Imagine that." He shifted his gaze to Lucien's scarred face. "Ye were never handsome, lad, not like that brother of yours. Pity ye are less so now."

Alessandra gasped.

Hoping she would hold her tongue, Lucien said, "'Tis most fortunate for you—and me—that how deeply a man buries his sword is not dependent upon his countenance."

Sully laughed. "Is that what ye proved in France?"

The leather of Lucien's saddle creaked as he tensed further, but though that last insult was grievous, he controlled himself.

Disappointment glanced across Sully's face, evidence he had hoped to antagonize his adversary. But before he could renew his efforts, a low rumble sounded across the land.

Lucien looked around. The meadow was empty, but not for much longer.

"See now, my lord Breville has returned from hawking," Sully announced as a party of riders crested the hill.

Lucien turned his steed toward them.

Heart pounding furiously, Alessandra also urged her horse around. Guessing her father was among those at the fore, she considered the half dozen who rode there. It was futile, though, for they were still too distant for her to match one with the description her mother had occasionally given.

"There," Lucien said. "Off center, left. He wears the green."

As the man with a hooded falcon perched on his wrist neared, he became a tall, stately figure whose russet-colored hair had yet to go gray.

Remembering to breathe when Lucien gave her hand a squeeze, she looked up at him from beneath her hood.

"Keep your head down and say nothing," he said and released her.

On the final approach, all but James Breville slowed. Breaking from the pack, he surged forward.

If he was surprised by the one who awaited him, he did not show it. He guided his mount to a place before his visitors, leaned forward, and peered at the De Gautier come back from the grave.

Staring at the man who had sown her, who had no knowledge of the harvest, Alessandra began to tremble. Here was her father, the one who had loved her mother. Kind, Sabine had insisted, though driven by past generations to hate his neighbor.

In spite of his forty or more years, he appeared to be in good form, and she could only hope the wrinkles at the corners of his eyes and mouth had been created by laughter, not anger.

In that moment, she who had once wanted nothing to do with him, yearned to know him. He was all she had—providing he accepted her.

He looked to Alessandra, narrowed his gaze in an attempt to see beyond her hood, then returned his attention to Lucien. Behind, his assembled men muttered in surprise, evidencing they also recognized the one they had thought dead.

As if sensing the tension, the hooded falcon on James's wrist bristled, causing its glossy feathers to rise.

James calmed the bird with a caressing hand. "I knew it," he said. "If a Breville could not bring you down, neither could a Frenchman."

"It is encouraging that not all believed me dead," Lucien replied.

James shifted his gaze to Lucien's sword. "You come armed. I take it you demand satisfaction?"

"Two years' absence cannot have changed things so much that you would expect otherwise."

"But they have changed."

Lucien did not answer.

With a jerk of his head, James indicated those behind. "Only you would stand alone against so many."

"I have done it before."

"And nearly died for it."

"Nearly."

James sighed. "Finally, we are at peace with the De Gautiers, and you return."

Lucien's sword wavered. "At peace?"

James blinked, and Alessandra thought it genuine surprise upon his face. "You have not yet been to Falstaff?"

"I came here first."

"For what?"

Sully pushed his way between Lucien's and Alessandra's horses. "Kin, milord." He nodded at her. "He says this one be of Breville stock."

James looked to Alessandra again. "Breville, hmm? Let me see you."

She raised a hand to push back her hood.

"In a moment," Lucien said. "First, I will hear more of this peace between our families."

James looked as if he might argue, but then he shrugged and urged his horse forward. "Come out of this cold and we will talk."

At Lucien's hesitation, he added, "As Brevilles are welcome at Falstaff, De Gautiers are welcome at Corburry. Set your suspicions aside and share a warm fire with me."

Alessandra saw no harm in it, but she felt Lucien's misgivings. However, he turned his mount toward the drawbridge.

"And Lucien..." James twisted around in the saddle.

"Aye?"

"There is no need for arms."

Slowly, Lucien sheathed his weapon.

Riding beside him, Alessandra marveled at the goings-on of the bailey they entered. Though it was fairly quiet this Sabbath day, it was a world unto itself with its towering granary, thatched barn and stables, odorous piggery, and sprawling smithy. And it appealed to every curious bone in her body.

Prior to reaching the inner bailey, the procession of men and horses split and disassembled. Only a handful continued on to the keep with their lord.

Passing over a smaller drawbridge, Alessandra looked for marbled walks, splashing fountains, and gardens with fruit-bearing trees and flowers. There was only the austere keep and lesser buildings—a world far removed from the elegance of Jabbar's home.

Let it be handsome within, she silently beseeched. It seemed ages since she had been surrounded by beauty.

James swung out of the saddle and tossed his reins to a squire, then waited near the keep's steps for his guests to join him.

Lucien dismounted, untied three of the four packs from his saddle, then came around his horse to assist Alessandra.

"Speak naught," he murmured as he set her to her feet.

"He does not seem so bad," she whispered.

He glared. "You do not know him as I do."

True, but her mother had known James and said he was kind. Thus far, Alessandra saw nothing to dissuade her of that.

In silence, she preceded Lucien up the steps.

When the man soon to learn he was her father stepped aside, allowing her a view of Corburry's immense hall, she pressed her teeth into her bottom lip. The great room appeared clean and orderly, but its only claim to beauty were its colorful wall hangings. All else was stark, including the castle folk who wore drab clothing with what seemed an air of indifference.

What dull lives these people must lead, she thought as she was swept with bittersweet longing for the harem and its tumult of spirited personalities. Had no one ever taught the English the importance of color and form? And where was the lively chatter and laughter that warmed a room as no fire could?

Aboard the ship, and later in the inns where she and Lucien had paused for the night, there had seemed no lack of gaiety and enthusiasm, though it had been of a different sort from that to which she was accustomed. So why was Corburry cheerless? Had someone died?

As the massive door they had passed through closed, a spot of color made its entrance at the far end of the hall. Lady Breville?

James seemed not to notice. He ascended a dais, settled his falcon on the back of an immense chair, and lowered himself into the seat.

Lucien halted ten feet back from the dais, caught Alessandra's arm, and steered her from his right side to his left. Doubtless, he wanted no interference with his sword arm should it become necessary to wield the weapon.

Those of James's men who had accompanied him inside positioned themselves about the hall as if in anticipation of trouble.

"Sit with me," James invited.

"I will stand," Lucien said, his gaze following the brightly garbed woman who mounted the dais and halted alongside James's chair.

"Lady Breville," James introduced her.

Lucien inclined his head, prompting Alessandra to do the same.

The woman acknowledged the visitors with a lift of plucked eyebrows. In spite of her haughty demeanor, Alessandra thought Lady Breville looked flustered.

"It seems the De Gautier has come back from the dead, dear wife," James said.

Her mouth tightened.

"What is this peace you speak of?" Lucien prompted.

James motioned a serving woman forward and accepted the tankard of ale she handed him. "Some for you, friend?" he asked.

Alessandra saw the hollows beneath Lucien's cheekbones deepen and the veins in his neck swell. "The peace," he said again.

James lifted the tankard to his lips.

Thinking she could not have seen right, Alessandra looked again. She was not mistaken. The bottom of James's tankard was fit with glass as if to allow him to keep his eyes on Lucien while he quaffed his ale.

He lowered the vessel to the chair arm, reclined, and clasped his hands across his middle. "We have been at peace with your family for nearly a year. There is no more fighting. No more bloodshed. Your family—"

"How did it come to be?"

"Your family and mine now come and go as we please without threat of injury," James continued. "The villagers and their crops thrive. Children play in the meadows where once they feared to go. Truly, peace has come to our lands."

Lucien's hand curled around his sword hilt, causing James's men to step forward.

James thrust his legs out and crossed them at the ankles. "Do you intend to undo what has taken so long to be done?"

"That depends on your answer."

Something between a groan and a sigh escaped James. "That over which our families have fought for well beyond a hundred years is now resolved. All rights and claims to Dewmoor Pass have been ceded to the Brevilles."

Lucien's hand tightened on the hilt. "Never would my father agree to it."

"He did not." James righted himself in the chair. "Neither could he, for Sebastian de Gautier is dead."

All went still a moment before a roar broke from Lucien. He dropped the packs, thrust Alessandra aside, and wrenched his sword from its scabbard.

The commotion following his charge toward James seemed like a warped dream. A scream—Lady Breville's?—and the ring of iron resounded throughout the hall. Bodies flew past Alessandra, one knocking her to the floor as men fell upon Lucien.

"Miscreant!" Lucien shouted, throwing an arm back and cracking his fist into the jaw of one of those who held him. The man dropped, but was replaced by two others who met with the same fate. In the end, it took four men to keep Lucien from rising again. Small victory, though, for they were unable to wrest the sword from his fist.

In a certain state of agitation, James came forward with dirk in hand.

Thinking he meant to slay Lucien, Alessandra thrust to her feet and lunged forward. "Do not harm him!" she cried, fear causing her to lapse into Arabic.

Had her father not halted midstep, she would not have reached Lucien first. Placing herself as a barrier between the two men, she met James's gaze. And realized she had lost her hood when his eyes shifted to the hair tumbling past her shoulders.

His dirk clattered to the floor. "Catherine," he choked. "Is it you?"

26

THE ANGRY WORDS Alessandra had been about to fling at her father slipped her mind as she watched hope and disbelief battle in eyes the same shape and color as her own.

It was Lucien who broke the silence that had blanketed the hall. "'Tis your daughter, you murdering swine," he shouted from where he remained pinned to the floor.

A shrill cry dragged Alessandra's gaze to Lady Breville whose eyes bulged and mouth hung agape. Then the woman rushed to her husband's side. "'Tis a hoax he works upon you, Husband. A lie!"

"No hoax," Lucien said. "No lie. Alessandra is the child James made with Lady Catherine twenty years ago."

James's gaze roved Alessandra's features, then once more settled on her hair. "My daughter?"

His wife grabbed his arm. "Catherine carried no babe when she disappeared!"

He shook her off, then stepped near Alessandra and touched the curve of her face. "You have my eyes."

She inclined her head.

He swallowed loudly. "But Catherine did not tell me she was with child."

"She did not know," Alessandra said, acutely aware of her accent, "but she carried me."

"Lies, I tell you!" his wife cried. "Mayhap she is Catherine's misbegotten child, but she is not yours, James."

Alessandra swept her gaze to her father's wife. "I am not illegitimate. My mother did not—"

"Do you open your mouth again, Agnes," James said, "I shall cast you out of the hall."

That name—Agnes—loosened Alessandra's knees. Could this be her mother's cousin? She recalled what Sabine had said of her, and considering Agnes had desired marriage to James, it made sense.

Having gained his wife's acquiescence, James said, "I must know all, Alessandra."

She turned to where Lucien lay beneath his captors. "First, release him."

"And give him another chance to slit my throat?"

"'Twas not what I had in mind," Lucien snarled.

"Ah, disembowelment, then."

"For a start."

James considered him, sighed. "The Brevilles are not responsible for your father's death. I assure you, Sebastian died of natural causes."

"Natural for whom? You?"

"I heard tale his heart gave out."

"I am to believe you?"

James glanced at Alessandra. "I suppose that would be asking too much. But when you return to Falstaff, your family will bear witness that I had naught to do with his death."

"What remains of my family?"

James muttered what sounded like a curse, though it was not a word Alessandra had encountered. "Have you not heard anything I have said, Lucien? We are at peace. Your family is well."

"I will not believe it until I see it."

"Release him," James commanded his men.

Warily, they rose and backed away.

In one fluid movement, Lucien regained his feet. Though he did not raise his sword, he kept it to hand.

"What now, Lucien?" James asked.

"Who of the De Gautiers made peace with you?"

"He who was thought to be Sebastian's heir, your brother, Vincent."

"And the terms?"

James appeared reluctant to speak, but said, "Next spring, our daughter, Melissant, was to wed Vincent."

"A De Gautier joined with a Breville?" Lucien exclaimed.

"'Twas agreeable to Vincent. But as you are Sebastian's true heir, it falls to you to wed our daughter to seal the peace."

Alessandra nearly protested. However, Lucien's next words made it unnecessary. "There will be no wedding."

"Your hatred threatens all the good we have achieved," James warned.

Lucien's upper lip curled. "I see no benefit in lying with one of your offspring."

If not for the hope he did not truly see her as a Breville, Alessandra would have been stung.

"The benefit is peace," James said.

"Too high a price. Better a battle than a Breville wife."

"You refuse, then?"

"I do."

After a long moment, James said, "Vincent, then. 'Twill still bind our families."

Agnes gasped, and her face turned more florid. "My daughter will not wed a landless noble. Melissant marries the heir or none at all."

"None, Lady Breville," Lucien said. "I would not allow my brother to make such an unsavory union."

"You arrogant——!"

"Agnes!" James barked.

She swung her gaze to him. "How dare you allow him to speak such to me."

James jabbed a finger toward the stairs. "Out!"

Her jaw worked, but she huffed and strode opposite.

When she was gone, James returned his attention to Lucien. "Very well. No marriage, but will you honor the peace?"

"I make no promises until I know what goes at Falstaff."

Although James's face mirrored detachment, Alessandra felt his uneasiness. "Then go," he said.

Lucien slid his sword into its scabbard, crossed to the packs, and retrieved them. He opened one and pulled out a letter. "From Lady Catherine to her aunt and uncle. It explains Alessandra."

Alessandra caught her breath. Another letter? He had not spoken of it. As her own letter had been left in Jacques LeBrec's home, it took all her control to not run forward and snatch it from him.

Wide-eyed, James said, "What of Catherine? Where is she?"

Lucien strode forward, dropped the packs at James's feet, and extended the letter. "She is dead."

Alessandra knew it well, but was chilled by that single word spoken to the man who had loved her mother.

"Dead?" James choked.

Lucien inclined his head.

Slowly, James unfolded the letter. "What form of writing is this?"

"Arabic. Alessandra will translate it for you."

"Arabic?"

"Catherine was sold into slavery after she disappeared from Corburry. She has been in Algiers all these years."

James's lips drew back. "Then the De Gautiers have known of her whereabouts—are responsible for thieving her away!"

Lucien laid a hand to his sword hilt. "We were wrongly accused. Only by chance did I encounter Catherine."

"He speaks true," Alessandra said as she moved to stand alongside her father in hopes of averting another attack. "Never did my mother say the De Gautiers abducted her."

"Who, then?" James demanded.

"She did not know."

"You think that absolves the De Gautiers of the crime?"

Firmly, she said, "They were not responsible."

He looked unconvinced, but shifted his regard to Lucien. "Then you are off to Falstaff?"

"I am, but be assured we are not done, Breville."

"What more is there to discuss?"

"Dewmoor Pass."

James shook his head. "The matter is settled. It belongs to the Brevilles."

"Perhaps."

James nudged the packs with his boot. "What are these?"

"Alessandra's dowry."

Surprised that Lucien did not intend to keep any of her mother's possessions for himself, Alessandra sought his gaze. "What of your share?" she asked.

"I have my reward." His cool eyes swept her face. "I am home."

Realizing he was about to leave her with strangers, she stepped near and gripped his arm. "Pray, Lucien," she whispered, "do not forget me."

She was certain his eyes softened. "How could I?" he murmured, then gently pulled her hand from him and turned away.

Lucien was at the door when James called to him. He looked over his shoulder.

"You will find much changed at Falstaff," James said. "Accept it and let us continue on in peace."

Lucien stood unmoving, as if trying to unravel the mystery of James's words, then he was gone.

Alessandra felt as if her heart were withering. Reminding herself of her vow to behave as a woman, not a child, she quelled the impulse to run after Lucien and assured herself she would see him again—even if she must go to him.

A knight approached James. "My lord, when he discovers Falstaff is but a shadow of its former self, he will be back."

"I am counting on it."

Disturbed by the exchange, Alessandra touched her father's arm. "Of what does your man speak?"

He turned to her and folded her in arms that might have been comforting had he not denied her the answer she sought. "Welcome, Daughter," he said. "Welcome to Corburry."

27

WHETHER THEY THOUGHT him apparition or flesh and blood, it did not matter. What mattered was that the Lion of Falstaff was home.

None opposed him when he rode into their midst—not the guard at the gatehouse, the men-at-arms within the walled fortress, or the few knights straggling about the great hall. Wide-eyed and slack-jawed, they let him pass.

Intent on the one who had yet to notice his arrival, Lucien ignored the gasps and whispers of disbelief as he strode toward the high table.

Vincent, who had not a responsible bone in his body—who must have been the one who had refused to pay the ransom—did not look up. He was too intent on the woman perched upon his knee.

Suppressing the desire to upend the table, Lucien slammed his palms to its top and leaned forward.

Vincent shot up from his chair, tumbling the wench to the floor. "Almighty! You are alive!"

"Disappointed?" Lucien snarled.

Vincent took a step back. His gaze darted left and right, but he would get no aid from his knights. Lucien's return had robbed him of his rule over them.

"Of course I am not disappointed," Vincent said. "I am surprised, that is all."

"I am sure."

"Lucien!" a woman cried.

He turned to the lone figure across the hall.

His mother stood wide-eyed, the glow upon her face evidencing she had come from the kitchens. "My prayers are answered," she said and dropped to her knees.

Lucien shot Vincent a warning look, then strode to Lady Dorothea and raised her to her feet.

Tears flowing, body trembling, she searched his face. "You have come home. My boy has come home."

In spite of France, slavery that had feasted on the pieces of soul it had stripped from him, James Breville, and Vincent de Gautier, Lucien felt himself soften. "'Twas a promise not to be broken, Mother."

She fell into his arms and, holding tight to him, sobbed into his tunic.

In spite of the questions to which he did not have answers, and the eyes that fell heavy upon them, Lucien let her cry.

Finally, she grew still and, between sharp, replenishing breaths, said, "Your father is dead."

"I have been told. What I wish to know is how he died."

"His heart grew old before my own. Now he is lost to me." Her voice cracked, and Lucien feared she would fall to crying again, but the appearance of a beautiful child distracted her.

The curly-headed girl, perhaps six years of age, tugged on Dorothea's skirt. "Mama."

Lucien's mother wiped a hand across her eyes and stepped out of her son's arms. "Ah, Giselle, have you come to welcome your brother home?"

The little girl shifted her blue-eyed gaze to Lucien. "He is not my brother."

Dorothea bent near. "Aye, 'tis Lucien come home from France, little one. Give him a kiss, hmm?"

Giselle crossed her arms over her chest. "He is not Lucien." She narrowed her gaze upon the crescent-shaped scar. "My big brother had a nice face."

Dorothea glanced at Lucien and, as if only then noticing the scar, frowned. But she quickly recovered. "'Tis Lucien, indeed. He is a warrior, and when warriors go into battle, sometimes they are injured. Now be a good girl and give him a proper welcome."

She stamped her foot. "I will not!"

Dorothea offered Lucien an apologetic smile. "Give her time. She will come 'round."

What Lucien longed to do was sweep his little sister into his arms. Before he had departed for France, she had often been underfoot, but he had rarely begrudged her his attention.

During long nights aboard the galley, he had calmed his soul with memories of her guileless giggles and yelps of delight, her innocent remarks and boundless curiosity. She had been a beacon, this miracle child who should not have been conceived, much less survived the arduous birthing by a woman well past childbearing age. But Giselle had, and she had been born to parents who, until then, had only been blessed with boys—five, of whom three had survived to adulthood.

"When you wish to ride on my shoulders again," Lucien said, "you will let me know, hmm?"

Something flickered in her eyes, and for a moment she looked near upon him, then she tossed her head. "Only my brothers get to be my horse."

"Well, if ever you wish to see what is up here," Lucien said, "I suppose you will have to pretend I am your brother."

Giselle glanced beyond his head, pressed her lips tight.

Dorothea nudged her daughter toward the stairs. "Summon Jervais," she said.

Giselle raised her eyebrows at Lucien, said, "My *brother*," and flounced off.

"She will be in your lap by nightfall," Dorothea said, then looped an arm through her son's and urged him to where Vincent and the others stood silent and watchful.

Upon the dais, Lucien seated his mother at his side, then dropped into the chair vacated by Vincent. "Leave us," he ordered the knights and servants.

They withdrew, and in their absence, a gaping silence grew until Dorothea said, "Tell us, Lucien—"

"Nay, Mother, when Jervais is here."

Dorothea inclined her head, looked to her middle son. "Sit with us, Vincent."

He fidgeted before taking a seat distant from Lucien.

When the youngest De Gautier son came off the stairs, there was an air of annoyance about him, but the moment his eyes beheld Lucien, he halted. And there he stood and stared until a smile broke upon his face. "How dare I not believe Giselle!" he cried and crossed the hall at a run.

Lucien rose to accept his embrace, and was surprised at the bulk and power his brother's once slender body had attained. Nicholas had not exaggerated.

When they drew back, Jervais said, "Tis a blessing beyond blessings that you are returned to us," and made the table his seat.

"Much has changed." Lucien marked Vincent with a glower. "And I would know all of it, but first I seek an answer."

Vincent rose. "I know your question, Lucien." His face was so pale it diluted his good looks.

For their mother's sake, Lucien presented a calm face. "Of course you know, but they do not, do they?"

Vincent looked to his mother and younger brother. "They thought you dead."

"We all thought you dead," Dorothea said. "When you did not return from France, and no word came, it was the only conclusion to be had."

"But word did come," Lucien said. "Aye, Vincent?"

Throat bobbing, the younger man stepped forward.

"What speak you of?" Dorothea asked. "Make sense, Lucien."

"All will be clear shortly, Mother."

Vincent's advance on the one he had almost mortally wronged was probably the bravest thing he had ever done, Lucien silently scorned.

Vincent halted before Lucien, and though his gaze wavered, he did not look away. "Lucien is making sense, Mother. I did receive word that he lived. And with it came a ransom demand."

Dorothea staggered and dropped into her chair. "You never told. You said naught of it!"

Vincent turned pleading eyes upon her. "How could I? The coffers were near empty, nowhere near enough coin to bring him home."

Lucien jerked. "Not enough coin?"

"After Father died, and when there was no word from you, I thought I was heir. I…thought it all mine."

"All yours!" Lucien strained to keep his fists at his sides. "What did you do with it?"

Jervais supplied the bitter answer. "He gambled it away. Almost every last bloody coin."

"I tried to get it back," Vincent protested. "I tried everything to make your ransom."

"And for that," Jervais said, "we are now reduced to near poverty."

It was as Breville had warned. Much had changed at Falstaff, the loss of Dewmoor Pass the least of its troubles. Lucien looked to his youngest brother. "Explain."

Where he perched on the table's edge, Jervais crossed his arms over his chest. "You tell him, Vincent." He jutted his chin at the one to whom he was no longer subject. "Tell the heir of Falstaff who now holds the greater portion of the De Gautier lands."

At that moment, Vincent could not be said to be handsome. The beauty that had forever eclipsed his brothers was reduced to a vague shadow of manliness.

"Each time I thought I had him," he bemoaned, "the knave took another piece. I should have stopped, but I thought the next time my luck would run better and all would be restored."

Now Lucien understood the scarcity of knights when he had entered the hall. Untold numbers of De Gautier vassals now answered to another lord. Though he knew the name of their new liege, he demanded, "Who holds our lands, Vincent?"

"Breville," he said low.

Lucien's arms began to shake with the effort to keep them at his sides.

Accept it and let us continue on in peace, the miscreant had said, knowing full well what awaited Falstaff's true heir.

Lucien threw himself on Vincent, making the floor their battleground. He heard his mother's cry, but it was not enough to pull him back up over the edge he had gone over.

By the time he realized Vincent made no attempt to defend himself, as if accepting the beating as his due, he had landed at least a dozen blows. Breathing hard, knuckles stained with his and Vincent's blood, he thrust upright and looked down at his brother who would surely regret he had not thrown up an arm to protect that beautiful face. It was a mess, and it would look worse once the bruises came into their own.

"Do it!" Vincent demanded, peering up at him through swelling lids. "End it. 'Tis no more than I deserve."

"It is far better than you deserve," Lucien barked and wrenched his tunic off over his head.

Behind, he heard Dorothea and Jervais gasp.

"This"—Lucien jabbed the scar on his face—"and this"—he jerked around to present his back to Vincent—"is no more than you deserve."

Vincent groaned. "Dear God, I did not know!"

"Did not know!" Lucien swung back around.

"I tried not to think about it."

"Well now you get to think about it, and I hope you ever shall."

Wiping the back of a hand across his bloody mouth, Vincent raised his head. "After what I have done, you would let me live?"

"You may not have the backbone of a De Gautier," Lucien rasped, "but you are still my mother's son."

Vincent flinched. "I am also our father's son—and your brother."

"That you will have to prove."

Vincent pulled his battered body into a sitting position. "How?"

Lucien left the question unanswered. "What did Breville promise you for marriage to his daughter?"

"How do you know of that?"

"What did he promise you, Vincent? Falstaff?"

"Nay, Lucien! Falstaff and its immediate environs I—you still hold. He offered lasting peace."

"Naught else? No dowry? No return of the property he stole?"

Slowly, Vincent gained his feet. "It was agreed that with the birth of a child made of Melissant and myself, he would gift all De Gautier properties back to me."

"And Dewmoor Pass?"

"Holy rood, Lucien! Is it not enough that he will restore the lands? Have not both our families lost too much over that useless pass?"

"It is ours!" Fearing he might attack Vincent again, Lucien swung away. "I will have the lands and the pass back," he said, looking from his mother's distressed face to Jervais's expectant face. "Be it by blood or guile, I will have them back."

"You speak the same nonsense our father spoke," Vincent protested. "You would rather spill blood than accept peace through marriage to a Breville."

Slowly, Lucien came back around. "Certes, it is not the way of one who gambles away his family's wealth, but it is the way of warriors. That is what *I* am."

Vincent averted his gaze. "I know what it is to be at peace. Do you?"

Much to their father's disappointment, Vincent had always been better at words than weapons, and as these had the potential to strike deep, Lucien once more gave him his back.

"What do you intend?" Jervais asked.

In the past, making war on the Brevilles had been the only means of retribution. Now, the loss of vassals and household knights hindered such a solution. Or did it?

Lucien raked a hand through his hair, fervently wished he had brought Alessandra to Falstaff first as she had pleaded. Judging by James's reaction, she might have played a powerful role in restoring De Gautier lands—a useful pawn, the same as Sabine had made him.

"I must think on it," he said, and felt fatigue settle deeper into his bones.

Jervais laid a hand on his shoulder. "I stand with you. Together, we will restore the De Gautier name."

Lucien looked to his other brother. "Have you the stomach for it?" At Vincent's hesitation, he muttered, "I thought not."

Vincent opened his mouth, closed it on whatever he had been tempted to say, and strode from the hall and out into the last of day.

Lucien crossed to his mother. "I have need of a bath."

"Of course. I shall have water delivered to the solar."

That place where his mother and father had slept and made their children. Where Dorothea had birthed her babes. Where, when young, he and his brothers had gathered around their father to hear tales of the cowardly Brevilles and the fearless De Gautiers.

"'Tis yours now," Dorothea said.

Hastened from his memories, Lucien acknowledged it was, indeed, his. And one day he would share it with a wife as his father and generations before him had done.

Visions of Alessandra arose. Alessandra in the great bed, red hair spread upon their pillows. Alessandra in the chair before the fire, a babe in her arms.

He dragged a hand across his stubbled jaw. "I must needs shave."

"I shall do it," Dorothea said, and hurried across the hall.

"What *is* up there?" a petulant voice asked.

Having not seen Giselle's return to the hall, Lucien was surprised to find her staring up at him.

Despite fatigue and the ominous emotions beneath his skin, he summoned a smile for her. "Magic." He lifted a hand, stirred the air above his head. "Up here, one can fly."

She tapped her pursed mouth. "But only birds can fly, Lucien."

With her naming of him, the ache in his heart eased. "And little girls who have big brothers with broad shoulders."

She raised a sharp little eyebrow that he did not doubt would one day set many men aback. "I have not said you are my brother."

"True, but mayhap you are ready to pretend I am."

She looked as if she might once more denounce him, but she raised her arms. "I think that would be all right."

Trying not to smile too wide lest she pridefully changed her mind, he plucked her up, told her to hold back her skirts, and settled her on his shoulders.

"Ooh," she crooned, "'tis magic, as you said."

"Would you like to try to fly?"

Her whole body shrugged. "I do not know how."

"Hold your arms out to the sides."

"But I might fall."

"I will hold you steady." He clasped her legs more tightly.

"Very well, but if I fall, 'twill prove you are not my brother."

"I am prepared to accept the consequences."

She laughed and raised her arms out to her sides. "I am ready, Lucien."

His troubles and fatigue much lightened, he carried her about the hall amid giggles and gleeful cries and the silent refrain, *I am home.*

28

❧◈❧

A<small>S</small> J<small>ABBAR HAD</small> wept upon Sabine's deathbed, so did James when Alessandra finished translating her mother's letter—or nearly so. He was too English to allow any to witness his tears, though the back he turned to her quaked with silent sobs.

The letter had been addressed to Catherine's aunt and uncle, but its message was clearly meant for James. It recorded her abduction from Corburry, her first months in the harem, the birth of Alessandra, the intervening years, the sickness thieving her body, and Lucien's role in delivering Alessandra to England.

Only one detail was missing, Alessandra had realized when she came to the last, beseeching line of the letter. Her mother had not mentioned her great love for Jabbar. She had been wise not to, for there was no doubt James had loved her deeply. No good would come of him learning of Catherine's feelings for another man.

For hours, Alessandra and James sat alone in the great hall, even now forgoing the evening meal as they attempted to bridge the lost years.

Though there were some facets to James's personality that might take years to understand, Alessandra was soon assured of one thing. As her mother had said, he was kind, his one failing the same as Lucien's— the legacy of hate between their families.

Still, he spoke often of the new peace, reveled in the word each time he uttered it, and expressed concern over whether it would last now that Lucien was home.

Tentatively, Alessandra posed the question uppermost in her mind—what would Lucien find upon his arrival at Falstaff?

Though James attempted to turn the conversation, he eventually yielded the truth.

"You won the land from his brother?" she repeated.

"Fairly, I vow, and with good intentions."

"What was that?"

He smiled. "Surely you can guess."

"Peace?"

"Aye. Had it been Lucien, I might never have attempted such a thing, but it was simple with Vincent. The idea was to gain what the De Gautiers treasured most and offer it back to them at a price."

"The price being peace."

He inclined his head. "And a grandchild that would forever join our families."

"Vincent was agreeable?"

"As agreeable as a De Gautier can be."

Alessandra looked past him to a tapestry that depicted men engaged in battle. "Lucien will return," she said, "but I do not think it will be in peace."

James also considered the tapestry. "The battle at Cresting Ridge in the year 1342," he said. "The De Gautiers lost six men, the Brevilles five. Breville victory by the death of a lad too young to heft the sword he carried."

A shiver stole up Alessandra's spine for what the tapestry represented—a repulsive gloating over death.

James sighed. "I fear you may be right. Still, I pray Lucien will put aside his pride and reconsider marriage to Melissant."

Alessandra's silence was her undoing.

Her father gave her a searching stare. "What happened between you and De Gautier?"

She felt herself blush. "I…" She clenched her hands in the blanket James had earlier sent for when she had begun shivering. "Lucien was kind to me."

Her father chuckled. "Not likely. Tolerant, perhaps. Never kind."

She shook her head. "You are wrong about him."

"I pray I am. But you have not answered my question."

Though he was her father, it was not easy what he asked. "I am chaste," she said.

James covered her hands with one of his. "As hoped, but what of your feelings for him?"

Should she tell him of her love for his enemy?

The appearance of James's wife saved Alessandra from responding. Stepping from the stairs, the woman crossed the hall with a young woman and boy on her heels.

Frowning, James stood. "I had thought you would await my summons."

Agnes halted before him. "And I had thought you would summon me sooner." Her gaze flickered over Alessandra, dismissed her. "With darkness upon us and no meal laid, it has fallen to me to interrupt your conversation."

James's jaw worked. "Which you have succeeded in doing."

The young woman stepped forward, smiled sweetly. "Is it true, Father"—she nodded at Alessandra—"she is also your daughter?"

James put a hand beneath Alessandra's elbow and urged her to stand.

Reluctantly, Alessandra gave up the warmth of the blanket, feeling anew the draft of cool air that crept in through every crack in the hall. Even on the deck of the ship, with the night wind blowing through her clothes, she had been warmer. But then, Lucien had been at her back, arms encircling her. Would they ever again?

She sighed, wished her father would call for a fire to be set in the hearth.

"Aye, Melissant," James said. "She is my daughter and your half sister."

"Is she also mine, Father?" the boy asked.

What seemed pride leapt off James's face as he looked upon the lad who appeared ten or so years aged. "Aye, Ethan, she is."

Alessandra wondered if she ought to embrace this brother and sister as she had done her father. But uncertain as to how such affection would be received, she linked her hands before her.

A frown aged Ethan's young face as he considered Alessandra's mouth. "Mother says she speaks strange. That she has the sound of the infidel."

A look passed between Agnes and James, his fit with displeasure, hers with defiance.

Turning aside her mother's warnings about her cousin, Alessandra silently sympathized with Agnes. It could not be easy to live in the shadow of one whom James had so loved, especially her childhood rival.

James set a hand upon Ethan's shoulder. "'Tis true Alessandra speaks different—with a song in her voice. But she is Christian, the same as you and I."

"Let me hear," Ethan said.

Alessandra smiled. "It is most pleasant to meet you, young Ethan." She shifted her regard to his sister. "And you, Melissant."

They both stared.

"What of our daughter's betrothal, James?" Agnes asked.

James stepped forward and took Melissant's hands in his. "I am sorry, but Lucien de Gautier's return has spoiled our plans."

"I am not to wed Vincent?"

"It seems not."

Alessandra did not think the girl looked disappointed. Indeed, her eyes brightened.

"But perhaps Lucien," Agnes said.

James snapped his gaze to her. "Do you forget he declined?"

"He may reconsider once he learns there is more than peace to be gained in wedding Melissant."

The land, Alessandra thought. "You are wrong," she said. "Lucien will take back his lands by force before he will bend a knee to a Breville."

Agnes turned to her. "You cannot know that."

"But I do. I——"

"Because you have lain with a man does not mean you know his mind," Agnes said.

And she had sympathized with this woman? Alessandra gathered words to respond to the accusation, but James said, "Stand down, Agnes."

"'Tis true," she pressed. "Look at her. Do you not think a man like De Gautier would not take what she blatantly offers?"

Alessandra glanced down her attire, then up to compare it with what Agnes and Melissant wore. It seemed little different from their gowns. In fact, the cut of hers was more modest.

What then? Her hair hanging unbound past her shoulders? Agnes's was mostly concealed by a jeweled cap, and Melissant's braids were pinned on either side of her head over her ears.

While Alessandra had been occupied with discovering what made her so different from the other women, James had moved to stand before his wife.

"You are behaving the shrew, Agnes," he said. "Alessandra is my daughter, and——"

"As is Melissant. And do not forget you also have a son from me."

He bent his head near hers. "Henceforth, you will keep your nasty thoughts inside your head or suffer my displeasure."

The standoff was abandoned only when Agnes spat, "Very well, but do not forget to whom your first duty is."

"To the Breville name, as it has always been."

Her eyebrows soared. "You know 'tis your children of whom I speak."

"Of which Alessandra is the firstborn."

"If what she says is true, which——"

"It is true, Agnes. And 'twould benefit you to accept it."

Though the woman closed her mouth, the way she crossed her arms over her chest said the discussion was far from over, and she had no intention of embracing the trespasser in their midst.

James turned back to his children, smiled tightly. "Methinks a tourney would best introduce Alessandra to the gentry. What think you of that?"

"Aye, Father!" Ethan exclaimed.

"Alessandra?" James asked.

"A tourney," she mused. She had heard tales of such celebrations but knew little of them. "It sounds interesting."

"Then it will be done. A month hence, Corburry will host its first tournament in a decade."

29

"Where is the sun?" Alessandra bemoaned, keenly feeling its absence as she had every day this past fortnight. She was nearly a month at Corburry now and had yet to see a full blue sky or feel the sun's heat upon skin that was often covered in prickly bumps.

At first, it had been an interesting change from the Maghrib, but now it was almost monotonous. Though the green of England was beyond compare, the price paid for such beauty seemed too high.

"I thought never to tire of rainbows," she muttered. "Now I am nearly sick of them."

"Come away from the window," Melissant urged.

Lifting her chin from her hands, Alessandra looked over her shoulder.

Dressed in a gown of lustrous velvet, its buttons loosened as a defense against the overheated room, her sister sat upon the bed as far from the fire as possible. Propped in her lap was an illuminated tome, its warped and discolored pages attesting to its respectable age.

Alessandra smiled as she reflected on their friendship. In spite of Agnes's attempts to keep James's daughters apart, the girl was a bit of a rebel. At every opportunity, she sought out Alessandra, begging for tales of Algiers and life in the harem in exchange for demonstrations of the English way of things.

Having a sister filled a void of which Alessandra had been unaware, while the void left by Lucien's absence grew more terrible with each passing day.

His silence was almost unbearable. Though James's men kept an eye out for his vengeful coming, thus far, their efforts were for naught.

"Come," Melissant beckoned again. "I wish to show you something."

Alessandra straightened from the window, but was tempted instead to the hearth she rarely allowed to go cold. Taking up the poker, she stoked the fire, then reached to add another log.

Melissant groaned. "Must you? I am near to burning up."

Alessandra paused, and for what seemed the hundredth time, said, "I have hardly been warm since leaving the Maghrib."

Her sister lowered her book. "'Twill be a miserable winter if you do not soon adapt."

"I cannot believe it could get any colder than this. Rarely have I seen my breath upon the air, and now each morn when I awaken, it is there when I come out from beneath the covers."

Melissant giggled. "And yet you sleep almost fully clothed."

"Did I not, I would be like the frost upon the window, and you would find me dead come morn."

"Methinks you need a man to warm you." At the widening of Alessandra's eyes, Melissant quickly added, "'Tis what Hellie tells me when I complain of the cold."

She referred to the robust cook who had groused about modifying the foods her lord's daughter ate, but who had finally complied when Alessandra became sick in her presence.

Silently, Alessandra conceded the woman was right. Were Lucien to share her bed, there would be no need for covers or fire.

"Shall I guess who occupies your mind?" Melissant asked.

Alessandra straightened from the hearth and moved toward the bed. "No one occupies my mind."

Melissant drew up her knees and settled her chin on them. "No one but Lucien de Gautier."

Alessandra nearly tripped over her toes. "Wh-what makes you think that?"

Her sister smiled knowingly. "A good guess, aye?"

Though Alessandra had been fairly open about their escape from Algiers and the events up until Lucien had rescued her from slavery, she had downplayed their relationship. What had revealed her?

Lowering herself to the mattress, she pulled the coverlet over her legs. "It is wrong of me, I know—improper, you English would say—but I cannot stop thinking about him."

"You love him?"

Alessandra nodded, forgetting what Melissant had earlier told her of playing coy with men.

"And he you?"

"It seems not. Perhaps had I remained Alessandra, daughter of Jabbar, he might have come to love me, but I am Alessandra Breville, daughter of his enemy."

Melissant looked to the bitten nails of her right hand. "Methinks father should offer you in marriage to keep the peace."

Alessandra shook her head. "Lucien would refuse me as surely as he did you."

"One does not know until one asks."

"I know." Wishing she had not been dissuaded from throwing another log on the fire, Alessandra dragged the coverlet around her shoulders and buried her nose in it.

A knock preceded Ethan's entrance. Cheeks flushed, the boy thrust his head around the door. Beaming, he said, "A messenger has come from Falstaff."

Alessandra sprang from the bed and rushed forward to pull the door wider. "He brings word of Lucien?"

Ethan frowned. "What did you say?" Though he was becoming accustomed to her accent, it bemused him when she spoke too fast.

"She asked if the messenger brings word of Falstaff's lord, Lucien de Gautier," Melissant interpreted.

Ethan rolled his eyes. "Nay, the message is that the De Gautiers shall attend the tourney."

Alessandra gripped the door's edge. She had not known James had issued them an invitation. What did Lucien's acceptance mean? That he would overlook the loss of his lands, embrace peace?

"Does Mother know?" Melissant asked.

"Not yet. She is with the physician and will not allow any to enter her chamber until he is finished."

Melissant grimaced. "She is being bled again?"

Ethan nodded.

Alessandra shuddered at mention of that repugnant thing English noblewomen did to attain a pale complexion. Melissant had described the procedure, admitting she had undergone it herself—and been sick for days thereafter. Now she opted for painting and powdering her face to achieve a similar look.

Alessandra thought both methods unsavory and refused Melissant's offer to instruct her in applying paint and powder. She had always preferred her skin honey-colored, and now without sun, it was much too pale. Even Agnes's taunts and Ethan's teasing about her freckles would not make her give in to the bleaching Melissant suggested.

But though kohl for her eyes and rouge for her lips would suit her better, she hesitated to apply them, as she had not seen them worn by her stepmother or Melissant.

Ethan touched Alessandra's arm. "It is not something you have eaten again, is it?"

"What? Oh, nay, Ethan. I am well."

He shrugged and ran back down the corridor.

"Father says things meant to be are, and not meant to be are not," Melissant said as she crossed toward Alessandra. "Mayhap you and Lucien de Gautier are meant to be."

Alessandra wished to believe it, but she feared disappointment. Had the messenger carried a missive from Lucien to her, she might have chanced it, but it was as if he had completely forgotten her. "Nay, Lucien has made it clear he has no thought for me other than as a Breville."

"We shall see." Melissant pecked her on the cheek, stepped into the corridor, and tossed over her shoulder, "Do you not put another log on that fire, it will surely die."

Arriving in the hall before the evening meal, Alessandra halted at the sight of Agnes and Melissant poring over journals she had only ever seen in the company of the steward.

Pale, appearing weakened by the bloodletting, Agnes flipped through the pages, muttered something, and pushed the journal in front of Melissant.

Sabine had said it was not uncommon for English noblewomen to be versed in household accounting, but Alessandra had given it little thought. Intrigued, she watched as mother and daughter discussed the entries.

"Figure these two." Agnes tapped the top of the page.

Alessandra, who had a flair for calculating without need for quill and parchment, itched to know the numbers.

Quill in hand, Melissant wrote out the figures and, shortly, provided the answer. "Two hundred seventeen."

Annoyance spotting Agnes's pale cheeks, she clipped, "Two hundred twenty-seven. Where is your head today, child?"

Melissant groaned. "Elsewhere. Why must I know the books? It is our steward's duty."

Agnes harrumphed. "As you will someday run your husband's household, you must know the numbers the steward puts before you."

"Why?"

"I have told you—so you will not be cheated. 'Tis your duty to your husband to keep an eye on all that is his. Did I not do it for your father, much would be lost to thieving."

"Is it not duty enough to bear my husband's children? Surely he can do this better than I. I detest numbers."

Agnes looked ready to vent her anger, but the bit of color in her cheeks drained, and she lowered her head into her hands. "If I have to explain it one more time, I shall scream."

Melissant placed a hand on her shoulder. "You let him take too much. Why do you not just use powder and paint?"

Agnes started to lift her head but quickly returned it to her hands. "I must needs look my best, else the memories that have gained strength with the coming of Catherine's daughter will supplant me entirely." As if pained, she rolled her head side to side. "What am I to do about Alessandra? What?"

Guilt gripped Alessandra—guilt that James's memories could hurt so much and had grown with her arrival at Corburry, and guilt at not revealing her presence. It was a private moment, one that would never include her.

Hoping to withdraw without being seen, Alessandra turned and gasped when her foot bumped the table she had stood alongside.

"Alessandra!" Melissant called. "I did not see you there."

Alessandra came back around, looked first to Agnes.

Though the woman did not look up, her heartfelt groan revealed her chagrin.

"I was just…" Alessandra raised her palms. "I did not mean to intrude."

Melissant beckoned. "Come assist me with helping Mother to her chamber. She is not well."

As Alessandra started forward, Agnes raised her head. A moment later, her body followed. Swaying, she narrowed her eyes on Alessandra. "I am no old lady to be cosseted and carried about." Chin high, she came around the table on legs that made it appear she had imbibed too much, and walked past Alessandra.

When Alessandra was certain Agnes was far enough up the stairs she would not hear, she said, "I am sorry."

Melissant sighed. "It is not your fault." After stacking the journals, she came around the table and halted before Alessandra. "The only one to blame is whoever stole your mother away. Hopefully, one day he will be found out."

Alessandra hoped it as well, for she would not have Lucien and his family forever burdened by suspicion.

"Unfortunately," Melissant continued, "Mother has given me the task of overseeing supper preparations. Would you like to help?"

Another lesson in being an English noblewoman. At least it sounded more interesting than spinning wool or embroidery. "I would."

Within moments of stepping into the cavernous kitchens, Alessandra knew she belonged. It was not the wonderful smells wafting from bubbling pots. It was not the joyous clatter of cooking utensils. Nor was it the laughter and chatter of cooks and kitchen maids. Though all these things made her feel welcome, it was the glorious heat that appealed to her every cold place. It was so intense, it raised a sweat on her brow and caused her clothes to cling—just like in Algiers when she had ventured to the rooftop at midday.

"It is wonderful," Alessandra breathed. Having never entered a kitchen, it being considered beneath harem women, she was deeply curious.

Wandering from Melissant's side, she leaned over a cook's shoulder to peek into the pot he stirred. "What is it?" she asked.

He stepped aside to give her a closer look. "Spiced wine custard, milady. One of yer father's favorites."

And soon hers, Alessandra thought as she inhaled a breath of it. "How is it made?"

"Ye truly wish to know?"

"Of course."

He handed her the spoon. "Taste it, then I'll tell ye."

Uncertain, Alessandra looked around. Across the room, Melissant stood with elbows on a huge block table at which two women kneaded dough. She winked, nodded for Alessandra to try the custard.

Alessandra dipped up a spoonful, blew on it, tasted. "It is delicious." She returned the spoon to the cook. "Now tell, how is it made?"

"Ye warm good wine, cast yolk of eggs in it, and stir awhile, but let it not boil, milady. When 'tis thick, ye toss in sugar, saffron, salt, mace..." He frowned. "Ah, galingale, then flower of Canelle."

Impressed, Alessandra thanked him and crossed to Melissant who now stood at a spit lined with roasting hares.

"More sauce," Melissant instructed the man tending the meat. "It would not do for them to be dry."

He reached for a bowl of honey-colored sauce.

"What do you think?" Melissant asked Alessandra.

"I like it. Had I known it was such an interesting place—and so very warm—I would have ventured here sooner."

Face aglow from the heat, Melissant took Alessandra's arm and drew her away. "What were the kitchens like in Algiers?"

"I do not know. I was not allowed within."

"Why?"

"Food preparation was the duty of slaves, often overseen by the chief eunuch, but never the master's wives or daughters."

"Ah, heavenly! How I detest this hot, smelly place. But Mother says a wife must assure her husband's food is good and plentiful."

Alessandra tried to temper her smile. Of all things she had thus far encountered in England, she thought the kitchen among the best—and possibly household accounting. To test the steward's numbers would be more enjoyable than what she had thus far learned of being an English lady. Of course, those things paled next to Lucien. More than anything, he made England appealing. Without him...

Shaking her head, she returned her attention to the busy kitchen.

30

Aт LAST, HE had come. The other participants having arrived hours earlier, Alessandra had nearly given up hope Lucien would attend the tournament.

Though her first sight of him was from the window of her chamber, and he was too distant to make out his features, she knew him by the head and shoulders he sat above most others.

Despite his loss of property, his was an impressive entourage, numbering twenty or more, all outfitted in gold splashed on red. Banners of the same colors fluttered in the stir created by the speed with which they approached Corburry's walls.

Would he come to the keep this eve to dine with the others? Or would he stay in the encampment outside the walls?

"Lady, come back to your bath," called Bernadette, Alessandra's recently acquired maid.

"I will not catch chill," Alessandra said as she followed Lucien's advance.

"For certain, not in this chamber," the twelve-year-old girl muttered.

Alessandra grinned. The temperature suited her, even with the draft from the window. It was heavenly to be without garments and to not feel the English cold.

"Come, milady, I must needs rinse the soap from your hair. There is much to do ere the banquet."

Not until the walls stole Lucien from sight did Alessandra comply. However, as she drew alongside the wooden tub, she paused.

The water from which she had emerged upon hearing the thunder of hooves was murky gray. The English way of bathing was something she did not think she would ever grow accustomed to. Rather than sitting on stools, allowing filth to be scrubbed from one's body before finishing with a dip in water, one soaked, bathed, and rinsed in the same fouled water.

But though forced to use a tub, there was one thing upon which she could not compromise—the frequency of her baths. Worse than their mode of bathing, the English more often used heavy perfumes to mask the scent of unwashed bodies.

Days earlier, when Alessandra had called for heated water, Agnes had refused to allow the servants to deliver it. Thus, Alessandra had fetched the water up the stairs herself. If not for James's intervention, she might still be doing so. Regrettably, his interference had added fuel to Agnes's fire.

"Come, come," Bernadette urged. "I must rinse your hair."

"I am not going back in the tub," Alessandra said, then knelt beside it, leaned forward, and instructed the maid to pour what remained of the fresh water over her head.

After it was done with much grumbling, Alessandra stood, crossed to her dressing table, and lowered to the stool.

"Ah, milady, have you no modesty?" Bernadette dropped a robe over her mistress's bare shoulders.

Alessandra looked around. "There is only you in this room with me."

"Aye, but 'tis improper for you to wander about with nary a stitch of clothing."

As Alessandra fit her arms into the robe's sleeves, she humored herself by casting Bernadette in the role of serving girl in a bathhouse. It would terrorize the poor thing to see so many naked women.

With an adeptness that surprised Alessandra, Bernadette made quick work of pressing the moisture from her lady's hair and arranging it in thick braids that she wound around Alessandra's head like a coronet. It was a compromise, for Alessandra refused to don the weighty headdress Agnes had sent to her. She was not ashamed of her hair's color and had no intention of hiding it beneath that contraption.

An hour later, Alessandra fingered the jeweled necklace that had been her mother's, finding consolation in knowing it had once been warmed by Sabine's skin. Though tempted to wear belled bracelets and anklets as well, Agnes's unmerciful chastisement of days earlier when Alessandra had worn but a single bracelet, precluded that.

Alessandra rose from her dressing table and began pacing her chamber. Though daunted by the great number of people she would soon face, it did not compare with the possibility of seeing Lucien again.

Melissant had promised to send word if he appeared, but thus far, none had come to announce his entrance into the great hall.

Glimpsing her reflection in the mirror, Alessandra halted. No paint, she had insisted, but had yielded to a light dusting of powder to cover her freckles. A mistake. What little color remained in her face was concealed beneath pasty white.

"God's rood," she muttered James's favorite expression of astonishment, grabbed a cloth, dipped it in the washbasin, and scrubbed at her face.

Relieved to see the freckles resurface, she pronounced, "Better." And she would have been content with the transformation had not the small wooden box on her dressing table caught her eye.

She lifted the lid and considered the kohl and rouge—simple enhancements compared with painting and powdering. Once more, she consulted her reflection and found it wanting.

When a knock sounded a short time later, Alessandra was pleased with her handiwork. Knowing it was likely her father who was to escort her belowstairs, she opened the door.

To her discomfort, James's smile faltered at the sight of her. However, he quickly recovered and offered his arm.

"Something is wrong?" she asked. "The kohl?" Though she had more lightly applied it than when she had lived in the harem, it might still be a shock to those unaccustomed to the look.

James shook his head. "Everything is perfect. You are beyond lovely, Catherine's daughter."

Unconvinced, she peered down the front of her gown to the raised hemline. "I know I should not have"—she put a foot forward to show him the space between gown and floor—"but I feared if I did not shorten it, I might trip and embarrass you."

James eyed her stockinged ankle. "I have always wondered why women wear gowns so long. 'Tis not practical, is it?"

She smiled. "Were it permissible, I would choose a caftan and trousers instead."

James laughed. "Pray, give me fair warning ere you wear such garments in Agnes's presence."

Alessandra looped her arm through his, and as she walked beside him down the corridor, said, "Father, will the house of Falstaff be represented at the banquet?"

"Methinks you are asking if Lucien has arrived," he said as they began their descent of the stairs.

With the excited buzz of hundreds of guests floating up to them, Alessandra said, "Why would you think that?"

He looked sidelong at her. "On the way to your chamber, I intercepted Melissant's messenger."

Inwardly, she groaned. "What was the message?"

"He is here."

Gripped with apprehension and excitement, she asked, "Has he come in peace?"

"As far as I can tell. Still, I have set men to watch him and those accompanying him."

"Then you and Lucien have not spoken?"

"We have not."

Alessandra sighed.

James halted a half-dozen steps up from the hall. "You think he has come to make trouble?"

She shrugged. "I would not be surprised if he moves to reclaim what was taken from him."

"Neither would I."

"What will you do?"

He patted her hand and led her down the last steps. "I have always intended that De Gautier lands be returned, but it must be by way of marriage to a Breville."

"The peace is important to you."

He nodded. "The feud ends with me. That is the promise I made Catherine ere she disappeared. Though many times since I have broken it, as when I believed the De Gautiers responsible for her disappearance, I am determined to secure this current peace."

Alessandra wanted to know more, but found herself before an audience whose conversation rippled into silence.

"Smile, Alessa," her father used the pet name he had adopted for her shortly after her arrival at Corburry. "Let them see that Catherine lives in you."

She pushed a smile to her lips and lifted her chin.

Before her, nobility flanking nobility, men and women considered her lined eyes and the hem of her gown. The faces of the former reflected appreciation, while those of the latter more often shone with disapproval.

As only once before had she been faced with so many intent upon her—at the slave auction in Tangier—Alessandra almost wished her father had ordered her to pull out the stitches in her hem and wipe away the kohl.

"Allow me to introduce my daughter," James boomed. "Lady Alessandra Breville."

A murmur of acknowledgment rose, along with whispers and judgmental mutterings. Though some stepped forward, most remained aloof.

"Worry not," James whispered. "Once I have taken you around and all know your charm, they will clamor to stand alongside you."

Agnes's sudden appearance boded no good. However, her eyes shone with satisfaction rather than disapproval. "Your daughter is most becoming, James."

Alessandra's suspicions echoed those her father voiced. "Are you laying down your sword, wife?"

"Wrongly you have judged me," Agnes said. "Never did I take it up."

"Is that so?"

Increasing her smile, Agnes slipped her arm through the one to which Alessandra held. "Come." She tugged James free. "The steward wishes a word ere the banquet commences."

"Whatever for?"

"Several knives have gone missing."

James's eyebrows met.

Knives and spoons were precious articles, Alessandra had learned during her first meal at Corburry. They represented a good portion of the portable wealth of a castle, and it fell to the steward to hand the utensils out prior to each meal and collect and count them afterward.

James motioned his younger daughter forward. "I should not be long," he assured Alessandra. "In the meantime, Melissant can introduce you." Agnes on his arm, he disappeared among the throng.

"Clever," Melissant said, eyeing the hem of her sister's gown. "Though I would never be brave enough to do it myself."

"Bravery had naught to do with it," Alessandra said. "It is a matter of function."

"You need not explain it to me. Now come, there are scores to introduce you to ere the call to feast."

Alessandra leaned near. "And Lucien?"

Melissant grinned. "As was my message, he is here. Though I have yet to lay eyes upon him, I am told he has created a stir." At Alessandra's frown, she added, "Turning up alive when all thought him dead."

Having to content herself with that, Alessandra allowed herself to be led through a whirlwind of introductions. To her further discomfort, she was followed and watched closely by a man wearing the lavish robes of one who held high office in the Church.

"Who is that?" she asked after Melissant extricated them from a group of giggling young women.

Melissant followed her gaze. "Bishop Armis."

"There is only one of him?"

"Thank the heavens. Why do you ask?"

"He seems everywhere at once."

"Ah, I imagine the good bishop wishes to be certain you share the Holy Church's beliefs, not those of Islam."

What must he think of me clothed and made up as I am? Alessandra wondered. "And if I were of that faith?"

Melissant's mouth flattened. "Do not even think such thoughts, Alessandra. Did your mother never tell you the Church is tolerant of only one religion—theirs?"

Alessandra was surprised by her vehemence. True, Sabine had spoken of the Church's staunch position, but she had never detailed the consequences of holding conflicting religious beliefs. "I do not understand."

Melissant steered Alessandra away from the bishop. "I shall explain later."

A man who looked to be a male rendering of Agnes, though some years older and sporting a good-natured demeanor, appeared before them. His stare engulfing Alessandra, he said, "I would not have believed it had I not seen it with my own eyes."

In spite of his advanced years, he was handsome. Short, liberally peppered hair waved back from a face that captured the elements of masculinity without sacrificing beauty. The trim beard tracing his jaw was silver gray, his mustache raised with a smile.

"Uncle Gavin." Melissant stepped forward and kissed his cheek.

He slid his gaze from Alessandra to his niece. "You have grown since last I was at Corburry." He ruffled her hair as if she were a pet.

"Did you visit more often, you would not even notice."

"True, but then I would have to endure your mother's matchmaking."

Melissant giggled. "It would be good for a laugh, would it not?"

"At my expense."

"How are Grandmother and Grandfather?"

He shrugged. "Well, I would guess. They have been in London at court for over a month now."

"Stuffy," Melissant said, then asked, "Does Mother know you are here?"

"I have just come from her."

"I am sure she was surprised to see you since you so dislike these events." Melissant turned back to Alessandra. "As you know, this is my half sister, Lady Alessandra."

"Catherine's daughter." He stepped from his niece's side and caught up Alessandra's hand. "You are even lovelier than your mother." He brushed his lips across the backs of her fingers.

He would have known her, of course, Catherine having been raised in his home following the death of her parents.

Gavin released her hand. "So, what did she tell you of me?"

Alessandra searched her memory for mention of Agnes's brother, with apology said, "I fear I do not recall."

He shrugged. "Ah, well, as I was several years older than she and not often around due to my knighthood training, it does not surprise she would have forgotten me."

"I—"

"Pray, excuse me." He peered past her. "There is an old friend with whom I must speak." He inclined his head and stepped away.

"Let us hope it is a lady friend he seeks," Melissant said.

"He is not wed?"

"He is not and has never been."

"But surely he is most eligible?"

Melissant pursed her lips. "Mother said he loved once and lost to another, and he waits to find such love again."

Alessandra was struck with sorrow, for Gavin as well as herself. Would she also wander the rest of her days in search of the love Lucien denied her? Would she grow old never knowing the happiness of a love returned?

"Do not worry over him. Uncle Gavin is content with his lot." Taking Alessandra's arm, Melissant pulled her through the crowd, a moment later halted.

There, two strides distant, stood Lucien.

Alessandra's heart lurched. Such fine clothes he wore, and so well groomed was he that he hardly seemed the man who had brought her out of Algiers. But it was he, the same brilliant eyes that had once shone with desire now as flat and condemning as when she had revealed her parentage.

As he scrutinized her more thoroughly than Bishop Armis had done, his eyes also lit with disapproval. On the ship, he had warned her about the use of kohl and forbidden her to stitch up her hem, saying it was not English. She knew that now.

Pressing a smile to her lips, she pulled free of Melissant and stepped forward. However, before she could greet him, the call to feast came.

The press of men and women eager to take their places at the well-laid tables forced Alessandra back, and she bumped into her sister.

"'Twas him, was it not?" Melissant said with awe.

Alessandra turned to her. "Aye, but where did he go?"

"Likely to his table, as we should be doing."

Alessandra's discomfort doubled upon finding herself seated beside the bishop. When he stood and said grace, she knew without raising her bowed head that he watched her. When she answered a question put to her by the knight on her other side, she sensed the man attended to their words. Then there was Lucien.

A lady on either side of him, he sat below the dais at a side table—likely the first time a De Gautier had dined with a Breville, Alessandra mused. But she corrected herself upon recalling that, in his youth, he had been James's prisoner.

Turning her attention from Lucien, she marveled as she often did over the experience of dining among men. Most were without manners, including her father. They overfilled their mouths, spoke before swallowing, wiped dribbled chins on sleeves, and seemed more likely to loose a belch than suppress it. For this, she guessed women of the harem dined separate from men. Still, she preferred dining amongst them, for during meals that always took too long to draw to a close, they were a good diversion—at least, for a while.

Boredom descending, Alessandra turned to Sir Rexalt and once more engaged him in conversation. The man was talkative and inclined to bouts of laughter, and he often touched her hand and arm. Though the latter seemed innocent enough, it unsettled her.

When her father stood between courses to toast Lucien's return to the living, Alessandra glanced at the man she struggled to shake from her thoughts—and met eyes brimming with reproach.

"I welcome home to England," James bellowed, "he who has delivered unto me my daughter born of my dear, departed Lady Catherine—Lucien de Gautier." He raised his goblet. "To everlasting peace and the union of our families."

Lucien remained seated while the other men in the hall rose—all but two seated near Lucien.

Relations? Alessandra wondered. Though smaller in stature, the features of the younger one were too similar for him not to be Lucien's brother. And the other was surely the middle brother, Vincent. Lucien had said he was handsome—the cause of two broken betrothals—and Melissant had concurred, telling that he was beautiful. He was.

She returned her gaze to Lucien. Although a half smile turned his mouth, she felt the anger beneath the facade.

In unison, goblets were carried to a hundred pairs of lips. However, few found their mark as Lucien surged upright.

"To the return of my lands!" He raised his vessel high. "And then peace." Eyes fixed on James, he took a long draught.

Silence enveloped the hall, the tension Lucien had brought to it increasing tenfold until James lightened it with forced laughter.

"Do you hope to escape marriage, young Lucien, the return of lands that now belong to me will cost you much coin."

Coin that all knew the De Gautiers lacked due to Vincent's gambling.

Lucien's smile broadened. "Better coin than a Breville," he said.

Gasps sounded around the hall, mostly from women who cast pitying looks in Melissant's direction.

Alessandra swept her gaze to her sister who appeared more like a girl than the young woman she had earlier. Coloring prettily, she sat erect beside her brother, mouth trembling, moist eyes on the giant of a man who had insulted her.

Anger at Lucien's callousness brought Alessandra to her feet. "A shared sentiment," she called.

Lucien shifted his cool gaze to her. "Is it? Then what of you, Lady Alessandra? Would you also find such a match objectionable?"

"Indeed." Though the word did not reflect what was in her heart, she threw it at the arrogant man who had forgotten her in the weeks gone by.

His jaw shifted, eyes narrowed.

Had the speculation about their relationship been spoken aloud, it could not have been more tangible.

"We shall settle this in the lists tomorrow," James said.

Lucien looked to his host. "Do you think you are up to it, old man?"

James's mouth pinched white. "I will be there. Will you?"

Lucien inclined his head. "'Tis my only reason for attending the tourney."

After a long moment, James raised his glass-bottomed tankard, quaffed his drink, and sat.

The others followed suit.

It took quantities more wine and ale before the life of the banquet returned. Regardless, throughout the festivities that followed—the music of jongleurs, songs of minstrels, and dancing—a pall hung over Alessandra.

From the shadows of an alcove, she watched an actor perform a mime and wondered if the morrow would bring bloodshed.

She searched out Lucien who was flanked by his brothers on the far end of the hall. Though he lounged against a wall, gaze fixed on the mime, Alessandra knew he was less interested in the performance than she.

Then, as if aware of her regard, he looked her way.

She stepped deeper into the shadows and hugged her arms about her. Who would be the victor on the morrow? A father she was growing to love, or the man who possessed her heart?

31

"I DO NOT SEE Lucien's," Alessandra whispered.

Melissant peered over the ladies crowded before the canopied table that displayed the contenders' banners and crested helms. "There." She pointed to the far end of the table where the De Gautier red and gold fluttered in the morning breeze.

Alessandra nodded. "I see it, but why is his last?"

"You would ask that after what happened yestereve?"

Then this was the penalty James levied against Lucien.

"Oh, look!" Melissant pointed again. "Sir Simeon's helm is being removed."

Excitement rippled through the women as they attempted to guess what had warranted the removal of the intricately embossed helm.

"I do not understand," Alessandra said.

"It means a lady has accused him of wrongdoing. Thus, he is banished from the lists."

"He will not be allowed to compete?"

"Only to watch, though such disgrace will likely keep him from the tournament altogether."

Alessandra briefly considered this as a means to prevent Lucien and James from publicly carrying out their private battle, then sighed. That would only fuel Lucien's anger. If he did not battle with the blunt-tipped, dull-edged weapons of tournament, he would likely battle with those that let blood.

Pushing her way between two older ladies, Melissant gained for herself and Alessandra a place before the helms. "Are they not marvelous?" she exclaimed.

While she chattered over the decorated helms, Alessandra craned her neck to better see the one Lucien would don. Directly beneath his banner, several helms rested on the table, red and gold plumes projected over their crowns.

As the ladies began to drift toward the pavilions to watch the opening ceremony, Alessandra took the opportunity to draw nearer. Hitching up skirts that skimmed the ground—after her reception last eve, she had left their hems be and her cosmetics in their pots—she advanced on the De Gautier panoply.

She reached to the helm that was surely Lucien's and discovered the metal was warm. Sun, she realized, amazed she had not noticed it had come out. Peering over her shoulder, she saw the clouds had begun to disperse.

She smiled. At last, evidence of England's earthliness.

"He will defeat your father, you know."

Alessandra looked around, and her gaze clashed with heavily lashed blue eyes. Vincent de Gautier.

"You speak to me?" she asked, thankful he stood on the opposite side of the table.

"I do."

"Why?"

Vincent's lower lip dropped, enlarging his white smile. "Curiosity. My brother is much changed from the man who left for France. Now I am beginning to understand why."

Did he imply she was responsible? Farfetched. If she had touched Lucien's life in any way, it was only briefly, as proven these past weeks by his silence and last night his contempt.

"Methinks you ought to look elsewhere for answers," she said. "Namely, the war he fought on French soil and the slavery he was pressed into. Therein lies your answer, Sir Vincent."

His smile slipped. "'Twas not what I referred to. That side of him I understand."

"I do not believe you do. Indeed, I doubt there are many who understand that side of him."

Melissant edged near Alessandra. "Ah, 'tis you, Sir Vincent," she drawled.

"My lady." He inclined his head.

Her mouth compressed into a lipless line.

Vincent must have found something amusing about her behavior, for his smile returned. "I take your leave," he said and pivoted away.

"Knave," Melissant muttered. "That I do not have to wed that whoremonger is evidence enough of God."

"Now who speaks heresy?" Alessandra teased.

Melissant crinkled her nose. "'Tis true. He would have made an unsatisfactory husband."

Though she had never expounded on the matter, it had remained an item of interest for Alessandra. "Surely you find him attractive?"

Melissant pulled the golden plume atop Lucien's helm through her fingers. "Who would not? Unfortunately, Vincent is neither responsible, nor faithful, his only gift a face over which women make themselves fools. God willing, I shall wed a man who wisely guards his coin and shares only my bed."

Though the Christian law of one man to one woman seemed a wonderful institution, Alessandra had learned it was not uncommon for married Englishmen to bed other women. And yet they condemned the practice of polygamy. Hypocrites.

"You would do poorly in a harem," she said, despite Melissant's enthusiasm for tales of that exotic place.

Melissant grinned. "Then in England I must remain."

"Jousters make ready!" called a herald as he wound his way through the avenues of tents, rousing the knights within.

Linking an arm through Alessandra's, Melissant turned them toward the pavilions.

"A moment," Alessandra said. She turned back to Lucien's helm and quickly traced the sign of the cross above his visor's eye slit. "The Lord protect you," she whispered and swung back to Melissant.

"What did you do?" her sister asked.

Alessandra shook her head and started toward the pavilions.

"You are an odd one," Melissant said, drawing alongside her.

"Verily."

Shortly, Melissant groaned. "We are late." She jutted her chin toward the pavilions that were nearly filled to capacity. "Mother will be displeased."

Though Alessandra did not say it, she was disappointed when they did not join the other ladies. Instead, they were seated in the center pavilion reserved for the Breville family and visiting dignitaries. And that included Bishop Armis whose seat provided him a full view of Alessandra. Beside him sat Agnes, smile false, eyes hawking Alessandra's every move.

Once the mass was sung, the parade commenced.

The display was like nothing Alessandra had seen. As host of the tournament, her father came first. Resplendent in Breville blue, he led four camp marshals into the lists, all senior knights chosen to oversee the contest. They were followed by heralds who cried encouragement to the combatants.

The participating knights, riding two by two, outfitted in burnished armor and long spurs, each preceded by a banner bearer, sat atop warhorses. Though the destriers of the lesser knights were modestly arrayed, several wore complete head-and-neck armor, elaborately worked muzzles and stirrups, double reins, and richly decorated coverings that Melissant called trappers.

As the first of the knights completed the circuit of the tilt—a wooden barrier erected to separate jousters and prevent their horses from colliding—and passed by the pavilions, he began to sing. The melody was taken up by the other knights and ladies in the pavilions, causing the lists to quake.

Then something more peculiar happened. Married and unmarried ladies began removing items of clothing—stockings, hair ribbons, gloves, girdles, even sleeves torn from their gowns.

Hoping for an explanation, Alessandra turned to Melissant, but her sister was bent over and in the process of removing her stockings.

Alessandra looked back at the knights. As they pranced their horses before the pavilions, ladies leaned forward and tied their castoffs to the tips of proffered lances. Even dignified Agnes joined in.

What is the meaning of this? Alessandra wondered. *And where is Lucien?*

She stretched her neck to see past the contestants who waited to enter the lists, but could not pick him from among the armored knights.

"Be mindful where you place your favor," Melissant said, "else you may find yourself pursued by one you would rather not."

"Is that what the ladies are doing?" Alessandra asked as she watched Melissant's Uncle Gavin accept an array of items. "Showing favor?"

"Aye, and so shall I." Melissant held up her stockings.

"To whom will you give them?"

Melissant fluttered her lashes. "Methinks the youngest De Gautier quite fair."

"Jervais? He also competes?"

"Of course."

"And Vincent?"

Melissant shrugged. "He is likely too busy consorting with joy women to prove himself a man."

"Joy women?"

"See yon woman with her skirts hiked high?" She pointed toward the tents of competing knights, then put her mouth near Alessandra's ear. "For but a coin, she will give him what a lady would never allow."

"Truly?"

"Would I play you false?" Melissant sat back in her chair. "Now tell me which knight you intend to favor. Perhaps Lucien de Gautier?"

"Never," Alessandra blurted.

"Father says that is a word one should *never* use."

Alessandra folded her hands in her lap. "Methinks Lucien would rather dangle the stocking of a joy woman from his lance than that of a Breville."

"Well, you must choose someone." Melissant cogitated, then said, "Sir Rexalt."

Alessandra recalled the good-natured knight who had dined beside her during the banquet yestereve. Though she was not attracted to him, he had been amiable and pleasing to the eye. "Aye," she said, "Sir Rexalt it shall be."

"The ribbon in your hair will do nicely."

Alessandra fingered it. "Not my sleeve?"

"Only if you wish to ruin your gown. And then the poor knight will think you are most besotted."

As Alessandra began to unbraid her hair through which she had woven the red ribbon, Melissant jumped to her feet and waved her stockings. "Come hither, Sir John!"

Smiling broadly, the knight led his horse in a caper as he neared the pavilion.

"What of Sir Jervais?" Alessandra asked.

Melissant looked over her shoulder. "I have two stockings, have I not?" Then she tied one of her favors to the lance Sir John leveled at her.

"Much honored, Lady," he said and urged his horse onward.

Blushing prettily, Melissant sank into her chair.

When next Alessandra looked up, she glimpsed the end of the procession, which surely numbered in excess of sixty knights. Waiting to enter the lists, Lucien sat atop an enormous destrier draped with an emblazoned trapper. Unlike its rider, the animal wore no armor.

Visor raised, Lucien peered across the lists, though never did his eyes rest upon the center pavilion where Alessandra sat.

Her indignation flared that he did not so much as acknowledge her, that he forgot all they had shared in favor of his godforsaken revenge.

"I do not believe it," Melissant said.

"What?" Alessandra asked.

She pointed toward Lucien. "Sir Vincent also competes."

Alessandra had been too intent on Lucien to notice his brothers bringing up the rear of the procession. Side by side, Vincent and Jervais waited for their turn to enter the lists. "Perhaps you have judged Vincent too harshly," she suggested.

Melissant harrumphed. "I do not think so."

Not for the first time, Alessandra wondered if she also judged wrongly. Lucien was entitled to his anger. After all, when he had left England, he had been heir to prosperous lands, only to return to an estate far diminished by the actions of his brother and James Breville. She only wished he would not direct his anger at her.

His banner bearer going before him, Lucien angled his lance upright and spurred his horse forward. Vincent and Jervais followed.

Though it was by no means an esteemed position to be the last to parade the lists, many of the ladies grew more enthusiastic with the De Gautiers' arrival.

"I am told they are fierce fighters," Melissant said. "Lucien and Jervais, that is. Ere he left for France, Lucien was a favorite among the ladies."

Jealousy warmed Alessandra. "You have never witnessed their skill yourself?"

"Nay, 'tis rare the Brevilles and De Gautiers come together any-where other than on a battlefield."

Until now. Of course, Lucien might well turn the lists into his own private battlefield.

So caught up was Alessandra in watching Lucien that Sir Rexalt would have passed by unnoticed had Melissant not elbowed her.

Gripping the ribbon, she stood and beckoned to him.

His seemingly perpetual smile widened. "Lady Alessandra." He lowered his lance. "I am grateful for your kind regard."

Head bent to the task of securing the ribbon between the sleeve and girdle of two other ladies, Alessandra sensed Lucien's gaze. Guilt crept over her, but she reminded herself that as he did not want her favor, he had no right to care whom she bestowed it upon.

Sir Rexalt hoisted his lance, waved it jubilantly, and urged his destrier forward.

Alessandra looked to Lucien who had just completed his parade at the tilt, and their eyes met. Was the anger in his simply that, or jealousy, too?

As she sank into her seat, Lucien rode to the far pavilion and lowered his lance for the favors women clamored to bestow. Like brightly colored streamers, more than a half-dozen articles adorned it when he advanced to the center pavilion and halted before Alessandra. However, he did not lower his lance, even when the lady beside Agnes waved him to her.

The din of the pavilions lapsed into murmurs, and Alessandra realized she was onstage as she stared at Lucien. In spite of the scar tracing his cheekbone, the hard planes of his face, and a mouth that offered no hint of a smile, he appeared a most attractive man.

Thinking that if he would only give her some encouragement she would gladly tear both sleeves from her gown, she offered a tentative smile.

He urged his destrier past and gained several more favors before exiting the lists.

Jervais and Vincent also paused before the center pavilion.

Ignoring the latter, Melissant tied her second stocking to the youngest De Gautier's lance.

Though Vincent certainly had no need of more favors, he ill disguised his disappointment at being snubbed.

"Did you see Mother?" Melissant whispered as the lists cleared. "I thought she might snatch my stocking off Jervais's lance."

Alessandra frowned. "She does not like him?"

"She does not know him."

"Then?"

"He is not the heir, and only an heir will satisfy her."

And Lucien was the De Gautier heir. Yet he had made it clear that not even for the return of his lands would he wed a Breville.

A herald crying the commencement of the contests started the clamor anew. "Come hither he who wishes to do battle!"

Trumpets blared, and favors that had escaped being bestowed upon knights were scattered to the sanded ground.

With the appearance of the two champions chosen to joust first, there was a collective gasp.

As Alessandra watched Lucien and James being led upon their destriers by their squires to opposite ends of the lists, it seemed her heart stopped beating. Doubtless, it was a fitting opening to the tournament for these two adversaries to face off after the events of yestereve, but it boded ill.

Facing each other, Lucien and James lowered their visors and made ready for the confrontation.

When the squires moved away, the chief marshal called, "In the name of God and King Henry, do battle!"

All in the pavilions surged to their feet and shouted when the knights and their destriers came to life. As they raced down the lists toward each other, the ground trembled, sand sprayed, and all Alessandra could do was join her hands in prayer.

Bent low over their saddles, Lucien and James raised their shields and leveled their lances at one another. A moment later, the splintering of wood sounded like the crack of thunder.

Alessandra clapped her hands over her ears and watched wide-eyed as the destriers struggled to regain their balance, both riders brandished broken lances and scraped shields, and the spectators shouted with excitement.

Though Melissant had described the contest of the joust, Alessandra had not expected such a horrific, primitive display.

Lucien and James turned their destriers and cantered back to position where they were met by their squires who handed them new lances.

Once again, they rushed at each other and met the same fate, both sustaining broken lances and battered shields. And again—with the same result. Finally, each having broken three lances, it should have been called a draw, but the contestants called for fresh lances and rode a fourth time.

The moment before they met, James swerved just enough to cause him to miss his mark and to take the impact of Lucien's lance across his shield. Propelled out of the saddle, he slammed to the ground and narrowly escaped his destrier's hooves.

Melissant's shriek was muted by the roar of the spectators as James struggled to his feet.

Dear Lord, Alessandra prayed, *let it be done that I might wander the garden. That I might put my nose in a boring book. Anything but watch grown men behave as animals.*

Melissant turned to her. "Now Father must pay De Gautier a ransom for his horse and armor."

"Whatever for?"

"'Tis the price of the victor."

A commotion in the lists returned Alessandra's and Melissant's attention to it. Armor dulled by dust and the scratch of sand, James thrust his sword toward Lucien. A challenge?

Alessandra stepped alongside her sister. "Is it not done?"

Around the thumbnail she chewed, Melissant said, "It seems not."

Lucien slid his visor back. "First, the ransom," he shouted.

Those in the pavilions quieted to await James's response.

"Name it!" his voice rang from the depths of his helm.

"De Gautier lands."

James shoved his visor back. "You know the price. Coin will not buy them back."

Hearing his blood thrum in his ears, Lucien glanced at Alessandra. "Nor Breville wife," he said, then silently cursed her for the sun in her hair that reminded him of gentler moments and emotions he had never thought to feel, that stirred jealousy at the remembrance of her awarding her favor to Sir Rexalt.

"'Tis your last insult," James shouted, sword glinting in the sun. "Come down from your horse, De Gautier!"

Dancing his destrier sideways, Lucien said, "For a price."

James laughed. "The lands are mine. Only under my terms will they be restored to you."

"And only under my terms will I enter swordplay with you, old man. And here they are—should I be victorious, you agree to sell the De Gautier lands to me for the price you paid. Should I lose…" He glanced at the pavilions. "…I will agree to your peace through marriage."

Those last words were bitter, but they were only words, he assured himself. He had spent these past weeks in merciless training for this confrontation, and if his sword arm remained as true as he had honed it, he need not worry over the humiliation of being forced to wed in order to regain his lands. Certes, he would better Breville, and however many others it took to raise the money.

Though Breville obviously burned to test his skill against Lucien's he lowered his sword. "Naught, then."

Lucien smiled. "You need not fear my sword, Lord Breville." He drew the weapon from its sheath. "As you can see, 'tis dull-edged for the tourney and will draw little blood. Too, I will be gentle with you."

James's sword swept the air again. "I fear no man's sword," he shouted, the visible portion of his face flushed.

Drawing his quarry in, Lucien resheathed his sword. "You fear mine, else you would trust yours to keep my lands. Perhaps your sword arm has grown infirm with age?"

James's struggle was short-lived. He hurled his sword to the sand, bellowed, "Bring me a blade that will pierce this knave!"

Lucien's blood surged. "My terms, Breville?"

"Aye, and your blood!"

Lucien called for his own cutting sword and, amid shouts from the goading crowd, dismounted and slapped his destrier's rump. It was time to take back his lands.

The contents of her belly churning, throat dry, Alessandra looked to Melissant. "True weapons are not permitted," she repeated what she had been told.

Melissant jerked her chin. "'Tis not looked kindly upon by the Church."

Both turned to Bishop Armis.

He appeared unconcerned by the challenge being taken up. In fact, he seemed eager where he leaned forward in his chair, staring at the combatants with the same intensity a worldly man might show a comely wench.

Even more obvious was Agnes, her eager smile, sparkling eyes, and shifting carriage evidencing she was not averse to a contest that might see one or both men wounded, perhaps dead.

It appalled Alessandra, this bloodlust echoed by men and ladies alike.

"What say we dispense with armor?" James said. "All but the breastplate."

Lucien accepted the honed sword his squire handed him, motioned for the young man to remain. Unhurriedly, he peered down one edge of the blade, twisted his wrist, peered down the other. "We may dispense with armor altogether if you like," he finally answered.

James hesitated, then said, "For the love of the ladies, the breastplate remains."

"As you will."

Immediately, the squires began the process of removing the armor piece by piece.

Alessandra looked to the bishop again, but still he did not move. Thinking to appeal to him, she started to step around Melissant, but her sister pulled her back.

"What are you doing, Alessandra?"

"I would speak with the bishop. Surely he cannot allow this to go forward."

Melissant shook her head. "He, more than any, enjoys such sport. You will only anger him if you interfere."

"But if I do not, who will?"

"None. These contests are a part of England. You cannot change that."

Alessandra looked back at the lists. The squires and varlets were carrying away the armor. All that remained were the breastplates and arming doublets to which they were attached.

"Fools," she hissed.

The chief marshal called for the contestants to take position, then cried, "Be worthy of your ancestry. Do battle!"

32

T HE CLASH BETWEEN Lucien and James was an unspeakable thing to witness. Hugging her arms about her, Alessandra forced herself to watch, tensing with each meeting of steel on steel.

Though Lucien had the advantage of height, James appeared a good match, his greater experience surely making up for the ten inches he lacked.

Lucien was the first to draw blood, his blade piercing James's mailed sleeve and causing the links to color red.

Amid the roar of approval, James cursed, retreated, raised his shield, and lunged again. "Get your fill, De Gautier," he yelled, "for that is all you will ever have of a Breville."

Lucien landed another blow, but in denting his opponent's breastplate, left himself open.

James seized the moment, swung, and slashed through Lucien's unprotected thigh.

Blood discolored Lucien's chausses, but he continued to hack and slice. His sword tip caught his opponent's jaw, cut downward, and snagged the edge of James's shield and sent it flying.

Thus, James's fate was questionable, but he pressed on and was granted a swipe at Lucien's arm. More blood, alternately Lucien's and James's.

The crowd became more frenzied, their cheers and excited voices closing in on Alessandra until she could hardly breathe. Teeth clenched, her mind reeled with every prayer she had ever memorized, while tears slid down her cheeks.

When the shifting battleground moved in front of the center pavilion, she stepped back, but not before her father's blood flecked her and the others in the front row.

Alessandra gaped at the pattern of red across her bodice, cried, "No more!" and pushed past Melissant who also appeared horrified to find herself marked by battle.

"You must stop this!" Alessandra entreated the bishop. "Now!"

He swept a hand before him. "You block my view, child."

"Your view? Is it not the edict of the Church that only weapons of peace be used at tournaments?"

Nostrils flaring, he said, "Remove yourself from my presence."

Alessandra did not. Thus, Agnes stood, snatched her arm, and jerked her aside. "'Tis the way of men" she hissed. "Now take your seat or I will have you returned to the keep."

"But it is wrong! A tournament—"

Agnes shook her. "'Tis no longer a tournament. A vendetta is what it is, and one that ought to have been settled long ago."

Alessandra broke free. "Not this way. Not with blood."

"Aye, with blood, you little fool. As much blood as it takes to bring the De Gautier dog to heel."

Alessandra stilled. Stared. Though her mother had said England was where her daughter belonged, it seemed no better than Algiers. Worse. This woman was James's wife, yet it mattered not that he was injured or doing injury to another—the De Gautier dog as she had called Lucien.

"You are a pitiful excuse for a Christian," Alessandra said, fully aware her voice carried. Then she met the bishop's imperious gaze. "As are you."

She heard the crack of flesh on flesh before she felt the burn. Dazed, she touched her cheek where Agnes had slapped her, looked to the woman.

Agnes's expression was reminiscent of another, one who had shown little emotion in the face of Sabine's death. One whose eyes had challenged Alessandra to prove her wrongdoing. One who would have been more content had it been Alessandra whose veins coursed with poison.

She blinked to dispel the face of the woman who could not possibly stand before her, but it persisted, dragging her back to a time she had tried to convince herself was past.

With a cry, she fell upon the one who had murdered her mother—who, this time, would pay.

A chair collapsed beneath the force of their combined weight, and they crashed to the floor of the pavilion. As the commotion around them rose, Alessandra fit her hands around Leila's neck. Against her fingers she felt straining muscles; her palms, the vibrations of a scream; her thumbs, the swift flow of blood that ought not to flow. But it was not Leila's face that stared in horror at her. It was Agnes's.

Alessandra's hands slackened, and in the next instant she was gripped beneath the arms and lifted.

Feeling as if jerked from a terrible dream, she looked over her shoulder into Lucien's beautiful eyes.

How had he come to be here? What of the contest with her father?

She turned to him. "I thought…Leila…" She shook her head, then pressed her face against the heat of his armor.

His arms came around her, and it was the most wonderful thing she had felt in weeks. She heard her father's voice, Agnes's shrieks, the bishop's condemnation, and the chatter of the crowd. But she refused to give up Lucien, holding tight to him and praying he would not reject her.

"Quiet, woman!" James shouted.

Agnes finished her accusation, claiming Alessandra had attacked her without cause, then fell silent as the bishop asserted that the *infidel* had insulted Agnes and himself and been corrected with a slap that in no way made recompense for what had been spoken against them.

"Lord Bishop, I assure you my daughter is a Christian," James said in a strained voice that reflected veneration and humility. "Her mother raised her in our faith. 'Tis simply a matter of England and its ways being foreign to Alessandra. But she will learn. I implore you, accept my apologies for her conduct."

Alessandra lifted her head to protest her father's apology, but Lucien pressed it down and hissed, "Be silent."

"I do not believe she is without taint of the infidel," the bishop said. "Methinks she ought to be questioned to determine the truth."

Alessandra felt Lucien tense further.

"I attest to her purity of heart, Lord Bishop," James said. "Each morning, she attends mass and offers prayers to our Lord. She knows the Bible and quotes scriptures. She—"

"Yet she shows her body like a trollop, lines her eyes with the black of the devil, speaks out of turn, shows no respect for the clergy or her elders, and has just attacked your good wife."

"Lord Bishop, do you speak of the gown she wore yestereve, it was improperly hemmed. By the time it was discovered, it was too late to correct. As for the cosmetics, she has been told it is improper and does not wear any this day. The rest she will learn."

The bishop snorted. "You excuse her sin as trivial, yet even now she wantonly clings to a man not her husband."

"She is frightened, Lord Bishop. This is her first tourney, and surely a shock to one gently raised."

"You do not understand the gravity of the situation, Breville. Your daughter could be tried as a heretic. She—"

"No doubt," Lucien said, "you are also shocked to see blood shed in a manner condemned by the Church, my Lord Bishop. Verily, it is the reason you did not protest, is it not?"

What was clearly a threat caused the bishop to sputter. "But she...I..."

"No harm has been done," Lucien concluded. "Though methinks it best that Lady Alessandra attend no more contests."

"Aye, for the best," James agreed.

After some moments, the bishop begrudged, "Very well. This matter is concluded."

"What of the attack upon my person?" Agnes cried. "Look at my throat. I will be bruised—"

Whatever James hissed, it silenced her.

Lucien turned Alessandra toward the steps and, an arm around her waist, aided her descent from the pavilion. But as they started toward the castle, James stepped into their path.

"I will take my daughter."

Alessandra lifted her gaze up her father's battered figure and face. No longer the warrior provoked to foolish rage, he looked weary and gaunt. Old.

Wordlessly, Lucien guided her around James and away from the lists.

"Did you not hear me, De Gautier?"

Lucien halted, looked over his shoulder. "I hear well, Breville. Do you?"

From the lists came the booming voice of the chief marshal as he announced the points for each of the contestants. Twice he named Lucien the victor—once in the joust, once in foot combat.

Alessandra felt dirtied. Lucien had won, gaining the ability to purchase his lands from her father, but it seemed such an unholy thing.

"The ransom for your horse and armor will be high, Breville," Lucien said, then continued forward and across the drawbridge.

"As expected," James said, following, "but it will not be near enough to buy back your lands."

The muscles of the arm around Alessandra tightened. "Be assured that by the end of this tourney, I will have amassed enough to have much—if not all—of it back."

"Not even you have the endurance to challenge enough comers to raise that much," James retorted.

Lucien said naught, and the remainder of the walk to Alessandra's chamber was covered in silence.

Once there, she sank down on the mattress, drew her knees to her chest, and peered through narrowed lids at the two men who stood over her.

It was not only her father who bore the marks of battle. Lucien's breastplate was dented, the mail of his arming doublet in disrepair, and the stain of blood was abundant.

She shivered.

James drew the coverlet over her. "Are you ill, Alessa?"

"She is in shock," Lucien said.

James touched her cheek. "Aye?"

"I am fine," she whispered.

"Keep her away from the tournament," Lucien said and pivoted.

"Halt!" James called.

Lucien paused.

"I have not thanked you for intervening with the bishop," her father said. "Truly, I am grateful."

"I did it for her, not you."

"This I know. Thus, I would encourage you to wed my daughter that there be no more bloodshed. "

Mouth compressed, Lucien said, "'Tis Alessandra you offer?"

She felt as if struck by a bolt of the blue lightning that often preceded rain in England. Would Lucien truly consider a match with her?

"Though I do not wish to relinquish her," James said, "if it keeps the peace between us, I shall give you her hand in marriage."

Alessandra held her breath.

"Nay, Breville. I would rather spill blood than wed a Breville to gain back what was stolen from me." He turned and strode from the room.

Alessandra stared at the empty doorway, keenly felt Melissant's humiliation of yestereve, then the longing to run after Lucien and repay him with every vile word—Arabic and English—to which she could set her tongue. Instead, she hugged the coverlet tighter.

"You love him," her father said.

She met his gaze where he bent near. How had he guessed? Did it show upon her face?

Awash in humiliation, she sought another topic. "Why do you fear the bishop?"

Unmindful of soiling the bedclothes, James lowered to the mattress edge. "Very well, we will not speak of Lucien and you, but do not think you fool me, Catherine's daughter."

"What of the bishop?" she persisted.

Worry lined his brow. "If he determines you are a heretic—"

"I am a Christian. More than he!"

"It does not matter. Many Christians whose only crime was in being different have suffered persecution, have even been put to death. You must suppress those things Arabic if you are to assuage his suspicions."

"It is not fair."

"It is not, but neither is Bishop Armis. He is a powerful man of the Church and easily inflamed."

Feeling her stubborn streak surface, knowing it best to keep it hidden, she lowered her eyes. "I will try to suppress my upbringing, but it will not be easy."

Though anxious to return to the lists where the future of the De Gautier lands lay, Lucien paused in the great hall that was silent but for servants who made it ready for the next meal.

He feared for Alessandra, and she gave him good cause. Still, there was some good to be found in the attack upon Lady Agnes that had so roused the bishop. No longer would Alessandra witness the battles in the lists, which was as Lucien wished it, for he would not have her see the animal he must become these next days to gain his lands.

Recalling James's taunt, he ground his jaws. *Not even you have the endurance to challenge enough comers to raise that much coin.*

The same might have been said for the amount of soul given to survive the ordeal of slaving a galley. But Lucien had survived, and his scarred body was testament to it. The question was, had he enough soul left to endure the quest to retrieve all his lands? If so, at the end of it, might he find himself soulless?

Vowing he did have enough soul and it would be intact, hoping James Breville would not be swayed from keeping his daughter away from the tournament, Lucien braced his mind and body for the day ahead.

33

THE TALK WAS of Lucien's triumphs that evening. Though conspicuously absent from the banquet, his deeds filled the mouths of men and women. Even those who had lost to him regaled listeners with accounts of the blows they had traded during jousting and foot combat and the ransom paid for their horse and armor.

Sitting alongside Agnes's brother, Gavin, Alessandra tried not to think of Lucien and the further injuries he must have sustained. Tried but failed, though over and again she told herself she did not care what became of him and he was undeserving of her concern. All lies.

Averting her thoughts, she returned to swinging her foot beneath overly long skirts for which she had finally found a use. The soft peal of bells fastened about her ankle that were hidden beneath her hem eased her anxiety and gave her something to smile about each time they caused someone to glance her way.

It was rebellious, and the bishop would disapprove if he learned whence the sound issued, but the satisfaction of resisting some things English seemed worth it.

"You will be found out," Sir Gavin spoke near her ear.

She met his gaze. "Whatever are you talking about?"

He grinned. "I may be mistaken, but methinks I hear the sound of bells coming from 'neath your skirts."

"Aye, Sir Knight, you are mistaken." She swung her foot more vigorously.

His grin softened into a charming smile. "Forgive me. It just seems something your mother might have done."

She stilled. "Tell me what she was like as a girl."

"Ah, now 'tis silent." He tilted an ear to the air. "Methinks the wearer of bells has departed the hall."

Alessandra gave her foot a shake. "She is still here—merely curious."

Pushing aside his food, he began to relate Catherine's sorrow when she had first come to live with his family. Her grief for her parents was not short-lived, but eventually she had settled in and light had returned to her eyes. In relating her antics and the rivalry between her and his sister, he became animated. He chuckled, grimaced, and became teary-eyed when he spoke of the last time he had seen her—a few months following her marriage to James.

"Though she was my cousin, I considered her a sister," he said. "Indeed, methinks I was closer to her than my own sister."

Alessandra smiled. "Thank you for telling me. It is easier knowing my mother had you for a friend."

"Though she did not speak of me, apparently," he murmured, and she glimpsed hurt in his eyes.

Alessandra touched his arm. "I am certain she thought of you often. It is just that when she spoke of England, it was usually as my father's wife. Rarely did she mention her childhood."

Gavin leaned back in his chair. "Now you must tell me of the Catherine who mothered you."

As she opened her mouth to comply, meal's end was called.

"Later," Gavin said and stood.

Assisted by his hand beneath her elbow, Alessandra rose. "I am indebted, Sir Gavin. You have been very kind."

He snapped a bow, then strode to the hearth where the senior knights had gathered.

Left on her own, Alessandra turned to search out Melissant and found a red-faced Agnes before her.

"You will remove those pagan bells at once!"

Determined she would not be bested by this bloodthirsty woman who had struck her, Alessandra said, "I know not what you speak of."

"Nay?" Agnes grabbed Alessandra's skirts, clearly intending to expose the anklet to any who watched, including Bishop Armis.

Alessandra caught Agnes's wrist. "You would expose my legs when the good bishop has directed they remain covered?"

Agnes jerked at her hand. "I would show what is hidden beneath your skirts."

"I have my ankles, knees, and thighs," Alessandra said, "none of which are appropriate to bare." She pulled Agnes' hand from her skirt, then stepped around the woman. Bells softly tinkling, she crossed to where Melissant stood before a group of minstrels who tuned their instruments.

Having observed the encounter, Melissant's face was pale. "No doubt, Mother will forbid me your company again," she bemoaned.

And again, Melissant would appeal to their father, who would over-rule Agnes.

"I wish she did not hate me so," Alessandra said. "Previous to this day, I did naught to earn her enmity, yet she behaves as if I have grievously injured her."

Melissant sighed, said softly, "You have, Alessandra. You remind our father of your mother, whom he makes no secret of having loved above all others. Ere you came to Corburry, my mother was lady of the castle and had Father's affection. Now she is once more eclipsed by Lady Catherine."

Alessandra nearly protested, for it seemed unfair that she should be blamed for something over which she had no control. But then she recalled the day she had come upon mother and daughter while they studied the household accounts. The older woman's pain at being second in James's life had been clear, but Alessandra had overlooked it, exerting little effort to not become entangled in Agnes's jealousy.

As hard as it was to admit, especially now with even greater animosity between them, she had made a mistake in not heeding the older woman's feelings.

"I am sorry," she said. "I should have been more understanding, should have held my tongue better and discouraged Father from lavishing so much attention upon me. Truly, it is not my wish that your mother be reduced to such a state." She started to turn away. "I shall apologize."

Melissant pulled her back. "Just now, I do not think she would be receptive."

A glance over Alessandra's shoulder confirmed it. The bishop her companion, Agnes looked entirely unapproachable. "Then later," she acceded.

Shortly, music sang upon the air as the minstrels played a tune that brought the young people to their feet.

From the sidelines, Alessandra and Melissant watched others take up the dance that soon turned vigorous.

"It surprises me," Alessandra said. "I did not know the English could dance so. The steps Lucien taught me were slower and more controlled. This reminds me—"

"Lucien taught you to dance? When?"

She had not meant to reveal that. "On the ship. He schooled me in many things English, dance being one of them."

Melissant smiled. "Only the slow dances, I wager—those where he held your hand and turned you about."

Recalling Lucien's warning, Alessandra did not mention he had also shown her the more intimate peasants' dance. Her toes curled in her slippers in remembrance of his body brushing hers, pressing, withdrawing.

Deciding it best to turn the conversation, Alessandra nodded at the dance floor. "What is this dance called?"

Melissant laughed, but obliged. "The tourdion."

"It is livelier than the other dances."

"Would you like to try?"

Alessandra longed to, but was reluctant in the presence of the bishop and Agnes. "Nay, I am content to watch."

"Liar."

Alessandra sighed. "That I am."

"Resist as long as you can," Melissant said and crossed to a group of young noblemen. Shortly, a partner in tow, she joined the others on the dance floor.

As Alessandra watched the quick, vibrant steps of the couples who smiled broadly and spilt laughter, she struggled to keep the music from sliding beneath her skin. But it found its way in, tempting her feet to move and body to sway.

She closed her eyes to block the sight, but behind her lids arose the women dancers of the harem. Gossamer garb billowing, they turned and twisted, leapt and sprang, bent and arched, spread arms wide and drew them close. And there Alessandra found herself, joining them with abandon that would surely earn her Jabbar's reproach. But all that mattered was now. This moment. The dance.

She lifted her arms, circled her hips, and gave her feet to the rhythm.

Marvelous! her body sang.

Deeper the music pulled her into its embrace, tighter it wrapped around her.

More! pealed the bells about her ankles.

Laughing, she dropped her head back. And in the midst of unfolding joy, acknowledged something was not right.

Where was the caress of light garments, the brush and tickle of unbound hair catching in eyes and mouth?

The garments she could do nothing about, but her hair...

She pulled free the pins that secured the braids to her head and dragged fingers through the crossed sections of hair. As it tumbled past her shoulders and joined her in the sway of the dance, she once more raised her arms and teased the air with her fingers.

Beyond slightly raised lids, she glimpsed a large figure, felt the heat it radiated, then the brush of hands. She laughed and whirled away—only to find it once more in her path, and this time a hand gripped her arm.

Alessandra opened her eyes and startled to find before her the one person she had not expected to see this evening—Lucien. But a Lucien who no longer wore the turban and robes of a eunuch. A Lucien whose stern countenance dropped her back down in England.

Breathing hard, she looked past him into faces that reflected shock, among them Agnes's and the bishop's. Even the musicians whose instruments had gone silent, stared at her. The couples who had been dancing moments—or was it minutes—before, stood on the outskirts of the dance floor, leaving Alessandra and Lucien near its center.

"Give me your hand," he said.

Realizing that what she had done had not been in her head, she returned her gaze to his. "I do not know…"

"Your hand," he repeated.

When she remained unmoving, he reached and lifted it in his own. Then, with a nod to the minstrels who scrambled to accommodate him, he led Alessandra into the first of the dances he had taught her.

"Smile," he said, "and do not forget your feet."

She did as told, focusing on his face so she would not have to look upon the others who surely condemned her for her behavior.

Though Lucien was hardly pleasant to look at, numerous cuts, bruises, and abrasions causing his crescent-shaped scar to pale in comparison, she could not imagine anyone she would rather rest eyes upon. Whence had he come?

"Lucien?"

"Later," he quieted her.

Not until well into the dance did the other couples return to the floor, and the dance that followed—another lively number—lessened the rapt attention with which they were regarded.

"Now?" she asked.

"Later."

Telling herself to be content with being so near him, she concentrated on the steps he guided her through. It still amazed her that one so large could move as smoothly as he did. As on the ship, he made her feel one with him, the meeting of their hands the point at which they flowed together.

With the commencement of the next dance, Lucien ushered her from the floor and into an alcove.

Alessandra smiled up at him. "Once again, you save me. I thank you."

He did not return her smile. "Did your father not warn you of the punishment of heretics?"

She felt her insides sink. Though his displeasure was deserved, she did not need to be told. "I am not a heretic," she said, squinting to pick out his features amid the shadows.

"You learned naught from what happened today, did you?" he snapped. "You don the bells and flaunt the dance of an infidel without thought of the consequences."

She swallowed the lump in her throat. She had purposely worn the bells, but the dance had just happened. "I do not understand why you care," she said. "I hear nothing from you for weeks, and when you finally appear, you ignore me as if we never shared a kiss."

Lucien caught her chin and lifted it. "We shared more than a kiss, Alessandra."

His acknowledgment made her mouth go dry. "Did it mean anything to you?"

"Had it not, I would have left you to your dance and the bishop's denunciation."

Meaning he still felt something for her? "If that is true, why do you cause your body to suffer so much abuse when what you seek could be had by wedding me?"

"I am not craven, Alessandra!"

Images of him exchanging blows with her father rose before her. "Certes, not in battle. Indeed, you are very nearly an animal—one who chooses bloodshed and preservation of the De Gautier name over peace."

"You do not understand," he said gruffly.

She pulled free and stepped back, causing the bells to peal softly. "I do understand. You do not love me as I love you. And even if you did, you would not allow yourself to feel it past your loathing of the Brevilles."

Whatever might have shown upon Lucien's face was lost in shadow. "There is one rule of war you would benefit from knowing," he said. "Never let your enemy know the emotions which drive you, for he will turn them against you."

War. Enemy. Emotions. His choice of words felt like a fist to her belly. "It is good to know you and I are at war, Lucien de Gautier," she said. "Until now, I had not realized I was your enemy."

Lucien stared at her, hated himself for being responsible for the hurt upon her face. It was true she was his enemy, but not in the broader sense of the word. She was the enemy of his heart. But if it would keep her from the lists and mock carnage, he would not disabuse her of the notion. Once he regained his lands, there would be time aplenty for explanation.

"All Brevilles are my enemy," he said. Words only, but intended to send her away until the time was right.

Alessandra drew herself up to her full height, turned, and walked opposite.

Brave shoulders, Lucien thought. They did not slump or sag, but remained squared as if she went into battle. But something was missing—bells. Her departure had not been accompanied by their music.

Catching the glint of gold where she had stood, he scooped up the anklet. It was still warm from her flesh. Accursed bells. They were the reason he had come from his tent in the first place. Having left the banquet early, Vincent had mentioned the speculation caused by the sound coming from beneath Alessandra's skirts.

Though Lucien had ached from head to foot, his body demanding rest, he had once again appointed himself her savior and arrived in the hall to discover her the center of attention. Like the others, he had stared at her exotic dance. Unlike the others, he had momentarily slipped into memories of the first time he had laid eyes upon her.

He had not intended to dance with her, but to drag her from the dance floor. But it had seemed natural—and safest—to take her into his arms. And he had savored every moment.

Lucien stepped into the light, opened his palm, and considered the miniature bells. Alessandra would not know it, but he would carry them into the tournament on the morrow. A favor ill-gotten, but his.

Alessandra closed the door of her chamber, leaned back against it, and released the sob she had barely kept down. Though she hated the self-pity gripping her, she could not prevent tears from spilling over.

"What more must I do to gain his love?" she addressed the darkness. He cared for her, but not as much as she cared for him.

Wiping the back of a hand across her eyes, she started to move away from the door, but halted at the sound of laughter.

Straining to hear who passed outside the door, she recognized Agnes's voice. To whomever she was with, she spoke husky words, then laughed in a way that sounded of intimacy.

Did Agnes intend to cuckold James? Did she seek to lessen the pain of his love for Catherine by spending time in another's arms?

Once the couple had passed by, Alessandra eased open her door and peered down the corridor. And blinked in surprise.

It was James to whom Agnes spoke words of love, his arm around her that guided them toward their chamber, he who paused and covered her mouth with his, his voice that said, "I do love you."

Agnes tipped her head farther back. "Even though I am not Catherine?"

He heaved a sigh. "Foolish woman. How you anger me, how you test every whit of my patience, how you make me want to shake you 'til your teeth clack." Another sigh. "Of course I love you, but stop asking me to prove it. I have done enough."

She rose to her toes and pressed her lips to his, then walked beside him to their chamber.

Gently, Alessandra pushed the door closed. It was a side to both Agnes and James she had not expected. Well they played the warring lord and lady of Corburry, but there was tenderness, too—as there had been between her mother and Jabbar.

The difference was that if Agnes and James remained faithful to each other, there would be no other with whom to share their affections. On the other hand, though Jabbar had loved Sabine, his other wives and concubines had time and again come between them.

Alessandra sank down on her bed and dragged the covers over her. "I see, Mother," she murmured, better understanding Sabine's insistence that her daughter was unsuited to life and marriage in Algiers.

One man, one woman. Lucien and Alessandra.

Dare she continue to hope?

34

Alessandra had intended to stay away—had not wanted to witness more bloodshed—but the final day of the tournament had drawn her back to the lists. It was not that she wished to join in the revelry. Rather, she thought it might be her last chance to see Lucien before he returned to Falstaff.

Lest her father caught sight of her, she hid her hair beneath the hood of her cloak and kept her head down as she moved among the crowd. Eschewing the pavilions, she made a place for herself at the sidelines where lesser nobles and villeins watched.

The jousts that followed, and the occasional foot combats, were tame compared with the battle she had witnessed between Lucien and her father. In fact, Alessandra found much of it interesting, though she still thought it a primitive means of proving one's valor.

Vincent de Gautier's entrance into the lists caused a stir. Surprised, Alessandra listened as the chief marshal announced his victories. Of the four jousts in which he had participated, he had lost only one—to Melissant's uncle, Sir Gavin.

In the evening, Alessandra had heard only tales of Lucien's victories, each bringing him closer to his goal of regaining his lands. Having been privy to none of Vincent's and Jervais's successes, she had assumed they had not prevailed.

Now, curious as to how this De Gautier fought compared with his older brother, Alessandra watched as he readied himself at one end of the tilt. The cry "do battle" sounded, and Vincent and his opponent sent their horses charging toward each other. Then the crack of their meeting...

Lances broken, Vincent and the other knight took up position again, and again met midway down the tilt. This time, Vincent unseated his opponent who tumbled to the ground amid the clamor of armor.

"Fairly downed!" the crowd shouted.

Vincent thrust his lance high.

Alessandra looked to the center pavilion where Melissant clapped and shrieked, and to which Agnes put a quick end.

It seemed Melissant was not immune to Vincent. Because he had redeemed himself with this show of valor?

Two jousts later, Jervais also proved he was capable, gaining ransom from his opponent after only one run down the lists.

How close were the De Gautiers to regaining their land? Alessandra wondered, thinking the ransom of horse and armor must be quite high.

The chief marshal interrupted her ponderings with the announcement of a break in the tournament and the promise of two challenges Lucien had accepted to be played out following the respite.

Hungry for the vendors' savory meat pies and pastries, the crowd dispersed, leaving Alessandra staring toward the tents pitched nearby.

Resisting the urge to seek out Lucien, she turned and walked into a wall—of sorts. A chuckle rose from the chest before her and a hand whipped back her hood.

Sir Gavin grinned. "I thought 'twas you."

She reached to retrieve her hood, but he stayed her hand.

"So like Catherine," he said. "The looks, the spirit...She lives in you."

"Pray, Sir Gavin," she beseeched, "if I am seen, my father will insist I return to the keep."

"And we would not want that, would we?" He released her.

Snatching the hood over her hair, she said, "As it is the last day, I am determined to see the end of it."

"Then you will also see my joust."

She frowned. "I had thought you finished. Yestereve you said——"

"I could not resist one more try. But tell me, will you bestow a favor upon me, little cousin?"

She raised her eyebrows. "A favor from me?"

He laughed. "You need not tell me I am too old, Lady Alessandra. 'Twould be in remembrance of Catherine only."

Alessandra's next words leapt from her before she could think them through. "Were you in love with my mother?"

He looked taken aback. "As I have said, Catherine was like a sister— well loved in that respect. No other."

Alessandra blushed. "I am sorry. That was rude of me." She pulled off one of the embroidered red gloves Melissant had given her and handed it to him. "For my mother." Instantly, she regretted the loss of warmth, for though it was another sunny day, the air was cool.

He tucked the glove beneath his belt. "I will do it honor. Now I must needs seek out the brew ere it is all drunk."

Alessandra watched him depart, then once more considered the tents. If she discovered which was Lucien's, would he receive her well? She feared not, but headed for them.

Weaving among those who had eschewed food in favor of watching the preparations of the knights, she quickly located the De Gautier tents of red and gold. Outside the center one, Lucien's squire polished his lord's armor. Was Lucien inside?

Alessandra continued forward and was grateful the squire was so intent on his task that he did not look up as she passed.

Outside the tent, she paused to listen for sounds from within, but it was quiet. Had Lucien joined the others who filled their bellies? She peeled aside a corner of the flap.

Back to her, scars more obvious than they had been the night she had ventured to the eunuchs' quarters, Lucien sat on a stool with his head bowed while his younger brother applied a pungent, herb-soaked cloth to his injuries. Did he sleep, or simply rest?

Alessandra stepped inside. Meeting Jervais's startled gaze over Lucien's head, she lowered her hood.

He frowned, but did not react in any way that might alert his brother to her presence.

Footsteps muffled by carpets laid upon the dirt floor, she advanced as Jervais once more dipped the cloth in a bowl that teetered on the small table at his side.

Halting at Lucien's back, Alessandra reached to Jervais. He narrowed his lids, but passed her the cloth, which she pressed to a livid swelling on Lucien's shoulder. As she held it there, she looked nearer upon his back. And began to tremble as she took in the numerous scars crisscrossing his shoulder blades, the backs of his upper arms, his lower back, and beyond—the welts he would carry with him into death disappearing beneath the waistband of his chausses.

Lucien came around so swiftly she did not realize he had turned until his face was below hers and her legs trapped between his.

"Oh, Lucien…" She swallowed hard to dislodge the anguish seeking to deny her voice. "I knew it was terrible, but not…" She shook her head, and that slight movement drew her eyes to more recent injuries obtained during the tournament.

These past days had left bruises, gashes, and scabs upon his arms and torso, all of which must have caused him pain, for they were not yet the scars of some distant injury. Any one could have been the end of him, whether some vital organ was struck or infection set in. And yet he continued to accept challengers and subject himself to deadly punishment. For De Gautier lands.

Meeting his reproachful gaze, she silently cursed him, his precious lands, the De Gautiers, even her own family.

"All this," she hissed, "to avoid wedding a Breville."

His shoulders rose with a deep breath. "I cannot think of a more worthy cause. Can you?"

Striving to hold back tears, she said, "Once I might have, but now?" She stepped back, and Lucien let her go. But as she made for the tent flap, Jervais stepped into her path. "Brother?" he called.

She peered over her shoulder, saw Lucien close his eyes as if he might return to whatever state he had been in previous to becoming aware of her presence.

He lifted his lids, said wearily, "Stay, Alessandra. We will talk while Jervais armors me."

She turned toward him. "'Tis clear where your heart lies, Lucien de Gautier. And I want no part of it."

He raised an eyebrow. "Not even a small piece? What of the love you professed?"

She drew a deep breath. "I do love you, though I am almost ashamed to once more speak the words."

The silence between them stretched, then Lucien snatched his tunic from the carpet and dragged it on over his head—doubtless, so she could not look further upon what he had not meant her to see.

Gaining his feet, he said, "Leave us, Jervais."

Behind Alessandra, the tent flap rustled.

Alone. How long since she and Lucien had shared a space with no others? Too long.

As if his body were one great ache, he stiffly strode toward her. "You are missing a glove," he said, eyeing her hands clasped at her waist.

"So I am."

He halted. "Given as a favor?"

"It was."

"Sir Rexalt again?"

"Nay, another."

"What of my favor?" He reached up and brushed the hair back from her face. "What will you give the one you love to remember you by when next I do battle?"

Reminding herself she was angry, she fought the impulse to turn her mouth into the calloused palm that grazed her cheek. "What would you have me give you? My girdle? A stocking? What say you to a glove that has sadly parted ways with its match?"

He drew his hand down her jaw, lingered upon her throat. "A memory is all I want."

She knew she should spurn him as he had spurned her, but she could not move—even when he began to work the brooch fastening her cloak, nor when the garment slipped from her shoulders to her feet.

"You should not," she breathed.

He lowered his head until his mouth was a moment from hers. "To whom do you belong, Alessandra?"

Him. Only him. She lifted her arms and cupped his bruised face. "Pray, do not enter the lists again, Lucien. Take me to wife, and the lands will be yours."

He brushed his lips across hers. "I cannot. Now tell me—who, Alessandra?"

She was tempted to fall back into anger, to stamp a foot and pout, but it was a woman she aspired to be—a woman to this man. "I belong to you, Lucien de Gautier."

How she loved that mere words from her mouth caused his mouth to curve.

"Are you certain 'tis love you feel for me?"

"I am."

He drew his head back. "Look at me, Alessandra. I am no prize. Every place, I am scarred. Even before the crescent was cut into my face, I had not the beauty of Vincent, not even Jervais."

She touched it, traced its path to the corner of his eye. "You are not handsome like Vincent, nor Rashid," she acceded, then drew her hand down and pressed it to where his heart beat. "Here, though, you are most beautiful—or will be if ever you let yourself feel it. It is that which I love."

Lucien longed to believe she truly was different from the two to whom he had been betrothed. Since the day he had arrived at Corburry to participate in the tournament, he had watched her closely when possible. And never had he seen her look at Vincent with the same cow-eyed longing as other women did. On the first day of the tournament, when he had seen her viewing the banners and helms, she had seemed reluctant—even annoyed—at Vincent's attempt to engage her in conversation. And when he had left her, she had done something out of sight of all.

Only later had he discovered what it was. When he had accepted his helm from his squire, the smudge of a cross where it broke the perfect polish had caught the light of the sun. Alessandra had blessed it.

The renewal of faith in womankind had begun to spread through him. But then she had given her favor to Sir Rexalt.

As much as the need to regain his lands, jealousy had driven him to fight that day, and to fight over and again these last days. From it, he had gained the strength to defeat his challengers and accept new ones, even when the weight of his armor threatened to bear him to the ground.

"I am yours, Lucien," she said again.

"I am glad," he said and pulled her against him. "Now, the favor."

He parted her lips beneath his, lightly drew his fingers down her spine, splayed them against the small of her back. "Mine, indeed," he said and deepened the kiss.

Alessandra slid her arms around his neck, her hands into his hair, and pressed herself nearer.

Gripped by the discomfort he had experienced on the ship when he had lain with her in the cot, he stepped back. "I must armor for the joust."

Hurt flashed across her face, and she caught his arm. "No more, Lucien. I beg you, stop now."

"I cannot."

Anger, frustration, and fear took their turns on her face, then she asked in a rush, "Do you love me?"

On that, neither could he accommodate her. "Alessandra, I will be late to the lists."

Her teeth snapped. "If you truly cared for me, you would not do this. You would lay down your arms and reject further challenges."

His own anger stirred. "You give me an ultimatum?"

She looked stricken, but said, "I do."

Lucien pulled his arm free. "Then you lose."

She dropped her chin, but not before he glimpsed moisture in her eyes. Turning her back on him, she scooped up her cloak.

As Lucien watched her jerk the garment around her shoulders, the misery coming off her yanked at his caged emotions. But as much as he wanted to explain all to her, there was not time. Nor was there any guarantee all would fall into place despite what James had agreed to in the heat of anger. Brevilles were treacherous like that.

Lord help me, he silently beseeched, *I am weary.*

The tent flap parted.

"Pardon." Jervais said. "The bishop comes this way."

Alessandra swung back to Lucien, her fear-widened eyes reminding him of the night she had come to the eunuchs' quarters.

"Someone shadows you," he said, then addressed his brother. "Delay him."

Jervais inclined his head and departed.

Lucien stepped forward, refastened Alessandra's brooch, and pulled her across the tent.

"You intend to hide me here?" she asked. "Where?"

He drew her to the far side of the tent, released her, and swept his dagger from its scabbard. Punching the blade's tip through the heavy canvas, he sliced an opening waist-high to the ground. Once assured none lurked on the backside of the tent, he said, "Go," and thrust the canvas aside. "We will not be caught again."

She bent, paused. "Lucien—"

"Alessandra, this time the punishment will not be mine." He gave her a push. "Go!"

It was no empty threat. Unlike in Algiers when he had been beaten like an animal, most—if not all—of the blame would be hers for being alone with a man not her husband.

"Just tell me this," she beseeched. "Do you or do you not love me?"

He glanced toward the tent flap, beyond which could be heard the voices of the two outside. "Love is an emotion reserved for children. And we are not children, Alessandra."

Did something in her eyes die? he wondered even as he named himself a cur. Later, he told himself. Now was not the time to work out the emotions he had battled with ever since he had first laid eyes upon her.

Jaw quivering, she said, "Farewell, Lucien," and disappeared through the opening.

He retrieved a stool, placed it before the torn canvas, and lowered himself just as Bishop Armis entered.

"You are alone, De Gautier." The man made no attempt to hide his surprise.

"You expected otherwise?"

"I thought you might be enjoying a woman's company." He stepped forward, his gaze searching the corners of the tent.

"I speak of a joy woman, of course." The bishop brushed his fingers across the dusty top of the trunk containing Lucien's belongings.

"Then you have mistaken me."

"'Twould seem so." Bishop Armis looked up. "You will, of course, provide us a good show this afternoon, hmm?"

Lucien resisted the urge to demonstrate his prowess that very moment. "Certes, a performance worthy of you, most esteemed bishop."

"I look forward to it." The man inclined his head and swept from the tent in a flurry of silken robes.

Lucien eased his heavy shoulders. Something was unfolding. Something that would do Alessandra harm if she did not tread more carefully. Pondering what it might be, and who the players were, he strode to the small box he had earlier tossed on his cot. He lifted the lid and picked out the belled anklet to which he had added a length of chain. He considered it, then fastened it around his neck.

Since the night Alessandra had left it behind, he had worn it beneath his armor, the noise of the crowd and the clank of metal masking its soft peal. He was certain it had brought him good fortune, and just as certain his purse would be more heavily weighted within the hour. Enough to buy back De Gautier lands.

Then he would explain all to Alessandra. And, God willing, she would still have him.

I am sick of it all, Lucien silently acknowledged as he wheeled his horse around to discover the fate of his fallen opponent.

The man lay motionless, his left pauldron—that piece of articulated shoulder armor which Lucien's lance had broken free—thrown to the opposite end of the lists.

Lucien thrust his visor back and waited with the crowd as the squire of the downed man dropped to his knees, lifted his lord's visor, and peered inside.

The long silence boded ill.

Had the knight broken his neck in the fall? Lucien wondered as he was shot through with regret, guilt, and something near self loathing. Though it could be said to have been a fair joust, and many would see it as confirmation of his mastery of the game, he wanted to shout to the heavens at the injustice of it.

Searching the crowd, he located Alessandra's hooded figure. Though her face was in shadow, he knew her eyes were on him, and he imagined the accusation that must be there.

No matter his reason for returning to the lists, he was an animal and, like an animal, had taken the life of another—a man who was not even an enemy, unlike those Lucien had killed in battle in the name of his king. If it was hate, not love, that now shone from Alessandra's eyes, it was deserved.

No more, he vowed, and flung the remains of his lance to the ground. He had reestablished himself, returned honor to his family's name, and he and his brothers had taken enough ransom to buy back their lands. There was nothing more to be gained.

A groan rent the silence, followed by sighs of relief from the onlookers.

Releasing a breath he had not realized he held, Lucien swung his gaze to his opponent and saw him begin to flounder as his senses returned.

Three varlets were summoned and, shortly, the knight was carried away on an elongated shield.

Lucien's final opponent entered the lists.

A red glove fluttering from the shoulder strap of his armor, Sir Gavin Crennan took his position as the chief marshal called out the challenge.

What had possessed Alessandra to give the glove to her cousin? Lucien wondered as jealousy growled through him. Not only was the man too old, but they were related within the degrees prohibited by the Church.

A token favor only. It had to be.

"Take position, Sir Lucien," the chief marshal commanded.

Lucien looked around. "I am finished," he called, and snapped the reins and cantered his destrier to the center pavilion where James sat.

"Lord Breville," he said, "as agreed, De Gautier lands for gold. This eve, if you will have the papers drawn, I shall deliver the entire sum to you."

James rose. "My offer stands, Lucien. Do you take a Breville to wife, the lands I will give you, and that which you have gained these past days will keep you in good stead for a lifetime."

"You are mistaken to believe a Breville bride is all it would take to keep peace between our families."

James's nostrils flared. "Dewmoor Pass?"

Lucien nearly laughed—at himself. Since his return to Falstaff, he had hardly thought of the pass that had caused so much bloodshed.

Thinking of it now, it seemed ludicrous that so many battles had been fought over a piece of land comprising fewer than fifty hectares.

"Keep it, Breville," he said, then turned and left the lists.

Rigidly, Gavin sat his destrier before the tilt as a murmur arose from those who were to be denied the final De Gautier match.

Tenfold more aware of the heat of his armor, the sweat trickling down his back, the flush creeping up his neck, he breathed deep. Then he forced a smile, doffed his helm, and shouted, "Alas, 'twould appear the Lion of Falstaff fears my lance and blade." He laughed. "As well he should." He drew his sword, gave his destrier a jab of his spurs, and triumphantly trotted the lists.

The onlookers tittered. Though Gavin knew he was regarded as one of the most competent of jousters, he also knew his chances had been little better than the chances of the others defeated by De Gautier.

Returning his sword to its sheath, he urged his destrier away from the lists.

I am well, he assured himself as he headed for the stables. But still anger brewed until everything he laid eyes upon was splotched red.

When he dismounted, his squire appeared before him. "I will take him, Sir Gavin." The young man reached for the reins.

The desire to strike him surging through Gavin, he jerked the reins and stepped around the boy. "I will tend him myself. Go enjoy the festivities."

"But—"

Gavin halted and, keeping his back to his squire, thundered, "Leave me. Now!"

"Aye, my lord!"

Regretting his outburst, Gavin led his destrier into the stables. "All is well," he muttered and, to prove it, smiled and lifted a hand to an approaching knight.

The man nodded as he passed by.

Feeling as if his mouth might crack wide, leaving a gaping hole out of which his emotions would howl, he slowly—carefully—lowered the smile.

"I am not angry," he tried again. "I am disappointed. That is all." With more assurances, he might have convinced himself of it, but Agnes appeared, she who would rub his nose in the humiliation dealt by Lucien de Gautier.

"The miscreant!" she hissed. "Who does he think he is?"

Once more beset with the urge to strike out, he fought down the desire, for his sister must never know of his demons. Though their appearances were rare, when they did rise up, they wreaked havoc on his and others' lives that haunted him with memories he could not bear to examine.

"'Tis De Gautier of whom you speak?" he said.

"Who else would I call 'miscreant'?"

"Your husband, perhaps?"

She laughed. "Only when he disagrees with me."

Which was fairly often.

Gavin led his destrier to the far stall and began to tend the animal's needs. "He gave forfeit, did he not? What better victory than that, Agnes?"

"What better victory?" She snorted. "Knocking him from his destrier, bringing him to his knees."

He unbuckled the saddle. "I am content," he lied, wishing she would leave him.

"He humiliated you, and yet you tell you are content?"

"I am."

Her face brightened. "Do you know what will be said of you?" When he did not respond, she answered, "They shall say De Gautier forfeited not because he feared your lance or sword, but because he deemed you unworthy."

Gavin moved around the horse so she would not see his seething.

"Of course, methinks he did it for Alessandra." She grunted. "Lucien's homecoming was bad enough, but her arrival has stolen any hope of Melissant wedding the De Gautier heir."

Gavin looked across his destrier's back. "What has Alessandra to do with that? 'Tis Lucien's decision to wed, not hers."

"Ah, but Lucien and Alessandra are enamored of one another. Do you know where she went after she spoke with you during the break in the tourney?"

Gavin had not known he'd had an audience when he had unhooded Alessandra. It made him terribly uncomfortable. "I do not know where she went."

"To *him*—his tent. If he weds a Breville, it will be that one, not my poor Melissant." She shook her head. "What am I to do, Gavin?"

Alessandra had given him her favor, then gone to another…

Trying again to shake off his demons, Gavin strode around the horse and laid an arm across Agnes's shoulders. "There will be one more worthy of Melissant than Lucien de Gautier. 'Tis for the best he does not wed her."

She pulled away from him. "Do you think that is what I wish to hear? From you who would have fallen at the feet of a De Gautier had your challenge not been rejected?" She swung away, crossed to the stall portal, but stopped herself with a hand to the frame.

She stood there a moment, then turned back. "Forgive me." Her eyes glistened. "Alessandra's coming has been difficult for me."

"I can imagine," he pushed the words past his constricted throat.

Agnes nodded. "She has brought with her Catherine's ghost, and I know not how to battle it. But I shall." As if gaining strength from her declaration, she smiled and left Gavin to his own private battle.

He held the demons back until he was certain she was out of earshot. Then, eyes painting everything red, he pulled the saddle from his destrier and threw it against the wall. While the horse whinnied and sidled away, he hurled buckets, brushes, reins, a whip—anything he could lay hands to—until his demons were exhausted. Collapsing against the wall, he slid down it. There he sat, minute after godforsaken minute, weakened by the fit that had possessed him.

When he finally rose from the straw-covered floor, a voice within whispered, *Something must be done.*

Knowing his demons hungered, that if he did not feed them, they would eat him from the inside out, he said, "So it shall be. And soon."

35

"It could all be yours, and the land," Vincent said as he sifted through a pile of coins, "if you wed the red."

Lucien did not comment until his squire, struggling under the load of armor, exited the tent. "The red, hmm?"

"Aye, the red," Jervais agreed with Vincent.

Lucien dragged his arming doublet off over his head. "Her name is Alessandra." He tossed the mailed garment to the cot. "And I shall wed her once order is restored to Falstaff."

Vincent jerked. "If that was what you intended, then why...?" He shook his head.

"Why not accept Breville's offer?" Lucien supplied, then picked a coin from the pile and turned it front to back. "For one thing, De Gautier pride."

"Which you have little enough of, Vincent," Jervais pointed out.

Vincent shot to his feet and lunged toward his younger brother, but Lucien stepped between them. "Enough!" he growled.

Vincent tore his gaze from Jervais. "I do not need him"—he jabbed a finger—"reminding me of my mistakes. I am paying for them, and will no doubt continue to pay the remainder of my life."

Lucien knew that, among other things, Vincent referred to jousting, a contest abhorrent to him. Prior to attending the tournament, he had voluntarily submitted to weeks of grueling practice alongside his more capable brothers. Yet for all the humiliation and pain he had borne, he had not heretofore uttered a word of protest.

Though Lucien was certain it would be a long time before he could completely forgive his brother for his wrongdoing, he had been proud of the man Vincent had struggled to become.

"We will speak no more of this," he said. "Come dawn——"

A skittering sound caught his ear, and he looked over his shoulder at the opening he had slashed for Alessandra's escape. A shadow moved across the red and gold stripes.

Alerted to Lucien's discovery, his brothers started across the tent, but Lucien stopped them and motioned for them to continue speaking.

Too late. The shadow dissolved, and by the time Lucien thrust his head through the opening, only the trampled scrub evidenced an eaves-dropper had been there.

"Who was it?" Vincent asked.

"The bishop?" Jervais suggested.

Lucien considered a long moment, muttered, "Possibly."

Following the repast, the return of De Gautier lands took place behind closed doors. An hour after entering the lord's solar, the parties emerged.

Carrying the documents, a brother on either side, Lucien traversed the great hall. His eyes flickered over Alessandra, then he passed through the doors with nary a word to those who watched.

Alessandra slumped where she sat before the blazing hearth. On the morrow, before first light, Corburry's guests would depart en masse. Would Lucien leave without further word to her, believing the ultimatum she had given him in anger?

"You look unhappy," Sir Gavin said, reminding her they had been conversing before Lucien's appearance. "Is it something I said?"

She met his kind eyes. "Nay, I——"

"'Tis what was not said," Melissant interrupted.

Alessandra turned to find her sister over her shoulder. "What speak you of?"

Melissant winked at her uncle. "I believe our Alessandra hoped to have words with Lucien De Gautier."

Wondering how her sister could speak so boldly of matters of the heart in front of Sir Gavin, Alessandra said, "You are mistaken."

"I do not think so," Melissant replied in a singsong voice.

Grinning, Sir Gavin said, "So, 'tis Lucien de Gautier who occupies your mind. I should have guessed."

As both Melissant and Gavin appeared firm in their beliefs, Alessandra decided it was useless to protest further. "We are friends. He was good to me when he brought me out of Algiers."

Melissant plopped down beside her. "Good to you? Is that all?"

"Melissant!" Alessandra exclaimed.

"You have your mother's foolhardiness if you think you can tame that one," Sir Gavin said.

"Perhaps she does not wish to tame him," Melissant suggested.

Sir Gavin chuckled, mussed his niece's hair. "What of you, Melissant? Would you want him tame?"

"I do not want him at all!"

"But 'twas you who were to wed the De Gautier heir."

"Aye, Vincent. And good riddance to him."

"But now Lucien is heir," he pointed out.

"A better choice," she said, and added, "were I inclined to make a choice."

Grateful the conversation had shifted from her involvement with Lucien, Alessandra glanced around the hall and found it emptying as the guests moved to bed down for the night. Which she should also do to rise early enough to seek out Lucien before he departed.

Out of the corner of her eye, she glimpsed Agnes and Bishop Armis. They stood at the far end of the hall, their intent gazes making her feel like prey.

She rose and turned to bid good eve to Melissant and Gavin, and discovered her sister had wandered off to a side table to pick at a platter of cold meats and cheeses.

She looked back at Sir Gavin whose eyes were closed. She touched his shoulder. "Good eve."

His lids opened. "Good eve, Lady Alessandra."

As she turned to go, a serving girl appeared before her.

"I've a missive for you, milady," she whispered and placed a parchment into Alessandra's hand and scampered off.

It had to be from Lucien.

Though her heart fluttered, she grimaced. The girl had tried to be secretive but had not succeeded, for the feeling of being watched was stronger than ever.

Curling her fingers around the missive, she looked into Sir Gavin's questioning eyes and said again, "Good eve."

Out of sight of the hall, she threw her skirts over her arm and took the stairs two at a time. Once inside her chamber, she went to stand before the fire and opened the missive.

It was from Lucien, his boldly scrawled initials overlapping the final sentence. She read the note through, then pressed it to her breast.

He wished her to come to his tent, urging her to be cautious so she might slip from the keep unseen and suggesting she mingle with those who headed for their camps outside the castle walls.

Quickly, she donned the cloak and hood that had allowed her to attend the tournament unnoticed. Of course, it had not fooled Sir Gavin.

Keeping him in mind, she descended to the hall. From the shadow of the stairs, she searched for him and found him absent. She continued to the kitchens where some of the servants looked up from their toil, but allowed her to pass without question.

Night's crisp air greeted her when she stepped outside.

Rubbing her hands over her arms, she traversed the inner and outer baileys. At the portcullis, it proved easy to merge with a group of departing nobles, and moments later she skirted them and ran toward the encampment.

She paused as she neared the red-and-gold striped De Gautier tents, looked cautiously around, then toward Lucien's tent from which light shone. Smiling, she hitched up her skirts and hurried forward, only to stumble.

She thought she had tripped on her skirts, but instead of falling forward, she was dragged backward.

Her cry of surprise caught by a hand that clapped over her mouth, fear cut a jagged path through her. Desperate to free herself, she twisted and thrust her elbows into the chest of the one behind—a man, as told by his grunt of discomfort.

Gripping her more tightly about the waist, he continued to drag her opposite Lucien's tent.

Alessandra kicked a leg back and connected with a shin. When that failed to result in her release, she sank her teeth into the fleshy palm that bruised her mouth. But to no avail. Her captor held tight as he maneuvered her from the camp toward the bordering wood.

Did he intend to violate her? Murder her? Who was he? Had he followed her from the keep? Had he been among the nobles she had trailed out of the bailey?

The crunch of leaves and the shadow of trees alerted her to their entrance into the wood. Heart beating so hard she thought it would burst, she reached over her shoulder and raked her nails down the man's face.

He growled and shifted his hand so that it also covered her nose.

Alessandra tossed her head in an attempt to dislodge the hand, but it bit more deeply into her face. She opened her mouth and screamed against it, but the sound was heard only in her head.

As unconsciousness crept over her, weakening her struggles, one lucid thought made it through. Embracing it, she became deadweight in her captor's arms.

As she hung there, she sensed his uncertainty. Then, blessed air. Desperation entreated her to gulp the precious stuff, but she forced herself to draw slow, shallow breaths. Her hazy senses slow to clear, it was not until she felt the cold, moist earth that she realized she had been lowered to the ground.

Fearful the night was not dark enough for her to risk opening her eyes, she lay still and waited to discover what the man intended.

He whistled softly, and she heard the sound of approaching horses.

Lifting her lashes slightly, she saw the dark silhouettes of three horses and two riders heading to where she lay. Her captor, his back to her, motioned them forward.

Struggling to keep her breathing even, Alessandra commanded herself to devise a plan before the man's accomplices reached them. But all she could think to do was run and scream in hopes of drawing the attention of someone in the camp.

She rolled to her stomach, jumped to her feet, snatched up her skirts, and lunged toward the flickering lights.

A shout sounded behind her, then she heard her captor give chase.

Her hair flying out behind her snagged something. A branch? Or the grasping fingers of the one in pursuit? She ran faster, felt the roots of her hair pull free, and knew it was the man.

The blood pounding in her ears echoed by the hooves of riders bearing down upon her, she sent forth a prayer that just this one time she would not trip over her long skirts. Then she screamed. It sounded pitiful, wheezing from her and cut short by the need to draw more breath to fuel her flight.

When her feet touched meadow, her heart soared. *Nearly free*, she told herself, then an arm turned around her waist, lifted her, and held her like a rag doll against the side of a galloping horse.

As the animal was wheeled around, Alessandra saw the woods rise up before her again—refuge for those who meant to steal her away.

Shortly, she was dropped to the ground.

Where she lay in a heap, she heard voices that sounded strangely and impossibly familiar.

Am I dreaming? she wondered and rolled onto her back and stared up through her tangled hair at those above her.

"I want her gone from here," spat one of them. "Now!"

Though she was certain she knew the voice, she could not place it.

There was an answering murmur, then one of them dropped to his knees beside her.

Alessandra knew the face, but it made no sense. Closing her lids, she whispered, "I always could outrun you," then yielded to unconsciousness.

"She did not come?"

Lucien dragged his gaze from Corburry's darkened keep, took up the reins, and looked over his shoulder to Jervais. "She stayed true to her word," he said.

Jervais urged his horse near. "She will change her mind. Within a sennight, you will have word from her."

Lucien tapped heels to his destrier and maneuvered to the head of the De Gautier procession. As it had been nearly impossible to sleep through the night, they would be the first to depart Corburry. It suited him, leaving ahead of the dawn and ensuring their arrival at Falstaff before the noon hour.

"Even so," Lucien said when Jervais sidled near, "'tis probably best Alessandra remain a Breville."

"For whom?"

"Both of us."

"But—"

"She has made her decision, Jervais. Leave it be." Lucien jabbed his heels into his mount's sides and left his brother and the others behind.

Falstaff, he told himself as the cool air ran through his hair. His former holdings restored, it was there he would find peace. In time,

Alessandra would fade from memory until all that remained would be the occasional encounter that was bound to happen as long as there was peace between the De Gautiers and the Brevilles.

However long that might be.

36

"She is awake, my friend."

The accented voice drifted into Alessandra's consciousness. She groaned, blinked against the light of a sun muted by cloud cover, and turned her head toward the man who rose from beside a campfire. Not until he knelt beside her and pushed the hair out of her eyes was she able to bring him into focus.

Thinking she must be dreaming, she closed her eyes in hopes of awakening in her warm chamber at Corburry.

"Alessandra," he gave her a shake.

Funny that his voice is so clear, she thought.

"Do you hear me?" His warm breath caressed her cheek.

She lifted her eyes again, peered into familiar black orbs. "Go away," she breathed. "You do not belong in England." Rubbing her hands up and down her chilled arms, she curled into a ball to try to warm herself.

"Neither do you belong here," he said and shook her harder.

She returned her gaze to him and found his features undeniably distinct. His black eyebrows drawn together, mouth a tight line, he looked more real than any dream she had ever had. And the four lines scoring his right cheek…

"Rashid?"

His mouth softened. "Yes, Rashid."

She sat up so abruptly, her head clipped his chin. "It cannot be," she switched to her native language with an awkwardness that surprised her. Though she continued to think in Arabic, more and more she spoke the English language without conscious effort.

Rashid caught her hand. "It is me," he said and placed her palm against his jaw.

"What are you doing in England?"

"I came to take you home."

The events of the night past rushed at her. It was Rashid who had abducted her from the camp. He who had stolen the breath from her when she had fought him. But what of the other two? She had known one of them—or thought she had—but could not recall who it was.

"Why did you come for me?" she asked.

His nostrils flared with a hint of the anger she had glimpsed the night he had beat Lucien. "Algiers is where you belong. As my bride."

His bride, not Lucien's. Realizing Lucien had likely departed Corburry by now, she closed her eyes. He would have gone believing she had spurned him.

"Alessandra?" Rashid jogged her. "We are returning to Algiers."

That was what she had wanted when Lucien had forced her to accompany him to Tangier, but now she wanted something different. She could not return to the life she would have as Rashid's wife. She needed freedom, not to be cosseted and locked away without consideration of her own feelings.

Even though women were also regarded as chattel in England, their lives seemed fuller—running the household, checking the accounts, enjoying outings where they were not required to hide their faces, and all other manner of independence she was not permitted in a harem. Despite England's cold weather, strange food, and primitive means of men proving their valor, she belonged here. More, she belonged with Lucien, even if he would not have her.

"I cannot," she said and pulled her hand away. "Algiers is no longer my home, Rashid."

Abruptly, he stood. Coloring suffusing his face, he said, "You think you belong in this godforsaken country of little sun and accursed cold?"

She deserved this. After all, he had come across an ocean to return her to Algiers.

He reached down and yanked her upright. "Are you still mine, Alessandra?"

"Yours?" Had she ever truly been his? Regardless, now she was not, for he was not Lucien. Wishing there were an easier way to tell him, she said, "I am sorry, Rashid, but England is my home."

He thrust his face near hers. "I have asked if you are still mine!"

"I am not."

"Then it is true you lust after De Gautier. Have lain with him."

The truth would hurt him, but it would be worse to lie. "I am still chaste, but 'tis Lucien I love."

Only the fury that leaped in his eyes and her quick reflexes saved her from the hand he raised to her. Gripping his wrist, she stared into his eyes and tried not to tremble with fear.

"I will not allow you to strike me, Rashid," she said as evenly as she could manage.

His nostrils flared, then he thrust her back so that she dropped to the blanket she had been lying on. "You are a witch and a whore, just as my mother tried to tell me." He gripped his forehead. "I should have listened."

Alessandra pushed to her feet. "You know that is not so."

"What I know is that you betrayed me. And for that, I would not be faulted for ending your life."

His words frightened her, but she calmed herself with the reminder of who he was to her and put a hand on his shoulder. "You could not do that to me. We are friends, and shall always be."

"Friends!" He threw off her hand and lurched away.

It was then Alessandra saw who had accompanied Rashid to England. Perched on a rock, a knee drawn up, an arm draped over it, Jacques LeBrec gave her a slow smile.

Once more, she considered this must be a dream, for what else would bring together these two men?

Jacques stood. "*Cherie!*" He sauntered to her, caught up her hands, and brushed his lips over the backs of her fingers. "You are surprised, no?"

"This is not possible," Alessandra whispered.

"But it is! I am here." He laughed. "The same as your betrothed."

She glanced at Rashid, felt his anger, then returned her gaze to the very real person of Jacques LeBrec and snatched her hands from his. "You sold me into slavery!"

He shrugged, said, "*Pardon,*" then attempted to coax understanding from her with the same smile he had used to gain her trust in Tangier. "But now I am redeemed, eh? Soon you will be back in Algiers, as was your wish."

Drenched anew in memories of the slave auction, she spat, "Redeemed? Never!" and launched herself at him.

It was Rashid who saved him from her fists. He grabbed her from behind, forced her to the ground, and straddled her. "I demand your obedience, woman!"

"You demand?" she gasped. "I am not your wife, nor am I of your faith that I must obey your every word."

"You are not my wife yet, but you shall be."

"I am not leaving England!"

"Indeed, you are," he said, then covered her mouth with his.

Alessandra was too stunned to move, but when he began to grind his mouth against hers as if that might evoke a response, she jerked her head aside. "Cease, Rashid!"

"You wanted it once."

When she had kissed him on the rooftop to prove she was not attracted to Lucien. She swallowed the lump in her throat. "Not like this."

"How?" he demanded. "Tell me how De Gautier pleasured you, and I will do better."

When she did not answer, he put his mouth to her ear and nipped her lobe.

Alessandra would have protested anew, but Jacques dropped to his haunches beside them and said in lingua franca, "Rashid, my friend, this is not the time or place to tame her."

Although Alessandra expected Rashid to turn his anger on Jacques, he stood and stalked away.

"Heathen," Jacques muttered as he helped Alessandra up to sitting. Then he put an arm around her as if to offer solace.

She pulled free and scooted away.

With a rueful smile, he gained his feet. "Eventually, *cherie*, you will have to forgive me."

"Never!"

He tsked. "That is a very long time."

"It is forever."

He sighed, returned to the fire, and picked a piece of dried meat from the platter beside it. "I thought I was making amends by leading your betrothed to you," he mused, then held up the meat.

She shook her head, asked, "How did you come to be with Rashid?"

He popped the meat in his mouth, chewed. "You must know I suffered terrible guilt selling you at auction."

"I know nothing of the sort."

"I did, *cherie*. But when I saw the English captain had bought you, I knew you would be fine. You had family in England, and I thought it likely you would escape once you reached its shores."

"And Rashid?"

"Two days after you set sail, he came to me—quite angry." He glanced at the other man who had distanced himself and was now at prayer. "Talk was still fresh of the fiery woman sold at auction. Thus, he learned I had offered you for sale."

He grimaced, rubbed a hand over his throat. "There was a moment, *cherie*, when I feared my life was over. Then, Blessed Virgin, I remembered something."

"What?"

He crossed to where a pack sat beside the rock he had earlier perched upon. Shortly, he returned to her and dropped a folded letter in her lap.

Alessandra knew it was the one her mother had written her that she had been forced to leave behind upon being sold into slavery.

"Read it." He jerked his chin.

"I know what it says."

"Then you also know it is how Rashid and I discovered your whereabouts. It was—"

Rashid's wail rent the air.

Jacques rolled his eyes. "It was not so difficult."

"But the letter said I was to be taken to my aunt and uncle. How did you find me at Corburry?"

He sank to his haunches. "I am not at liberty to say."

"What do you mean, 'not at liberty'?"

"Alessandra, you are an intelligent woman. You can figure it out."

"I would prefer you save me the trouble."

"My word I have given. I cannot."

Glowering, she dragged the blanket around her shoulders to ward off the morning cold.

Glasbrook, she thought. Her mother had instructed Lucien to deliver her there, where Sabine's aunt and uncle—Agnes and Gavin's parents—lived. Thus, it was to Glasbrook that Rashid and Jacques would have gone first. But who had sent two strangers on to Corburry? The aunt and uncle? Sir Gavin?

Not Sir Gavin. He was too wise to be duped by two of obvious foreign descent. It must have been his unsuspecting parents. Still, it made little sense.

A memory niggled at the back of Alessandra's mind, but though she tried to pry it free, she lost hold of it.

"I cannot think now," she said.

"It will come to you."

She would have pressed him further, but Rashid returned.

"Arise, Alessandra."

Taking the blanket with her, she stood and was surprised to see his eyes were filled with tears.

"It has been difficult these last months," he said. "Forgive me." Then he put his arms around her.

Would he allow her to return to Corburry, then?

"Everything I knew has changed," he said. "You are all I have left of what was good in my life. I need you."

His sorrow tugged at her heart, made her wish she could love him as he loved her, but there was Lucien. Only Lucien.

Rashid pulled back. "We will wed as soon as we reach Algiers, then you will become my first wife as you were always meant to be."

If he was set on returning her to Algiers and she had any hope of escape, she must allow him to believe she would go willingly. Only then might she catch him off guard.

She nodded, leaned in, and over his shoulder, met Jacques's bewildered gaze.

"We must go." Rashid set her back from him. "There is a ship that leaves for the Mediterranean in four days. We shall be on it."

She summoned a smile she hoped revealed none of her true feelings.

Placated, his face once more boyishly handsome, Rashid turned to Jacques. "Clear the camp. I will bring the horses."

A half hour later, they rode east.

37

"My lord, the Brevilles ride on Falstaff."

Lucien's first thought was that Alessandra had come, but the captain of the guard's brow was too furrowed. He pushed away the ledger he had been examining. "In peace?"

"Armored, my lord, with knights abounding."

Lucien surged to his feet. Despite Breville's talk of goodwill, he intended to continue their feud. Indeed, Lucien would not be surprised if it had been in his mind even as he had signed over the De Gautier lands two days past. And for what? The knave now possessed Dewmoor Pass, and without contest.

"Secure the castle," Lucien ordered.

"'Tis being done now," the man said.

Throwing off his fur-lined robe, Lucien called for his squire.

The young man came running. "You would have me arm you, my lord?"

"For now, I require only mail tunic, boots, and sword."

The squire disappeared and quickly returned. In the center of the great hall, amid knights and family members, Lucien donned the mail, shoved his feet into leather boots, and secured his sword.

"I thought 'twas finally over," Dorothea said, placing a hand on her eldest son's arm.

Lucien shifted his jaw to ease its tension. "You are not the only one who was duped, Mother."

She lowered her head, whispered, "It will never end."

He tilted her face up, pressed a kiss to her pale cheek, and called for his knights to follow.

On the roof of the gatehouse, Lucien and his brothers stared out at the assembled Breville knights. There was no question they did not come in peace.

"Are the cannons ready?" he asked the captain of the guard.

"They are being loaded now."

Lucien turned back to contemplate Breville's first move.

"I cannot believe it," Vincent said. "It must be a misunderstanding."

Jervais grunted. "No misunderstanding. Typical Breville trickery."

James Breville, a knight on either side of him, broke formation and urged his horse forward. "Lucien de Gautier! Where are you, man?"

Lucien moved to the center of the embrasure. "I am here!"

James lifted his visor. "I want her back!"

Lucien narrowed his gaze on him. "Of what do you speak, Breville?"

After some silence, James called, "Very well, I will play your game, but know that you will die on your knees."

Though Lucien was tempted to return threat for threat, he knew he must not give in to anger—at least, not until it was time to take sword in hand. "I play no game. That I leave to you who professed to want peace and now rides against me without provocation."

"Without provocation! You De Gautiers steal my daughter as you stole my wife and dare say I am unjustified in seeking your deaths?"

Struck with fear as vicious as that felt when he had lost Alessandra to the streets of Tangier, it took Lucien a moment to respond, and when he did, he did not care that his voice was strained as of one not fully in control of his emotions. "She is missing?"

"Missing?" James spat. "Just as your father took Catherine, you took Alessandra, you milk-livered wretch."

Overlooking the insult, for which he would have once made the man pay dearly, Lucien said, "Your accusation is false, Breville. I am coming down." He turned and found Jervais in his path, a bow with a nocked arrow at his side.

"Do not trust him, Brother. It may be a trap."

Realizing he preferred it be that than the jagged-edged truth, Lucien said, "If it is, you need not worry as to whose blood will spill."

Jervais raised the bow. "I will watch your back."

Pain at the center of his chest, Lucien descended to the bailey and motioned for the portcullis to be raised. When it was waist high, he ducked beneath it and strode the length of the drawbridge.

"Tell me all of it," he demanded, halting before James who had the look of a man teetering on an edge he should not go near.

Sword before him, James leaned forward in the saddle. "Where is my daughter?"

Lucien flexed his hand on his sword hilt. Even with Jervais and others on the wall ready to defend him, there was much danger in leaving the blade sheathed where he stood alone before his lifelong enemy, but this time was different from others. This time, there was Alessandra to consider, she who would benefit none from another De Gautier-Breville clash. Indeed, such a delay would surely be to her detriment.

Easing the tension from his jaw, Lucien said, "I did not take Lady Alessandra."

"You deny sending her a message ere you left Corburry?"

"The message was sent, but that is all."

"She did not come to you that night?"

"She did not."

James arced his sword, stopped its point a foot from Lucien's chest.

Struggling against warrior senses that urged him to return aggression for aggression, Lucien told himself the timing must be right, else all would turn bloody before the walls of Falstaff. And if that happened, Alessandra could as easily be lost to her family—to him—as those whose lives would stain the soil beneath his feet.

"You lie," James growled. "You took her, likely sold her into slavery as your father sold her mother." He pressed the sword nearer.

The timing would get no better. Sweeping his dagger from its scabbard, Lucien lunged to the side, gripped James's arm, and wrenched him out of the saddle. As the Breville knights hastened their mounts forward, Lucien withstood the thrust of the older man's unbalanced body and forced James's sword down.

Face to face with his old enemy, Lucien pressed his dagger's blade to Breville's throat and shot a warning look at the knights, one of whom was Sir Gavin.

"Hear me well," Lucien rasped. "As my father was not responsible for your wife's disappearance, neither am I responsible for Alessandra's."

James's eyes bulged. "I am to believe you?"

"Lest you forget, 'twas I who safely delivered her to you."

"Before you knew what had become of your lands!"

Lucien ground his teeth. "Once I learned she was of your blood, I did think to use her against you, but I could not. I brought her directly to you, my family's enemy."

Breathing heavily, James said, "Why did you do it? Why did you leave her untouched and hand her over without a demand for ransom? Through her, you could have had Dewmoor Pass."

There was no searching for an answer. It was close at hand—rather, close at heart—as it had been for longer than Lucien had realized. But though that did not make it easy to admit, especially now that Alessandra was gone and the words could not first be spoken to her, he put down his pride. "I love your daughter," he said and thrust James back.

Sword tip raking the packed earth, Breville regained his balance and, a hand to his throat where Lucien's blade had scored a thin line, said, "If that is true, why did you not accept marriage to her?"

"For De Gautier lands? Two reasons, one being pride."

"The other?"

"Would you take to wife a woman you loved and have her always believe you did so only for gain?"

Suspicion narrowed James's lids, but he nodded. "I see."

"Do you? Then you no longer believe I stole her?"

"At the risk of being made an unpardonable fool, I will take your word you did not."

Lucien drew a deep breath that did little to ease the strain in his chest. "I am glad to hear it. Now leave your men without, and we will talk in the keep while I make ready to join your search. I would know everything." Lucien turned away.

Shortly, James appeared in the hall amid the bustle of those of Lucien's household who made ready for his departure. Accompanied by Sir Gavin, he halted before the dais where Lucien consulted with a senior knight.

Lucien looked around. "When did Alessandra disappear?"

"Melissant discovered her missing yestermorn after the tournament," James said.

"She should not have ventured out at night," Sir Gavin said. "It is the same as when her mother was taken."

Lucien frowned. "You believe she disappeared the night before?"

"It would follow," Sir Gavin said with a shrug. "You send her a message, and she is gone the next day. Likely, she was caught out in the open as she sought to answer your summons."

"How did you know the message was from me?" Lucien asked.

Sir Gavin smiled. "The look on her face when she received it. Did you know she loves you?"

Lucien returned his regard to James.

"My men spent all day yesterday scouring the countryside," James continued, "but without result."

"Did you set dogs to track her?"

"I would have, but there is malady among them. Too, once I was convinced you were responsible, it seemed an unnecessary exercise."

Lucien grunted. "And now it may be too late to pick up her scent."

"Aye, but if her fate is the same as her mother's, whoever took her is headed for the nearest port."

— 310 —

Lucien inclined his head. "Then we ride on London."

"Too obvious," Sir Gavin said. "More likely, they will go by way of Southampton."

Lucien considered the older man's wisdom, nodded. "Still, I would send on to London to be certain."

"Two parties, then?"

"Two parties," Lucien agreed. "My men and I will take Southampton. James?"

"I go with you."

"Then I shall take my men to London," Sir Gavin said.

Vincent stepped forward. "And I shall accompany you."

Sir Gavin snorted. "With your dice?"

"With my sword, Crennan," Vincent growled. "Like it or nay, you will suffer my company."

Pleased Vincent had not backed down, his determination to redeem himself growing each day, Lucien said, "Let us delay no longer. We will have to ride hard for all the ground that must be covered this day."

A half hour later, the two parties thundered across the land before Falstaff. One toward London. One toward Southampton.

38

"I T WILL BE good to be back in Algiers," Rashid said where he lay behind Alessandra, his chest against her back. "This cold is not fit for humans."

She stared into the fire, reflected that even if she never fully adapted to the climate, the cold of her body was far preferable to the cold of her heart.

Beyond the fire, Jacques lay on his side beneath a blanket, watching her as he had done throughout the day.

He was her hope. In spite of what he had done to her in Tangier, his concern for her welfare seemed genuine. He had truly believed he was making amends by leading Rashid to her. Now that he knew different, it was possible he could be convinced to aid in her escape.

She offered a tentative smile.

His face showed momentary surprise, then he returned the gesture.

"Are you awake, Alessandra?" Rashid asked.

Though tempted to feign sleep in the hope he would loosen his hold on her, she said, "I am awake."

"What are you thinking?"

"How nice it would have been to stay at the inn we passed earlier," she lied. "As you say, it is cold."

He rose onto an elbow and rolled her to her back. "Do I not keep you warm?"

"It is not you, Rashid. It is the weather."

He swept the hair off her brow. "There are other ways to be warm," he said and drew a finger down her throat to the neck of her gown. "I am thinking we need not wait until we are wed."

The suggestion shocked her, for never would she have expected this of him. She summoned what she hoped was a regretful smile. "We are not alone."

He glanced at the Frenchman. "We could be."

"Nay, Rashid. I…wish to be pure on our wedding night in accordance with your faith."

"But you do not share my beliefs."

"It is also the Christian belief."

His eyes delved her face, then he kissed her. "If that is what you desire."

Alessandra was grateful he did not linger over the intimacy, else she might have had to pretend a response she did not feel.

"You love me, do you not?" he asked. "As your mother loved my father?"

Only as her childhood friend. Never as a woman should love a man. Never as she loved Lucien. "I have always loved you," she half lied.

He smiled, closed his eyes as if to impress her words upon his mind, then said, "Our parents' love was great. I am certain my father continues to mourn Sabine's death."

Mention of the loss of her mother made her ache, remembrance of the circumstances under which she had died stirred her anger. Knowing it best not to let Rashid see how deeply she was affected, she determined to ask the question to which she yet lacked an answer. "What was your mother' punishment, Rashid?"

Pain, revealed by firelight, lined his face. "Leila is dead."

Alessandra knew she should not feel relief, but she did. The murdering woman could injure no others.

"How?" she asked, though she was not certain she truly wished to know.

His dark eyes became distant. "For my sake, Father agreed to return her to her family for what she had done—to be finished with her forever—but she would not let it be."

"What do you mean?"

"She asked for a farewell embrace, and when Father complied, she tried to stab him. He wrested the dirk from her and, in anger, turned it on her." He swallowed loudly. "She died laughing, Alessandra. It was the most gruesome thing I have seen—laughing and cursing Father, Sabine, you, even me."

Alessandra cupped his jaw. "I am sorry. I know it must hurt."

His bitter smile turned sweet. "Of course you do."

"And Khalid?" she asked.

He gave a short laugh. "He would be dead now had he not disappeared."

"He left Algiers?"

"That surprises you?"

"Algiers is his home. But why do you say he would be dead?"

"You do not know it was he who aided De Gautier in your escape?"

She knew, but feared confirming Rashid's belief should Khalid resurface. "No, and I do not believe it."

"Believe it, Alessandra. He is the one who purchased a eunuch who was not a eunuch, who did not give punishment where punishment was due."

"How do you know that?"

"That he did not bastinado De Gautier as ordered?"

She nodded.

"Had Khalid obeyed me, the Englishman could not have escaped, much less taken you with him. He would have been crippled—or nearly so."

"Was that what you wished?" she whispered, horrified at the ease with which he spoke.

"Do not look at me like that," he snapped. "What I wanted was to see him dead—and he would have been had I not feared what you might think of me."

Risking further inciting him, she asked, "Why do you want me, Rashid?"

He lay back. "You have been mine since the beginning. From the moment your mother pulled aside the blanket and let me see the girl child within."

"But you could not have been more than two."

"About that, but I remember. My mother had been sent away because of Sabine."

Alessandra nearly told him the reason Jabbar had banished Leila that first time—for trying to poison her mother—but there was nothing to be gained in burdening him with another terrible truth.

"To stop my crying," he continued, "Father promised me that one day you would be mine. Perhaps it would have appeased me, and I would have shed no more tears, but your mother would not let me hold you. She said I was too young, that I could look but not touch."

"And so Leila came back."

"Yes, and even she tried to keep me from you, but I was determined to claim you. And I finally did."

"As you are claiming me now."

"There is nothing dishonorable in it. It is as Allah wills a woman to be."

"And if I do not wish to be claimed?"

His eyebrows descended. "You will be happy with me. As first wife, the harem will be yours to govern, and do you give me a son, you will be mother of my heir."

What Alessandra had once accepted with wide-eyed innocence was no longer enough. She wanted a husband and children, but not with Rashid. No longer did he figure into her world, having been left far behind the day Lucien had entered the harem. The boy in Rashid might have understood that, but not the man.

She closed her eyes and turned her face away. "I am tired. It has been a long day."

Without further words, he once more curved an arm around her.

Alessandra lifted her lids a fraction and met Jacques's gaze that was just visible above the blanket he had pulled up over his nose.

You are going to help me get out of this, she silently told him.

As if he heard, he nodded.

Something did not fit.

For what seemed the hundredth time, Lucien paced the camp, working forward and backward what was known and what was not. When, at last, his worn mind found the fit, he cursed and strode to where Breville and the others made their beds around the campfire.

"Surely your father taught you stealth in murdering a man in his sleep," James muttered when Lucien knelt beside him.

"Tell me," Lucien rasped, "did you ever discover the means by which Catherine was stolen from Corburry?"

James lifted his head, squinted at him. "Nay, I returned early morn from a two-day trip and found her missing. Some time between eve and dawn she was taken."

"You do not know if she received a message that would have summoned her out of the castle during the night?"

"How would I know that? 'Twas assumed a De Gautier had taken her from our bed."

Lucien thrust to his feet. "You assumed wrong, Breville, just as we assumed wrong in thinking Alessandra's captor would take her to Southampton."

The man sat up. "What say you?"

"We ride!"

Shortly, in the dark of middle night, the Southampton-bound party turned their mounts toward London.

39

"*Mon dieu*," Jacques blurted as he swept his gaze over the room into which the rotund woman had led them.

Peeking out from her hood, Alessandra agreed with his assessment, but kept her head lowered as Rashid had instructed.

"You want, I could send a girl up to sweep it out," the woman said.

"No." Rashid pushed Alessandra ahead of him. "It will suffice."

The woman peered at him, trying to see his face beneath his hood, then returned her regard to the Frenchman who had so charmed her she seemed to have forgotten the not-so-distant defeat suffered by the English at the hands of the French.

"If there be anything ye need"—she gave a gray-toothed smile— "ye'll let Anna know, hmm?"

"Of course, mademoiselle," Jacques said. "I will come to you directly."

With an immense swing of her hips, she turned back down the corridor.

Rashid closed the door behind him and tossed back the hood to reveal his distinctly Arabic countenance. "Now we wait."

For the ship that, on the morrow, would deliver Rashid to his homeland, Alessandra reflected. Though he did not know it, she would not be with him—providing the plan hastily conceived with Jacques succeeded. It had to, since her scheme of delaying their journey had failed.

Knowing the time constraints they were under to reach the ship before it departed, she had done her best to slow their progress these past days. But despite feigned malady, a saddle that mysteriously came uncinched, and the disappearance of their provisions, Rashid had not slowed. Now they were in London, and the morrow would tell what was to be her fate.

Misinterpreting her silence, Rashid said, "It is only for one night."

She lowered her hood and looked to where Jacques stood at the window. "Only one night," she echoed.

Missing their exchange, Rashid crossed to the bed, patted the lumpy mattress, and threw back the blanket to reveal frantically scattering insects. He yelped and lurched back.

"This you prefer to sleeping out-of-doors?" he demanded.

Alessandra hastened forward and brushed the insects to the rush-strewn floor. "At least it will be warmer, and there is food to be had belowstairs."

"Such a primitive lot," Rashid grumbled. "It will be bliss to be back in Algiers."

"It will," she absently agreed.

He snapped his gaze to her and smiled. "Perhaps it will not be so bad," he said and gingerly lowered to the mattress. "At least it is soft between the lumps."

Jacques started toward the door. "I will see what food can be had. You are hungry, yes?"

"Very," Alessandra answered.

"You, Rashid?"

He grimaced. "Not for English fare."

"Sorry, my friend," the Frenchman said. "You will have to wait until we reach the Maghrib to satisfy your craving." He slipped Alessandra a cryptic look, and was gone.

Having feared Rashid would not allow him to leave alone, she released her breath.

In the silence, Rashid's eyes appreciatively considered her, making her intensely aware it was the first time they were truly alone since he had taken her from Corburry.

Alessandra removed her cloak, draped it over the back of a rickety chair, and wandered to the window to peer down into the filthy street. Moments later, Jacques emerged from the inn and took off at a run. Dragging fingers through her hair, she watched until he went from sight.

Hurry, she silently urged, then shifted her gaze to the bits of gray water visible between the buildings that separated the inn from the harbor. Somewhere out there, was the ship that would return Rashid home.

She heard the bed creak, then his footsteps over the grit and dry rushes covering the floor. Halting at her back, he put his arms around her.

Alessandra tensed. Surely he did not intend to become intimate with Jacques soon to return? She looked down at where he clasped his hands over her abdomen.

They were nice hands. Though smaller than Lucien's, Rashid's were so smooth and unblemished she imagined they would glide over her like silk. But it was the rasp of Lucien's worn, calloused hands, their strength and familiarity, that she longed to feel. Between silk and coarse wool, she would choose the latter.

"You will soon forget him and think only of me," Rashid murmured. "Trust me in this, Alessandra."

How had he known? And what of her ruse these past days—affecting an attitude of acceptance and favor toward him?

"What speak you of?" she clung to her deception.

He brushed aside her hair and placed his lips near her ear. "Though you say you love me, I know it is not true. Still, I am certain you will come to feel for me as your mother felt for my father, and all that fire of yours will belong to me."

"But I do love you, Rashid."

He touched his mouth to her ear, trailed it down her neck to her shoulder. "As a brother, but soon as your lover."

She tried to turn to him, but he gripped her firmly about the waist and drew his other hand up her ribs.

"You think the Englishman would make you happy." He nuzzled her nape. "But once I lie with you, you will feel different."

How vain, Alessandra thought, then reminded herself of the culture in which she had been raised, where a man was the supreme master. His wives, especially if there were many, magnified his self-importance with their eagerness to gain his sexual attention.

Still, Rashid seemed in an amiable mood, and Alessandra thought it might be worth the risk of reasoning with him. She owed it to him to try one last time.

"Rashid, your mother, my mother, even Jabbar said I would not make you a good wife. Surely you have not forgotten?"

He let her hair fall back into place and turned her to him. "They were wrong."

"They were not. These English you detest—I am one of them. I always have been, always shall be, and England is where I belong."

His smile was indulgent, though also bitter. "With me is where you belong. You are mine—"

"I am not a possession. I am your friend, and that is all."

"You will be more when we are wed. I promise you, it will be the same as what was between Jabbar and Sabine."

She wanted to shake him, to loosen his crazy ideal of love. Instead, she said, "Yes, Rashid, my mother did love your father, but I am not Sabine. Never will we have the great love our parents had. Friends is all we will be, and perhaps not even that if you force me to return to Algiers."

He pecked a kiss on her lips, then released her and returned to the bed. He removed his cloak, spread it on the mattress, and laid down. "Join me?"

"Did you hear nothing I said?"

He clasped his hands behind his head. "I heard, and the discussion is done."

"But we have only just begun."

"Done, Alessandra. I will speak of it no more."

"But—"

"Enough!"

Fighting tears, she swung back to the window and silently bemoaned, *He leaves me no choice. None at all.*

40

"Vincent!" Lucien dropped to his knees and turned his brother.

Lids lowered, blood caking his face from the gash on his forehead, Vincent did not respond.

Lucien pulled him into his arms, called again, "Vincent!"

James and Jervais's entrance into the tent went unnoticed until Jervais lowered beside his brothers.

Eldest and youngest exchanged glances, then Lucien put an ear to Vincent's mouth, watched for the rise and fall of his chest, and prayed for breath.

Was it his imagination, or did life, indeed, flutter through his brother?

Lucien lifted his head and found Vincent staring at him through half-hooded eyes.

"I am sorry, Lucien," he mumbled. "I tried…"

Lucien clasped his brother nearer. "You are alive. That is all that matters."

"No time," Vincent's muffled voice rose from Lucien's embrace. "You must reach her ere he does."

"Sir Gavin," Lucien said as he eased Vincent to the ground.

"Aye, 'twas he who attacked me."

Lucien looked to James, conveying what the man refused to believe—until now. Sir Gavin's undoing had been the words he had spoken in the great hall at Falstaff that had festered at the back of Lucien's mind until they finally drew near enough to be examined.

She should not have ventured out at night, he had said of Alessandra. *It is the same as when her mother was taken.*

The man could not have known how Catherine had been stolen from Corbury. Then the miscreant had thrown them off his trail with the cool logic that Alessandra's captor would flee by way of Southampton.

"Why did Crennan attack you?" Lucien asked.

Vincent raised a trembling hand and touched the wound. "I found the letter."

"What letter?"

"When I questioned him as to the leisure with which we rode on London, he became defensive. We argued, and when he went to bathe in the stream this night—it is still night, is it not?" At Lucien's nod, he continued. "I stole into his tent and went through his belongings. I found the letter—" He rolled onto his side and retched.

When he was finished, Lucien carried him to the cot and sent Jervais for a basin of water.

Vincent shuddered, feebly hugged his arms about himself. "You waste time."

Lucien dragged blankets over him. "Tell me about the letter."

Not until Jervais returned did Vincent find the strength to comply. As Lucien mopped his brow, cleaning away blood and perspiration, Vincent said, "The letter you gave me…to have delivered to Alessandra the night ere our departure. He had it, Lucien."

Lucien looked around. "Now are you convinced, James?"

Breville momentarily closed his eyes. "How could I have known? We were friends. Does this mean Agnes knew his plans?"

Lucien turned back to Vincent. "What happened next?"

"He discovered me here. I confronted him with the letter, and he struck me."

"And left you for dead," Lucien said bitterly and thrust to his feet. "Now that Sir Gavin is found out, he has surely gone to London to make certain his plans for Alessandra do not go awry."

"Before I lost consciousness," Vincent said, "I heard him mutter something about Marietta. A woman?"

"A ship," Lucien guessed, then motioned for Jervais to attend to Vincent. "Do you ride or stay, Breville?"

Face hardened by fury, James said, "I ride. Crennan is mine."

Rather than argue as to who had first rights to the man, Lucien met Jervais's anxious gaze. "I trust no other with Vincent," he said. "There will be other times for us to do battle together." Though he prayed this would be his final battle, that his family would finally know peace, he also knew it was unrealistic. If not the Brevilles, there would be others who challenged the De Gautiers.

He turned on his heel and strode from the tent.

Outside, Sir Gavin's men waited to discover what had transpired while they slept. Though the arrival of Lucien and James had sent them scrambling for their weapons before they realized who rode on their camp, they remained none the wiser as to the reason for their coming.

And Lucien had no intention of wasting time explaining it. Soon enough they would learn of their lord's sins.

Calling for his men to gain their saddles, Lucien mounted his destrier. It would be morning before they reached London. But, God willing, Crennan was not far ahead.

Alessandra, he silently entreated, *be impetuous, be wild, be reckless. Do not go quietly.*

Though he knew she might this moment be aboard a ship sailing south, he had to believe she was still in London, waiting for him to come to her. And if she was not...

I will go into Algiers and bring you out again, he vowed. *You are mine, as I am yours.*

41

THE BLOW LANDED.

Remorse flooding Alessandra, she sat up and turned to Rashid who lay upon the pillow as if he still slept. In a way, he did.

She looked to a grinning Jacques whose weapon—a rotted board—was propped upon his shoulder.

"You hit him too hard," she said.

"No more than he deserved. Besides, it will assure he does not come to before he ought."

Alessandra rose and crossed to the window. "Soon it will be light."

"Thus, there is no time to waste." Jacques tossed the board to the bed, hurried to the door, and opened it a crack. A moment later, he crept out. When he returned, he shouldered a large trunk.

Alessandra bolted the door behind him and went to the table where quill and parchment awaited her. While Jacques bound and gagged Rashid and fit him into the trunk, she lit a lamp and set to writing a letter—one of apology, explanation, and reminiscing of a childhood that belonged in the past.

"Farewell, old friend," she whispered and signed her name.

"I am ready," she said after placing the letter in Rashid's hand.

Jacques closed the trunk lid and secured it.

"You have punched enough holes that he will be able to breathe well?" she asked.

"Plenty. He will not want for air." He heaved a sigh. "Now I am forgiven, no?"

Alessandra was jolted back to the reality of her relationship with the Frenchman. Though she was still vexed at having been sold into slavery and stolen from Corburry, he seemed truly repentant and had acted to right the wrongs.

"Nearly so," she said honestly.

He pretended nonchalance. "You will let me know when it is *nearly so* no longer?"

She summoned a smile. "I shall."

Jacques crossed to the pallet and retrieved his cloak. As he settled it about his shoulders, he glanced from her chemise to her stockinged feet. "Dress quickly. I shall return shortly and not alone."

A quarter hour later, he entered the room ahead of two men of great size and frightening countenance. Caps pulled down over their ears to ward off the cold of a gusty English morn, they looked with interest at Alessandra.

Grateful she had covered her own head, she peered at them from beneath her hood and wondered where Jacques had unearthed such unsavory characters.

"There." Jacques nodded at the trunk. "Carry it to the dock, and you will have your reward."

"Who be the lady?" asked the older of the men.

Jacques strode to her and put an arm around her. "My wife, gentlemen, Madame Felice LeBrec."

The younger ruffian elbowed the older. "Sooner done, the sooner we have our coin."

The older one grunted, lumbered to the trunk, and hefted one end. Shortly, Rashid was borne from the room and began a hazardous journey down stairs that protested loudly beneath their weight.

Leaving their few possessions in the room since they would return before journeying to Corburry, Jacques and Alessandra followed the hired men through and around the dirt and garbage of streets beginning to awaken to morn.

In contrast, the docks were already teeming with life. Everywhere, men made ready for the departure of the ship that would carry Rashid far from England.

Walking beside Jacques, Alessandra marveled over the berthed vessel. Though Nicholas's ship had been splendid, it hardly compared with this one. "*Marietta*," she read the gold-lettered name.

Jacques led her to the railing along the edge of the dock. "Wait here while I see to Rashid."

Huddled in her cloak, the moist air chilling her cheeks, she watched him direct the men to the area where baggage was stacked and waiting to be hauled aboard.

Without a care for the contents, they dropped the trunk to the dock, making her wince in anticipation of the bruises Rashid would suffer from such handling.

Jacques paid them from a pouch and started to walk away, only to find the men blocking his path. Haggling and angry words followed, but finally the Frenchman dropped more coins in their palms and the men retreated.

After speaking briefly with one of the crew who also received payment, Jacques returned to Alessandra. "Thieves," he muttered. "I had to pay those men twice what they agreed upon yesterday."

"You expected better?"

His scowl ascended to a smile. "Foolish, no?"

She looked to the ship. "What now?"

"If I had my way, we would start for Corburry, but since you refuse to leave Rashid to his fate, we wait."

Of their plan, it was the one thing on which Alessandra had not conceded. Bound and gagged, Rashid might not make his presence known, and he would certainly not survive the long voyage in the trunk. Thus, Jacques would accompany the trunk to the cabin Rashid had reserved, extricate him from the trunk, and leave him bound and gagged on the cot. Rashid would be discovered, but not until after the *Marietta* sailed.

Over the next half hour, during which the docks swarmed with passengers eager to begin their voyage, Alessandra decided it was a good thing Jacques had struck Rashid so hard. Otherwise, his awakening and subsequent commotion might have foiled their plan.

Gripping her hood to keep it from being blown off her head, she watched as two sailors carried the trunk up the sharply inclined ramp.

Jacques patted her hand. "I shall return shortly, *cherie*." He strode the dock, mounted the ramp, and went from sight.

Alessandra settled her elbows on the railing, cupped her chin in one hand, and looked down into the cold, murky water.

Finally, there came the call to board, and the travelers advanced up the ramp.

Where was Jacques? she worried as she searched the deck for sight of him. What was taking him so long? Might Rashid have regained consciousness and overpowered him?

Then she saw him. At the top of the ramp, his progress hindered by the upward surge of passengers, he waved his arms, seemingly in a frantic manner.

A quick check of her person revealing the hood had fallen to her shoulders, she whipped it over her hair, but he waved more vigorously and shouted something she could not catch. As she strained to make sense of what he was saying, a hand settled to her shoulder.

She turned.

A friendly smile awaited her. "Good day, Alessandra."

She gaped. What was Sir Gavin doing here? Had he and her father tracked Rashid to London? She glanced past him, but saw no other familiar faces.

Then a piece fell into place, and she heard again the words of the man who had lifted her onto his horse after she had run from Rashid at Corbury.

I want her gone from here. Now!

She had known the voice, but only now did its owner register.

Too late, she understood what Jacques had tried to tell her. More, she understood the reason Sir Gavin had never mentioned that Rashid and Jacques had come to Glasbrook in search of her.

When Melissant had asked after her grandparents the night Alessandra had first met Sir Gavin, he had said they had been in London for more than a month. Thus, they could not have been present when Rashid and Jacques arrived at Glasbrook. But Gavin had surely been, and for reasons known only to himself, he had assisted Rashid in abducting her, which meant he had also...

Realization striking like the back of a hand, Alessandra lunged away in hopes of losing herself among the throng, but Gavin caught her cloak. The neck of the garment cutting into her throat, she was dragged back and his arms came around her. "So you know," he said.

Pulling the cloak away from her neck, she searched out Jacques and saw he continued to struggle against the crowd.

Once more pretending defeat, she stilled, and when Gavin turned her toward him, clenched a hand and punched him between the eyes.

He released her and dropped back a step.

Ignoring the pain cramping her hand, she thrust through the crowd, building a wall between her and the man who would soon be fast upon her heels.

Where she was going, she did not know, but it would not be toward the ship she was to have boarded.

Denying herself a look behind lest that moment was all it took for Sir Gavin to overtake her, she left the docks and turned onto a familiar-looking street.

As she ran, she was reminded of Tangier and her flight from Lucien. The irony of it was she would not be running now had she not run from him then, for there would not have been a Jacques to lead Rashid to her. But there would still be Sir Gavin, he who had surely abducted her mother and sold her into slavery.

The ramshackle inn in which she had spent a sleepless night peeking at her from between two larger buildings, she headed for it and, shortly, clambered up the stairs to the room at the end of the corridor. It was locked. As she searched the pouch upon her girdle, she looked over her shoulder and nearly cried with relief to discover she was not followed.

She fit the key in the lock, but as she turned it, she heard pounding on the stairs. And there was Sir Gavin, taking the last steps to the second floor.

Alessandra lunged into the room, slammed the door, and locked it.

Without haste, Sir Gavin advanced, as evidenced by his shadow that crept beneath the door and spread to the toes of her shoes. She jumped back.

"Alessandra, open the door."

A weapon. She searched the room for one, but there was only the board with which Jacques had knocked Rashid unconscious. She snatched it up, retreated to the window, and held it behind her in hopes of once more catching Sir Gavin unawares.

He knocked. "Alessandra, my dear, I must speak with you."

How harmless he sounded!

"Please. There are things I need to explain."

Indeed there were.

He put his weight to the door, but though it strained and creaked, it did not give. He tried again, this time using thrust.

Fearing the lock would not hold, she closed her eyes. "Lord, I need another angel." Preferably, in the form of Lucien.

The sound of splintering wood snapped her eyes open.

The door swung inward, hit the wall, and rebounded.

Throwing a hand up to avoid being struck by it, Gavin pushed the door away and stepped inside. Fixing his gaze on Alessandra, he paused in the middle of the room.

"You are afraid of me," he said. "You should not be. I would never hurt you."

Though slivers pierced her where she gripped the board, she curled her hands more tightly around it. "Is that what you told my mother—that you would never hurt her? You do not think she was injured when you stole her from my father and sent her into slavery?"

A corner of his mouth drew up into something of a smile. "You are guessing, Alessandra."

She shook her head. "I know it was you. Just as I know you intended to also steal me from my father."

His gaze shifted to the floor, and he stared at it as if considering her words, then he held out a hand. "Give it to me."

"What?"

"That which you have behind your back."

The shadows thrown by the dim lamp having revealed the board, she brought it forward. "Do not come any nearer."

He crossed his arms over his chest. "Do you want to know why I did it?"

"I do."

"You asked if I loved Catherine. I did. And when she chose James Breville over me—"

"You were cousins!"

He shrugged. "All those years watching her grow, waiting for her to come of age…Then Breville took her from me. And she did not even love him."

"Neither did she love you."

His nostrils flared. "Given a chance, she would have come to love me."

Alessandra clenched her teeth. It would do more harm than good to throw in his face the love her mother had felt for Jabbar.

"When she wed James," he continued, "I promised myself I would turn my heart and head elsewhere. And I was succeeding, but then Catherine summoned me. I hastened to her at Corbury, believing she meant to tell me she had made a mistake in wedding James—that it was me she loved." His mouth bent with bitterness. "She thought I teased when I went down on my knees and kissed her hands. She laughed, said I must be serious if I was to aid her in obtaining a birthday present for James."

Feeling his anger mount, Alessandra took a step back.

"She was oblivious to my feelings, always treating me like a brother when it was her husband I should have been." He pressed fingers to his forehead as if he suffered pain. "While I sat beside her in the gardens as she chatted about whether a new sword or a saddle would make a better gift, it occurred to me that if she could not be mine, neither should James have her."

"So you sold her into slavery." Alessandra could not keep condemnation from her voice.

"She should not have flaunted her happiness! A little regret was all I asked."

"You were her friend. How could you betray her?"

"She betrayed first!"

"But she did not know what you felt for her. You never told her."

He blinked. "She should have known. I could not have made it clearer."

"Except with words."

Abruptly, he turned to the table where the lamp burned dimly. Pressing his palms to it, he hung his head between outstretched arms.

The open doorway beckoned to Alessandra, but she could not go until she knew everything. "How did you lure my mother from Corburry?"

"She did not tell you what happened?"

"Nay."

"James was visiting one of his vassals when she summoned me. Otherwise, it would have been impossible to do what I did. Knowing I could not spirit her away without being seen, I sent her a message from James that asked her to meet him at the stream at dusk. A tryst, you see. And like a lamb, she came."

"And you abducted her."

He looked around. "I stole upon her and bound her up. Though I was careful so she would not know it was me, I have ever feared she might have guessed, and for that, I led Rashid and Jacques to you. If Catherine had known and told you, I did not doubt you would reveal me."

"She never knew."

"I guessed as much when I met you." He straightened, pushed a hand through his hair, and stepped toward her.

Hoping to delay his advance, she taunted, "You are proud of what you did."

He halted. "Haunted, but never proud. For an entire day, I fought the demons that plotted against her, but once the idea was in my head, they would not let it go. Do you not see?" His tone was pleading. "It was not me who did it. It was them. What I would have given to have her back the day after I sent her into slavery!"

Though he spoke in riddles, Alessandra unraveled enough to understand it was not evil that drove him, but unrequited love and an unbalanced mind. "If that is true, why have you done the same to me?"

"As with your mother, I fought it, and again I lost."

"But why harm me? I am not my mother."

"You looked at me the way she did. You were her all over again, tearing at my heart, making me want something I could not have."

"You wanted me?"

"I wanted Catherine. But in you I could have had her, or nearly. However, you only wanted De Gautier, as I discovered when I heard you had gone to his tent after giving me your favor."

Alessandra gasped. "'Twas you who set the bishop upon me, you who sent him to Lucien's tent."

"The bishop?" He shook his head. "Nay, that would have been Agnes."

Did he speak true? Insecure in James's love, had Gavin's sister purposely set out to do her harm? Of course she had.

"You betrayed me with De Gautier," Gavin continued.

"I did not. The favor I gave you was in remembrance of my mother. You said so yourself."

Uncertainty came and went on his face. "Aye, but you led me to believe differently. Thus, with your betrayal still fresh and hurting, I had to act quickly when I overheard a conversation between De Gautier and his brothers."

"What was said?"

"Enough to make me realize you must disappear the same as Catherine."

"But I know Lucien sent the message that summoned me to him. It was not you."

He smiled. "A timely coincidence. I had planned to have a message delivered to you later that night, but then De Gautier accommodated me. It was perfect, throwing suspicion on his family for the second time. And it would have worked if…"

"What?" Was her father this moment making war on Lucien?

Gavin shrugged. "I am not selfish, Alessandra. What I did to your mother and you was not only for myself."

"You make no sense."

"Just like Catherine, you took from another woman for your own gain."

"What are you talking about?"

"When Catherine wed James, she not only wounded me, but Agnes."

Agnes who had wanted James for herself.

"She loved James. It was always assumed they would wed. So what I did in sending Catherine away also helped my sister."

Alessandra shook her head. "But what have I to do with it?"

"Melissant," he hissed. "She was to wed the heir of Falstaff. Then you came and took that from her."

"She did not wish to wed Vincent."

"Agnes wanted it, and if not Vincent, then Lucien would have done. 'Tis the same, can you not see? Catherine again."

He was mad. "It is the same only because you make it so."

"Not I. You, Alessandra. You made it so!"

Certain he was approaching an edge over which he might also take her, she did not argue further and asked instead, "Did Agnes know what you had done? Did she aid you?"

When he finally answered, his anger seemed to have dimmed. "At the time she did not know, but I told her years later."

"And?"

He gave a bark of laughter. "She did not believe me, did not appreciate all I had done for her. Now she shall."

"Because of my disappearance."

"Aye. But enough of this. Tell me how you convinced the Frenchman to assist you in escaping Rashid."

"I can answer for myself," came a voice from the doorway.

"Jacques!" Alessandra exclaimed.

Sir Gavin cursed and, keeping her in his peripheral line of sight, turned to the Frenchman. "Where is Rashid?"

"Comfortably settled on the *Marietta*, and soon bound for the Maghrib."

"Not without Alessandra."

Jacques stepped into the room. "*Oui*. Alessandra stays in England."

Gavin drew his sword. "She goes."

"It is over, Crennan. Run, and you may escape the wrath of the Brevilles and De Gautiers. Stay, and you will become well acquainted with death."

"I am no coward! I have never run from anything—"

"Except the truth," Jacques interrupted.

Gavin charged.

Jacques answered, letting fly a dagger that struck his attacker's sword arm and caused Sir Gavin to shout and drop his weapon. But it did not stop his advance, and the two slammed into the wall and went down amid flailing arms and legs.

As they fought over the dirt-encrusted floor, Alessandra searched for a means of aiding Jacques, but their violent shifting—one moment he was atop, the next Sir Gavin—made it impossible for her to correctly land a blow.

"Run!" Jacques cried.

She started to obey, but she could not leave him.

When the two rolled into the table, nearly upsetting it, she hastened forward lest the lamp overturned. But as she reached to snatch it to safety, a leg kicked the table and dropped the lamp amid rushes that burst into flames eager for the hem of her skirts.

Alessandra jumped back. The acrid scent burning her nostrils, she looked to Gavin and Jacques who continued to fight as if unaware the room would soon be engulfed and them with it.

She flung the board aside, bent, and grabbed the first shoulder that came to hand. "Cease! The room is afire!"

A fist struck her temple and knocked her backward. Dazed, she lurched up onto her hands and knees, but as she crawled toward Jacques and Gavin, fire rushed into her path.

"Jacques!" she screamed. "Gavin!"

"Alessandra!"

She jerked her chin around, and through the billowing smoke, saw the figure of a man burst into the room. Lucien.

She made it to her feet and fell into the arms he wrapped around her. Then he was lifting her against his chest.

"Jacques!" she protested as Lucien ran for the door.

"I will come back for him," he said and traversed the smoky corridor and stairs.

The air outside struck Alessandra as wonderfully fresh and clean, though it had not seemed so earlier. Looking up, she saw a crowd had gathered before the inn.

"Your daughter," Lucien said, setting her to her feet before James who immediately pulled her close.

"Are you well, Alessa?"

She coughed, nodded, peered over her shoulder. And saw Lucien plunge back into the burning inn. Gasping, she tried to pull free.

James hugged her nearer. "He will come out."

He could not know that, and it did not seem likely when flames burst from the window of the room she had shared with Jacques and Rashid.

Whimpering, she turned her face into her father's chest. *Dear Lord,* she silently prayed, *bring Lucien out. And Jacques. Even...aye, even Sir Gavin.*

"Accursed Gavin," her father muttered. "By blood, he will answer for his every crime against me and mine."

Then he had learned his brother-in-law was responsible for her abduction. And likely Sabine's.

"And Agnes," he choked. "Agnes..."

Gripped by his pain, she tilted her head back and met his gaze.

"Did Agnes have a hand in it?" he asked.

That Gavin had told Agnes of what he had done all those years ago seemed no longer relevant. Too, he had said his sister had not believed him. As there was no need to ruin more lives, and Agnes should not be made to suffer for her brother's sins, Alessandra shook her head. "Nay, Father, she did not know."

Hope flickered in his eyes. "You are certain?"

"Sir Gavin voiced his regret that his sister was unaware of what he had done for her."

She felt a breath of relief go out of her father.

A shout brought her head around. Though Lucien's face was smudged black, his hair singed, never was there a more welcome sight than that of him emerging from the inn with a man over his shoulder.

Alessandra pulled out of her father's arms and ran to where Lucien gently lowered Jacques to the muddy street.

"Stay back!" he snapped.

Ignoring him, she sank to her knees beside him, and saw the reason he did not wish her so near.

Jacques was badly burned, his beautiful clothes charred and smoldering, face red and puckered where fire had tasted him, and the eyes he opened to peer at her were glazed.

"Forgive me?" His mouth trembled violently as if he attempted one of his charming smiles.

"Of course," she exclaimed. "Completely."

He raised a hand toward her, but it fell to his abdomen.

Alessandra entwined her fingers with his. "You will be fine, my friend."

"No, *cherie,* I will not."

"Do not—"

"Did you know I have never lain with a woman? Never."

Alessandra swallowed. "I did not know."

"Were I man enough, methinks you would have been the first."

She glanced at Lucien, saw the displeasure upon his face, and returned her gaze to Jacques.

"Tell me," he rasped, "could you have loved me?" His plea was followed by a bout of coughing.

Lucien silent beside her, Alessandra leaned down and said, "I could have." It was a lie, but he was right. He would not be fine.

"That"—he gasped—"is the sweetest lie I have ever heard. It makes me…very happy." His lashes fluttered down.

It seemed a long time before Alessandra or Lucien moved, but when they did, Jacques had passed. Oblivious to his audience and the clamor of men running for water, he bore silent testimony to bravery gone awry.

Face wet with tears, Alessandra looked up at Lucien, and only then realized he had brought out only one man. "Sir Gavin?" she asked.

"Dead."

For the best, she acceded, then began to sob as she was swept with all the fear, anger, and sorrow of these past days.

Lucien helped her to her feet and pulled her into his arms. "I am sorry for your friend, Alessandra. I wish he could have been saved."

"After all the deception he worked upon me, he helped me escape Rashid."

Lucien raised his head. "Rashid was part of this?"

She nodded.

His brow grew more lined, and she was certain he sought to make sense of the connection between Rashid and Gavin. "Was he in the room as well?"

"Nay, he is on the ship. Jacques bound him in his cabin and was returning to deliver me to Corburry when Sir Gavin found me on the docks." She frowned. "How did you know where to find me?"

"A long tale better told later," he said.

"But how did you know I was at the inn?"

He rubbed a smudge of ash from her face. "We were passing by on our way to the docks when we saw the smoke. Something told me it was here I would find you."

"My prayers," she whispered. "I prayed you would come."

"Do you still want me, Alessandra?"

He seemed so uncertain, it tugged at her heart. Always he had been confident and in control, but now she saw some of the boy Lucien must have been before the war between the Brevilles and De Gautiers had consumed him.

She cupped his face in her hands. "I have never stopped wanting you."

"Even when I became an animal in the lists?"

"Even then."

He reached into the neck of his tunic and pulled out her anklet of miniature bells. "I wore these that day. To keep you close."

She touched them. "I thought them lost."

"What does it tell you, Alessandra?"

"That you love me," she ventured. "Do you?"

He lowered his head, kissed her. "I do."

He did not say the words, but it was enough. For now.

"This is hardly the place to ask," he said, "but I need to know. Will you marry me, Alessandra Breville?"

She caught her breath. "But you said—"

"I could not have you believe I wed you only for the land."

So it had been more than foolish pride. "Is that why you sent me the message?"

"It is. When you did not come…" He momentarily closed his eyes. "You are the one for me, Alessandra. Will you marry me and tame the beast?"

"Yes," she said. "I will marry you, Lucien de Gautier."

42

Rashid could not have chosen a better day.

The missive that had first been delivered to Corburry had followed the Brevilles to Falstaff where they had journeyed for the celebration that would culminate in vows spoken before the chapel.

It was Lucien who had brought the travel-weary letter to Alessandra in the chamber where she was being prepared to pledge her life to his. It was he with whom she had shared the three lines of Arabic after sending Melissant and the others away.

Now, hours later, she reflected on Rashid's words. As Jabbar had made his son a satisfactory match with the daughter of a wine merchant, Rashid had released Alessandra from their betrothal, forgiven her as he hoped she would forgive him, and wished her well as she started life anew in England. Terse, perhaps, but it had settled her unsettled places, and the day had passed as beautifully as hoped.

Now, on this autumn eve, with a storm raging outside Falstaff's keep, Lucien and she would finally become one. And not too soon, for he had insisted on courting her these past months to prove himself worthy and further put James at ease over the man who would become his son-in-law.

"If you make me wait much longer," he called, "Vincent will have his wedding night ere I have my own."

She laughed and, pulling fingers through her braids, unraveling them so her crimped tresses draped her shoulders, moved her thoughts to dear Vincent, who aspired to recapture Melissant's hand in marriage—and to get around the obstacle of Agnes.

Though Alessandra knew it was wrong, she was tempted to give aid in doing away with that impediment, as she had done away with her own.

No longer need she fear Agnes would conspire with the bishop to name her a heretic. There was peace between them, owing to the older woman's gratitude that Alessandra would not disclose to James her knowledge of Catherine's abduction. True, Agnes had not believed her brother's claim, but both women understood the revelation would be detrimental to her marriage.

As for Vincent…

Firmly, Alessandra set aside the idea of speaking on his behalf. It was a battle he must win on his own, and she was fairly certain he would want it that way.

Deciding she had made Lucien wait long enough, she peeked around the screen and saw he was seated before the hearth. Back to her, he leaned forward with his forearms propped on his thighs, reminding her of when she had come to his tent during the tournament. This time, his back was not bare, the scars he did not wish her to see hidden from her eyes.

Stepping out from behind the screen, she smoothed her embroidered chemise and wondered how long before it fell at her feet. And shivered, but not with cold.

She crossed to Lucien, laid her hands on his shoulders, and bent forward. "Are you ready for me, my lord?"

He chuckled. "Should I not be the one asking that of you?"

She slid her hands down his chest to the hem of his tunic and lifted it. As her fingers brushed his abdomen, he caught her wrists.

"Come stand before me," he said and started to pull her around.

She resisted. "First, I would look nearer upon your back. It is part of you, and as we are now wed, I would know all of you."

"Not that," he said, the humor gone from his voice.

"I have seen it before."

"Not tonight, Alessandra."

"Surely you are not ashamed of it?"

He looked over his shoulder, and it was displeasure, not passion, in his eyes. "It was not by cowardice I earned those stripes, but by mettle."

"This I know, but I would have you trust me."

He looked ready to refuse, but his eyes softened and he released her and started to raise his tunic.

Alessandra stayed his hands, gripped the hem, and drew the garment off over his head.

With her gaze, she traced the scars, with her fingers, touched them, with her mouth kissed them. And when the tension went out of Lucien, she slid her arms around his neck and put her lips to his ear. "You know not how long I have wanted to be like this with you."

"Then why do you waste time at my back?" He swiveled and captured her between his legs.

"Why?" She peered into his upturned face. "Because I once heard a concubine say that to love a man is to love all of him, from the soles of his feet to the ends of his hair. And I do love all of you, Lucien—the boy who defied my father, the warrior whose scars delivered him into my mother's hands, the man who brought me out of Algiers, the husband who shall ever be my home." She slid her hands into his hair, stepped nearer, and pressed her abdomen to his chest.

He groaned. "This is not progressing how I planned."

She raised an eyebrow. "How did you plan?"

"Words first. Ones that have waited too long to be spoken."

"Then speak them, my lord husband."

He urged her to her knees. Pupils wide and dark, only a narrow ring of amethyst to attest to the color of his eyes, he lowered his head. "I love you, Alessandra Breville de Gautier."

There was something so sweet in the birth of those words that she did not want to let go of them, and so she closed her eyes and savored them until he began to kiss around her mouth. "Tell me again," she beseeched.

He did—over and over until she said, "Words first. What comes second?"

He began unfastening the buttons of her chemise. "I will show you." When the garment dropped to her feet, he stood and swept her into his arms. "Now, Alessandra mine," he said, "we make love." And he carried her to bed.

Excerpt

Baron of Godsmere

The Feud: Book I

England, 1308. Three noblemen secretly gather to ally against their treacherous lord. But though each is elevated to a baron in his own right and given a portion of his lord's lands, jealousy and reprisals lead to a twenty-five year feud, pitting family against family, passing father to son.

The Decree

England, 1333. The chink in Baron Boursier's armor is his fondness for a lovely face. When it costs him half his sight and brands him as one who abuses women, he vows to never again be "blinded" by beauty. Thus, given the choice between forfeiting his lands and wedding one of his enemies to end their feud, he chooses as his betrothed the lady said to be plain of face, rejecting the lady rumored to be most fair.

The Enemy

On the eve of the deadline to honor the king's decree of marriage, the fair Elianor of Emberly takes matters into her own hands. Determined none will suffer marriage to the man better known as *The Boursier*, she sets in motion her plan to imprison him long enough to ensure his barony is forfeited. But when all goes awry and her wrathful enemy compels her to wed him to save his lands, she discovers he is either much changed or much maligned. And the real enemy is one who lurks in their midst. One bent on keeping the feud burning.

2

Barony of Godsmere, Northern England
Autumn's end, 1333

To stop the wedding, she would have to kill the groom. Or so Agatha sought to convince her.

Peering up from beneath the ragged edge of the thick shawl she had drawn over her head, Elianor of Emberly considered the man who approached astride a destrier blacker than the dregs of her ink pot. Though Bayard Boursier was fairly complected, he seemed no less dark than his mount. From his perspiration dampened hair that flipped up at the nape to his unshaven jaw to the merciless heart that beat beneath an ebony tunic, he was kin to the night.

El ground her teeth over the king's plan to ally the bitterest of enemies. Had Edward learned nothing from the mistake of five years past when her aunt had been made to wed into the Boursiers—one that had turned the families' hatred more foul?

"A pox on you, Edward," she muttered as she glared at the king's agent of misery, a man whose appearance hardly improved the nearer he drew, one made worse by the black patch covering his left eye.

A fearsome groom he would make for Thomasin de Arell whom, it was told, he had chosen to take to wife and would do so within the next six days to avoid forfeiture of his lands. But providing all went as planned, *The Boursier*, as he was better known—as if the whole of him could not be contained within his given name—would not have the De Arell woman. Nor would he have El, though until three days past, she had feared he would choose her. Thus, she had laid plans to avoid a sacrifice possibly greater than that offered up with her first marriage.

Despite the shawl's heat that was too much for a relatively warm day, she shivered as memories of her husband crawled over the barriers erected against them.

She shook her head. Murdoch Farrow, to whom she had been wed five years ago at the age of sixteen, was dead. And, God forgive her, she had nearly danced to be free of him. Just as Thomasin de Arell would rejoice in being spared marriage to Bayard Boursier.

As he drew closer, she lowered her gaze. But one peasant among the many who thronged the market in the town outside Castle Adderstone's walls, she feigned interest in the foodstuffs offered by a merchant—an old man whose bones and joints were prominent beneath a thin layer of skin. A moment later, his hands shot up and, in concert with his voice, expressed annoyance over his dealings with a stout woman whose heavily loaded cart evidenced she was from the castle kitchens.

El slid her gaze past unplucked chickens suspended by their legs to the riders who skirted the gathering, and hazarded another look at The Boursier. She groaned. Having only seen him from a distance when he had brought his men against her uncle's, he was larger than thought. Beneath a broad jaw, his neck sloped to expansive shoulders, chest tapered to sword-girded hips, bulky thighs gripped his destrier, hosed calves stretched long to stirrups.

Curling her toes in her slippers, she assured herself she could do this. Though he had chosen Thomasin de Arell, still her family—the Verduns—must ally with the loathsome Boursiers, meaning it fell to her uncle to wed this man's sister. However, if El's plan succeeded, the Boursiers would be expelled from these lands, as might the De Arells.

Pricked by guilt that the De Arells might feel Boursier's wrath for that which would soon be worked upon the latter, she reminded herself of the raid upon Tyne five months past. A dozen villagers' homes had been burned with half their crops, and all evidence suggested the De Arells were responsible for the atrocity visited upon the Verduns' people.

The flick of Boursier's reins drew El's gaze to tanned hands that appeared twice the size of her own. Familiar with the cruelty of which a man's hands were capable, she told herself this one would not get near enough to hurt her as her departed husband had done. Still, her heart pounded with emotions she had struggled to suppress since her wedding night when she had realized Murdoch found her tears pleasing.

Boursier was less than twenty feet distant when the sun came out from behind the clouds, and she was surprised to see his looks lighten. She would have said his hair was deepest brown, but sunlight revealed it to be darkly auburn. And the one visible eye was pale, though she could not tell if the gaze he swept over the town folk was blue, green, or gray. Regardless, his soul was black.

Doubt prying at her purpose, she silently beseeched, *Lord, can I do it?* Not that she believed God would condone her plan, but neither was she certain he would condemn her.

She shifted her regard to the diagonal scar above and below Boursier's eyepatch. Though deserved, he surely loathed the Verduns and De Arells for an affliction without end.

When he was nearly upon the stall behind which El stood and his gaze settled on her, she forced herself not to react in any way that would attract more attention—all the while praying the shawl provided enough shadow to obscure her face. Not that he had ever seen Elianor of Emberly.

Though questioning disturbed his brow, he urged his destrier past.

She eased the air from her lungs, swung around, and hastened to the hooded one who awaited her near a stall piled high with cloth.

Despite broad shoulders that fifty years of life had begun to bend, the woman who looked down upon El had something of a regal bearing.

It was also present in high cheekbones and the dark, sharply arched eyebrows Agatha raised to ask what need not be voiced.

El glanced beyond her at the great fortress that flew the red and gold colors of the House of Boursier, and nodded. In the guise of a kitchen wench, she was ready to steal into Castle Adderstone. Or so she prayed—or should have.

Six days she must hold him. Then, for his refusal to wed his enemy, his lands would be forfeited. Unless she failed.

I shall not, she promised herself.

Even now Boursier was likely feeling the effects of the draught she had slipped into his drink a half hour past. That had been no easy task, one nearly rendered impossible when the cook had approached her. Blessedly, as she tensed for flight, someone had called him to the storeroom.

In his absence, she had stirred Agatha's preparation into the cup that was to be delivered to Boursier's bedchamber, the lord of Castle Adderstone's habit of wine before bed having remained unchanged since Agatha had endured a year in his household.

"'Tis just ahead," Agatha said low, raising the torch to burn away the cobwebs blocking their passage.

El peered around the older woman at stone walls laid not by man, but by God. Here was the place to which Boursier was destined. Carved out of the bowels of the earth outside his own castle, the shaft with its branching passages had been dug by Verduns and De Arells twenty years past when, for several months, they had joined against the Boursiers. El's own grandfather had assisted with the undermining that had brought down a portion of the castle's outer wall—a short-lived victory.

Months following the thwarted siege, she had visited Castle Kelling and bounded onto her grandfather's lap. Only one arm had come around her. Bayard Boursier's father had taken the other.

"This is it, my lady," Agatha said as she turned left off the passageway onto another, at the end of which lay an iron-banded door with a grate at eye level.

El considered Boursier's prison. "It will hold him?"

Agatha fit one of several keys into the lock and pushed the door inward. "'Twould hold three of him."

El accepted the torch offered her, stepped into the chill cell, and grimaced. The stone walls were moist with rainfall that seeped through the ground above. To the right, a rat scuttled into shadow. Ahead, three sets of chains and manacles hung from the walls. Were Boursier of a mind to be grateful, he would be glad he had only to endure this place for the six days remaining of the two months given him to wed his enemy.

As El turned out of the cell, she wondered again how Agatha had learned of the passage formed from the mine of that long ago siege, the entrance to which was a cavern in the wood. More, how had she obtained the keys? Unfortunately, the woman's secrets were her own, but El would not complain. While wed to Murdoch, she had benefitted from those secrets in the form of sleeping powders.

Meeting the gaze of the one in the doorway, she said, "Aye, it will hold him."

Agatha drew from her shoulder the pack that would sustain Boursier and tossed it against the far wall. "You are ready, my lady?"

"I am."

With a smile that revealed surprisingly white teeth, Agatha turned to lead her into the devil's lair.

"I know what you do."

Bayard had wondered how long before she stopped hovering and spoke what she had come to say. He returned the quill to its ink pot and looked up at his half sister who stood alongside the table.

Jaw brushed by hair not much longer than his, she said, "You will not sacrifice yourself for me."

He wished she were not so perceptive. Though she had attained her twentieth year, she regarded him out of the eyes of the old. Yet for all the wisdom to which she was privy, she was a mess of uncertainty—the truest of ladies when it suited, a callow youth when it served. And Bayard was to blame, just as he was to blame for her broken betrothal. Had he not allowed her and her mother to convince him it was best she not wed, the king could not have dragged her into his scheme. Of course, it truly was advisable that she not take a husband.

"Pray," she entreated, "wed the Verdun woman, Bayard."

He would laugh if not that it would be a bitter thing. "I assure you, one Verdun wife was enough to last me unto death." He curled his fingers into his palms to keep himself from adjusting the eyepatch.

Her brow rumpled. "Surely you do not say 'tis better you wed a De Arell?"

He shrugged. "For King Edward's pleasure, we all must sacrifice."

Her teeth snapped, evidence it had become impractical to behave the lady. "Then sacrifice yourself upon a Verdun!"

Never. Better he suffer a De Arell woman than Quintin suffer a De Arell man. Of course, he had other reasons for choosing Thomasin. The illegitimate woman was said to be plain of face, whereas Elianor of Emberly was told to be as comely as her aunt whose beauty had blinded Bayard—in more ways than one. Then there was the rumor that Elianor and her uncle were lovers and, of equal concern, that she had given her departed husband no heir. He would not take one such as that to wife.

"Hear me," Quintin said so composedly he frowned, for once her temper was up, she did not easily climb down from it. "As Griffin de Arell already has his heir, 'tis better that I wed him."

Feeling his hands begin to tighten, he eased them open. Regardless of which man she wed, regardless of whether or not an heir was needed, she would be expected to grow round with child.

He forced a smile. "'Tis possible you will give Verdun the heir he waits upon." And, God willing, she would have someone to love through what he prayed would be many years.

Quintin drew a shuddering breath. "I will not give Magnus Verdun an heir."

He sighed, lifted his goblet. "It is done, Quintin. Word has been sent to De Arell that I ride to Castle Mathe four days hence to wed his daughter." Though the wine was thick as if drawn from the dregs of a barrel, he drank the remainder in the hope it would calm his roiling stomach and permit a fair night's sleep.

He rose from the chair. As he stepped around his stiff-backed sister, he was beset with fatigue—of a sort he had not experienced since the treacherous woman who was no longer his wife had worked her wiles upon him.

"Make good your choice, Bayard," Quintin warned.

He looked across his shoulder. "I have made as good a choice as is possible." Thus, she would wed Verdun, and the widow, Elianor, would wed the widower, De Arell, allying the three families—at least, until one maimed or killed the other.

"You have not," Quintin said.

Pressed down by fatigue, he stifled a reprimand with the reminder she wished to spare him marriage into the family of his darkest enemy. "If I give you my word that I shall make the De Arell woman's life miserable, will you leave?"

She pushed off the table. "*Your* life, she will make miserable." She threw her hands up. "Surely you can find some way around the king!"

He who demanded the impossible—who cared not what ill he wrought. Though Bayard had searched for a way past the decree, it seemed the only means of avoiding marriage to the enemy was to vacate the barony of Godsmere. If he forfeited his lands, not only would Quintin and her mother be as homeless as he, but the De Arells and Verduns would win the bitter game at which the Boursiers had most often prevailed. Utterly unacceptable.

"I am sorry," he said, "but the king will not be moved. And though I have not much hope, one must consider that these alliances could lead to the prosperity denied all of us."

Her jaw shifted. "You speak of more castles."

He did. When the immense barony of Kilbourne had been broken into lesser baronies twenty-five years past to reward the three families, it was expected licenses would be granted to raise more castles. However, the gorging of their private animosities had made expansion an unattainable dream.

"Accept it, Quintin."

She opened her mouth, closed it, and crossed the solar. The door slammed behind her, catching a length of green skirt between door and frame.

Her cry of frustration came through, but rather than open the door, she wrenched her skirt loose with a great tearing of cloth—their father's side of her. Later, she would mourn the ruined gown—her mother's side of her.

Though Bayard had intended to disrobe, he was too weary. Stretching upon his bed, he stared into the darkness behind his eyelid and recalled the woman at the market. Not because of the comely curve of her face, but the prick of hairs along the back of his neck that had first made him seek the source. In her glittering eyes, he had found what might have been hatred, though he had reasoned it away with the reminder that his people had suffered much amid the discord sown by the three families. And that was, perhaps, the worthiest reason to form alliances with the De Arells and Verduns.

Curiously aware of his breathing, he struggled to hold onto the image of the woman. As the last of her blurred, he determined it was, indeed, hatred in eyes that had peered at him from beneath a thick shawl. A shawl that made a poor fit for a day well warmed by sun.

3

The squire made a final, muffled protest and slumped to his pallet.

"Now The Boursier," Agatha said, pulling the odorous cloth from the young man's mouth and nose.

For the dozenth time since slipping out from behind the tapestry, El looked to the still figure upon the bed. Though the solar was dark, the bit of moonlight filtering through the oilcloth showed he lay on his back.

El crossed to the bed. "Does he breathe?"

"Of course he does." Agatha came alongside her. "Though if you wish—"

"Nay!" She was no murderer, and holding him captive would accomplish what needed to be done.

"Then make haste, my lady." Agatha tossed the coverlet over Boursier's legs so they could drag him down the steps of the walled passage. And drag him they must. Though the older woman was relatively strong of back and El was hardly delicate, there was no doubt Boursier would still outnumber them.

El put her knees to the mattress and reached to the other side of the coverlet upon which he lay. As she did so, her hand brushed a muscled forearm. She paused. It should not bother her to see such an imposing man laid helpless before his enemies, but it did. Of course, once she had also pitied Murdoch. Only once.

Returning to the present, she began dragging the coverlet over his torso. When she reached higher to flip it over his head, his wine-scented breath stirred the hair at her temple and drew her gaze to his shadowed face.

By the barest light, something glittered.

She gasped, dropped her feet to the door.

"What is it?" Agatha rasped.

El backed away. "He…" Why did he not bolt upright? "…looked upon me."

Agatha chuckled. "It happens." She pulled forth the cloth used upon the squire and pressed it to Boursier's face. "But let us be certain he remembers naught."

Would he not? Of course, even if he did, the glitter of her own eyes was surely all he would know of her. Heart continuing to thunder, El watched Agatha sweep the coverlet over Boursier's head.

"Take hold of his legs," she directed.

El slid her hands beneath his calves. Shortly, with Agatha supporting his heavier upper body, El staggered beneath her own burden. Boursier seemed to weigh as much as a horse, and by the time they had him behind the tapestry, he seemed a pair of oxen. Perspiring, she lugged him through the doorway onto the torchlit landing.

"Put him down," Agatha said as she lowered his upper body.

With a breath of relief, El eased his legs to the floor.

Agatha closed the door that granted access to the keep's inner walls and jutted her chin at the wall sconce. "Bring the torch."

El retrieved it, and when she turned to lead the way down the steps, a thud sounded behind. She swung around.

Agatha had hefted Boursier's legs, meaning his head had landed upon the first of the stone steps. "Nay!" she protested. "We must needs turn him. His head—"

"What care you?" Agatha snapped, lacking the deference due one's mistress. But such was the price of her favors.

Still, El could not condone such treatment, for a blow to the head could prove fatal. "We turn him, Agatha. Do not argue."

"My lady—"

"Do not!"

Agatha lowered her eyes. "As you will."

El assisted in turning Boursier and, shortly, Agatha gripped him about the torso. His feet taking the brunt of the steps, they continued their descent. At the bottom, Agatha dragged him through the doorway that led to the underground passage.

"Give me the key, and I will lock it," El said.

Continuing to support Boursier, Agatha secured the door herself.

Trying not to be offended, El led the way through the turns that placed them before the cell.

When Agatha dropped Boursier inside, once more having no care for how he fell, El glared at her.

From beneath a fringe of hair that had come loose from the knot atop her head, Agatha raised her eyebrows.

El held her tongue. She supposed the rough treatment was the least owed one whose grievance against Bayard Boursier was great. Agatha had spent a year in his household serving as maid to his wife who had also been El's aunt. For one long year, Agatha had aided Constance when Boursier turned abusive, and comforted her when he took other women into his bed. Given a chance, it was possible she would do the baron mortal harm.

El fit the torch in a wall sconce, then aided in propping Boursier against the cell wall. She tried not to look upon him as she struggled to open a rusted manacle, but found herself peering into his face. And wishing she had not.

She returned her attention to the manacle and pried at it, but not even the pain of abraded fingers could keep from memory her enemy's dimly lit face—displaced eyepatch exposing the scarred flesh of his left eyelid, tousled hair upon his brow, relaxed mouth. All lent vulnerability to one who did not wear that state well.

"Give it to me." Agatha reached for the manacle.

El jerked it aside. "I did not come to watch," she said and glanced at Boursier's other wrist that Agatha had fettered. Wishing the woman would not hover, she pried until the iron plates parted, then fit the manacle. As she did so, his pulse moved beneath her fingers—weak and slow.

Alarmed, El asked, "How long will he sleep?"

"As I always err on the side of giving too much, it could be a while. Perhaps a long while."

"But he will awaken?"

Agatha shrugged. "They usually do."

Murdoch always had.

"And most content he shall feel," Agatha added.

As Murdoch had felt, which had many times spared El his perverse attentions, just as what she did this night would spare the De Arell woman Boursier's abuse.

El extended a hand for the keys and, at Agatha's hesitation, said firmly, "Give them to me."

The woman's nostrils flared, but she surrendered them.

El met the upper plate of the manacle with the lower. It was a tight fit, one that might make it difficult for blood to course properly, but she gave the key a twist. As she rose, she looked upon Boursier's face and the eyepatch gone awry. She struggled against the impulse, but repositioned the half circle of leather over his scarred eyelid.

Behind, Agatha grunted her disapproval.

El considered the pack of provisions. There was enough food and drink to last six days, after which she and Agatha would release Boursier.

Though she wished she did not have to return to this place, Agatha was of an uncertain disposition—not to be trusted, El's uncle warned. Not that the woman would harm the Verduns. She simply did not take direction well, firm in the belief none was more capable of determining the course of the Verduns than she. Thus it had been since Agatha had come from France eleven years past to serve as maid to El's aunt.

"We are finished," Agatha pulled her from her musings.

El knew they should immediately depart Castle Adderstone, but something held her unmoving—something she should not feel for this man who had stolen her aunt from another only to ill treat her. "What if he does not awaken?" she asked.

"Then death. And most deserving."

Once more unsettled by Agatha's fervor, wishing it had been possible to take Boursier on her own, El frowned in remembrance of how quickly the woman had agreed to help—and how soon her plans had supplanted El's. Grudgingly, El had yielded to Agatha, who was not only conversant in this place, but had possessed the keys that granted them access to Castle Adderstone.

"Do not forget who he is," Agatha said, eyes glittering in the light of the torch she had retrieved.

El peered over her shoulder at Boursier who was no different from Murdoch—excepting he was mostly muscle whereas her departed husband had been given to fat. And that surely made this man better able to inflict pain and humiliation.

Lord, what a fool I am! she silently berated herself for feeling concern for one such as he. *It is no great curiosity that Murdoch made prey of me.*

"Never shall I forget who he is," she said.

Agatha lowered her prominent chin, though not soon enough to obscure a childlike smile.

Telling herself she did not care what pleasure Agatha took in Boursier's suffering, El stepped from the cell.

As Agatha pulled the door closed, she beckoned for the keys.

"Nay," El said, "I shall hold to them."

The woman's lids sprang wide. "You do not trust me, my lady?"

El longed to deny it, but said, "Forgive me, but I do not." She locked the cell door.

Feeling Agatha's ire, she followed the woman from the underground passage, taking the light with them and condemning Boursier to utter darkness. A darkness that would not lift for six days.

About The Author

Tamara Leigh holds a Master's Degree in Speech and Language Pathology. In 1993, she signed a 4-book contract with Bantam Books. Her first medieval romance, *Warrior Bride*, was released in 1994. Continuing to write for the general market, three more novels were published with HarperCollins and Dorchester and earned awards and spots on national bestseller lists.

In 2006, Tamara's first inspirational contemporary romance, *Stealing Adda*, was released. In 2008, *Perfecting Kate* was optioned for a movie and *Splitting Harriet* won an ACFW "Book of the Year" award. The following year, *Faking Grace* was nominated for a RITA award. In 2011, Tamara wrapped up her "Southern Discomfort" series with the release of *Restless in Carolina*.

When not in the middle of being a wife, mother, and cookbook fiend, Tamara buries her nose in a good book—and her writer's pen in ink. In 2012, she returned to the historical romance genre with *Dreamspell*, a medieval time travel romance. Shortly thereafter, she once more invited readers to join her in the middle ages with the *Age of Faith* series: *The Unveiling, The Yielding, The Redeeming, The Kindling,* and *The Longing.* Tamara's #1 Bestsellers—*Lady at Arms, Lady Of Eve, Lady Of Fire,* and *Lady*

Of Conquest—are the first of her medieval romances to be rewritten as "clean reads." Look for *Baron Of Blackwood,* the third book in *The Feud* series, in 2016.

Tamara lives near Nashville with her husband, sons, a Doberman that bares its teeth not only to threaten the UPS man but to smile, and a feisty Morkie that keeps her company during long writing stints.

Connect with Tamara at her website www.tamaraleigh.com, her blog The Kitchen Novelist, her email tamaraleightenn@gmail.com, Facebook, and Twitter.

For new releases and special promotions, subscribe to Tamara Leigh's mailing list: www.tamaraleigh.com

Made in the USA
Columbia, SC
12 May 2025

57852938R00221